W9-CLY-014

TERMINAL

TERM

INAL

RODERICK **GORDON**   BRIAN **WILLIAMS**

Chicken House
Scholastic Inc./New York

Text copyright © 2013 by Roderick Gordon.
Inside illustrations © 2013 by Kirill
Barybin except Bartleby Kitten © 2013 by
Roderick Gordon and spade, shovel, and machete
chapter-ending spots © 2009 by Brian Williams.
www.tunnelsthebook.com

All rights reserved. Published by Chicken
House, an imprint of Scholastic Inc., *Publishers
since 1920.* CHICKEN HOUSE, SCHOLASTIC, and asso-
ciated logos are trademarks and/or registered
trademarks of Scholastic Inc.
www.scholastic.com

Published in the United Kingdom in 2013
by Chicken House, 2 Palmer Street, Frome,
Somerset BA11 1DS.
www.doublecluck.com

No part of this publication may be repro-
duced, stored in a retrieval system, or transmitted
in any form or by any means, electronic, mechanical, photocopying, recording, or otherwise,
without prior written permission of the publisher.
For information regarding permission, write to
Scholastic Inc., Attention: Permissions
Department, 557 Broadway, New York, NY 10012.

Every effort has been made to trace or contact
all copyright holders. The publishers would be
pleased to rectify any errors or omissions brought
to their notice, at the earliest opportunity.

Walt Whitman, *"Salut au Monde!"*, first published in *Leaves of Grass*, Second Edition (1856) •
Helen Hayes, published in *Guideposts* (January
1960) • Song lyrics from "You Are My Sunshine"
by Jimmie Davis and Charles Mitchell (1940)

Library of Congress Cataloging-in-
Publication Data Available

ISBN 978-0-545-47964-6

10 9 8 7 6 5 4 3 2 1   13 14 15 16 17

Printed in the U.S.A.   23
First American edition, November 2013

The text type was set in Vendetta.
The display type was set in Squarehouse.
Book design by Kevin Callahan and
Whitney Lyle

This is not my true country, I have lived banish'd
from my true country, I now go back there,
I return to the celestial sphere where every one
goes in his turn.

"Salut Au Monde!" by Walt Whitman (1819–1892)

■ ■ ■

The truth is that there is only one terminal
dignity — love. And the story of a love is not
important — what is important is that one is
capable of love. It is perhaps the only glimpse we
are permitted of eternity.

Helen Hayes, actor (1900–1993)

PREVIOUSLY, IN SPIRAL ...

WILL AND DRAKE learn from Eddie, the former Limiter, that the Styx race is entering the Phase, a stage in their life cycle that has occurred only two or three times down the millennia. A new Phase would mean the rapid production of an army of Styx Warrior Class Limiters, with devastating consequences for England as they cut a swath through the Topsoil population.

Drake's father, Parry, mounts a military operation to destroy a warehouse in which the Phase is taking place. It is thought that all the Styx women have been eliminated and that the Phase has been averted, until a security video on a hard drive reveals that two have managed to escape the net. One of these women, Alex, goes to ground in Topsoil England, while the other, Vane, travels to the inner world. Each of them intends to restart the Phase, although a successful outcome is far from guaranteed.

That's the good news.

The bad news is that Styx mythology tells of a possible second reproduction cycle, effectively a backstop plan in the instance that the Phase is not able to proceed. This would have even worse implications for the human race because it would spawn the far deadlier Armagi, killing beasts capable of rapidly adapting to different environments and of regenerating after injury.

As Will and the team regroup to plan their next move, Danforth has come up with his own plan to defect to the Styx.

But when he makes his move, he brings about the death of Chester's parents and entombs everyone in the Complex, Parry's government stronghold deep in a Scottish mountain.

After the team eventually manages to escape from the Complex, Parry and Eddie remain Topsoil with members of the Old Guard and Eddie's former Limiters, their mandate to track down and kill Alex. Anticipating that her sister, Vane, is going to attempt to use the population of New Germania as the hosts in a new Phase, Drake leads Will, Elliott, Sweeney, and Colonel Bismarck on a mission to the inner world. Their task is to seal the Ancients' passage and the Pore, the only two ways in or out of the inner world, with nuclear explosions.

However, before the devices can be detonated, Drake and his team are surprised at the Pore by Vane, Rebecca One, and a squad of Limiters.

Colonel Bismarck is shot dead by the Limiters and, in the ensuing struggle, help comes from an unexpected quarter. To Drake and the others' complete surprise, Jiggs has shadowed them to the inner world and now springs into action. He slashes the throat of one Limiter, and then takes a second out of the running by sweeping him over into the Pore with him. Drake is forced to do the same with the Styx twin, but is still able to remotely detonate the nuclear bomb as he falls toward the zero-gravity belt.

Sweeney loses his life because he is too close to the electromagnetic pulse from the nuclear explosion and it fries the circuits in his head. As he topples to the ground, he crushes a test tube in his pocket and inadvertently releases a deadly virus sourced from the Eternal City, which wipes out not just every human and Styx present in the inner world, but virtually all other species. Will and Elliott survive the virus because they have been vaccinated against it, but they are now sealed in Dr. Burrows's "Garden of the Second Sun," seemingly with no way to return Topsoil.

And on the surface in a remote cottage on the Pembrokeshire coast, Old Wilkie and his granddaughter Stephanie care for Chester as he tries to deal with the death of his parents.

Although the Phase in the inner world has been forestalled, Alex's efforts on the surface have borne fruit, and the deadly Armagi are spawned.

This final installment in the Tunnels series picks up the story just minutes before the nuclear explosion in the Pore, as Jiggs battles for his life. . . .

PROLOGUE

THE BATTLE WOULD END with one of them dead.

Hands gripped wrists, arms taut as metal hawsers, muscles shaking from extreme exertion.

They strained and resisted, man and Styx testing each other time and time again as their blades reflected the sun far above, which grew ever smaller as they continued to fall.

The Limiter's lips were drawn back and his teeth bared as he swore in the Styx language, but Jiggs was completely silent.

They'd been locked in mortal combat from the first instant that Jiggs had swept the Limiter over into the void with him. The Styx had lost his long rifle early on when Jiggs kicked it from his grip, but in the blink of an eye he'd drawn out his scythe. In any case, at such close quarters a bladed weapon would always be the preference.

Without the element of surprise to help him, Jiggs had known that dispatching the second Limiter wasn't going to be easy. The first had been caught completely unawares as the perfectly placed strike with a combat knife severed his jugular. The Limiter had died with a frown on his face, still asking himself how the thin, bearded man had been able to appear from nowhere.

And now Jiggs was pitted against the second Styx soldier as they performed the macabre acrobatic display. Their deadly intent bound them together like shackles because neither would release the knife hand of the other, as that would spell instant death. So the contest went on, both adversaries knowing there was to be no intervention from a comrade, no relief from the topography, because it was just them and the rushing air.

Physically, they were pretty evenly matched: Both had that strength of sinew and honed muscle that years of service had brought, Jiggs in the jungles of the world where he had been sent for solo recon missions, the Limiter from his lengthy tours in the Deeps.

But, little by little, the Limiter was beginning to gain the upper hand. He seemed to have reserves of energy that went beyond those of any human. As they grappled with each other, turning slow spirals through the air, he'd managed to clamp Jiggs's legs together with his own in a scissor move. And now that Jiggs was caught in this inflexible lock, the Limiter was pushing with all his might, applying pressure to his opponent's back. Jiggs could feel his spine beginning to strain — he didn't know how much more of this it could take.

And the vicious curved scythe was moving closer and closer to his neck.

The sun was growing ever more remote and the shadows beginning to merge as Jiggs caught a rush of color in the corner of his eye. Because the void was cone-shaped, the chances of hitting the sides were increasing the farther they fell, and Jiggs had seen precisely that — he'd glimpsed the forty-five-degree gradient coated with a dark brown residue, which several months earlier Dr. Burrows had said was some kind of naturally occurring bitumen.

Jiggs knew that a collision with the side could be his salvation — as things stood, he was losing and needed to buy himself some breathing space. And quick.

Then they crashed into the slope, rolling over each other as they tumbled chaotically down it, quickly becoming pasted in the sticky bitumen. Due to the marked reduction in gravity at that depth in the void, they weren't so much falling down the slope as bouncing down it, in a manner similar to the motion of a pebble carried along the bed of a river.

Yes! Jiggs thought, as the Limiter lost his grip on his legs.

Then they entered a stretch of the slope covered with the stunted trees, branches whipping their faces as they tumbled through them, and the struggle growing even more confused as they strove to hold each other at bay.

Rolling off a small escarpment, they found themselves thrown into midair again.

Jiggs's defense seemed to waver, as though his arms were giving out. The Limiter seized the opportunity. Twisting his upper body, he drove his scythe at Jiggs's neck in one almighty effort.

Although Jiggs managed to deflect it, the tip of the scythe caught him along the collarbone. As it ripped through the material of his combat jacket, he was fortunate that the shoulder strap of his Bergen prevented it from doing much harm to the flesh beneath.

But the Limiter had drawn first blood. Believing the battle had turned in his favor, he immediately went for a second strike at his opponent's neck.

Exactly what Jiggs had been hoping for.

He'd allowed the Limiter his small victory because he had seen what was fast approaching.

And just as Jiggs had intended, the Limiter had been so distracted that he hadn't spotted the massive outcrop of rock they were about to cannon into as they gravitated toward the side again.

At the last moment, Jiggs arched his body, controlling their flight. Then they hit the rock.

With a resounding crack, the Limiter's skull took the impact full on. His body went slack — given a few seconds he might have recovered, but Jiggs wasn't about to allow that to happen.

He rammed his combat knife into the Styx's chest, just below the clavicle.

As he detached himself from the lifeless Limiter, Jiggs didn't have time to dwell on his victory. There was only one thought in his mind; he knew he was already far below the nuclear device that Drake and Sweeney had secured to the side of the void and then primed ready for remote detonation. And he knew that he had to put as much distance between himself and the device as he could.

Before it went off.

Jiggs didn't feel any guilt over saving his own skin. There was nothing he could do for Will and the others back at the top of the Pore — he was too far away to help them now.

XIV

Grabbing the booster rocket from a side pocket of his Bergen, he spun the valve around to full thrust and, aiming it behind him, fired it up. A blue flame sprouted from the end of the propulsion unit, and he took off like a firework.

At the breakneck speed he was traveling, he exited the void in a matter of seconds and then shot out into the huge cavern beyond, as endless as the night sky. Although they were still many hundreds of miles away, his trajectory was taking him straight toward the suspended bodies of water behind which ethereal lights flickered. Jiggs had already witnessed this illumination on the first leg of the journey to the inner world, and knew that it was being produced by triboluminescence in the crystal belt, where mountain-sized lumps of crystal ground against each other like some sort of perpetual motion machine. And this was also generating the rumbling sound that filled his ears. But, at that precise moment, Jiggs didn't care which way he was heading — he just had to get himself clear of the blast radius.

With the booster still on full thrust, he braced himself for the explosion, counting the seconds. He continued to count until he'd reached a full minute, then two minutes, then three. At that point he stopped, wondering if Drake and the Rebecca twin were still facing each other in some sort of standoff, or even if they had agreed to a truce, unlikely as that seemed. Perhaps there wasn't to be an explosion after all.

Then the atomic device detonated.

As the roar shook every bone in his body, he braced himself

for the first wave from the one-kiloton bomb — the blast of light and searing heat. He knew better than to look at it, making sure his head was tucked well down and that his eyes were protected by his arm. The heat on his back was so intense he really thought that his Bergen and clothing might burst into flames.

He didn't have time to worry further about this as the shock wave caught up with him. The wall of compressed air felt precisely as if a giant hand had slapped him, flinging him forward with such impetus that he could barely draw breath. He was reminded of the first time he'd gone on a roller coaster as a child; the sensation of falling at precipitous speed was identical, but this ride seemed to have no end.

Daring to remove his arm from his face as he sped along, he caught a brief glimpse of the torrents of light from the blast rebounding and reflecting from the far-flung corners of the huge chamber before him. As the whole area lit up, it was so vast and endless it made him feel vertiginous. The glittering masses of water and gargantuan crystal spheres were revealed in all their glory — perhaps as they'd never been before in this secret place deep within the planet.

And what made absolutely no sense to him was, for the instant in which the veil of darkness was lifted, he could have sworn that the line of crystal spheres was remarkably regular, as if they weren't simply some artifact of nature. And there was also something curious about the stretch of cavern wall he'd glimpsed through the haze in the extreme distance — it appeared to be marked with grids of lines, or raised sections of some description.

"Pull yourself together!" he growled at himself. There had to be a rational explanation — the patterns he'd noticed must be due to the superheated air currents. Either that or the shock wave from the explosion had temporarily scrambled his vision.

And it had been one hell of an explosion. He peered over his shoulder, quickly locating the dull red glow that marked ground zero. Where the void had previously been, the rock had fused into one massive plug of silicate and completely sealed the way into the inner world, just as Drake had predicted it would.

"Crikey!" Jiggs cried, flinching as a white-hot lump of rock shot not ten feet away from him. As more of these missiles followed, he realized it was fallout from the explosion, like a shower of miniature meteors. But the main barrage was over almost as soon as it began, and he was far enough away for it not to be a serious hazard.

Even though there was no "up" or "down" in this place, Jiggs didn't need his finely tuned sense of direction to tell him that the explosion had sent him in completely the wrong direction. He checked his position in relation to the crystal belt. If he was to have a hope of navigating his way back to the outer surface again, he needed to find the mouth of the second void, called Smoking Jean, which they'd used on their journey to the inner world. He tried to use his booster to adjust his flight path, but such was his velocity that even several minutes with the propulsion device at full thrust made little difference.

But he had no option but to persevere if he ever wanted to get home again, so he kept using the blaster, all the time referencing his position against the still-glowing blast site.

That was when he noticed something curious. A streak of green light appeared in the distance, then faded away. Jiggs was wondering if his eyesight was acting up again when, several seconds later, it was followed by a second streak, although this time it was yellow.

"Flares?" Jiggs wondered aloud.

Of the team, only he, Sweeney, and Drake had been carrying flares in those particular colors. The green flare was a signal to report to an emergency rendezvous, while the yellow one meant that the sender needed help — in effect it was a distress flare. Sending both up at once made no sense at all.

Jiggs frowned, briefly considering the possibility that something on the drifting corpse of the Limiter he'd killed had been set alight in the blast. But it was highly improbable that it would have been those precise colors. No. Jiggs quickly decided that it had to be either Drake or Sweeney, or one of the others. *But who?*

And he knew the flares must have gone off because of the intense heat, so there was no point in sending a countersignal. Whoever it was had to be in trouble.

He didn't think twice about what he must do.

"We never leave anyone behind," Jiggs said, already setting himself on a new course to intercept where his team member — or perhaps members — were bound. There was enough propellant in the booster tanks for the detour, so that wasn't a concern. His main worry was that he'd miss his speeding target, whose flight path would eventually take it into the huge suspended masses of water or even beyond them, into the crystal belt. But in the endless black canvas of this huge space, broken only by the flickering muted light, it was tantamount to looking for a needle in a haystack, at midnight.

Taking out his light-intensifying monoscope, he put it on his head and adjusted it for the ambient light levels. Although Drake had tried his best to make him adopt one of his proprietary lenses, Jiggs had stuck firmly to his Soviet-made nightscope. The electronics may have been primitive compared to Drake's design, but it had seen him through two decades of active service, and he knew how to repair it in the field if it malfunctioned.

But now all Jiggs was seeing through his monoscope was chunk after chunk of slow-moving rock that had been flung out by the explosion. Then, finally, he spotted something that looked more promising, and for a few seconds he continued to track it through his scope. It was farther out than he'd expected, but nevertheless Jiggs angled his booster so he could home in on it, praying that it wasn't just another hunk of itinerant rock.

Jiggs finally steered himself onto a parallel trajectory, then closed the distance with blips from his thruster. As he made out more through his monoscope, he was filled with hope when he saw what appeared to be one of the team, judging from the Bergen and the booster rocket trailing behind on the end of a lanyard. With a final burst of speed, he was near enough to take hold of the drifting form. He seized the Bergen, which was still smoldering in places, then turned the body toward him.

"My God! It's you, Drake!" he cried.

But it wasn't just Drake — there was someone else with him, although this second person was so badly hurt as to be almost unrecognizable.

Jiggs concentrated on Drake to start with. Even from a cursory inspection, Jiggs could tell that he was in a very bad way. Patches of his fatigues had been blasted completely away, and the flesh underneath scorched black. Some of Drake's hair was missing, and his head was covered in angry red blisters from the crown and down one side of his face. Jiggs felt his neck for a pulse — he found one, but it was very weak. He must have been in close proximity to the bomb when it detonated, which explained why he'd been moving so fast. And it also probably meant that he'd been bathed in radiation.

Then Jiggs moved on to the second person, twisting the head around so he could see the features.

It was Rebecca One.

Drake had obviously employed the same tactic as Jiggs and swept her over into the void to take her out of the running. Then they'd been involved in a struggle, which explained why she was tangled up in a coil of rope attached to the side of Drake's Bergen.

Jiggs didn't bother to check her for a pulse. Her body was so charred that there was no question the Rebecca twin was dead. "Hah! Fashion victim!" he observed, as part of her coat crumbled at his touch. "That's what you get for wearing black around a nuclear explosion," he added without a shred of sympathy.

He was correct — the nonreflective surface of her matte black Styx coat had done an admirable job of absorbing the pulse of heat and light. And, as Jiggs tried to disentangle her arm from the rope, it cracked as if it were made of charcoal. He could see that, of the two, she'd come off far worse than Drake. Indeed, she must have helped him by shielding much of his body from the blast.

Jiggs quickly searched the twin's body for anything useful, but other than a few items in the pouches on her belt, it was difficult to tell what was her and what were the remains of her incinerated clothing. Everything had been fused together by the heat.

For a moment Jiggs simply regarded the slight body of Rebecca One. For someone so young, she had been responsible for so much suffering. "You don't deserve any last words," he snarled, then unceremoniously heaved her away into the darkness.

Jiggs was checking Drake's pulse again when he heard him trying to say something, although it was little more than a murmur. "Take it easy there, old man. Just you hang on." Jiggs tried to comfort him, forced to shout over the din of the crystal belt. He unhitched his medical pack from his belt, fishing out a Syrette of morphine. "Something for the pain," he said to Drake, as he jammed the Syrette against the injured man's thigh.

It was only then that Jiggs felt the moisture on his face and looked up sharply. He had become so accustomed to bowling along at speed through this low-gravity environment that he'd completely forgotten he and Drake were still very much on the move.

"No!" Jiggs just had enough time to yell as they plowed straight into a huge globule of water. Although Jiggs didn't have much of an opportunity to gauge its size, it was around twenty feet in diameter. At least, it was until they hit it.

Their momentum was such that it disintegrated into thousands of smaller droplets. And then there were more of these suspended megadroplets of all sizes in Jiggs's path. Coughing from the water he'd inhaled, he simultaneously tried to shield Drake's face, dodge the larger droplets, and fire up his booster, which had taken such a dousing that it had gone out.

As he attempted to protect Drake from another soaking, Jiggs's feet skimmed the circumference of a droplet the size of a house — this one didn't break apart but wobbled like a giant Jell-O mold. "Space surfing!" Jiggs exclaimed, as he managed to restart the booster, then frantically sought some unoccupied air space. He needed a safe place to stop and administer some urgent first aid to Drake.

In a clearing of smaller droplets, he made out an angular and familiar shape.

"What the . . . ?" he yelled. He really couldn't comprehend what he was seeing. He tried to use the booster to reach it, but overshot and had to backtrack. As he jetted them both closer, he was able to confirm his first impression.

It was a Short Sunderland — a seaplane that had been out of regular service for nearly fifty years and was these days more likely to be found in an aviation museum. It was a sizable aircraft, capable of carrying a good twenty-four passengers. One wing had been torn off, and the cockpit was badly damaged, but the rest of the fuselage seemed to be intact apart from a few holes in the tail section.

Still not believing what he was seeing, Jiggs maneuvered toward it as he remembered the Russian submarine in Smoking Jean, and what Drake himself had said about pores opening up on the surface from time to time. So could some twist of fate be the reason that this seaplane had been sucked down, too? Caught in a whirlpool that had brought it all the way down to this inner space?

Much of the white paint remained on the fuselage, although it was stained by patches of rust, particularly around the rivets. And long tendrils of some kind of black algae had anchored itself in clumps all over the exterior, waving in the air currents like fine black hairs.

Reaching the large float under the surviving wing, Jiggs braced himself against it, then with a push of his legs directed himself at a door on which EMERGENCY EXIT had been stenciled. He tugged on the handle. It refused to open, so he used his handgun to shoot out the lock and hinges. With another tug, the door came away with a burst of rust. Jiggs allowed it to float off, then entered the aircraft with Drake.

Although the windows amazingly weren't broken in this section of the seaplane, everything was damp inside — the fabric of the seats and the carpet almost rotted completely away and covered with a gray slime. In one of the rows Jiggs spied two skeletons. Their bony arms were clasped around each other, and from the way their skulls were touching, there was no question they'd been in a final embrace at the moment of death.

"I'd have done the same," Jiggs confided to them.

But he didn't have time to examine what else was in there as he gently laid Drake on the floor and set about tending to him. Battlefield triage was nothing new to Jiggs. Slipping off Drake's Bergen and removing the booster tied to his wrist, he methodically cataloged the areas that needed attention. Having worked his way along each of Drake's limbs and then the trunk of his body, he quickly found the injury to his shoulder.

"That's no burn. That's a bullet wound," he mumbled to himself, then glanced at the welts on Drake's head and the charred areas of his combats, which would need to be carefully removed to assess the damage to the tissue beneath them. "But it's probably the least of our problems."

He scanned the cabin around him as he voiced his concerns out loud. "Major trauma from third-degree burns . . . huge risk of infection from this septic environment . . . and unless there are any supplies here, just my Medikit to work with." He rolled up his sleeves. "Hey ho," he whispered grimly. "Off to work we go."

If Drake had any hope of pulling through, at least he was in capable hands. Jiggs was highly proficient in field medicine. In some of the places he'd been sent — often the middle of nowhere — he'd frequently been called upon to use his skills to save both himself and those around him.

But now Jiggs suddenly noticed his patient had stopped breathing.

"No you don't, old man. You're not going to die on me." He leaned over and gave Drake mouth-to-mouth resuscitation. "Not today," he said, as he began to thump Drake's chest to get his heart beating again. "Not on my watch."

PART 1

AFTERMATH

1

SCHRAACK!

The small skull split open under Will's boot, the hollow sound resounding through the empty New Germanian street. Will hadn't been looking where he was treading as he'd moved toward the pavement, and had completely failed to notice the diminutive skeleton stretched out in the gutter.

"Oh . . . my . . . good . . . God." Will swallowed as he stood over the skeleton, which had to have been that of a child. Although very little brain tissue remained inside the skull, the sight of the empty pupal casings spilling out was horrifying. The climate of this inner world with its ever-burning sun couldn't have been more favorable for the armies of voracious flies, which had stripped the flesh from the human skeletons in a matter of weeks. Eight weeks to be precise. And stripped it so efficiently that the stench of decay that once hung over the dead city had almost completely vanished.

Everywhere Will looked there were sun-bleached bones, mostly poking from crumpled clothes. Since the virus had also killed off all the mammals that would normally have scavenged on the remains, the bodies had lain undisturbed, still precisely where they had fallen.

Undisturbed except for the carrion-feeding birds. Avian species had been spared by the virus, and a little farther along the road Will spotted two fat crows playing tug-of-war over something beside a discarded hat. They didn't bother to move until he was almost on them.

"Get away!" he shouted, aiming his foot at them. Beating their greasy black wings and giving ugly calls, they grudgingly took to the air.

Will saw what the crows had been fighting over. On the tarmac was a human eyeball, so desiccated and discolored it resembled a rotten plum.

He couldn't stop himself from staring at the eyeball as it stared accusingly back at him, its ragged optic nerve strung out behind it like a tail, as though it were some kind of new animal.

"This is so wrong," Will whispered, suddenly overwhelmed by all the signs of death around him. People had clearly left their homes in their thousands to gather here in the center of the city, where they'd succumbed to the virus. They must have been desperately hoping that their government was going to do something to save them from the disease that could cause death in as little as twenty-four hours.

"Hey, dozy, what is it?" Elliott shouted. Finding that Will hadn't followed her into the large department store they'd been heading toward, she'd reappeared through the shattered glass of one of the doors.

"*We* did this," he managed to reply. "We're to blame for all this."

"We never meant for it to come to this," Elliott said, as she surveyed the bodies.

Of course Will knew that Elliott was right; Sweeney must have accidentally broken the test tube Drake had given him. It was never the intention to actually release the deadly virus. But it didn't make Will feel any better about what he was seeing.

Elliott shrugged. "They were doomed anyway. Most of them had been Darklit. Sooner or later, they'd have ended up as either hosts or food for the Phase." She was silent for a moment. "Perhaps this is better, Will. Perhaps we did them a favor."

He moved toward her, shaking his head slowly. "That's difficult to believe."

As soon as they were inside the shop, Will stopped to take in the fountain — a large bronze dolphin in the center of a circular pool set into the marble floor. Although the water had long since stopped spouting from the mouth of the dolphin, both it and the polished marble floors gave the impression of incredible affluence from a bygone age on the outer surface.

"This was quite some shop," Will said.

"Those people obviously thought so," Elliott agreed, as she left Will peering around at the cadavers on the floor, some with bags crammed full of items still clutched in their skeletal arms.

"They must have known things were bad, but even so they were grabbing whatever they could," he said as he poked one of the bags with the barrel of his Sten and expensive-looking lipsticks and face creams spilled from it. He laughed, though emptily. "They were even stealing makeup!"

"Come over here. You've got to see this!" Elliott shouted, her voice resounding through the huge main hall.

"Wow," Will said. There was an imposing statue at the end of the hall, on either side of which a pair of staircases swept up to the other levels of the shop. The statue, which was a good fifty feet in height, was of a woman dressed in a toga and proudly displaying a cornucopia of fruit.

But what stopped Will in his tracks was the enormous smoked-glass dome that served as the roof of the hall. In wonder he craned his head back to take it all in. Without anyone around to keep it clean, wind-borne grit was already building up at the edges of the dome and encroaching on the glass, but the effect was still breathtaking.

Will lowered his gaze from the dome, taking in the other floors on the way down, where he could just about make out all the different goods on display there.

"This place is ginormous — like Harrods or something. Where do we start?" he asked. He stepped over to a counter and wiped the layer of dust from its surface to peer at the range of meerschaum pipes arranged on crumpled velvet. Then he leaned over the counter as he examined the showcases behind it. The glass doors had been wrenched off, and many brands of cigarettes he'd never heard of were inside. *"Lande Mokri Superb. Sulima,"* he read, scanning along the row of old-fashioned packets. *"Joltams, Pyramide."* Then he noticed a dead body slumped by the base of the showcase, dressed in a pinstriped suit and with a packet still held tightly in its dried-out hand. *"Tch, tch!"* Will said, wagging a finger. "Those things will kill you, you know," he admonished the corpse.

"We can get everything we need here," Elliott called from another counter where she'd helped herself to two umbrellas — essential items in this world where the weather had only two defaults: blinding sunshine or fierce monsoons that descended with no warning at all. "Will, what do you reckon's through there?" she asked, indicating a row of doors along the side of the hall with signs above them proclaiming LEBENSMITTELABTEILUNG.

"One way to find out," he replied, already making straight for the nearest pair of doors and pushing them open.

If the reek of rotten food wasn't disgusting enough, the maelstrom of flies that Will and Elliott's entrance stirred up would have deterred most people from entering. But not Elliott.

"Must be something we can take?" she asked, despite the fact that the flies were everywhere in the food hall.

As Will waved the teeming bluebottles away from his face, he caught glimpses of the different counters selling cheese, food, and meat, their once-chilled displays now a mass of putrefaction and writhing with maggots. And not only was the once-pristine white-tiled floor smeared with filth, it was also littered with the remains of dead rats. They'd obviously thought they were onto a good thing until the virus had finished them off, too.

"Oh, God, let's just get out of here!" Will yelled, frantically swatting the flies away from him.

"But there's canned food over th —" Elliott was shouting and pointing, as a fly shot straight into her mouth.

"No way. We can get our supplies somewhere else," Will insisted, as he and Elliott stumbled back through the doors, which swung shut, sealing them off from the stench and insects again. Except for the one lodged at the back of Elliott's throat.

"Fly," she wheezed, pointing at her mouth. She was coughing and making noises like a cat trying to bring up a fur ball.

She looked so comical that Will began to chuckle. "Is that tasty?" he asked. Then he couldn't help himself, doubling up with laughter. This didn't amuse Elliott in the slightest, her face flushed from all the coughing.

"It's not funny, you creep," she managed to get out. Then she gulped loudly and grimaced. "Yuck. I think I swallowed it."

"Well, you did say we needed more meat in our diet," Will quipped.

Then she, too, was laughing and coughing and thrusting the stock of her long rifle at him, as he backed away, pretending to be terrified by her attack.

"Hey, spider woman, be careful with that, will you?" he yelled, as he sidestepped yet again, only just managing to avoid her rifle.

Will realized immediately what he'd said. They'd had the misfortune of meeting Vane, one of the Styx women, when they'd been ambushed at the top of the Pore.

Even the Styx themselves hadn't known the reason for it, but this inner world had energized Vane, enabling her to restart the Phase. But it was more than just that; it had allowed her to produce Styx Warrior Class larvae in numbers that were off the scale. But, as a consequence, Vane had begun to resemble a hideously bloated arachnid. And given Elliott's parentage, it wasn't surprising that she was particularly sensitive whenever the subject came up, to the extent that she and Will rarely discussed it.

Elliott was standing very still with her rifle still poised in midair, her expression stony. "What did you just say?" she demanded.

"I . . . I . . . that . . . that came out wrong," Will gabbled. He took a hasty step back as Elliott's expression turned thunderous.

"Spider woman?" she growled. "Just because I've got Styx blood in me doesn't mean I'm suddenly going to turn into one of those monsters."

"I know. I'm sorry," Will said.

Elliott cracked a smile. "Gotcha!"

Relieved that he hadn't really upset her, the boy nevertheless spun on his heels and dashed off.

Elliott raised her arm in front of her face and moved it in an impression of one of the ovipositors that had snaked from Vane's mouth. "Where are you going, juicy human?" she shouted after Will. In fits of laughter, she gave chase, and Will was laughing, too, as he careered between the shop counters in the direction of the staircases at the end of the hall.

Shouting and running together, they were the only two people alive in that once-bustling department store, now filled with nothing more than the dreams of the dead inhabitants of the metropolis.

On the landing at the top of the first flight of stairs, they paused to take stock of what they could see around them, still chuckling.

"Clothes up there," Will said, surveying the mannequins,

many of which had been knocked over by looters. "Want a new dress?"

"Not on this trip," Elliott replied, as she tried to decipher the guide to the various levels on the wall. "Essentials only. Some new sheets and towels would be a good start."

"That's boring," Will muttered under his breath, but nevertheless followed after Elliott as she climbed the stairs to the third floor.

"This looks promising," the girl announced.

"Yes. 'Ome furnishings," Will said in a voice that wasn't far off from how he remembered his auntie Jean's.

They began to explore the different aisles, wandering past suites of sofas and armchairs, all in matching fabrics and arranged around tables on which were vases of very wilted flowers.

Elliott noticed that in one of the far corners of the floor numerous Persian rugs had been stacked in piles, or hung from the walls like some sort of Eastern bazaar.

"Pillows," Will said, pointing to another area. "I think we need to be over there."

As Elliott turned to see where he was indicating, her gaze settled on a display of dining-room furniture.

"Will," she warned him in a voice that was barely a whisper, bringing her weapon to her shoulder.

They edged toward the figures sitting very upright around a dust-covered table. There were four of them, dressed in sand-colored combats, their long rifles cradled in their laps. And in front of each was a delicate teacup of fine bone china.

"Limiters," Elliott said.

"*Dead* Limiters," Will added, scarcely able to bring himself to look at their faces, on which their scarred skin had dried out and was drawn so tight that more than ever it resembled ancient, spalled ivory. "Why, *of all places*, would they come here to die?" Will asked.

Elliott shrugged. "Maybe they were on patrol when the virus got a grip? They were just caught out?"

"Yes, but look at them," Will said. "A Limiter tea party? That's pretty weird, isn't it?"

Even in the final minutes of their lives they had been perfectly controlled, choosing somewhere to take their last breaths together, drinking from teacups as they shared some water from a canteen. Their eyes were shut, and outwardly at least there was little sign that they been touched by the flies. Perhaps the insects were as unenthusiastic as Will was right then to venture too close.

"We should snaffle their rifles and any spare ammo," Elliott suggested, already peering at their belt kit with interest.

"Leave it for another time," Will suggested. "It's not as if they're going anywhere, is it?"

But Elliott wasn't deterred in the slightest as she went to the first of the Limiters and began to rummage through his pockets. "Don't be such a wuss, Will," she said.

"This footage was taken by a former member of D Squadron who lives just outside the town," Parry said, as he turned to the flickering images being projected on the flaking white paint of the wall beside him. With its vaulted roof, the dark cellar was packed with soldiers from the 22nd Special Air

Service Regiment. "It's the first film we've managed to get hold of showing the Armagi in action."

Parry stood to the side so the assembled audience could see the scene clearly of the outskirts of a town. "This took place in Kent over the weekend. First we have fires breaking out around the perimeter," Parry said, as the camera panned wildly from one flaming building to the next. "They were most likely set by an advance party of Limiters to flush people out of the buildings and corral them in the center of town . . . ready for the second phase." There were several seconds when the camera continued to track the fires as they burned.

"What are we looking for now?" someone asked.

"Watch the airspace above the town," Parry replied.

The cameraman had been a little slow to notice what was going on. But you really had to look for it, as not only was it dusk and the light dwindling, but the multiple objects streaking down into the middle of the town weren't easy to spot. The winged forms were almost transparent as they swept down from the sky at incredible speed.

"Those are Armagi," Parry said. "Hundreds of them."

A murmur passed through the audience as someone exclaimed, "Bloody hell!"

"But why did the Styx pick this location for a strike? What strategic value did it have to them?" someone else posed from the rear of the cellar.

Parry turned to the men. "There's no question that the town was a carefully selected target — the Medway power station, which supplies electricity to a large area of Kent, lies just to the north. The proximity of the power station to the town meant that to do the job properly and quash any resistance, they needed to hit both targets simultaneously."

As if to emphasize Parry's point, there was a huge burst of light, which threw the town buildings into stark relief for a split second. "And there goes the power station," Parry said. "As you know, this was far from an isolated incident. We've received numerous reports that the Styx are methodically working their way through the home counties as they head toward the capital, cherry-picking utilities, comms hubs — anything that'll cripple our country's infrastructure."

"So we stake out a potential target and wait for them to show up," a soldier suggested. "Then we've got ourselves a duck shoot as these suckers come in to land."

"And claymore the bejesus out of them," one of his comrades chirped up.

"Nice idea," Parry said, then took a breath. "Look, I know you all think you're the toughest mothers that ever walked the earth." A few men chuckled as Parry continued, "But don't underestimate these organisms — they're spawned from the toughest, most ruthless mother of them all. And here she is . . ."

The camera zoomed in unsteadily on a point outside the town where a small group of figures was watching the attack. "Here you've got some Limiters, but focus your attention on who's in the middle." Parry leaned forward so that the shadow of his extended hand fell on two particular figures. "The taller of that pair is likely to be one of the Styx females that eluded us at the warehouse attack. I say *one of* because I haven't had the kill on the second one confirmed by my son yet, and we don't know if more were generated."

As the camera zoomed in even closer, the Styx female was silhouetted against the flames, her insect legs poised above her shoulders.

"So that's the big bug?" someone in the audience asked as the camera remained on her.

"Yes, and we know from Eddie that her Topsoil name is Alex," Parry replied, then he indicated the smaller figure beside her. "And with Alex is the Rebecca twin. The two of them are the head honchos in the Styx hierarchy. If we had a way of neutralizing that unholy couple, this war might be brought to an end, and we could all go home again."

Parry's words hung in the air as the men thought of their families, from whom they'd been completely cut off for weeks. As Parry had ordered, they weren't allowed to have any contact whatsoever with the outside world. He had made it clear that it was necessary in order for the unit to operate without any interference from the Styx.

The wall beside Parry went dark for a moment, then became so bright that it lit up the faces of all the men in the cellar. "This is the morning after," Parry said quietly. "You can see the results for yourself." The view swayed with each step that the ex-soldier took as he moved through the now deserted town, recording the aftermath of the attack. In the harsh dawn light, all the bodies could be clearly seen where they'd fallen outside the buildings, very few of which had escaped the fire.

"And don't get me wrong," Parry said. "This is a war, a war on our home turf, and a war that we're going to lose unless we can find what the Armagi's weaknesses are."

·"Have you got any more gen on their deployment or capability?" a soldier asked.

"From sightings, we believe they hunt in pairs, whether airborne or on land. And one report raised the possibility that they might possess a highly developed sense of hearing — based on the fact that the sound of engines or gunfire draws them like moths to a flame. That's why suppressors on all weapons are now the order of the day."

The pager on Parry's belt vibrated, and he quickly held it up to read the message. He appeared to be in a hurry as he said, "And I hope to have more to tell you about their physiology very soon, gentlemen. If you'll excuse me now, the Captain here will finish the briefing and take any questions."

As images of the destroyed power station flashed across the wall, Parry made his way down the side of the cellar, squeezing past the rows of seated soldiers who, by their usual standards, were remarkably subdued. Unlike the regular army, SAS briefings were generally informal with all ranks joining in, often with some irreverent banter to lighten the mood. But the severity of the situation had shocked even this highly experienced and highly trained elite of the British Army.

Despite his lameness, Parry was in a hurry and took the stairs two at a time as he climbed to the ground floor, then exited from the low-lying building at a trot. Directly opposite were helicopters, hidden under camo netting. He turned right along the track that ran through the center of the compound.

The decision had been to divide the 22nd SAS Regiment into three units, each unit operating autonomously of the others from secret locations. It meant that at least some capability would be preserved if the regiment became contaminated with Darklit men, or the Styx sniffed out one unit.

With his knowledge of the Styx, Parry had been a natural choice to be given one of the new divisions to command. And he'd chosen these rarely used barracks, deep in the Herefordshire countryside, as the location for the division. As he hurried along now, he didn't have time to enjoy the rolling hills that lay all around, except to allow himself a quick glance in the direction of the main SAS barracks in Credenhill some seven miles away, wondering if the Styx had mounted an assault on them yet. If they had, they would have been sorely disappointed, as the site was being manned by a skeleton team with instructions to blow the whole place at the first sign of any trouble.

He continued along the track that ran through the middle of the compound, passing the mess hall, shooting range, and munitions dump until he came to an unremarkable-looking building without any windows.

A sentry had been watching the entrance. "Fizzog scan, sir," the man said, as he stepped forward. He held a Purger up to Parry's face and fired the purple light into his eyes. The sentry knew what he was doing, and was scrutinizing Parry closely for any signs that he'd been Darklit.

"So I pass?" Parry pressed him, in a hurry to enter.

"Yes, you do, with flying colors, sir," the sentry said. He swiped a key card through the reader at the side of the door, which opened with a definitive clunk to allow Parry inside.

Other than the fact that these old barracks had fallen out of use so many decades ago they'd been largely forgotten, this building was the main reason Parry had been so eager to locate his division there. It housed a former germ warfare testing facility, which was ideal for his purposes. He went through a series of rooms full of dusty equipment until he came to the main laboratory. It was divided into two by a partition of three-inch tempered glass, one side an airtight isolation chamber.

"You paged me — what's the latest?" Parry asked the orderly in a white coat, who was intent on what was on the other side of the window. The orderly opened his mouth to answer, but Parry had already activated the intercom at the bottom of the partition. "Got anything for me, Major?" he asked the Medical Officer himself on the other side of the thick glass.

The Medical Officer — or MO, as he was referred to — wheeled around. "Commander," he said, acknowledging Parry. "Glad you could come at such short notice, because there are a couple of things you need to see."

The MO stepped aside, revealing the Styx secured to a stainless-steel gurney by several restraints. He'd been discovered in the debris after the attack on the power station and helicoptered to the base for examination. He was bare to the waist, and his appearance — his rake-thin body and severe features — gave the impression that he was a Limiter.

"He hasn't regained consciousness yet?" Parry asked.

"Still out for the count," the MO replied, "although all his injuries have healed."

"They've what?" Parry said, as he leaned against the glass partition so he could study the man's head. "That's incredible. You're right. No trace of any wound at all." When the man had been brought in, his skull had been crushed on one side, and the enormity of that injury combined with the others he'd suffered made it seem unlikely he'd last for very long.

"So, unless a run-of-the-mill Styx has miraculous powers that mean a major injury heals in hours rather than months, then what we've bagged ourselves here is an Armagi," the MO suggested.

"They haven't, and it would appear that we have," Parry said, his eyes flashing with excitement. This was the break he'd been looking for — an opportunity to evaluate what they were up against. "The Styx do have amazing powers of recuperation, but nothing like this. So I have to agree he must be an Armagi. Have you found anything else unusual about him?"

The MO grinned. "From my external examination, he has a heart, lungs — all the body organs you'd expect, and in the right places. The only anomalies I've found are in his throat, where there's some sort of extra gland, and beside it a small protuberance I can't explain."

Parry guessed immediately what that was likely to be. "It's an ovipositor. Eddie told us that the Armagi could breed like the Styx females, so they probably impregnate hosts in the same way."

The MO pinched the Armagi's bicep. "And the density of his muscle fiber is off the scale. The man weighs a bloody ton, which is why it took four troopers to carry him in here. But all that pales into insignificance in relation to what I'm about to show you." The MO went to a bench behind where the man was laid on the gurney, and raised one end of a long stainless-steel dish so Parry could see the contents.

"My God!" Parry exclaimed. He wasn't sure whether he was more shocked by the fact that the MO had lopped off the Armagi's arm just below the shoulder, or that the Armagi had apparently grown a completely new one.

"Quite so. You asked for incontrovertible proof," the MO said, grinning. "So I began with some small incisions to his skin, which healed within seconds, and worked my way up to the removal of an entire limb. And, lo and behold, it grew back in around three hours, and appears to be right as rain again." The MO paused for effect. "And if you think that's impressive, here's something else I've just discovered."

Beside the amputated arm on the bench was a device in a khaki-painted crate, which the MO switched on. "I know it's not very scientific, but I came across this ancient piece of inter-rogation kit in the stores," he said. "Of course, it's only fit for a museum of human rights now that the Geneva Convention precludes the torture of POWs, but I'm not sure it would apply to these combatants."

The MO picked up a metal probe connected to the device by a cable. "I've set the charge at two hundred volts," he said, then extended it toward the Armagi and touched his forearm.

A small spark sprang across from the probe to the Armagi's skin when it was close enough. The MO didn't stop there, pushing the probe hard against the Armagi's arm. "Note the lack of a normal reaction at this voltage," the MO said. He was right — there was no convulsion of the muscles as there would have been with a human being, even when unconscious.

Instead the most curious thing happened. Spreading out from the probe where it made contact, the skin was becoming silvery and crystalline, as if diamond-shaped scales were spreading across the arm. Then the whole limb suddenly became transparent, and began to transform into something else altogether.

"We think it's changing into a wing," the orderly beside Parry said. Parry had to agree — the arm was flattening all the way up to the shoulder, and it certainly did appear to be more than a little birdlike.

The MO removed the probe, and the limb lost its translucency and immediately reverted to its original form. "So they shape-shift, and electrical impulses are somehow involved. Like nerve impulses, I presume."

"The Major has experimented with a range of different voltages," the orderly said, holding up his clipboard to show Parry the small sketches he'd made. "We got a wing, as you started to see there, and also something like a flipper."

"Sea, air, and land," Parry remembered. "Eddie told us that they can transform into different entities with different morphologies to suit whatever environment they're in."

"Yes, what we've seen here would bear that out," the MO said.

Parry's brow was furrowed as his mind raced. "So . . . ," he began, ". . . is this their Achilles' heel? Can we use electricity to defeat them?"

"Good suggestion. Why don't I up the ante and see what some more juice produces?" the MO replied. "I'll ramp it up to five hundred volts." He went over to the device on the bench and twisted one of the dials as far as it would go, then extended the probe toward the Armagi's hand. An even brighter spark arced when the probe was close to the skin, and the lights flickered in the room.

"There it goes," the orderly said, as the limb again began to turn transparent. But this time the fingers merged together, and what had been the hand elongated and thickened, with three vicious-looking claws appearing at the end.

"I've no idea what that is," the orderly said, as he frantically tried to sketch this new configuration.

Something caught Parry's eye. "Major, behind you! The arm!"

The severed arm had transformed, too, taking on precisely the same form, complete with the three deadly-looking claws at the extremity. It was too long for the stainless-steel dish and had tipped it over, so the limb flopped onto the bench, like a dead fish.

"Cut the current! Now!" Parry yelled as the severed limb twitched beside the dish.

In his haste the MO dropped the probe. Stooping to retrieve it, he'd just straightened up when the Armagi transformed completely.

In the blink of an eye, it suddenly had three pairs of

limbs branching from its thorax, like an enormous transparent arachnid. The limbs thrashed, tearing the leather constraints binding it to the gurney as if they were tissue paper.

The MO didn't stand a chance as he regarded the creature with stunned bewilderment.

His head came off with one short sweep of the Armagi's forelimb. The three claws were as deadly as they looked.

Then it sprang from the gurney and hit the dividing window with a resounding clang. Its claws penetrated the tempered glass, deep enough that it could hang from the partition. Then it struck at the glass again, as if it knew it wouldn't take long for it to break through.

"Burn out!" Parry yelled at the top of his lungs.

"Burn out?" the orderly stammered, frozen into inactivity by the huge spider's head with compound eyes that were staring straight at him through the window.

Parry didn't wait for the orderly, instead flipping up the cover on a panel under the intercom and twisting the key in it. Then he slammed his palm against the large button beside the key.

The isolation chamber was instantly filled with a solid wall of fire. It was a safety feature installed to sterilize it in the event of a mishap with a biological sample.

Parry and the orderly watched as the Armagi turned black and fell back into the inferno.

"Oh good God," the orderly was whimpering.

"The severed arm was affected . . . even though the current was being applied to the Armagi's body," Parry said.

The orderly could barely cope with what he'd just witnessed, let alone understand what Parry was trying to tell him. "But the Major . . . ," he gasped.

Parry seized him by the shoulders. "Pull yourself together, man. If there's a similar form of communication between the Armagi themselves, then our specimen might just have compromised our location. There might be others on the way!" He grabbed the radio from his belt. "EVAC!" he yelled into it.

2

"I LOOK A RIGHT WALLY in this," Will said, catching his reflection in a shop window as they labored along in the intense heat, their Bergens stuffed with all the bedding and towels they'd helped themselves to.

"Yes," Elliott replied absently, her nose buried in a map that she'd found on one of the Limiters.

"Oh, thanks," Will muttered. He paused to adjust the canary-yellow hat with a floppy brim that Elliott had picked out for him in the department store.

"No, I mean it looks just fine," she said. "It does the job and keeps the sun off your face . . . and, anyway, who's going to see even if you do look like a willy?"

"*Wally*," Will corrected her quickly, then surveyed the bodies in the street. "Can't we go back to our base? This place gives me the creeps, and it's just crazy to spend so long out when it's so bloody hot."

Elliott gave him a sympathetic nod, then dangled the map in front of him. "OK, but I just want to check something first." She glanced at the map again before pointing straight ahead. "It's this way."

She strode off, not only laden down by her Bergen and long

rifle, but carrying an additional two rifles she'd insisted on taking from the Limiters. For a moment, Will watched her go, and the way her hips swayed as she walked. She was growing up so quickly, and with her tanned skin and her long black hair, she'd never looked more beautiful. In the same way that the Styx seemed to be able to adapt to any environment they were in, Elliott was flourishing in their new home in the inner world.

And Will had her all to himself.

He allowed himself a smug smile, then the sweat running down the small of his back reminded him where he was. He wasn't happy about spending any longer in the city than was absolutely necessary, but he always found it difficult not to let Elliott have her way.

Will happened to glance at what appeared to be a luxurious hotel judging by the canopy over the entrance. A flock of the most obnoxious-looking vultures was perching on the red-and-white striped awning, their mean little gray eyes intent on both him and Elliott. "You're out of luck, boys — I'm not dead yet!" Will yelled at the birds. Wiping his brow, he indicated Elliott up ahead. "Though if she has anything to do with it, I'd stick around!" he added.

There was no way that Elliott could have missed the comment, but she kept doggedly leading them both on. Soon they found themselves in an area with a different feel to it. There were no shops here, but rather austere terraces of five-story buildings, many of which appeared to be offices or government departments from the engraved brass nameplates at their entrances.

As Will and Elliott progressed down yet another of these unremarkable streets, they both heard the tapping sound. The rhythm wasn't regular, but as they drew to a halt and listened, it didn't let up. In this eerie place, it was more than enough to put them on their guard.

As Elliott pointed up ahead, Will acknowledged with a single nod of the head. She was right that the sound seemed to be coming from their side of the street, although it was difficult to pinpoint precisely where as it reverberated off the buildings opposite. As Elliott silently cocked her rifle, edging cautiously along the pavement, Will kept his distance, his hands tight around his Sten.

Elliott reached the second-to-last building of the terrace, then crouched and brought her rifle up. Discarding his Bergen, Will had stepped off the pavement and into the road, where he was using the discarded vehicles as cover, all the time keeping an eye on the facade of the building. He realized how efficiently he and Elliott worked together; there was no need for them to speak, as each knew instinctively what the other was going to do in any given situation. The first time Will had witnessed that level of empathy was as he'd watched Elliott and Drake out on patrol in the Deeps. Will suddenly thought of their friend, who had to have perished when the nuclear device exploded, and the pang of grief was so intense that it made him take a sharp breath.

As Elliott heard it and turned toward him, Will avoided her gaze. He took up position at the front of a car, then concentrated on the upper windows of the buildings where the sound seemed to be originating.

There was no sign of anybody there, but the tapping didn't let up.

Just as Will expected her to, Elliott now moved from the pavement, stepping slowly backward as she trained her scope on each window in turn. Will was covering her with his Sten when, all of a sudden, she stopped and gave a small chuckle.

"What is it? What can you see?" Will whispered.

"Top floor, two windows in," she replied.

Squinting, Will located the sash window, then spotted the movement through the open section at the top. At that height the faintest of breezes was enough to ruffle the blind drawn halfway down the window. And it was the pull cord on the bottom of this blind, which was swinging repeatedly against the windowpane below. As Will watched, there was no doubt that it was the source of the tapping.

"False alarm," he said. "It's only the wind."

They both relaxed and straightened up.

"We're seeing ghosts," Elliott said, as she ejected the round from the breech of her rifle to make it safe.

"Well, what do you expect?" Will replied with a shrug. "This place is enough to make anyone freak. They're all dead — the New Germanians, the Styx, even the bushmen back in the jungle. All of them." He glanced disconsolately up at all the ranks of dusty windows, then at the Sten in his hands. "I don't know why we're even bothering to bring weapons with us. There isn't a single animal left that can hurt us. Apart from the fish, birds, and the bloody flies, we're all there is."

Elliott cried out, but Will didn't catch what she'd said.

"What is it?" Will gasped, only now noticing that she'd moved to the end of the street. He lost his hat as he broke into a run to catch up with her.

As he reached her at the corner, the huge plaza opened up before him, in its center the government building constructed in the form of a colossal arch. He'd spotted the top of the arch on a previous expedition into the city, but had never been this close to it before.

In the roads that bordered and intersected the plaza, there were numerous crashed cars and trucks, while others had been driven up onto the pedestrian walkways and simply left there with their doors open. And then there were military vehicles and tanks dotted around the base of the arch that looked like they'd been abandoned in a hurry, their guns facing in random directions.

"What's the matter? What have you seen?" Will asked.

She didn't answer, simply pointing.

He followed her finger, making something out in the lee of one of the legs of the arch. It was sizable, probably several hundred feet in height, and, as he shielded his eyes from the sun, he realized it was a statue of some description.

"You've got to be joking!" he spluttered all of a sudden. "That can't be who I think it is!"

"Oh, yes, it is. Have a closer look." Elliott passed Will her rifle so he could use the scope.

It was a huge statue of Tom Cox.

There he was, in all his glory, his nebulous outline fashioned in granite as black and pernicious as some giant rock waiting to hole a ship.

His hood was raised to his growth-infested forehead so the grotesque face and pupil-less eyes were on full view. What was worse was that the eyes had been carved from some form of limestone or lighter stone, so it really did resemble the traitorous renegade from the Deeps who had helped the Styx.

"Tom *bloody* Cox," Will said through clenched teeth, as he recalled how the monster of a man had cut him on top of the pyramid, then threatened to remove his fingers one by one. The statue was a reminder that Will could have done without.

And Will wasn't sure if he should be outraged or simply laugh because the sight of it was just so ludicrous.

Elliott was similarly affected. It had been nothing for her to shoot Cox down and kill him; while in his clutches she'd suffered indescribably until Drake had rescued her from the man — if *man* was the right word. "That's so sick that only she . . . *they* could have dreamed it up," Elliott said, spitting out the words as if they were poison in her mouth.

Will nodded because he knew better than anyone that Elliott was right — the Rebecca twins had been responsible for erecting the monument to Cox, merely because the fact that the fat Chancellor would have to look down at it every day from his official chambers had amused them.

"If we can figure out how to work one of the tanks, we could use the statue for target practice," Will suggested, then ran a finger inside his shirt collar, which was soaked with sweat. "And if this is what you wanted us to see, can we go home now?" he pleaded.

"I had no idea it was here," Elliott replied, then held up the map. "What's unusual about this is the Limiters marked

locations on it. They never do that — it was against their
SOPs. And there seems to be something important marked
not far from here."

"Really, who cares about *what* the Limiters did or why
they did it?" Will said, but not unpleasantly. "They're all
history now."

Elliott fixed him with one of her looks.

Will let his shoulders droop. "Elliott, you talked me into
coming to this horrible city for supplies and stuff we need.
And now you want to go on a sightseeing trip. I didn't sign up
for this."

"What's happened to you?" Elliott said. "Remember when
nobody could stop you from sticking your nose into everything, because you were curious? You've really changed."
She frowned. "What is it, Will? Are you getting old or
something?"

Will humphed. "I am . . . not . . . getting . . . *old*," he
enunciated slowly. "It's just that this bloody sun is roasting
me alive."

"A little bit of sun never hurt anyone," she said under her
breath, then did an about turn and began to jog down the side
of the plaza.

"But I'm not just *anyone*. I'm an albino!" Will called after
her. "And don't go running off again. I need to fetch my
Bergen first!"

With the giant arch now behind them, they were making their
way down one of the wide avenues that branched off from the
central plaza like spokes radiating from the hub of a wheel.

Will began to sniff as he caught the faint smell of burning in the air. Then they entered a section of the thoroughfare where the wind was swirling black ash over the chalk-colored surface of the road. This ash grew ever more dense until their boots were leaving tracks in it.

Neither of them saw fit to remark on this; some weeks before, they'd heard explosions and rushed to the top of the pyramid beside their camp. From there they'd watched thick yellow smoke billowing into the sky from a factory on the outskirts of the city, which had clearly overheated and gone up in flames. Spontaneous fires were commonplace in this inner world, where the unrelenting sun set whole swaths of the jungle ablaze almost on a daily basis. So there was no reason to believe that the same thing couldn't happen in the middle of the city itself, particularly as it was completely unattended.

Will drew to a halt by the central median in the middle of the six-lane avenue, Elliott stopping beside him. "Goes a hell of a long way," she said, trying to see to the end.

Will was admiring the impressive facades of the buildings on the opposite side of the avenue. "They'd done so much here," he mumbled. He was suddenly struck by the dismal fate that had befallen the once-thriving metropolis, built on the bare earth in fewer than seventy years. "You know, this is just like a place in London that Dad used to take me some weekends. I think it was Kensington, where the science and natural history museums are, but it was always so crowded with people and tourists," Will said, indicating the buildings that he'd been staring at. "I wonder if they're museums, too."

Elliott shrugged. "Whatever they are, something important was going on in this area according to the Limiter map." A building farther down from Will's supposed museums caught her eye. "What do you think that place is?"

It was Will's turn to shrug as he located the iron-framed building with large expanses of glass reflecting the sun. "Dunno. A whopping big greenhouse?" he suggested.

Unbeknownst to Will and Elliott, it was the tropical greenhouse where Vane had been impregnating New Germanians in their thousands before the plague had struck. Will peered over his shoulder at the parade of shops behind him, his gaze coming to rest on a boarded-up shop with the words MOST — CONFISERIE emblazoned above it in large gold letters. This didn't mean anything to him, but the model of a giant bar of unwrapped chocolate hanging from a bracket did. "That must be a candy shop," he decided, then chuckled sadly. "Museums and chocolates — Dad's two favorite things in life. He would've loved it here."

"That's odd," Elliott murmured, not taking any notice of what Will was saying.

"No, I think it really is a candy shop," Will replied, already making a beeline toward it.

"Odd that there are far fewer bodies in this stretch," Elliott said, raising her rifle so she could use the scope to check farther down the avenue.

As Will reached the shop, he found that the main window was protected by lengths of timber nailed across it, although someone had had a go at an area toward the bottom. Here the planking had been prized off and the glass behind it stoved in.

Will squatted down to peer inside, but couldn't see anything much where the display of goods must have once been.

As he stood up again, the soles of his boots crunched on hard candies all the colors of the rainbow, grinding them into the ash. "Someone got lucky," Will muttered under his breath. After weeks of eating little else but fish, his mouth watered at the prospect of finding something that came in its own packet.

Wondering if there was anything left inside, Will went to the door of the shop. To his surprise, as he turned the handle and pushed, it swung open before him. He didn't stop to consider why it should be unlocked as he tore inside and was greeted with a view of a shadowy shop interior that was straight out of a different century.

On the shop counter of polished dark wood were chocolate truffles on silver platters, and stands of lollipops of all different colors. He examined one of these lollipops — it was quite unusual in that the top spun around on the stick as he flicked it with a finger. Stuffing it in his pocket, he turned his attention to the shelves beyond the counter, which housed jars of wonderful-looking sweets. BONBONS, he read on one of the jars, and had put his Sten on the counter and was about to climb over to get to them when he happened to glance at the wall behind him. On the shelves there was the most amazing range of what looked like chocolate bars, box after box of them, and enough to keep someone supplied for a good few years.

"The mother lode!" Will laughed, rubbing his hands together in glee. Turning from the counter, he walked slowly beside the shelves as he helped himself to the different bars. He had no idea what was written on the wrappers, so he began

to tear them open to sample chunks. "Mint," he said to himself, as he tasted one bar with a picture of an iceberg on the packet. The bars were all rather soft from the heat, but he didn't mind in the least.

"This is too good to be true," Will said as he reached the end of the shelves and his gaze alighted on the crates of bottles stacked there. He picked one out that had a clear liquid in it and banged the bottle top down against the edge of the counter so it flipped off. The cap hardly had time to hit the floor before Will took a big swig of the fizzy contents.

"Ah, that's so good!" he exclaimed, his eyes rolling in ecstasy before he promptly downed the rest of the bottle. "Lemonade!" He immediately grabbed another two bottles and popped off the lids. "Elliott's not going to believe this," he said, rushing back toward the door with his bounty.

As he exited onto the pavement, he stopped dead on the spot.

There was a small figure standing there in some kind of protective suit, a gun in its hands. The barrel was shaking, but the weapon was pointing in Will's direction.

Blast it! My Sten! Will thought, kicking himself for leaving it on the counter. But it wouldn't have done him much good right now. He slowly raised his hands with the bottles still in them, the chocolate bars he'd been holding under his arm falling all around his feet.

The suit was an opaque white and appeared to be made from some type of plastic. The figure's head was totally enclosed in a cylindrical helmet with a flat top, and there was a filter at the neck from which Will could hear a low hissing noise. The helmet was clearly being fed with a constant supply of oxygen or air from the cylinder slung over the figure's back.

"Who are you?" Will asked, as his mind raced, wondering how anyone could have been left alive in the metropolis. He squinted at the rectangular area of clear plastic in the helmet, making out the frightened young eyes peering back at him. It was a young boy — probably no more than ten years old.

At least it wasn't a Styx, Will consoled himself. "You're . . . you're just a kid, aren't you? What on earth are you doing here?" he asked.

The child made no response, but kept the gun pointing at Will.

"Can you understand me? Just keep calm," Will said, trying his hardest to keep calm himself in the circumstances. "I'm not armed," he added. He suddenly realized that this was a ludicrous statement to make, with his bottles of fizzy lemonade still held high in both hands.

The boy's arms were shaking as he held the gun.

"Look, can't you understand me? We're not going to hurt you," Will said again in exasperation.

The boy began to gesticulate wildly with his handgun. It was an odd-looking weapon, a Broomhandle Mauser, similar to the German side arm from the First World War. And it was unwieldy for a child, which was probably why the boy needed both hands to keep it leveled at Will.

The boy stepped nearer to Will, jabbing the Mauser at him until the muzzle was less than a foot away from his face. There was sheer panic in the boy's young eyes, and it was difficult for Will not to notice how tightly his finger was gripping the trigger. That wasn't good.

There was the slightest sound, like a gust of wind. Then the click as a safety catch came off.

Elliott was there on the pavement beside the boy. Her rifle was to her shoulder, aimed directly at his temple.

"I want you to lower your weapon," she ordered him. "Nice and easy."

The boy jerked as if he'd been stung, but he kept his head resolutely toward Will.

"I said lower your weapon," Elliott tried again.

The boy still showed no sign of complying, although his eyes were flicking back and forth between Will and Elliott.

"Come on, kid, put it down," Will pleaded with him, then spoke to Elliott. "It's useless. He doesn't seem to understand anything."

"No, he doesn't," Elliott agreed. "And if he doesn't lower that weapon soon, I'm going to put a round into his wrist."

The boy clearly didn't like it that Will and Elliott were talking. He began to jab the handgun in Will's direction and shake his head, while his helmet steamed up a little on the inside.

There was another click.

"Ah, but we both understand you very well," a man's voice said. "And you're not going to shoot anyone, Fräulein." He was armed with another of the odd-looking pistols, and the end of the barrel was pressed against the back of Elliott's head. She rolled her eyes upward, furious that she'd allowed someone to sneak up on her.

The man was also wearing a protective suit. "Might I suggest that you lower *your* weapon?" he said in very formal English.

"Not a chance," Elliott replied coolly. "If I do that, we lose our leverage. Right now, if you open fire I may die, but my finger will contract. At this range, the kid is certain to catch a bullet. He'll go down, no question. Do you want to take that risk?"

There was a pause as the man thought this over. "And before he dies, the boy may also get a shot off at your friend, too."

"Maybe, maybe not," Elliott said.

Will took a breath. "If it's OK with all of you, I'd really rather not find out." The heat on the pavement was oppressive, and the sweat was trickling down his back as his arms began to tire from holding the lemonade bottles above his head. "Tell you what," he said, forcing a smile, "how about if I go first and put these bottles down?"

No one replied or seemed about to follow his suggestion, all gripping their weapons firmly. Without moving his head, Will slid his eyes over to try to see the man more clearly. "You're wearing that suit because of the virus, aren't you? But you don't look like a soldier."

"No, I'm not a soldier," the man answered.

Will frowned. "It's a no-brainer that you're New Germanian, but how did you survive the virus? And what are you doing here?"

"I might ask you the same question," the man countered.

"We came here from the surface to stop the Styx . . . to stop them breeding. It all went wrong, and a deadly pathogen was released. It was an accident," Will said, realizing how bad that sounded. "So who are you exactly?" he asked again quickly.

"I was a science officer at the *Institut für Antiquitäten*," the man said. "You would call it the . . . er . . . Institute of Antiquities."

Will's ears perked up at this. "Antiquities? So you know all about the pyramids and the ruins in the jungle?" he ventured.

"As much as we were allowed to, with the military breathing down our necks," the man replied.

Elliott cleared her throat. "Can we *please* stick to the point? We're in a situation here!" she said through clenched teeth.

Will ignored her comment, feeling a little light-headed from the heat of the sun. "My dad and I were studying the pyramids, too," he said. "In fact, we ended up *inside* one of them, when we were running from the Styx. The bloody bushmen let us in, but then gave us up. My dad was killed as a result."

"So that was you," the man whispered. For a second he didn't speak, clearly considering what he'd heard. "Then you can tell me something," he finally said. "What was the name of the army officer who took you by helicopter so th —"

"Bismarck," Elliott jumped in before the man had a chance to finish. "The Colonel helped us to escape in his helicopter so we could take the route back to the outer world. That's where we met up with him again — on the surface. He was our friend."

The man appeared perturbed by this. "*Was* your friend?"

Will nodded sadly. "He was killed by the Styx when they ambushed us. Just before the void was plugged by the explosion and the virus released."

"I knew Bismarck, too. He might have been in the military, but he was a good man," the New Germanian said. He took a step back from Elliott, but kept his pistol on her. "So you know about how the plague started. And both of you are exposed to the air, but neither of you are showing any symptoms."

"We were given shots against it," Will answered, scrunching up an eye as sweat trickled into it.

Will's answer seemed to have impressed the man, who was silent for a second. "So . . . so we'd have immunity against it, too, if you allowed us to take blood from you," he finally said.

"If it means it's not going to be splattered all over the pavement," Will replied, now focusing on the end of the barrel of the boy's handgun, "be my guest."

"OK," the man said, and without further ado both he and the boy holstered their weapons. He went straight to the boy, and spoke to him in hushed tones while inspecting a gauge on the cylinder on his back.

With a sigh of relief Will put the lemonade bottles by his feet. He was stretching his arms and rubbing his cramped muscles as he met Elliott's gaze. "What?" he asked. She hadn't yet lowered her guard, her rifle in a semi-ready position at her waist. Then she gave a small shrug and slung the weapon over her shoulder with the others she was carrying.

The man came over to Will, proffering a gloved hand. "I'm Jürgen, and this is Karl, my son." It felt a little strange to be spoken to by the cylindrical helmet, with only the man's eyes visible through a window of clear plastic.

Will introduced himself and Elliott. "We didn't think anyone else was alive," he said, the surprise that anyone had survived in the city only now sinking in.

"I think we're the only ones," Jürgen said. He chuckled as he glanced at the doorway behind Will. "And not even a plague can keep Karl away from a *Süßwarengeschäft* . . . a candy shop." His voice turned serious. "But now I need you to come with me," he added, also addressing Elliott.

She was immediately suspicious. "Where?" she demanded. "And tell me something first — how is it that your English is so good? The Colonel mentioned that all New Germanians learned it at school, but you have even less of an accent than he did."

"The scientific fraternity here in the city employed it as the main language in their everyday work and for record keeping," Jürgen replied without missing a beat. "It started out that way because most of the scientific journals in the archives that were flown into this world back in the nineteen forties were in English. And many of the scientists at the time were reacting against the Third Reich and only too happy not to use their native language."

"OK," Elliott said, still not wholly convinced that the man was to be trusted. "And where do you want us to go?"

"To the hospital. Karl and I have to return there before our air runs out, and that's where my brother, Werner, will be able to use the antigens in your blood to immunize us. You see, he was a doctor in the infectious diseases unit of the hospital," Jürgen explained. "When the first reports of the outbreak began to come in, he rushed my son and me into the quarantine ward just in time. That's why we're still alive." Jürgen paused. "So you'll come with us now?"

"Sure, let's go," Will said.

They moved off, a watchful Elliott following a few paces behind Will, who was walking with Jürgen and Karl. As they passed them, Jürgen indicated the buildings on the other side of the avenue, which Will had taken for museums. "When the plague swept through the city, the concentration of people was high in this area. We think they were rounded up and brought here for the breeding program."

"I suppose for Vane," Will guessed. "She was the Styx woman."

"I don't know anything about that," Jürgen replied, "but it's clear that the principal site for the breeding was in there." He swung around to look at the large greenhouse, giving his son a passing glance as he turned back to Will again. "I haven't let Karl go in there because the human remains left inside are indescribable. And we haven't begun to clear it out yet, but you can see that we've made a start in the streets . . . by burning the corpses on pyres."

"That explains all the ash," Will said.

"Yes, we're doing all we can to eradicate any pockets of virus." There was despondency in Jürgen's voice as he continued. "It may be too late for the city, but we're hoping that our people in the remote outposts are still safe from the disease. With time, the high levels of ultraviolet light from the sun should destroy any free-living virus, although Werner is worried the avian species might have become the vector — the birds might be carrying it to the far reaches of this world. So we might be hoping in vain."

Will raised his head to the bright sky, watching a lone vulture flapping languidly across it. "Yes, because the birds have been eating the flesh," he said, then frowned. "I just hope they don't spread it to the surface."

"The odds of a bird making it through are pretty slim," Jürgen answered, then pointed down a side road as they came level with it. "The hospital is this way," he said.

Several streets on, Will saw two large wheelbarrows in the middle of the way. One was stacked high with jerrycans containing gasoline or something similar — the smell was strong in the air as they passed them. On the second barrow were several layers of bodies — skeletons still wearing their stained, tattered clothes — all heaped untidily on top of each other.

But Will didn't dwell on this because, at the major crossroads thirty feet away, he spotted what appeared to be a small hillock rising from the surface of the road. As they came closer, he could see it consisted entirely of bones. The mound was as black as charcoal, and rose to almost the height of the first stories of the surrounding buildings. And dotted all over it were glowing red pits where fire still burned, wisps of gray smoke snaking from them until they became lost in the haze of the sun.

Will heard Jürgen speak as he led them toward the mound. "That this is how it should end," he said. And nobody else had anything to add as they walked in a solemn procession around its circumference. The smell of the burned bodies was so pungent that Will cupped his hand over his nose and mouth, trying not to gag at the smell, while Jürgen and his son in their airtight suits were completely insulated from it.

Will spotted a shoe lying on its side in the road, which had managed to evade the fire. He couldn't take his eyes off it. It was a woman's shoe, of highly polished dark blue leather with a shiny chrome buckle. The shoe looked brand new, as if it had been bought from a shop that day and hardly worn.

They continued on and, after a few minutes more, they'd reached the hospital, a gleaming white building that was very out of place against the drab stone facades that bordered it. As they entered through the main doors and went into the unlit interior, it seemed so dark inside now that they were out of the blazing sun. Their footfalls on the linoleum floor were the only sound in the entrance hall, where there were several waiting areas, with ranks of empty benches facing unmanned reception desks.

Jürgen had been silent since they had seen the pyre outside, but now he spoke again. "When we emerged from the quarantine area after a couple of days, we found that people had come here in droves, desperate for help from the doctors," he told Will and Elliott, a hoarseness to his voice. "How do you say it — they were 'packed in like sardines.' And that's how they died — many still standing up. So many that we had a struggle to get the doors open into this area."

Will could see that around the walls there were several more barrows of the same type as the one by the pyre, and knew that these must have been used to move the many dead, although they were now stacked with boxes of supplies.

Jürgen beckoned them over to a doorway leading from the main area. And as he took out a flashlight and turned it on, they followed him down several flights of stairs until they passed through a pair of swinging doors and into a large room. The walls were hung with polythene sheeting, and lengths of yellow cable ran between the temporary lighting that had been rigged up.

Jürgen lifted aside some of the sheeting to reveal a solid-looking door, then pressed a button on an intercom. Will heard the distant sound of a bell ringing. "Just letting my brother know we're back," Jürgen explained. Seconds later a voice came on the intercom. "Werner," Jürgen began, then the lights flicked on in the room and he proceeded to have a rapid exchange with his brother in German.

Elliott came alongside Will. "We don't know what we're walking into here," she whispered. "This could be a trap."

Will was dismissive of the suggestion. "But they need us more than we need them, don't they?" he replied.

"Werner says we have to bring you inside to take your blood under sterile conditions," Jürgen said, breaking into their conversation. "That means you have to be decontaminated, and this is how we're going to do it. Karl and I will go through first, then it's your turn. On the other side of these doors you'll find the primary sterilization chamber, where we wash down our suits and go under the banks of UV light before we remove them. In the next room is the secondary chamber, where we shower again and dress before we can enter the quarantine ward."

"But are we really able to go in there, too? We can wash, but what about any virus *in* us?" Will asked.

"My brother's an expert in these procedures, and he thinks

we can minimize the risk," Jürgen said. "Just remember that you have to leave all your clothes and equipment in the sealed boxes in the primary chamber before you go through the rest of the procedure I've described to you. Once you're finished, you should don the gowns I'll put out for you. And you should wear face masks to ensure that you don't exhale any virus into the ward."

"Got it. OK," Will replied, pretending to be comfortable about the process.

"We'll let you know over the intercom when you can enter," Jürgen said, hesitating before swiveling his cylindrical helmet in Will and Elliott's direction. They could see his eyes as he added, "And thank you for helping us. I can't tell you what this means to us . . . to me . . . it means Karl has a chance." Then he put his hand on his son's shoulder, guiding him away. There was a hiss of air, and the polythene sheeting around the room stirred as he pulled on the heavy door, and they both went in.

Twenty minutes later Jürgen's voice came over the intercom, telling them it was their turn. As Will came to the door, there was a clunking sound as solenoids drew back the bolts in the heavy steel door and he was able to open it. There was another rush of air — a higher air pressure was clearly being maintained in the quarantine ward to stop any air from leaking in.

Although everything was made of stainless steel, the interior of the first decontamination area had the feel of a changing room, with lockers and showers down either side of it. Will squashed his Bergen into one of the lockers, followed by his Sten. He began to unbutton his shirt, but then twisted around to Elliott, who was standing quite still in front of another locker. She'd been about to deposit her weapon inside a locker beside the other two Limiter rifles she'd been carrying.

"What's wrong?" Will asked.

"We're going into this completely empty-handed. No weapons . . . that makes me very uncomfortable," Elliott whispered.

"You stay here, then. I'll go in by myself," Will suggested. "They only need to take blood from one of us."

"No way! We stick together — at all times," she replied quickly, then sighed. "But we don't need to put ourselves in this position in the first place. If we make a run for it, they'll never catch us. And we can make sure they never find us again."

"Don't we owe them?" Will replied. "Whatever you say, we're partly to blame for what's happened. How long can they go on living like this until someone screws up and they get infected? Or they run out of power or water or something?" As Elliott didn't speak, Will added, "You're not very trusting, are you? Don't you think if Drake had been here, he'd have tried to help them? Help save the life of that little kid?"

Elliott seemed taken aback by this. "I honestly don't know," she said, biting her lip as she thought. "I suppose so. But if we do this and it goes wrong, it was your call, and it's on your head."

"Righty-ho," Will said, then added hesitantly, "um . . . one thing, though . . ."

Elliott was unbuckling her belt. "What's that?" she asked.

Will waved his hand at her side of the chamber. "No peeking, OK? You keep your eyes to your side, and I'll do the same. Deal?"

"Er . . . yes . . . deal," she confirmed, realizing what he was saying.

They went through the decontamination procedure in bashful silence, stripping down and washing, then standing under the banks of ultraviolet light as they faced away from each other. And all the time fresh air was being pumped into the chamber — they could hear it rushing through the vents.

Then, at the very moment the banks of ultraviolet lights went out, a voice spoke to them over the intercom by the entrance to the second chamber. "Move through to the next area now, please," it directed.

"Ladies first," Will said, keeping himself turned well away from Elliott.

They showered again in the cubicles on their respective sides, dried themselves down, and then put on the gowns and masks Jürgen had provided for them.

"Are you dressed now?" Will asked.

"Yes, all ready," Elliott replied, and only now did they make eye contact.

Still a little embarrassed by the situation, Will flexed his shoulders under the white gown. "Been a while since I washed in hot water like that. I feel all itchy."

Elliott nodded, trying to hide a smile. "Yes, I noticed you've got a rash on your back."

"Huh!" Will exclaimed, as the solenoids clunked on the door and they followed the order from the intercom to walk through into the quarantine ward itself.

"How do you know that? You cheated — you bloody well looked, didn't you?" Will hissed at Elliott as they stepped into the corridor on the other side of the door. He knew his face was burning; the problem with his milky complexion was that even the slightest degree of embarrassment showed itself.

Elliott giggled. "And you're really quite muscly, aren't you?"

A man appeared from a doorway farther down the corridor and began striding toward them. Jürgen, Will assumed.

"Yeah . . . well . . . you have great dimples," he whispered back at Elliott, grinning mischievously.

"Dimples? Where? Wha —!" Elliott burst out, but was forced into silence because the man was now close enough to hear.

"So we meet in the flesh. I'm Jürgen," the man said, giving them each a formal bow, but not offering to shake hands with them again, maybe because he still had a concern about making physical contact despite the thorough cleansing they'd undergone.

Dressed in blue overalls, Jürgen was a slight man, not much taller than Will. His blond hair was still damp from his own decontamination procedure, his long bangs hanging lankly in front of his blue eyes. He now brushed them to one side self-consciously. "I hope your skin isn't too sore after all the washing," he said, smelling the back of his hand. He indicated a rack of what resembled fire extinguishers by the base of the wall, but they were painted green with German lettering on them. "The showers you've just had contain germicide, same as in those tanks. It's an added precaution against the virus, but it can cause a skin reaction."

"Yes, Elliott noticed I had a rash," Will muttered, giving her a pointed look.

Trying her best not to smile, Elliott asked, "So what do we do now?"

"Werner's waiting for us in the laboratory. Please come this way," Jürgen said, turning on his heels.

As they set off down the corridor, Karl ran up and threw his arms around his father, hiding his face against him. With his fair locks, the child resembled his father, although he had dark smudges under his eyes as if he hadn't slept for a while. Still, with his face pressed against his father, he was sneaking the occasional look at Will and Elliott.

"Hi," Will said, but the boy didn't reply.

Jürgen began to walk slowly, his son still hanging on to him. "Karl doesn't speak. In fact, he hasn't said a single word since the day of the plague. You see my wife, his mother, didn't make it into this shelter in time. We know she was on the way here . . . but maybe the invaders picked her up for more brainwashing. They were in the habit of doing that to anyone who appeared to be in a hurry."

"I'm sorry," Will mumbled.

Jürgen continued to walk slowly, his voice unsteady at the memory. "Anyway, we couldn't wait for her any longer. We had no choice. We had to close the main door . . . or we'd have been overwhelmed by all the other people in here."

"You said *brainwashed*? You mean the Styx Darklit her?" Elliott asked gently.

"Darklit?" Jürgen said, repeating the unfamiliar word. "With the purple light?" He squinted and pretended to shield his face from a bright light. "Yes, we all had that. The people you call the Styx went through the city quarter by quarter, forcing us out of the buildings. Then they made us look at the purple lights, even Karl here." He ruffled the boy's hair.

Will exchanged a glance with Elliott, who was frowning. "That's not good news. We need to deal with whatever they've implanted in you," she said, putting into words precisely what Will was thinking.

"You can do that?" Jürgen asked. "How? And why?"

"I've got a piece of kit in my Bergen that was developed to neutralize the Dark Light," Will replied, referring to the Purger. "What they put in your head might be dangerous for you, or anyone with you. I was programmed to chuck myself off anything high enough to kill me."

"I see," Jürgen said with a nod. "Then we should deal with that later, but first there's a more pressing matter to address." He steered Will and Elliott into a room crammed with medical equipment. A man looked up from his microscope. *"Guten Tag,"* he said.

"English, Werner, you need to speak in English," Jürgen reminded him.

Although Werner had his brother's blue eyes and similar features, he was taller and far thinner. He was obviously the elder of the two, his blond hair very patchy on his scalp.

"OK, in English," he said.

"You need some of our blood?" Will asked.

"That's right. I've been working to identify the viral bodies so I can isolate them," Werner explained, inclining his head at the microscope. "So far I haven't been successful." Then he got to his feet and pulled on a pair of rubber gloves. "You see, this ward you're in was established because there was always the specter of a new bacterium or viral strain seeping into our world from the surface. And because we would lack any natural resistance to it, it was feared that it might rip through the population. This plague that struck us was too virulent for our doctors to do anything in time."

"But you know how to prepare a vaccine from our blood?" Will asked.

Werner nodded. "The antigens in you will mean that I have a ready-made vaccine to inoculate us, and any other survivors we find, against the plague." He asked Will and Elliott to sit down, then used syringes to extract samples of blood from each of them. He told them that once he'd prepared the vaccine, either he or his brother would test it out first because if it went wrong then they couldn't both afford to be incapacitated at the same time.

"That'll be me, then . . . the guinea fowl," Jürgen said, nodding sanguinely.

"I think it's *guinea pig*," Will corrected him.

"So you don't need us any longer?" Elliott asked.

"No, but if you're agreeable, would you mind staying until we know the vaccine is viable? I might need some more samples," Werner said. "What's the English expression? Better safe than sorry."

"OK . . . but how long do you want us to stick around?" Will asked, eager to leave the city and return to their base in the jungle.

"Forty-eight hours maximum," Werner replied, already taking their blood samples over to a centrifuge as he began his work.

Jürgen escorted Will and Elliott from the laboratory and down a corridor, past several doors. "We have some rooms for you along here." He indicated the right-hand side of the corridor. "These are all isolation rooms, self-contained living quarters with their own distinct air filtration so you can remove your masks in them to eat and drink."

They'd passed several of these isolation rooms when Will caught sight of something through the inspection window in one of the doors that made him pull up sharply.

"I don't believe it!" he exclaimed as he saw the figure perched on the edge of the sleeping cot, its skin rough and whorled like the bark of an old tree. "That's a bushman, isn't it? How did you get him to come here?"

"I've never seen one alive before," Elliott said, going to the window to peer in.

The bushman had his head toward her, his small brown eyes the only recognizable human feature until he opened his mouth and she saw his pink tongue. He appeared to be saying something.

"But why is he here?" Will pressed Jürgen.

"I was one of a small team in the Institute of Antiquities that has been working with the indigenous population — or the tribespeople, as we refer to them — for the last decade," Jürgen replied. "We established contact on an expedition and kept it from the military, who had it in their minds that they were hostile. Actually, they had no idea *what* was in that sector of the jungle, but if they had known, they would most likely have mounted an operation to round them up."

Jürgen took a breath. "It was regrettable that several service-men lost their lives when they were mistakenly considered to be a threat to the pyramids. We were able to prevent any further deaths by talking to the tribespeople and making them understand."

Will was shaking his head as he realized something. "So that's why they left me and my father alone," he said.

"That's correct," Jürgen confirmed. "As for this tribesman, he was smuggled into my institute several weeks before the plague hit, and I couldn't just abandon him. I didn't know if he was vulnerable to it, too."

"We found a few of them dead in the jungle," Will said.

"Werner thought that might be the case. Most vertebrates are susceptible. And the tribesmen's physiology beneath those radically different epidermal layers is essentially the same as ours," Jürgen said.

Elliott didn't seem convinced by this. "They're human?" she asked. "They don't look it."

But Will's mind was teeming with questions. "You said that you've been working with them? On what, exactly?"

"The origins of their civilization, the pyramids, and the ruined city," Jürgen replied. "Progress has been slow because communication with them is so rudimentary. You see those drawings on the table in front of him?"

Will and Elliott peered at the sheets of paper covered with pictures, similar to the pictograms carved on the exterior of the pyramids. "Hieroglyphs?" Will asked.

"Yes. Right from the start, we figured out that it was the best way to have any sort of meaningful exchange. You see, their language is very basic . . . very limited."

"My dad was able to talk to them, but it didn't get us any-where," Will said, remembering the moment inside the pyramid.

"That's why this tribesman was at the Institute, to make recordings. We'd made the breakthrough that they communi-cate with each other using a whole other set of sounds that are barely audible to the human ear. It's —"

"It's sort of high-pitched, like a buzzing noise," Will cut in.

Jürgen nodded. "That's absolutely right."

"And it's even more difficult to hear because they move at the same time . . . they rustle," Will said, then fell silent as he stared into the middle distance. He still felt bitterness toward the bushmen about the way they had treated him and Dr. Burrows. "I picked up on it when they took us prisoner — just before they shopped us to the Styx."

Jürgen turned to him. "You know, the bushmen weren't . . . aren't your enemy. They don't want to get involved in anyone else's conflicts. If they gave you up to the invaders, then it was because they believed they had to in order to protect their pyr-amid. That's what they do. That's *all* they do. They protect their pyramids. Endless generations have been the guardians . . . the caretakers of something they don't seem to really understand." Jürgen went to the observation window and held up his hand to the bushman, who held up one of his, although it resembled a bundle of twigs.

Will noticed that there were pieces of his skin scattered all around where he was sitting, like shredded leaves. "What's that by his feet?" he asked.

"Their epidermal layer — their thick skin — is an evolu-tionary adaptation. It's both camouflage and a screen against the sun's harmful rays. But in here, away from the sunlight, the outermost layer isn't necessary, and some of it begins to dry up and slough off."

Jürgen was obviously keen to show Will and Elliott to their rooms, and began to edge along the corridor, but Will was lost in his thoughts and oblivious to this. As Elliott took him by the arm to get him moving, he said, "I'd love to know what you've learned from these people."

"I'd be very happy to take you through . . . ," Jürgen said, tailing off as his son appeared. The boy thrust something into Will's hand before running off again. It was a brightly colored lollipop that rotated on its stick, like the ones Will had seen in the shop.

Jürgen smiled. "You are honored indeed. Those *Kriesel* lollies are Karl's absolute favorites. You can eat it in your room, where you can take your mask off."

"I certainly will," Will said, spinning the top of the lollipop with his finger and smiling after the boy.

Although the isolation rooms were small, the sleeping cots were comfortable enough, and the canned food was a welcome change from Will and Elliott's usual fare in the jungle. Jürgen was the first candidate for Werner's vaccine, suffering nothing more than a slight headache after he was injected and his body began to produce antigens against the disease.

After twenty-four hours, Werner carried out tests on his brother's blood to establish whether he'd acquired immunity against the virus. Even though the tests proved he had, Jürgen didn't venture outside the quarantine ward, but instead kept

Will and Elliott company, talking about his research on the bushmen and the ruins his team had found on expeditions into the jungle.

Werner then vaccinated himself, Karl, and the bushman. The growing sense of excitement was almost palpable among the New Germanians, but then, halfway through the second day, there was an incident. Will was roused from his sleep by a crash and then voices in the corridor outside. Putting on his mask, he hurried from his room to find Elliott already there, with both of the New Germanian brothers. They were by the door to the bushman's room, peering in through the observation port.

"What is it?" Will asked.

"We don't know yet," Werner mumbled. "We need to go in."

Jürgen nodded in agreement.

Werner forced the door open, then quickly entered with his brother. That was when Will had the first glimpse.

The bushman had passed out against the door, blocking it. Whatever was wrong with him, it must have come on when he'd risen from his cot; he'd obviously knocked over a small table when he'd fallen, which accounted for the crash. He was breathing quickly, and his skin was dripping with sweat.

And it *was* skin — every last scrap of the outer layer of barklike hide had peeled off, and hunks of it were scattered over the cot and the floor around him.

There was no mistaking that he was human now — he was a wiry but fully grown man. But, at odds with this, his skin was very pink, like a newborn child's. And all over his body there were spots of blood, similar to abrasions, where shedding of the whorls of tough outer hide had caused hemorrhaging.

Jürgen and Werner each took one of the bushman's arms and carried him back to his cot.

Will saw then that he had absolutely no hair. Or eyebrows, for that matter.

"But has this happened before?" Will asked. "All the outer layers dropping off?"

"No, not with any of the other tribesmen we had with us in the Institute," Jürgen replied, as his brother took hold of the bushman's wrist.

"His pulse seems strong enough, but the rate is very elevated," Werner said, as he timed it using his watch.

Jürgen looked concerned. "It must be a reaction to the vaccine."

"I can't see why. I ran some *in vitro* tests on his blood beforehand, and there was nothing to sugg —"

"Wait — look!" Will said, as the bushman stirred, his eyes opening groggily. "He's coming around!"

The bushman tried to lift himself up, but Jürgen spoke soothingly to him, urging him to stay where he was. Although he probably didn't understand what he was being told, the bushman relaxed and laid his head back on the pillow. His eyes were flickering open and then closing as if it was a struggle for him to remain conscious.

Jürgen held a glass to the bushman's lips, helping him to drink some water. "He's very hot," he said.

"Maybe he's contracted a mild fever, or he's just become dehydrated," Werner suggested, as the bushman had some more to drink.

Jürgen nodded. "That would explain why he fainted. And why he seems to be improving now."

The bushman was indeed showing signs that he was recovering rapidly; he refused any more water and pushed the glass away as he attempted to speak.

There were words in the guttural language that Will had heard before, but in between these the buzzing sound was now far more audible. And this was becoming even more audible with every second. It was as if his voice box was also going through a transformation. Quite suddenly, the pitch of the buzzing sound dropped, and well-defined and ugly sounds came from his throat.

"What the —!" Will exclaimed, taking such a sudden step back that he collided with the wall.

Elliott was similarly shocked, too stunned to speak for the moment.

Jürgen and Werner turned toward them, giving them questioning looks.

"What is it?" Jürgen demanded.

From the words she'd been able to recognize, the bushman had been asking what was wrong with him.

In the Styx tongue.

And as Elliott, because of her father, was fluent in the Styx language, she was able to answer the bushman in it. "Don't worry. We'll find out what's wrong," she said to him, the eerie sound of her words filling the room as if someone was tearing old parchment.

"*Mein Gott*," Werner said.

"*Mein Gott*, indeed," Will said under his breath.

Elliott switched back to English for Will and the two astounded New Germanians. "I can understand some of what he's saying. He wants to know what's wrong with him."

Despite the fact that he was so weak, on hearing Elliott speak in the Styx tongue the bushman's eyes had flicked wide open. He heaved himself up from his cot and, before anyone could stop him, had thrown himself at her feet. With his face pressed to the floor, he continued to repeat the same words.

"They have returned," he was saying over and over again.

Will was dumbfounded. "All the time, the bushmen were talking in Styx. But at such a high pitch, no one knew it."

He looked from the groveling man on the floor to Elliott, and back to the man again. "If he can speak Styx, then maybe he's part Styx like you. And maybe your blood . . . your Styx blood in the vaccine caused this . . . changed him. But how? And why?"

3

AS THE SUN BEGAN its final descent, long shadows were beginning to crawl over London, where street after street was yet again without power. People were barricading themselves in their houses and preparing themselves for another night of fear, hunger, and cold. But they didn't know whether they were defending themselves against the lawless gangs who were running amok without the police or army to stop them, or something far more sinister, if the rumors doing the rounds were to be believed.

In some neighborhoods the residents had organized themselves into local militia, using vehicles to close off roads, and wielding brooms, garden implements, and even saucepans to scare off anyone who tried to enter their areas without good reason.

But in West London there was one bastion of apparent normality. The Westfield shopping center, Britain's largest mall, was somehow still connected to an active grid, and the light flooding through its windows proved to be irresistible to those too terrified to remain at home.

No one had thought to turn off the sound system, and piped music was playing in the background as, at regular intervals, a forced, DJ-smooth voice gave a pre-recorded message about forthcoming but long-out-of-date promotions. The shops themselves were definitely off limits with their security grilles firmly across them. Some still had goods in the window, but others had been vacated and the stock removed until, it was hoped, conditions returned to normal.

All along the walkways in the shopping center, people in sleeping bags or swaddled in blankets were settling down for the night. It was reminiscent of scenes from the Second World War when the underground platforms had been used as air-raid shelters. There may have been electricity to keep the lights burning, but the heating was another matter, and it was bitterly cold inside the building. A succession of small fires had been lit and were being stoked with empty packaging or whatever else could be found to keep them going, as empty-eyed faces stared into their meager flames.

Bound up in their own misery, none of them took much notice as a woman passed by. Tall and elegant, she threaded her way between the untidy clumps of people, her high heels clicking on the polished floor. If they had paid her any attention, they would have observed that she wore an expensive fur coat with the collar turned up, and that two men with hoods obscuring their faces were like twin shadows as they followed silently behind.

A child, no more than six years old, made straight toward her and planted himself insolently in her path.

"Oi, rich lady, got anything to eat?" the boy demanded.

The woman, Alex, stared down at him with undisguised disgust. "What?" she said.

"I said, got anything to eat?" the boy repeated, this time jabbing a dirty finger impatiently at his mouth as if he was talking to someone too stupid to understand him.

Her dark-rimmed eyes blazed with anger, the muscles in her razor-lean face tightening so that she looked more like a sculpture than a human being. "Yes . . . ," she growled, ". . . you!"

But as she finished speaking, a flood of lacteous saliva slopped over her black lip.

Not taking his eyes from her, the boy inclined his head and made a coarse noise as if he was vomiting, then swaggered away. He knew he was still in earshot as he added, "Gross old minger."

Alex quickly put her hand to her mouth, not to wipe it, but to make sure the fleshy tube twitching like a snake inside her cheeks wasn't about to show itself. She turned to one of the Limiters behind her. "I don't know what it is with children these days — they show no respect," she said. "Make a note that I want to teach that little brat a lesson myself, will you? I've got a grub with his name on it."

The Styx soldier gave a small nod to show that he understood.

As she caught the jaunty tune coming from the mall's speakers, she cocked her head to one side. "Is that 'The Girl from Ipanema'?" she asked. It was so upbeat and at odds with the fluorescent-lit scene of despair around her that she was unable to stifle a laugh as she began to head toward a retail unit at the far end of the shopping center, outside which another pair of Limiters was waiting. As soon as they saw her, they pulled up the shutter so that she could enter. She strode through the front of the empty shop and straight into the storeroom at the rear.

On some packing crates, Rebecca Two was sitting very close to Captain Franz. The instant that the girl realized someone had come into the room, she quickly pulled away from him.

Alex stood inside the doorway, shaking her head disapprovingly.

As Captain Franz got to his feet, there was a distant look in his eyes that spoke of many sessions with the Dark Light. He'd been provided with a Styx Limiter's long black leather coat and, with his strikingly blond hair, Alex would have been the first to admit that he was extremely handsome. But the problem was that he happened to be human.

"We're moving out. Come along," Alex said. She marched through to a door at the back of the storage room and hammered on it. It opened immediately, and with Rebecca Two, her captain, and the two Limiters following behind, she stormed outside into the darkness.

The only sound was the tapping of Alex's heels on the pavement as she led them at some speed through a succession of streets. They hadn't yet reached their destination when she beckoned Rebecca Two to come alongside her.

"Did I just catch you canoodling with that New Germanian? You weren't holding his hand, were you?" she demanded.

"Er . . . yes, I was," Rebecca Two admitted sheepishly.

Alex was shaking her head again as she walked briskly down the darkened road. "You're not even fourteen yet. Do you think th —"

Rebecca Two tried to interrupt, but Alex wasn't having it. "No, you listen to me," she said. "I know you're going to tell me you're a Styx so your age in human years is irrelevant. And looking at you now . . ." She cast her eyes over Rebecca Two beside her. ". . . you're very much a young woman. But at the end of the day, he's not one of us — he's a human. And to cap it all, his poor little human brain has been conditioned so many times that he's been zombified."

"I know all that," Rebecca Two said.

Alex waited for the girl to continue, and when she didn't she went on, "I'm only watching out for you. We're in the same boat, you know. Even if it hasn't been confirmed yet, we both know that we've lost our sisters, our twins. We both know it in our bones. We can feel that emptiness inside us as if something's missing, that pain of separation."

They came to the Victorian church, and a Limiter rushed ahead to push open the large oak door for them. Inside, luminescent orbs had been set up around the walls, and there were many more Limiters. One of them had a man lying curled up on the ground by his feet.

"Who's that?" Alex asked.

"The vicar. He was hiding in the vestry when we arrived," the Limiter replied. "He's been trying to keep people out of his church."

"How very Christian of him," Alex said, peering quizzically at the man. "So he's unconscious?"

"No, he's not." The Limiter kicked the man. He gave a small cry and curled up even tighter, then broke into a torrent of mumbled prayers.

"Ah, excellent. I feel the urge." Alex shucked off her fur coat. She tugged at the neck of her crimson camisole to free her insect legs where they sprouted from the top of her spine. She continued to give Rebecca Two advice as she raised a foot and pushed the terrified man over with a thrust of her long heel. "I'm only telling you that whatever you think you feel for him . . ." She threw a look at Captain Franz standing quite still behind Rebecca. ". . . it's just not normal. Excuse me for a moment."

The vicar was still babbling his prayers, and too petrified to resist Alex as she fell on him. Grabbing hold of his hair, she pulled his head around. "He's young," she said. "And how nice to have a conscious but submissive one for a change."

Alex glanced up at Rebecca Two, giving her a pointed stare. "This is all these human flesh bags are fit for." She turned her attention back to the vicar, the ovipositor swinging from her mouth as it sought out his. It was then that he began to resist weakly, but it was short-lived as her insect legs gripped his head hard at the temples.

The last thing he said was "God save me," as the tube penetrated his mouth, the egg sac squeezing down it and deep inside him. When it had been done, he simply rolled over onto his side and curled up again. A reflex action to the obstruction in his esophagus was making him retch and cough as Alex got to her feet.

"Ah, that's a weight off," she said, slotting her egg tube back into her mouth. She sighed as she turned to Rebecca, juices flowing down her chin. "It's just that your behavior is frowned upon. Some would consider it to be unwholesome, *sick* even.

And I'm telling you now that one day very soon you're going to have to put this childish crush of yours behind you."

There was sadness in Rebecca Two's eyes as she nodded.

"It's not a difficult choice. We have great times ahead of us," Alex said. She leaned closer to Rebecca Two and lowered her voice conspiratorially. "I know how it is. I did my stint Topsoil with the Heathen, too, and one's thoughts can become muddled, confused. There's a temptation to go native — I experienced it, too. But you're a Styx, and that's where your loyalties lie. Not with some pretty-boy wimp that you're going to outgrow very quickly. No, you'll soon get over him.

"Now," Alex announced, as she strode down the aisle. She mounted the steps up to the altar, where she swung around as if to address a nonexistent congregation. "Where are my children? Because I want them to sweep through that shopping center like a plague of locusts. We'll show these flesh bags that nowhere is safe for them."

There, at the altar, her insect legs extended to their full length and came together, rattling, and then vibrating faster and faster, until the sound was a continuous hum. At the same time, Alex put her head back and opened her mouth, issuing a call that no human could hear.

On all sides of the church, the windows suddenly burst inward, fragments of stained glass showering down around the Limiters.

Armagi streamed in from all sides, alighting on the backs of the pews and gathering together in the aisle. Semitransparent beasts, as if made of liquid ice, the spiked feathers of their wings glittered under the light from the orbs.

Alex ended her call, lowering her head. "Ah, my children," she said. "My children have come to me."

With his ever-present escort of a pair of Styx Limiters, Danforth was doing his rounds of the floor, peering over the shoulders of the operators seated in front of their screens.

A red indicator began to flash above one of the desks, and the operator held her hand mechanically in the air. Danforth immediately went over to her. She had spotted something in a radio frequency sweep and flagged it for his attention. As he watched her screen, he repeated, "Interesting," several times, but became distracted as he heard a sound from several desks away. He turned just in time to see the operator, a man in his forties, tug off his headphones and then begin to get to his feet.

"Who said you could leave your post?" Danforth snapped, but the man didn't answer. For a moment he swayed on his feet, a remote look appearing in his eyes before he keeled over backward, taking his chair with him.

Tutting furiously, Danforth went to check on the man. Not noticing any signs that he was breathing, he felt his neck for a pulse. "He's dead," Danforth pronounced without emotion, gripping the man's chin to turn his head. "Don't suppose either of you feel like administering CPR to bring him back?" he asked, half glancing at his Limiter guards, who were hovering behind him.

"No, thought not," he answered himself, as they didn't respond. Danforth scrutinized the expired man's face, which had dark bruises under the eyes and was coated in a sheen of sweat. "Cardiac arrest due to extreme exhaustion and dehydration, I would hazard," he said, as he indicated the man's blue lips to his Limiters. "Get him out of here, will you?"

Straightening up, Danforth rubbed his hands distastefully together as if removing the man's sweat from them.

"What is it?" the old Styx asked, as he appeared beside the two Limiters.

Danforth glanced at the dead man's desk, at a picture of two young children playing in the cerulean waters of some tropical sea. They were obviously his children. "These people are only human," Danforth said dispassionately. "We've hotwired their simple little brains with the Dark Light, and they're performing their tasks adequately, but we're pushing them beyond their physical limits."

"Out of necessity. We need results," the old Styx said, but without antagonism. He had a grudging respect for Danforth, who was assisting them in realms of technology that would have been out of reach without his expertise.

And where they were now, just south of London in a government communications substation where electronic traffic could be monitored, it was proving to be a real boon to the Styx as they continued to strike at key targets. Of course, most forms of communication such as landlines, cell phones, any radio or television broadcasts, and the Internet had long since been shut down. But more specialized communications used by the military or via satellite link couldn't be stopped or jammed, and that's where Danforth came in.

He wasn't just another of the Darklit automatons who did only as they were instructed — his expertise meant that the

Styx could keep one step ahead of the limited military resistance that they were encountering from time to time.

Danforth was proving to be valuable, which was fortunate for him, or otherwise they would have dispensed with him many weeks ago.

And he'd also directed the Styx in which radar surveillance installations should be destroyed or kept in operation so that any interference from the international community could be detected early on and headed off. The Styx certainly didn't want a multinational task force throwing a spanner in the works as they systematically dismantled the country.

"Well, we've got a limited asset here, then," Danforth said, glancing around at the silent, drawn faces lit by their screens. "Many of these operators won't last much longer than a day or two without rest and some proper food."

The old Styx nodded. "Then let the important ones have a break. The rest, doing less skilled tasks, can work until they drop."

"Very good," Danforth said, although the old Styx had just passed a death sentence on the majority of the humans present in the room. "And I want to show you something." He led the old Styx back to the screen where a signal had been detected. Pushing aside the woman who'd been at the monitor, he leaned over the keyboard and typed rapidly on it. A list of numbers scrolled up over the screen. "It may be nothing, but someone's intermittently using analog equipment at this location." As he hit a key, a map came up with a pulsing circle. "The signal is originating from here." Danforth sent the coordinates to print, snatching the page as it came out and handing it to the old Styx. "Worth sending a patrol to investigate, don't you think?"

"Yes, we'll dispatch one immediately," the old Styx confirmed.

Danforth looked up at him. "And it's very close to where I advised you that *we* should be right now. It's on one of the main feeder routes to GCHQ Cheltenham." Danforth indicated all the operators in the room with a sweep of his hand. "Sure, we can detect and pinpoint transmissions from here, but the equipment they have in that installation — in the Doughnut, as it's called — is second to none. I know because I designed a hunk of it when the place was built. And with that equipment at your disposal, you can get inside the signals — even satellite-bound traffic — and eavesdrop to your heart's content. Even encrypted transmissions."

"Yes, your recommendation has been noted," the old Styx replied. "It's something that we'll have to deal with sooner or later, anyway, and it's irksome that we haven't been able to penetrate it before now and turn it to our use. The security measures to detect Darklit mules are extensive, and the military perimeter is formidable."

"So that's a yes? We're going for a strike?" Danforth asked.

"Yes, very shortly." The old Styx took a breath. His voice showed no emotion, although he narrowed his eyes just the tiniest degree. "That place has always been top of your list, Danforth. Is there an ulterior motive to your suggestion?"

Danforth smiled, but it was a malicious smile. "A few years back, I volunteered my considerable services, and they didn't even grant me a meeting. Much of that facility wouldn't be what it is today if it hadn't been for me. They have this coming to them."

"Now shine it like a comet of revenge," the old Styx quoted from Shakespeare's *Henry VI*.

"A prophet to the fall of all our foes!" Danforth said, adding the next line.

There was a moment when both men simply regarded each other, recognizing a kindred spirit, before the old Styx spoke. "I understand a man with that motivation." He wheeled to the two Limiters. "You were told to remove the body. Why have you not done it yet?" He spun on his heels and walked away.

Danforth was left with one of his Limiter escorts as the other dealt with the dead operator. Stifling a yawn, he did a last round of the floor, then began toward the windowless office that had been his home for the past month. Although he never slept for long, he would grab the occasional catnap when he could. Without turning on the light and still fully dressed, he went straight to the camp bed and lay down, while the Limiter remained in the corridor where he took up position.

Danforth yawned as he rolled over onto his side. The Limiter outside the room had no way of seeing what he was doing as he put his hand into his mouth and twisted one of his molars. With the tiniest click, the hollow crown came away.

At one time, when he would be posted abroad to advise the intelligence services of other countries on their electronic surveillance, there had always been the risk that he might be abducted and tortured for what he knew. Then the hollow molar had contained enough cyanide to kill him within seconds.

But if Danforth had a talent above all others, it was the ability to take a piece of electronic hardware and miniaturize it.

And that was precisely what he'd done in order to fit the state-of-the-art radio inside the tooth. "I knew I should have flogged Sony the patent," he said under his breath, as he activated the tiny radio with a press of his fingernail.

He didn't need to see the device, operating it through touch alone. By tapping the message in Morse code, the device began to record it. It was only a short message, but when it was ready Danforth pressed a preset number of times and it was sent, at a frequency that, not by chance, was in a blind spot for the detection equipment just down the corridor.

In any case the transmission had taken only a fraction of a fraction of a second — or, as the military called it, "a burp" — because the message was so highly compressed. Even if one of the operators in the main room had happened to pick up the transmission on their screens, they would very likely have put it down to a scanner glitch.

When he had screwed the tooth back in place, the small smile on Danforth's lips faded as he drifted off to sleep.

"Um. You can't do that," Chester said.

"Do what?" Stephanie was at the table by the window, leaning over a chessboard.

Rising from his armchair by the fire, Chester went to stand beside her. "Pawns only move diagonally when they're taking something," he said, as he cast an eye over the various pieces she'd left in random positions while she'd been practicing. "Your grandfather must have told you that."

"Yeah, but isn't that so totally lame?" Stephanie flipped the small chess piece over with one of her bright red fingernails.

"Prawns are like these boring little no-marks, nearly as useless as the stupid horses and castles."

"Pawns," Chester corrected her gently. "They're called pawns." He'd been gradually coming out of his shell after the trauma of seeing his parents die in the Complex. But it was a slow process and, in the beginning, even a sudden sound, such as a slammed door or a raised voice, was too much for him and could reduce him to tears. All Chester had wanted was to hide away under the blankets in one of the tiny bedrooms upstairs in the cottage, and sleep, and go on sleeping, because that was the only way he could escape his anguish.

The problem was that when he did eventually wake, there were a few untroubled seconds before he remembered what he was doing there. Then the terrible memories were back in a gush, and the pain was with him again. It was more than Chester could bear, as though something were devouring him from inside until all that remained was the loss and regret, and a crippling paralysis.

After a couple of weeks of this Chester had slept all he could, so he simply lay on his bed, staring up at the corners of the room. He felt even more lost and alone as the wind howled in from over the sea, rattling the tiles on the roof like drumming from a distant pageant. His mind wouldn't stop replaying, over and over, the fateful day on which his parents had been killed, as he analyzed and relived each tiny event leading up to the moment of the explosion, changing them slightly each time as he imagined what he might have done to prevent their deaths.

I should never, never have left her. If only he had stayed with his mother in the kitchen. Why had he left her alone when he'd gone to Drake? He should have clung on to her, not letting her out of his sight. *No! Dad! Stop!* Chester could have stopped his father from going down the approach tunnel to his mother, rugby-tackling him if necessary. If he had, his father would most probably be alive today, and perhaps his mother, too. Chester's version of the day became ever more fanciful until he was confronting Danforth in the tunnel, emptying a full magazine into the traitor as his Sten bucked in his hands.

"Take that, you stinking BASTARD!" Chester would growl behind his teeth, coming out of his open-eyed dream, drenched in sweat and his fists clenched with hatred for the man who had slaughtered his parents. He'd never wanted to hurt and kill someone so much, perhaps even more than the Rebecca twins and the Styx themselves. Although, when he thought about it, Martha wasn't far off the top of his hate list for what she'd put him through.

And even if Chester desperately needed to go downstairs, perhaps because he was thirsty and wanted some water, he would remain where he was, not caring that he was so uncomfortable. In any case, Old Wilkie often kept vigil during the night in a chair by the front door, armed with his shotgun in case the Styx decided to turn up. As depressed as he was, Chester was reluctant to have his brains blown out over the cottage walls as he blundered into the man. It would all be too much bother.

Then, much to his surprise, Chester found that he was beginning to crave human company, although at a distance. He found that it made him feel a little better to be around Stephanie and Old Wilkie, even though he would feign interest in his book so that he had an excuse not to talk to either of them.

This lack of communication with Stephanie and Old Wilkie made life rather difficult in the confines of the cramped cottage, where they were completely cut off from the outside world. They'd had the most miserable Christmas lunch Chester could have imagined, sitting for the most part in silence around the meal Old Wilkie had gone to such lengths to prepare. All it did for Chester was summon the memories of Christmases past with his parents. Unable to control his emotions, he'd used a bad headache as an excuse to leave the table, even before Old Wilkie had brought out the Christmas pudding.

"Pawns, whatever," Stephanie now said with a shake of the head, snatching the queen from the board to admire it. "These guys are the business because they can move in every direction and as many squares as you want. And they're more powerful than all the others, including the stuffy old kings, who are only good for running away and losing you the game. I mean, why can't you play with all queens? The game would be so, like, better."

"But then it wouldn't be chess," Chester reasoned. He started a sigh but morphed it into a humming sound, as if he was giving serious consideration to her suggestion, because he didn't want to upset the girl. He couldn't bear the thought of upsetting anyone; he still felt so torn up and bruised inside that he shied away from anything unpleasant. And watching her try to learn the game had brought home how much he missed Will, his longstanding opponent. "You can't go completely changing the game, but there are other ways to play it," he added.

Stephanie folded her arms in front of her chest and made a sulky face, but Chester could tell it wasn't genuine. "Maybe you should have a go at playing by my rules," she said, peering at Chester from under her red mane, which hung loosely in front of her face. This was a surprising new development because she usually took so much care over her appearance, but today was one of her designated "bad hair days," as she called them.

She'd informed her grandfather and Chester that, as it was only the three of them in the cottage, she wasn't going to all the effort of washing her hair every morning. It was too much of a "hassle," she said, because lugging hot water from the Aga stove all the way upstairs was such a chore, and there was no way she was prepared to take a cold bath. Besides — she'd gone on to tell them — as they were in the back of beyond and there was zero likelihood that anyone would drop in to see them, what was the point?

Chester wasn't sure whether to be flattered she was so relaxed in his company, or to be put out because she wasn't making an effort for him.

Stephanie returned the pieces to each end of the board, but not in their usual positions. "So, because we're playing *my* game now, pretend all these are queens. Except, of course, for the two boring kings." She looked up at Chester. "Get ready for a trouncing, Chucky boy."

"Well . . . ," he began, glancing back to his book left open on the armchair. He didn't want to get into this, but was unable to come up with an excuse at such short notice.

"Pull up a pew, and prepare to meet thy doom," Stephanie said, pointing at the chair opposite her. "You know, your face looks better," she said, as he was slow to do what she'd asked. "My moisturizer's really helping."

"Yes, thank you for that," Chester said, touching his forehead where the small scabs were healing. His eczema had broken out all over his face and hands like never before. Old Wilkie suggested that it was more than likely to have been triggered by what he'd been through, but Chester preferred to tell himself it was because of the damp in the cottage. "I'm less of a freak show now," he said uncomfortably.

Stephanie smiled. "You never w —"

She was interrupted as the door from the kitchen swung open and Old Wilkie entered, with someone who appeared to be a soldier following closely behind. The man was wearing an SAS windproof jacket with the hood up, which he now pulled back.

"Parry!" Chester burst out as he recognized the gray-bearded face and craggy features, and rushed over to him. "I had no idea you were here!"

"Hello, lad, how are you?" Parry said warmly, gripping Chester's hand in both of his. "Sorry to have left you out here for so long."

"We thought you'd forgotten us," Stephanie said.

Parry acknowledged her with a quick smile, then turned toward Chester again. "I came as soon as I had a chance.

Things have been a bit chaotic to say the least." As Parry spoke, Chester took in his beige beret, noticing the winged dagger on the badge. "Yes," the old man said. "I've been helping out the regiment. But, more important, tell me how you've been."

"Better, I suppose," Chester replied flatly.

"Oooh, I must look like such a mess," Stephanie mumbled as she began to tidy her hair, darting looks at the doorway where Parry had entered from in case someone else was about to come through.

"Have you heard from anybody? From Will or Elliott? Or Drake?" Chester asked. "Are they back?"

Parry had taken out his satphone and now passed it from one hand to the other. "No, but it's too early to give up hope on them yet. Who knows what they walked into when they arrived down there? Perhaps they got the job done, but met resistance on the way home," Parry answered in a measured way, although Chester caught the slight frown on his face before Stephanie butted in.

"But how did you get here, Parry?" she said. "We didn't hear you arrive."

"By chopper," Parry replied. "It's just about the only way to get around these days."

"So have we got the all clear now? Can we go home?" she was quick to ask.

There was no doubt how worried Parry was as his brow formed multiple Vs. His eyes found the radio on the windowsill. "Exactly how much do you know about what's been going on in the rest of the country?"

"Nothing, really," Stephanie said, also turning to glance at the radio. "We've only got that ancient thing. We can tune in to a handful of stations, but the signal's so weak here it's always, like, dropping out. I can't even get any proper mus —"

"That's because the Styx are continuing to target news dissemination," Parry interrupted, "by jamming the frequencies so nothing gets through." As he took a breath, Chester used the opportunity to speak.

"So it's bad, is it?"

Parry gave a humorless chuckle. "Bad doesn't begin to describe it. No one trusts anyone else, mainly because they're frightened and very hungry. Imports have stopped, so food's scarce, and in any case the transportation infrastructure has ground to a halt."

Parry shook his head. "There's rioting and looting everywhere in the country because what's left of the police force has all but given up. People are hiding in their homes, army towns are putting up fortifications as though they're minor fiefdoms, and gangs of vigilantes are taking it out on the nearest minority they can get their hands on. It's as though the country's been thrown back into the Dark Ages."

"But what's the government doing about this?" Stephanie asked.

"They haven't got the faintest idea how to put things right," Parry replied. "And it's no good going to anyone in Europe for help. They're terrified that it's going to spread to them, so they've simply shut us out."

"Then our attack on the warehouse didn't do much to stop the Styx," Chester said.

"No, unfortunately," Parry replied. "When the Rebeccas hightailed it, one twin remained Topsoil with a Styx female, while we believe the other traveled down to the inner world. So everything that Eddie warned would happen is becoming a reality."

Much as Chester wanted to shy away from any of this, he couldn't stop himself from asking the inevitable question. "You're talking about the Phase?" he said.

"We delayed it with our assault on the warehouse, but that only had the effect of cranking it up a notch, maybe into something even worse. Here on the surface it's more than just Limiters and Darklit humans we're up against now. They've got the Armagi with them, too."

"What are they like?" Stephanie put in.

"They look like Limiters until they transform, then they look like nothing on God's Earth. They're extremely effective killing machines, whatever environment they're operating in. I know that because we've seen them in action." Parry suddenly sounded very weary. "And as for precisely how we deal with them, I have to admit we don't have any answers at present."

Stephanie opened her mouth to speak again, but Parry cut her short. "I don't know how long we'll be safe here, because the Armagi may have detected my chopper on the way in. And also our latest intel is that the Styx have commandeered a number of key radar installations."

"Not safe here?" Chester mumbled.

"Yes, so I want you all to get your things together. You're clearing out with me when I go."

"We're really leaving?" Stephanie said, trying her best not to sound delighted.

"Yes, but not right away. Chester, I need you to come somewhere with me first. And make sure you wrap up warm," Parry said, already heading toward the door.

"We're going outside?" Chester said unenthusiastically, throwing a glance through the window at the gathering darkness outside. "Do I really have to come?"

"Yes, I need you with me," Parry replied. From his tone Chester knew that it wasn't an option for him to refuse, however unwilling he was to get involved again. "We're going to rendezvous with some contacts of mine. And don't bring a weapon with you — better that you're not armed," Parry added, before rapping his walking stick once on the floor, then turning to the front door.

Chester followed Parry's advice and put on a thick sweater and his warmest jacket. As he emerged from the cottage, the man was talking on a satphone, but it was different from the one he'd been carrying inside. He held up a hand to indicate that he needed to finish the conversation, turning slightly away so that Chester couldn't hear what he was saying.

As the chill wind bit into him, Chester began to boil up inside; much as he respected Parry, he was done with all this. He was just summoning the courage to tell Parry this, so he could go back inside, to his nice warm bed, when the old man abruptly ended the call.

"We need to get our skates on," he said, marching off across the gorse-covered field in the direction of the sea. With a groan, Chester followed after him. Parry was putting on speed and barely using his walking stick as they approached the cliff edge. And he seemed to be very familiar with the lay of the land as he followed the cliff along to where a track led down. The full force of the wind was on them now, and Chester was struggling as he negotiated the steps hewn into the rock. There was a thick rope to hang on to, but it was still a daunting task with only Parry's flashlight to illuminate the way. Then they arrived at the bottom.

"Keep your arms at your sides and your hands open," Parry told Chester, raising his voice to be heard over the bluster of the wind. "And don't make any sudden moves. You have absolutely no reason to be alarmed by what's about to happen."

"Alarmed . . . but what *is* about to happen? And why do I need to be here anyway?" Chester demanded, unable to keep the antipathy from his voice. He hadn't actually agreed to any of this, and now he was standing on a windswept beach in the dark. He just wasn't ready to become embroiled in another of Parry's schemes. The last one had resulted in everyone almost running out of air in the Complex, after that madman Danforth had blown it up and killed his parents.

"Look, I'm sorry to drag you along, old chap, after all you've been through," Parry said, giving Chester's arm a squeeze through his duffel coat. "But this is important, and you are important."

He pulled Chester gently after him as he set off down the incline of the beach. As their feet crunched on the pebbles,

Chester strained to see if anyone was there, his eyes slitted against the spray from the sea. But he couldn't see a soul on the foreshore, which disappeared off into the murky darkness to either side of him.

Parry stopped dead once they had covered about half the distance to the sea, then clipped his flashlight to his jacket.

"Now put your hands on your head. Slowly," he said to Chester. "And just relax. You're going to be fine."

Chester reluctantly followed Parry's example, part of him feeling very apprehensive, and the other part bitterly resenting this intrusion into his life. Into his grief.

"Call sign Delta Echo," Parry suddenly announced loudly, then said the words again at even greater volume so they would be heard above the sound of the wind and the crash of the waves.

From somewhere close by came a harsh, efficient response. "Yankee Alpha."

Shadows suddenly came to life all around them.

Chester glimpsed black-clad men bristling with weapons before his arms were seized and wrenched behind his back. He felt a tie go around his wrists, binding them tightly, before a hood was slipped over his head.

It was so evocative of the brutal way he'd been treated in the Colony when he was sentenced to Banishment that he began to struggle against his captors, twisting his body away from them.

Someone whispered into his ear, "Calm it, junior, or we knock you out cold." The voice was American, and Chester had no doubt that the man meant what he'd said. He let his body go slack, closing his eyes under the hood and allowing himself to be led down the rest of the beach and then into some sort of boat or inflatable. The vessel was tossed around by the waves as the low drone of an outboard started up, then he felt the forward motion. He was on the move.

Five minutes later, the vessel bumped into something, and he was hoisted out by men on both sides of him, his feet meeting with a firm surface. As he was frog-marched a short distance along it, he was telling himself that he must be on a ship, then the two men drew him to a halt.

"Hoods off and untie them," another American voice barked.

As his hands were freed and the hood was whisked from his head, Chester blinked, trying to make out where he was. A diffuse red light percolated through the sea spray. The light seemed to be coming from somewhere above. "Arms out wide, bud," one of the men beside Chester ordered, and he immediately obeyed.

The men searched him thoroughly, feeling along his arms and legs, and even telling him to lift each foot so they could check the soles of his boots. Then they produced some sort of scanner, which wailed to itself as they passed it over his body, particularly concentrating on his stomach. Not far away he could see Parry was going through the same treatment.

"All checks done. He's clean," one of the men beside Chester called out.

"Ditto this one," someone from Parry's escort reported back.

"Head for the ladder," Chester was told, as he was steered in the direction of the light.

Whatever he was on, it was pitching in the sea like something of considerable size. It wasn't a ship — he was certain of that. The larger waves were washing straight across duck walks on its deck, and the only structure he could vaguely make out as he came closer to it was around forty feet in height.

In the glow of the red illumination he spotted some large white letters on the tower that loomed out of the misty darkness before him.

USS HERALD, Chester read. Then the penny dropped. "A submarine?" he asked incredulously, as he began up the metal rungs on the side of the conning tower. "We're on an American submarine?"

"Yes, my friend, you're a guest on one of the U.S. of A.'s finest, most awe-inspiring nuclear subs," a gruff voice behind him drawled.

"Not much moving tonight?" Eddie asked.

"No. Nothing in or out," the man on the scope said, not looking up.

Several observation posts had been set up in buildings around the periphery of GCHQ, the government installation often referred to as "the Doughnut" because the circular structure closely resembled one, and Eddie was now checking in on each of them. This observation post had been established in the attic of an abandoned house, in which part of the roof had been removed so that there was an unobstructed view of the government installation several hundred yards away, one of the few that the Styx had yet bothered to put out of action.

And this observation post was typical of all the others, consisting of one of Eddie's former Limiters and a member of the Old Guard, who between them were carrying out the around-the-clock surveillance.

Moving to the opening in the roof, Eddie peered out at the lights in the Doughnut. Although London seemed to be receiving the brunt of the Styx attacks, he suspected it was only a matter of time before they did something about GCHQ as it continued to operate. The threat, when it came, would be from outside and not from the staff at the installation itself, because the moment that Parry's first reports warning of Darklighting had been lodged with the military, the Director of GCHQ had had the foresight to put into action the center's lockdown measures. Parry and the Director had known each other for several decades, so the Director had no doubt that it was something he should take seriously. He doubled up the personnel on all the access points to the Doughnut, put an extra military perimeter around it, and, crucially, he had implemented the use of Purgers for all incoming personnel long before most other sensitive locations had done the same.

And now, as the member of the Old Guard scanned the approach road through his binoculars, a cup of steaming soup from his Thermos within easy reach, Eddie took a last lingering look at him.

The Limiter, sitting in the corner of the attic, stirred from his trancelike state as he heard Eddie's voice.

"I'm going to check in on the next post," Eddie said, glancing at his watch before he headed toward the stairs leading down from the attic.

As he found the first step with his foot, he felt regret that the two men were part of a game that called for their lives. Their location had been handed to the Styx on a plate, and they were both to be sacrificed for the sake of appearances, but Eddie's face — as expressionless as ever — betrayed nothing.

"Thank you, both of you," he said, as he descended from view.

PART 2

TOWER

THE

4

THE BUSHMAN WAS BEING bounced around
in the seat next to Jürgen, who was maneuvering the
New Germanian half-track through the jungle at some speed.
It was a hefty eighteen-ton military vehicle, requisitioned
from a military compound in the city, and with its combination of wheels and caterpillar treads it was ideal for the
jungle trail, which a recent monsoon had turned into a muddy
stream.

There were numerous crates of apparatus in the rear of the
vehicle that the New Germanian brothers had hastily assembled for the expedition. Despite this, there was still plenty of
room for Will and Elliott to spread out.

As they sat across from each other on the side benches, Will
caught Elliott's attention. "He's doing it again," Will mouthed
at her, as he indicated the bushman in the front seat.

The bushman's new appearance had taken some getting
used to. He looked very different now, wearing a pair of blue
denim overalls, a boonie hat, and a pair of wraparound sunglasses, all very necessary to protect him from the sun since
he'd lost his extraordinary epidermal layer.

But this wasn't why Will was pointing at him. As he had done since the first moment Elliott had spoken to him in Styx, the man was forever sneaking glances at her, as if he couldn't keep his eyes off her. And each time Elliott returned one of his glances, he quickly averted his eyes.

He now did this yet again, peering at her over his shoulder. And, true to form, as Elliott made a move to acknowledge him, he whipped his head back around to the windshield again. Never once had he met her eyes.

Will leaned toward Elliott, waving her closer so she could hear him over the sound of the engine. "Reckon our bushman here has a massive crush on you," he suggested mischievously.

Elliott shook her head. "Don't be an idiot, Will."

Will was grinning. "We should give your new BF a name. We can't keep calling him *the bushman*."

Elliott didn't rise to Will's teasing as she thought out loud. "No, I get the feeling he's sort of frightened of me . . . for some reason," she said.

"I know! Woody!" Will burst out all of a sudden. "Yes, that's what we should call him — Woody . . . get it?"

Elliott groaned. "That's as bad as one of Drake's awful jokes," she said, smiling sadly. "I never thought I'd miss them as much as I do."

"And if Woody's leaves grow back, we can change his name to Russell," Will added, but in a flat voice, because like Elliott he was thinking about their friend Drake and how unlikely it was that he'd survived the nuclear explosion.

What Elliott had said about Woody, as he'd just been

christened, did have some credence, though. He did seem to be in total awe of her and, although he'd gone back to scanning the passing trees through his wraparounds as they continued their way through the thick jungle, he did seem to be only interested in Elliott. For the first twenty-four hours after Woody had regained consciousness, he'd repeatedly tried to throw himself at her feet. And all he would say were the same words, "They have returned."

The revelation that Elliott was half Styx — or half invader, as they insisted on putting it — had taken the two New Germanian brothers by surprise, because neither Will nor Elliott had considered her parentage relevant when they took Jürgen through the series of events that led to the release of the virus in the inner world. But the New Germanian brothers seemed to accept it after speaking in more detail to Elliott about the matter, and, in any case, by the start of the second day, Woody's fever had completely abated. He stopped babbling his set phrase in Styx and, indeed, clammed up altogether and became very withdrawn.

Werner's diagnosis was that Woody was suffering from shock because of his abrupt physical transformation. In an effort to help him readjust, Jürgen had spent time with the bushman in his room, trying to communicate with him as he had done previously using the medium of the hand-drawn hieroglyphs. At the very least, Jürgen wanted to make him understand that he was immune to the virus and could leave the quarantine ward whenever he wanted.

Then they had put that to the test. After many weeks of being cooped up inside, it was quite an occasion when the New

Germanian brothers, along with Karl and Woody, filed through the decontamination areas without suiting up. Nobody spoke as they emerged from the shadowy interior of the hospital and stepped from the main entrance, followed by Will and Elliott. The rains had come and washed much of the ash away so that the streets looked cleaner than before. It was almost as if the city had returned to normal, except that the mound of charred bones remained as a testament to the terrible impact of the plague.

As they stood in the glaring sunshine, everyone was looking at everyone else. Then Werner spread his arms like an opera singer about to burst into song and gulped down a large breath of air. He held it in for several seconds as if savoring it, then exhaled slowly and dramatically through his nose. For so many weeks all that the New Germanians and the bushman had known was the highly filtered atmosphere of the quarantine ward, but now they were free to go where they wanted in the city.

"Well, so far so good. I can't feel any symptoms yet," Werner finally announced, then began to laugh. "I'm kidding. The tests showed the vaccine is effective. We're going to be OK!"

Jürgen was laughing, too, and hugging his son — only Woody remained unmoved, angling his face to catch the sun's rays on his new skin.

Jürgen turned to Will and Elliott. "Without you, we might never have seen this day. It was only a matter of time before the reserve power ran out, and we'd have been exposed."

"No problem," Will answered, enjoying the moment with

them. "And now I'm going to raid that sweets shop. Anyone interested?"

On hearing this, Karl's eyes lit up.

Later that evening they had returned to the quarantine ward laden with several carrier bags of food that they'd scavenged. They didn't have to worry about sterilizing any of it now that they all had immunity. Jürgen had prepared a meal to celebrate their newfound freedom, and they were all sitting around the table feeling very contented when, without any warning, Woody started to jabber away ten to the dozen in Styx, as if it had finally sunk in that he was safe from the plague.

"I can't get it all," Elliott said, doing her best to understand what Woody was saying. "But I think it's about his people . . . he believes they could be still alive in . . . I don't recognize the word, but he may mean the pyramids. Far down inside them."

"Is that possible? After all this time?" Jürgen asked his brother.

"Anything's possible," Werner replied. "You said that they lived in the pyramids for months on end. Maybe they knew something was wrong as the jungle fauna began to die, and they confined themselves in good time." He looked across at Woody, who was still babbling away. "It all depends on the air circulation inside the pyramids. I think it's highly unlikely, but . . ." He trailed off.

Jürgen pondered this for a moment. "We can't just ignore

what he's telling us. If we can save more of the indigenous people, we have to act, and act quickly."

Will and Karl had been enjoying the *Kriesel* lollipops that they'd plundered earlier that day, when Will caught Elliott's eye. It seemed that their simple way of life back at the pyramid wasn't going to be restored to them quite yet.

And now here they were in the half-track, embarking on a mission to rescue more bushmen when they had no idea if any of them had survived for this long.

"This is where the main trail ends. We're on foot from here," Jürgen shouted, as he brought the half-track to a stop in a clearing that obviously served as a turning circle. As he shut off the engine and jumped from the vehicle, he glanced briefly in the direction they'd just driven from.

"So what do we do now? Wait for Werner and Karl to catch up with us?" Elliott asked.

"No, we go on without them," Jürgen replied, as he went around to the rear of the half-track and undid the tailgate. "They won't be here for a while yet, and they'll radio me when they're close. In the meantime, we can make a start on shifting some of the equipment over to the pyramid," he said.

Jürgen, Will, and Elliott each took one of the sizable crates from the rear of the vehicle, the low gravity enabling them to lift far more than they could have managed on the surface. They balanced these crates on the tops of their heads as Woody led them in a procession into the dense undergrowth. Nobody

really expected him to carry anything, but at least he used his knowledge of the jungle to steer them onto an animal track so they weren't forced to cut themselves a path using their machetes.

They had quite a distance to cover, and Woody seemed so determined to reach the pyramid that he kept increasing his pace. Each time Jürgen urged him to slow down. Finally they stepped from the treeline, and there was the pyramid. Still damp from the recent deluge, the droplets of water on it were catching the sun and sparkling like thousands of tiny diamonds.

"There's nothing like coming home," Will puffed. He edged farther out so that he could see the base he and Elliott had built in the branches of the nearby tree, and felt more than a twinge of regret. What he was actually thinking was, *I wish we'd never left it in the first place.*

Although lives had been saved as a result of their foraging expedition into the metropolis, part of him wished that he'd never let Elliott talk him into it. He didn't like to admit to himself that there was some truth in what she'd said about him growing old and set in his ways. He recognized that he was different — he'd lost some of his taste for adventure. Perhaps the constant struggle against the Styx had beaten it out of him, but right now, all he wanted was his simple life in the jungle back again, with Elliott, and without any outside interference from the New Germanians or babbling bushmen.

"Home," Will repeated, as he realized the significance of the word, and how very happy he'd been there with Elliott. With both the Ancients' passage and the void sealed, neither he nor

Elliott had any serious expectations that they'd ever return to the outer world again. This place, with their base in the tree beside the pyramid, and this world in the center of the world, had become the best home he'd known in his short life. And as it now seemed to be coming to an end because of these new people in their lives, his heart began to race with a sort of panic.

He'd earned this time with her. He'd done his bit in the fight against the Styx, and wanted to put all that behind him now. He felt so far away from his mother in the Colony, and his friend Chester. And as for Parry and Eddie, of course he wondered how they were faring in their search for the second Styx female. But he couldn't help feeling all that wasn't his battle any longer.

"Hello! I was speaking to you!" Elliott called, pulling Will from his thoughts. "You joining us today?"

"Yeah, sorry . . . I was miles away." Will smiled and hurried to catch up with her and Jürgen.

Still lugging the crates, they climbed up the side of the pyramid. They stopped short of going onto the flattened upper platform at the very top, instead following the ledge around on the tier just below, until Woody brought them to a halt.

"Back here again," Will said, surveying the very place where he and Dr. Burrows had tumbled in when the Styx had surrounded the pyramid in a bid to capture them. "There's an entrance here," he added for Jürgen's benefit.

"Yes, we were aware of that," the New Germanian replied, as they all put their crates down. "The invaders didn't get very far, did they?" Jürgen noted, as he began to inspect the damage inflicted by the Styx's attempt to blow a way inside the pyramid using charges. "Interesting . . . ," he said, passing his hand over what remained of the stones with the carvings on them, and then the underlying masonry that had been exposed, which was considerably darker in color. "Do you see the difference between the two materials?"

Although the outer facing stones had been blasted away, the supporting structure seemed to be completely unmarked.

"Yes, it does look sort of . . . sort of new underneath," Will agreed. "And the Styx explosives took out what my dad called the *moving stones*, but there are still those to show where they were." He was pointing at a row of ten squares visible on the otherwise smooth surface.

Woody let out what might have been a curse in the Styx tongue, although much of their language sounded precisely like that.

"Will, he wants you out of the way," Elliott translated.

"Fine," Will said, peeved by the bushman's brusqueness. Nevertheless he stepped aside for Woody, who went straight to the squares. Standing on tiptoe, he began to touch them one after another.

"My dad and I thought there had to be a combination to get in. We spent ages pushing the blocks in and out in different sequences to try to crack it," Will said, watching as Woody continued to touch the squares at lightning speed. "But I don't know what he thinks he's doing."

"We tried different sequences, too," Jürgen said, as he watched the bushman with rapt attention. "But the tribesman isn't doing anything that can affect a mechanical linkage. This must simply be some sort of ritual before opening the door."

"So you've never seen inside?" Will asked him quickly.

Jürgen shook his head. "Never. And the bushmen were careful not to let us observe them doing this," he said.

Woody had obviously finished the lengthy sequence. As he hopped quickly out of the way, there was a grinding sound.

"Get back!" Will warned. He wasn't about to be caught out again.

The wall below the squares and a section of the ledge just in front of where Will and the others were standing seemed to have simply vanished, revealing a flight of shallow stone stairs leading into the depths of the pyramid.

Jürgen was blinking with surprise. "I don't understand. Did the masonry just retract somewhere?" he asked.

"If it did, I didn't see it," Elliott said, equally bemused.

Everyone remained where they were except for Will, who had stepped to the edge of the opening and was peering down into it. "So that's where we went . . . that day," he said quietly.

Woody uttered a few words and was suddenly off, racing down the dusty steps.

"He said to follow him," Elliott translated.

"Hold on!" Jürgen shouted. "Tell him not to be so hasty, will you? If we blunder inside, we'll be carrying the virus straight in with us."

Elliott called to Woody, who held back for a moment on the steps as he replied quickly.

"He's saying what we want is farther in," Elliott told them.

"So we should take the gear with us and set up inside?" Will proposed.

Jürgen considered the situation. "I suppose we don't have a choice. We don't know how close the other tribesmen are," he said with a shrug. "Once we locate them, we can put up the decontamination tent and attempt some basic sterilization. And if that's not practical, we'll just have to administer the vaccine and hope for the best."

"Let's go, then," Will said, and Jürgen tugged a flashlight from his pocket and switched it on so they had at least some idea where they were putting their feet. Then the three of them picked up their crates and began down the steps, into the murky darkness.

"This is where Dad and I ended up," Will said, as they came to the bottom of the steps and found themselves on a level surface, their footfalls echoing around the enclosed space. He couldn't help but recall the roller coaster of emotions he had experienced the last time that he'd tumbled into this very same chamber with his father. Will's terror at being chased by the Limiters had been transformed into elation as he realized that by some miracle he and Dr. Burrows were suddenly out of their reach, even if that elation was short-lived as they were surrounded by less-than-friendly bushmen.

Then Will remembered what Dr. Burrows had discovered there. "Take a look at the floor," he said to the others. Jürgen shone his flashlight where Will was indicating.

"A mural," Elliott said. "Or is that what it's called only when it's painted on the wall?"

Will smiled. "Maybe it's a *flooral*, then." He turned to Jürgen. "Actually, it's carved into the flagstones, then painted. My dad reckoned that the people responsible for building the pyramids — the Ancients, as he called them — had trade routes through to all the continents. That's how they were able to put together this map."

Jürgen edged carefully around the carved outlines of the continents on the stone floor, as if he was worried that he might damage them by treading on them. "Yes, but this must be from several millennia ago . . . and it's all in perfect proportion. So how could they possibly have the means to compile a map with this level of detail or accuracy?" he asked.

As Woody suddenly reappeared with a burning torch, the chamber was filled with light.

"And you've got to see this," Will said, now that the flames were illuminating the rest of the space. He took Elliott and Jürgen to where the procession of large figures had been painted on the wall, the king and queen in their finery and decked with golden jewelry like something an Egyptian ruler might wear. "Dad thought this was amazing," Will said, as he remembered how Dr. Burrows had lit match after match as he studied all the figures.

"There's that symbol from Tam's pendant again," Elliott said, as she spotted the three converging lines on the king's crown, and then on a warrior's breastplate. "It's all over the place."

Will was about to answer when Woody began to jabber rapidly in Styx.

"He wants us to go with him," Elliott said.

Taking the crates with them, they followed the bushman to the end of the chamber and out onto a landing where they were presented with more stairs.

"I expected the other tribesmen to be farther down inside the pyramid, not up here," Jürgen mumbled as Woody led them up flight after flight.

"Last time, that's where they took us," Will remarked. "Right down into the guts of the pyramid."

As they came to yet another landing, Woody ushered them away from the stairs and into a low-ceilinged, circular chamber, approximately thirty feet in diameter. He was gesticulating at a point on the curved wall directly opposite the entrance. As there didn't seem to be another way in or out of the chamber, they left the crates by the doorway.

"If the rest of the tribesmen are through there, this would be an ideal location for decontamination," Jürgen said. Undoing the top of one of the crates, he began to take out several of the green canisters of sterilizing agent. "If worse comes to worst, I've got some syringes of vaccine ready in here," he said, as he lifted out a small attaché case.

Woody was chatting away ten to the dozen, desperately trying to attract their attention. "What's he want us to see over there?" Will asked, as light from the bushman's torch fell on something in front of him.

As they came nearer, they found that a small shelf projected from the wall at waist height. Angled at forty-five degrees there was a black panel set into it, which Will began to touch. "What on earth is this for?" he asked.

"Talk to me. What are you looking at?" Jürgen asked, as he hastily emptied the contents of another of the crates out onto the floor and began to arrange them for construction of a decontamination tent.

"Well, it resembles glass . . . black glass . . . or some type of highly polished mineral. It's got the Ancients' symbol cut into it, but the edges are rough, like gouges," Will said, exploring the three prongs of the trident symbol with his fingers. "If this is the same as the squares outside and opens a way through, Woody needs to show us how to activate it."

"Who's Woody?" Jürgen asked, although he was preoccupied with his efforts to erect the tent. By now the bushman had begun to pace impatiently up and down beside the wall, still speaking rapidly. "So have we definitely got a way in?" Jürgen called across, just as Elliott, avoiding Woody as he tore past her, lost her balance. She stuck a hand out against the side of the chamber to steady herself.

Pulses of cool blue light coursed for several yards around where she'd made contact with the wall, revealing an intricate network of lines and circles.

"Whoa!" Will cried out.

They were all too startled to speak, the only sound in the chamber Woody's flaming torch as it crackled away.

"Tell me I didn't just imagine that," Will whispered, hardly daring to breathe.

Dropping the aluminum tent pole he'd just slotted together, Jürgen hurried over and shone his flashlight along the wall beside Elliott. "No, I saw it, too," he confirmed, then he slowly stretched his hand out to touch the wall.

Will was already tapping one of the large blocks of masonry where he was. "Whatever it was, it's gone. And I really don't get it. This is just stone!"

"Where did those lights come from, then?" Elliott asked, still thoroughly confused.

"They were more like sparks," Jürgen said, as he stooped to examine the wall at its base. "And I agree with you, Will. No question that it's stone." He took his hand away and rubbed the dust between his fingers. "Even if the phenomenon we just witnessed could be explained by some sort of electrostatic discharge, how did the masonry conduct it like that? I saw . . . shapes . . . designs."

Will stepped closer to the small ledge. "Maybe this has something to do with it." He was pushing on the panel to see if he could make it move in any direction, when Woody began to speak excitedly.

"What's he prattling on about?" Will asked Elliott.

"I can't understand him. He's speaking too quickly," Elliott replied. She held her hand over the shiny panel. "Show me how this works. Does it open a door?" she said to the bushman in Styx.

For the first time, Woody looked her straight in the eye.

Before she knew what was happening, he'd grabbed hold of her wrist. He forced her hand down onto the panel, ramming her fingers into the three-pronged symbol.

There was a flash as intense as that from an arc welder's torch. Elliott was thrown backward onto the floor of the chamber as if she'd received an electric shock.

"No!" Will shouted, rushing to Elliott's side and helping her to sit up. "Are you OK?"

She closed her fingers into a fist and then splayed them open again. "I'm fine. Doesn't hurt at all," she replied with some surprise. "But that was really weird."

Will was angry now. "You're saying!" He swung around to the bushman. "What the h —?"

The floor of the chamber shook.

Jürgen went into a crouch, thinking there was more to come. "Earthquake," he said. "They're quite common in this part of . . ."

But it wasn't an earthquake, and he knew it as he trailed off.

With the howl of displaced air, the ceiling above them disappeared, and they were drenched in sunlight. Shielding his eyes from the glare, Will had an uninterrupted view of the clear sky. "What?" he gasped.

Before any of them knew it, the walls on either side of the panel disintegrated. The oddest thing was that the only sound was the rush of wind all around them. Their eyes hadn't had time to fully adjust to the light, but from what they could see there was some kind of giant wave moving away from them, away from the pyramid, and at a rate of knots. A wave of stone and dust sweeping through the giant trees of the jungle.

With Karl carefully holding a case filled with additional syringes of newly prepared vaccine on his lap, Werner had been driving the small *Kübelwagen* along the jungle track.

But as Karl pointed urgently at something, Werner began to apply the brakes.

The boy had spotted that the sky above the trees was suddenly full of birds, as if they'd all taken flight at the same the time. Great flocks of them were wheeling and intermixing at some speed. And as he'd been watching them, these flocks dispersed to make way for something else; these weren't birds, but a variety of differently sized projectiles with hard, irregular outlines. Because Karl had been so quick to notice something extraordinary was happening, Werner wasn't caught completely by surprise as a sizable piece of masonry spiraled down and crashed onto the hood, making the whole vehicle bounce on its springs.

He'd just brought the *Kübelwagen* to a complete stop when a length of tree root struck the windshield, shattering it. As the bombardment continued like a freak hailstorm, Werner shouted at Karl to get out. Then he protected the boy with his body as they both hunkered down against the side of the vehicle.

Without any of them uttering a word, Will, Elliott, and Jürgen together began to shuffle forward, beyond where the wall of the chamber had originally stood.

"What *is* this? One second we were inside, the next we're out here," Will said finally, still reeling at the sudden development.

"Unbelievable," Jürgen was repeating over and over, as they stepped to the edge of the pyramid and peered down at the tiers below.

"It looks completely different. All the stones with carvings have gone," Will observed. "It's as though it was hidden by a layer of stone." He was right; the pyramid's appearance had been transformed in only a few seconds, and the darker substructure was now fully visible.

"Unbelievable," Jürgen said once again, his voice oddly flat.

They were all feeling rather numb as they struggled to find an explanation for what they'd just experienced.

"But how come we're still here . . . and alive?" Elliott burst out. "Why didn't we get swept off the pyramid, too?"

Neither Will nor Jürgen answered her, their eyesight still adjusting to the sunlight and allowing them the first glimpse of something else that confounded them. As the veil of dust retreated into the distance, they could see that the jungle had been stripped away, as if a plague of locusts had devoured everything in its wake. But there weren't even any uprooted trees — simply acre upon acre of bare earth, with the occasional piece of vegetation strewn across it.

"The jungle's just disappeared," Will said. He shielded his eyes, straining to peer farther into the distance. "Do you see? There's nothing but empty ground right over to the other pyramids."

Elliott gave an odd laugh as she drew Will's attention to the area below them, to the churned-up soil around the base of the pyramid. "That's where our camp was."

Jürgen was shaking his head. "None of this makes the slightest bit of sense. It was as though there was an explosion here. But why didn't we feel or hear anyth —?" He fell silent as his walkie-talkie crackled and his brother's worried voice came over it. Jürgen listened for a moment, muttering, "Oh, thank God." He looked quickly over at Will and Elliott to tell them what he'd just heard. "Karl and Werner were pelted by debris in their vehicle, but they're both safe." He spoke into the radio again. "Werner, as far as we can tell it seems to have originated from here, but . . ."

The radio crackled and Werner was saying, "Hello, hello, are you there?" but Jürgen was holding it away from his ear.

Just as Will and Elliott were doing, he was staring into the distance, at the intersecting point between the three pyramids.

Where something was causing the soil and the crust to be thrown skyward in a huge spout.

There was a low rumble as, all of a sudden, an enormous needlelike structure erupted from the ground itself, thrusting up higher and higher.

"Just when I thought this couldn't get any weirder," Will said under his breath.

Soil and rocks were spilling from the top of the structure as it reached its full height, several times that of the pyramid they were on.

"A tower?" Elliott murmured.

"Werner, er . . . let me get back to you," Jürgen muttered into the radio. "No, I'll call you. You and Karl stay exactly where you are until I do." Werner's anxious voice could still be heard over the radio as Jürgen simply switched it off.

"Where's the bushman?" Elliott asked, as she noticed he wasn't with them.

"There he goes," Will said, spotting the lone figure making its way purposefully over the bare earth in the direction of the tower. "I reckon we need to get after our friend Woody and make him give us some answers." Squinting at the tower in the distance, Will chuckled. "Besides, we need to take a closer look at that!"

■ ■ ■

Parry was escorted down through the airlock first, followed by Chester. Once inside, they were taken through to the bridge where Chester was peering around at the various terminals manned by the crew. Some of the men looked up from their instrumentation panels to give him and Parry curious but fleeting glances, as if they knew they weren't meant to show too much interest. Chester felt light-headed; he'd been plucked from a seventeenth-century farmers' croft that relied on a generator in an outhouse for its electricity, to a state-of-the-art nuclear submarine stuffed to the gills with electronics. And it belonged to the world's leading superpower, no less.

It was all rather unreal, as if he were in a film. Except in a film you couldn't get a sense of how rank it smelled, with so many men in an enclosed space. It reminded Chester of when he and his parents had joined a long-haul flight on their way home from their vacation one summer.

Two people in dark blue suits suddenly appeared. "Homeland Security," the young woman announced, flashing a badge at Parry.

"Watch the birdie," the man accompanying her said, as he aimed a device at Chester and Parry in turn.

"Facial recognition. They're making sure we are who we are," Parry said to Chester, as the man scrutinized a screen on the back of the device and turned to his colleague.

"Both positive," he said.

"Me too?" Chester asked Parry. "But how do they know who I am?"

Parry was about to answer when the woman held up something. Chester recognized it immediately.

"It's one of Danf —!" he began to exclaim, catching himself before he uttered the name of the man he most reviled in the world. "It's a Purger," he corrected himself quickly.

"Yes. Nothing like having your own technology turned on you, is there?" Parry said.

"Please don't talk. Focus on this point here," the woman snapped, indicating the small lens at the top of the small cylinder with her finger.

"Sorry," Chester muttered as she played the purple beam into his eyes, then Parry's.

"They haven't been Dark Lighted," the woman confirmed, typing the result into her PDA.

"Actually, it's *Darklit*," Chester piped up before he knew what he was saying.

The woman shot him a frosty look as another man came up to them. "Commander," he said to Parry. From his age and insignia, Chester guessed who he was before he shook hands with them both.

"Good to meet you, Captain," Parry said.

"And you. I apologize for the inhospitable welcome. I hope our squad of marines didn't play too rough with you," the Captain replied. "Things being what they are, those procedures are now standard drill before anyone's allowed on board. Even my crew members aren't exempt when they return from dockside."

"Quite right," Parry said. "Last thing you want is a suicide bomber in a confined space like this."

The man from Homeland Security was clearly concerned about the time as he glanced repeatedly at his watch.

"Looks like you gentlemen have somewhere to be," the Captain said.

"Yes, the comms link is up and running, Commander," the man in the blue suit said.

One of the marines remained behind as the rest of the escort withdrew. Parry's satphones and walking stick were given back to him before he and Chester were taken from the bridge and through several sections of the submarine. The blue-suited man from Homeland Security ushered them into a surprisingly small cabin, which had a table in its center on which three screens had been set up in a row, with some sort of camera mounted on top of the middle one. Parry told Chester to take a place at the table as he remained standing, talking to the blue suit in hushed tones.

With no idea why he was there or what was about to happen, Chester leaned back in his chair and slipped his hands into his jeans pockets. He looked from one screen to the other, each of which was showing the United States Naval emblem against a blue background.

Taking a breath, he glanced at the marine stationed by the cabin door, who was holding his assault rifle at the ready position across his chest.

"AR16," Chester said out loud, recognizing the weapon from one of his video games. The marine simply frowned at him, so Chester quickly looked away, nodding to himself and muttering, "Yes, AR16."

A tone chimed from a speaker somewhere in the room, and Parry and the blue suit quickly took their places at the table beside Chester.

The screens were blank except for the words TRANSMISSION STATUS with a countdown clicking away the seconds. As the countdown hit zero, the title changed to ENCRYPTION LEVEL ONE, then there was a moment of digital static as random blocks of color flashed over the displays. The picture finally settled down to show a scene very similar to the one in Chester's cabin — a desk or tabletop with three chairs arranged along it. A man holding several files of papers wandered into view.

"Bob Harper," Parry said. "Good to see you after so long, you old devil!"

As the man leaned toward where the camera was mounted on top of the middle screen, Chester saw that he was balding and wore wire-rimmed glasses.

"You too, Parry," Bob replied, but not as warmly as Chester might have expected if they were really such old friends. But Chester could tell that Bob had other things on his mind as he opened one of the files and extracted several documents, which he arranged very precisely on the tabletop. Then he looked up again. "Right, that's me locked and loaded. And a very good afternoon to you all," he said, with more enthusiasm than before. He squinted at the blue suit on Parry's right, then at Chester. "And you must be, er, Chester Rause."

"Rawls," Parry put him right. "How are the kids, Bob?"

There was a slight lag between the picture and the sound, which meant that Bob's lips had stopped moving but his words were still being relayed. "Well, thank you. With one at MIT and the other a Wall Street attorney, I've given them notice that they can provide for their old pa when I finally hang up my spurs. And you know Debbie would send you her love if I was able to tell her we were talking. When you're next over this side of the pond, you must come to stay with us again, Parry." Bob rubbed his chin in a troubled way. "After all this has gone away."

"That's a definite," Parry said.

No one spoke for a moment as Bob cast an eye over his documents. "We've got a frosty but sunny day here in Washington. What's the weather doing where you are, Parry?"

"Oh, other than it's the middle of the night here, Bob, do you need to ask? This is England; inevitably it'll rain before morning," Parry replied drily.

But Bob wasn't listening. From the noise in the background, Chester could tell other people had entered the room. A well-built man, younger than Bob and wearing a charcoal-gray suit, came into view. He inspected the screens and the table to make sure everything was as it should be, then moved out of the way to allow someone else to take the central seat.

Chester's mouth gaped open, his eyes nearly popping out of his head.

It was true that in the last year he'd spent a great deal of time underground, but it would have been impossible for him not to recognize the man on the screen in front of him.

One of the most famous people alive on the planet, and certainly the most powerful.

"Is that . . . ?" Chester tried to ask, but no sound came from his throat.

He shot a glance at Parry, who gave him a quick nod.

"Good day, gentlemen," the US President greeted them while scanning one of Bob's briefing notes on the table. When he finally looked up, he ran his eyes over the blue suit and Parry, his gaze coming to rest on Chester.

"Hi," the President said.

DRAKE'S FACE was sickly white, but the creases under his eyes and around his mouth were bloodred. And although his arm with the wounded shoulder was in a sling and he had numerous dressings on his burns, none of these was troubling him as much as his mouth, which he was now reaching inside as he probed his swollen gums. Despite the fact that the pain was making him wince as he touched them, he chuckled to himself.

"A man walks into a dentist's and sits in the chair." It was difficult to understand what Drake was saying because his fingers were in the way, but he went on regardless. "The dentist says, 'What can I do for you, sir?' The man replies, 'You've got to help me; I think I'm a moth.'"

Drake paused for a moment as he pushed against a tooth in his lower jaw and felt it shift in his gum. "The dentist says, 'But you can see I'm a dentist, and you need a doctor. So why did you come in here?'" Drake had taken his hand from his mouth and was examining the blood on his fingertips. "The man replies, 'Well, your light was on.'"

Jiggs gave a chuckle. "That's an old one," he said, as he took hold of Drake's good arm and wrapped a cuff around it. He was using an ancient sphygmomanometer, a blood pressure meter, which he'd found in the medical bay. "I can always tell when things are at their worst because you start with the jokes." Jiggs smiled. "Remember that time Parry was away, and Sparks, Danforth, and I had to drive you sixty miles across Scotland to the nearest hospital, through the heaviest snowfall that winter, because your appendix had ruptured? What were you — maybe sixteen years old? Even though you were in terrible pain, you told nonstop jokes the whole way."

Drake nodded, leaned his head forward, and shook it. "How about this for a snowfall?" he said. His hair had begun to grow back after he'd trimmed it all off some months before to disguise his appearance, but a few tufts of it now sprinkled down over the surface of the table.

"Bleeding gums . . . hair loss . . . I'm afraid they're all symptoms of chronic radiation sickness," Jiggs said. He inflated the cuff around Drake's arm, then let out some of the air as he listened with a stethoscope before taking a reading on the meter.

Drake wasn't paying any attention to what Jiggs was doing, instead staring into the middle distance. "The choices I've made in the past have meant that I've had some pretty close calls, and I'm not blaming anyone for the way things have turned out." He wasn't looking for a response from Jiggs, and Jiggs knew it. "I never anticipated a retirement trout fishing in the Cairngorms, but . . ."

"Are there any trout in the Cairngorms?" Jiggs put in.

"You know what I mean," Drake replied. "Where was I . . . ? But . . . but I always figured when my number was up, it would be quick." He clicked his fingers. "I thought I'd catch a bullet, or be blown up. So, tell me, is this how it's going to play out for me, quietly and painfully? A repeat to fade?"

"First the easy bit: The slug that caught you in the shoulder broke your clavicle, but it's only a minor fracture. So it's nothing serious." Jiggs sighed and began to put the antiquated meter back into its wooden box. "As for the radiation exposure, you'll have good and bad days. But you'll grow weaker as the nausea and the vomiting become more frequent, and the internal bleeding intensifies. I'm afraid it's all downhill from here."

"No, please tell me the worst, won't you, doctor?" Drake said wryly. He picked up an old bottle of iodine tablets Jiggs had also found in the medical stores. "Will these have made any difference?"

"They'll have helped to flush out some of the isotopes, but you were exposed to a massive dose of ionizing radiation. Even if we were on the surface with all the facilities there, not much more could be done for you." Jiggs shook his head. "I'm sorry."

"So it goes," Drake said resignedly, taking in a breath before he continued. "I suppose, sooner or later, we're all drawn to the big light, like a moth. It's just that my big light happened to be a nuke, and it fried me." He began to laugh, but it turned into a coughing fit, and it was a moment before he could speak again. "If I'd known it would come to this, I would never have paid so much attention to my diet." He leaned back in his chair and let out a long sigh. "Jiggs, old friend, really — what's the point of carting me all the way Topsoil again? You may just as well leave me here."

Jiggs gazed around the main area of the fallout shelter, a place constructed deep in the Earth that Will and Dr. Burrows had originally discovered, and which Drake himself had been to before when he'd come to rescue Will and Elliott. "A very long time ago," Jiggs began, "I promised your father that I'd look out for you. I intend to keep that promise."

He gestured toward the kitchen where he'd been preparing their meals from the fifty-year-old canned food. "And, in any case, I can't leave you here. The diet of corned beef in this place is enough to see off the strongest of us."

"But why take me back?" Drake asked. "What difference does it make if I pop my clogs on the surface or down here?"

Jiggs wasn't to be swayed. "Against all the odds and with those savage animals snapping at our heels, I've got you this far." Jiggs paused for breath. "So let me tell you one thing for sure; there's no way in hell that I'm just going to desert you. We are setting off up that river *together*."

After Jiggs had managed to resuscitate Drake in the wrecked Short Sunderland and stabilize him sufficiently to move him again, he'd set off for Smoking Jean. He only had the weakest signals from the radio beacons that Will and Drake had left on previous occasions to guide him, but when combined with his phenomenal sense of direction they were enough. Burning almost every last drop of the fuel in the booster rockets, Jiggs had managed to get Drake up Smoking Jean and through into the inclined seam. Once there, Drake had been so weak that he'd been only able to travel short distances under his own steam. However, the low gravity allowed Jiggs to carry both him and their kit on his back.

But then they'd received unwanted attention from the Brights and monkey-spiders, which were highly sensitive when it came to detecting wounded prey. Drake's blood was like a magnet to them, and he'd had to pull himself together and help Jiggs fight them off time after time.

And just when they thought they'd traveled far enough up the seam to escape all the local predators, Jiggs had nearly walked into the first of the antipersonnel devices left behind by Limiters. He only spotted it because a more regular-sized spider had spun a web on the very fine trip wire strung across the route. Its presence in the seam was bad news, as it meant that a patrol had been sent to the fallout shelter, and that there would doubtless be more devices planted along the way. So progress had been excruciatingly slow as Jiggs was forced to check every inch of the passage for more trip wires, and once they arrived at the shelter he'd had to conduct a complete sweep of that, too.

"You heard me, didn't you?" Jiggs asked Drake, who appeared to have drifted into a reverie. "We're going up that river together. OK?"

"Yes, OK, whatever you say," Drake replied. He languidly raised his eyes to Jiggs, as even that small act was an effort. "At least I'll be able to report back to Parry that, as far as we know, our mission was a success. And find out how he's got on with the other Styx female."

Jiggs nodded, as Drake turned his head slightly toward the entrance corridor where the communications room was to be found. Both Will and Chester had used the ancient telephone there to make contact with the surface before.

"No way," Jiggs said instantly. "If you're seriously considering using that phone through there to make a call, you can stop right now. If they haven't cut the line, the Styx will be monitoring any traffic over it — you even as much as pick up the receiver, they'll suss that we're down here." His voice became gentler. "Drake, really, don't go near it. You're not thinking this through, are you?"

"No, maybe not, but I haven't got the luxury of time any longer," Drake said, as he rose to his feet. "The thought of dying is enough to make one impatient."

"Why don't you catch some shut-eye while I finish the repairs to the boat?" Jiggs suggested.

"No, I want to give you a hand," Drake replied, holding up his good arm with a smile. "Even if it's only one hand." He glanced in the direction of the bunk beds. "I'm not quite ready for the scrap heap. Not while I've still got *some* life left in me."

"No question that he's going straight to it," Elliott observed, as she sought out the small form of Woody trudging deliberately toward the tower. He wasn't the only thing moving in the place, as flies and insects with bizarre appearances buzzed furiously in the air, and an army of birds had already ventured back after the tumult. These birds were clearly having a heyday as they flocked to the fields of newly turned soil to gorge themselves on the exposed grubs and worms.

Elliott, Will, and Jürgen had wasted no time in following after the bushman, but it wasn't that easy to move at any speed over the ground. Not only was it very uneven, but as the sun dried out the clods of earth, they were crumbling away and shifting like sand under their feet.

Shielding his eyes, Jürgen squinted as he tried to see the other pyramids through the sun-hazed air. "It's incredible when you think that this was all solid jungle only moments ago," he said.

But Will's mind was elsewhere as he tried to make sense of what they'd just witnessed. "So the pyramids must have been covered in the stones with the carvings on them at some point *after* the basic structures had been built," he reasoned out loud, turning to Jürgen.

"But the oldest of the carved stones were at least three thousand years old," Jürgen replied.

"Right . . . ," Will said thoughtfully. "But my dad's theory was that the Lost City of Atlantis has been in this world all along, and he could still be right. The Atlanteans might have built on top of the original structures."

"That's a possibility," Jürgen agreed, giving a small shrug.

"And so the bushmen, the descendants of the Atlanteans, continued the tradition of recording their culture and history on the pyramids," Will went on.

Elliott was forging ahead, as if she wasn't the slightest bit interested in the discussion the other two were having. Will had still been talking, but trailed off as he and Jürgen caught up with her. She'd come to a stop where a fifteen-foot-deep trench blocked their way. "Incredible. One of the giant trees must have been ripped out here," Jürgen said, as they all regarded the bottom of the depression where there was a jumble of roots, some of them huge.

"You both think you're so clever, but you're actually unbelievably stupid," Elliott said sourly.

"Huh?" Will said.

"Well, who gives a toss about the Atlanteans now?" she snapped. "Why aren't you asking yourselves what could tear out a bloody big tree in the blink of an eye, and chuck it and the rest of the jungle so far away we can't even see it?"

Will was surprised by her outburst, but made no comment as he lowered himself down into the hole where he began to kick at the roots and dirt.

"Some form of traction beam?" Jürgen answered when Will remained silent.

"Traction beam?" she repeated. "Where would you find one of those — whatever it is — around here? Was it left by whoever built the original pyramids? Who was that, then?" she asked. "And, tell me, why did that pyramid underneath look so new?"

Nobody replied, Will continuing to scrape away at the dirt with his toe cap. "There's something solid down here," he said after a moment.

Jürgen slid down into the depression, too, and together they worked at uncovering a whole series of thick conduits or pipes running side by side. Roots were growing between them, and Will squatted down to tug out handfuls of the smaller ones. "Look at this," he said, as he brushed the dirt from one of the pipes. "They're made of the same stuff as the pyramid. And they look so new, too."

"Despite being buried here for what must be many millennia," Jürgen said. He raised a hand to indicate the direction of the pipes. "And it appears that they start at the pyramid and . . ." He swung around to face the opposite direction.

". . . run all the way over to the tower." He paused for a second. "It could be that the other pyramids are connected, too."

Rather than climb down into it, Elliott was circumventing the trench in the ground. Will noticed that she sounded quite frightened as she spoke. "So neither of you can explain to me what happened back there when I touched that panel? That wasn't electricity, or an explosion, so what was it? And can't either of you feel it — the power?"

"Huh?" Will swallowed, peering up at her. "What power?"

"In those pipes . . . in the pyramid . . . all around us," she went on.

Will and Jürgen exchanged glances.

"Elliott?" Will called, but she'd gone, moving even faster toward the tower.

"YOU'VE GOT YOURSELF a real situation over there," the US President was saying. "Our bases in England are on full DEFCON, and we're already well down the road of recalling military personnel and assets, particularly our fighter planes. We can't have those Styx getting their paws on them."

He pronounced Styx as *Stikes*, which prompted Chester's eyebrows to jump up for a moment, but he'd already upset the Homeland Security woman when he'd tried to correct her. And this was the President, after all, so he could pronounce it how he liked.

"We've implemented full-body monitoring and Purger checks on all arrivals at our airports and seaports, and anyone entering our borders," the President was saying. "After the atrocity on Capitol Hill, we were already on the lookout for suicide bombers, but now we're also screening for Darklit passengers, too. Bob tells me that we owe you one for supplying us with the schematics for the Purger. Also, and more important, you gave him the heads-up about the Stikes's activity early on, Commander, so we had a contingency plan ready to roll out when all this flared up last year. America is deeply indebted to you for that."

The President was looking intently at Parry now, who briefly bowed his head in response. Then the President knitted his fingers together and leaned back in his seat. "So what can we do for you, Commander?"

"Well, as you say, we're in real trouble over here," Parry began. "The UK has effectively been put into isolation by the rest of its NATO partners. Not one of them wants to gets close for fear of the rot spreading. To cut to the chase, sir, I'm reaching out to you for military intervention. I can't see how we can fix things here without a conventional land force taking control and weeding out the Styx."

The President lowered his gaze as if what he was about to say was difficult, but Parry carried on regardless. "Mr. President, sir, our two countries have always been united by their special relationship, and this is a dark hour for us — perhaps the darkest in our history. We need your assistance to help pull us through. And how we came to this crisis, well . . . I want you to hear direct from my friend Chester here about how the situation evolved . . . about how he and Will Burrows stumbled upon the subterranean city, and how while they were on the run from the Styx they uncovered their plot to deploy the Dominion virus."

Chester couldn't believe he'd suddenly been pulled into the conversation. He looked in desperation at Parry. He couldn't talk to the President about all this. He wasn't important enough.

"And because of the intel we obtained from Chester and Will," Parry continued, "we were ahead of the curve on the

Phase. I don't think there would still be an England to save today if these two lads hadn't been on the ground and running recon for us."

"Ah, yes, Chester," the President said, switching his gaze to the boy. Before he spoke again, the President pressed his lips together in an expression of sympathy. Chester had seen him do it on television in the aftermath of floods, bombings, and other large-scale disasters in America. "I understand that you recently suffered a terrible sacrifice in the pursuit of duty — the death of your mother and father. I am very sorry for your loss."

When Chester didn't answer immediately because he was so tongue-tied, the President looked uneasy, as if he'd got the facts wrong. "I'm sorry . . . about your mother and father . . . that is correct, isn't it?" he asked, with a quick glance at Bob.

Chester tried to say, "Yes," but combined it with a simultaneous "Um," so what he actually came out with sounded like "Yum." He wanted to punch himself. *Oh. My. God. The US President just told me he was sorry about my parents' death and I said "Yum" to him!*

The President made like he was searching for the right page in front of him to mask his discomfort. "Right, I've read Bob's briefing about the . . . the . . ."

Bob whispered in his ear at this point. "About the Colony," the President went on, "and also this Germanic world at the center of the Earth, and I have to admit I've been finding the whole yarn rather difficult to swallow. I get it that a group of underground — truly *underground* — insurgents have surfaced and are using their kitchen-table bioweapons and technology to bring your country to its knees, but the rest of what's been going down . . . it sounds like the plot from a bad sci-fi movie. So I'd like to hear your side of things, Chester, because you were there. You've lived through all this." He held up Bob's briefing note. "Convince me that it's real."

Chester's mouth gaped open as the cabin seemed to be swaying, although it had nothing to do with the rough sea outside.

Talk about being put on the spot.

The President of the United States was asking for his version of events!

How could he, mere Chester Rawls, formerly of Highfield, where he attended high school until he went on the run, even begin to tell the leader of the free world about what had happened?

"Chester," Parry prompted the boy when he failed to speak. "I know this isn't easy for you, lad, but just take your time."

"But . . . but where do I start?" Chester croaked, finally finding his voice.

"From the beginning," the President said. "We've got all the time we need."

Parry placed his hand on Chester's shoulder. "From when Dr. Burrows went missing, and you and Will found the tunnel under his house."

"OK," Chester said. He took a deep breath and began to tell his story.

■ ■ ■

Whenever Chester faltered, Parry was ready to step in and help out. And when Chester began to speak about the run-up to his parents' death in the Complex, he was finding it so painful that Parry took over and finished the account for him.

"And I don't have to tell you what the situation is today, sir," Parry said as he came to the end.

"Thank you, both of you. That's quite a tale," the President said, then leaned back in his chair. "Can you tell me something, Chester? You've been in the thick of this for longer than anyone. . . . These Stikes — I know they're not like us — but what's driving them? What's their ultimate goal? To stamp out all human life?"

"Well . . . ," Chester began.

"I suppose what I'm really asking is, can we negotiate with them?" the President added.

"Uh, negotiate?" Chester said, surprised by the question but considering it. "I don't believe they want *all* people dead — they just want to weaken us enough so that we're not a threat, and they can get control of the surface. It's like they think it belongs to them. I suppose you could try to negotiate with them — they're open to deals — but there's no way you can ever trust them. They don't think we're equal to them. They've been messing things up for us with plagues and sabotage for centuries."

The President was rubbing his chin. "So this current act of aggression isn't about money, or a bid to have their own country?"

"Their own country?" Chester couldn't stifle a chuckle. "You could offer them that, but you should know . . ." Chester was staring straight at the President. ". . . you should know that even if they accepted that as an offer, they'll come for you, for America, someday. Nothing gets in their way when they want something, and they want it all."

"OK, that's pretty unequivocal." The President picked up one of Bob's briefing notes and read a few lines before he looked up again. "Commander, let's cut to the chase, shall we? Your European neighbors are refusing to have anything to do with you, but you're asking my country to make a major military commitment to bail you out. And that's after all the financial support we've been forced to give Europe because its banking system was threatening to drag the US into one doozy of a depression."

"Sir, I . . . ," Parry began.

The President held up his hand. "Just a minute, Commander, I need to bring another party into the conference for this. Bob, tap them in now, please."

The display on Chester's far left went black for a second, and when it came back on there was a view of an oval table with a dozen or so people around it, many in uniform.

"Hi, Dave," the President said, also looking to his far left. "We've got you on visual now. Did you catch all that?" He turned back to the camera before he received a response from the new roomful of people. "Commander, I wanted your Prime Minister to hear our conversation. We don't have time for a game of grapevine."

Parry was unfazed by the turn of events. "Good evening, sir," he said to the man in the middle of the scene, who wore an annoyed expression, before scanning the other faces on either side of him. "I see you've got the War Cabinet with you."

Chester's mouth gaped open for a second time — as he'd stumbled through his story the British Prime Minister had been listening, and most likely watching him. He wondered who was going to pop up on the screens next.

The Prime Minister narrowed his eyes with all the arrogance of a disgruntled headmaster. "Commander, I don't appreciate you going over my head and speaking to the President direct. Why didn't you use the normal channels and come to my office first?"

Parry was unapologetic. "The normal channels? At a time like this? For two reasons. First, because I didn't know who I could trust. I didn't know who the Styx had gotten at. I believe you yourself had been Dark —"

"We all had a session with the Purger ages ago." The Prime Minster cut him short, with a blasé flick of the head. "The Cabinet and all the staff at Number Ten have had a clean bill of health for some weeks now."

Parry appeared skeptical at this response. "Not just one Purger session, I trust? You and your colleagues in the Cabinet should be checked at regular intervals throughout the day."

"I don't need you to advise me on my security measures," the Prime Minister said, raising his voice to let Parry know he didn't like to be challenged. "And your second reason, Commander?"

"Because we can't fix this by ourselves. We need outside

intervention from a nation that hasn't been contaminated by the Styx." Parry stopped abruptly, his brow creased by a deepening frown. "Can I ask where you are right now? That room looks familiar."

"If it's anything to do with you, I summoned everyone here to the inner sanctum at Westminster. I overruled my security team because I wasn't about to leave London and let these Styx fellows think they had us on the run."

Without any warning, Parry was out of his chair and shouting. "You blithering idiot! Didn't you read the communiqué I submitted months ago?"

"Commander, please," the President urged, trying to restore order.

"Yes, calm down, dear chap," the Prime Minister said, clearly amused at Parry's distress.

"No, you listen to me, and this is vitally important. Get out of there now!" Parry was speaking with such fervor, he was actually spitting. "Rather than heed my warning, you've gathered everyone together in the Houses of Parliament, where you're sitting ducks. You've played right into the Styx's hands. Chester and my son learned that the Eternal City — the massive cavern under Westminster — has a weakness in its roof that the Limiters might choose to exploit at any moment. They might blow it!"

"It's true," Chester said, but he was drowned out by the Prime Minister, who didn't bother to hide his sneer.

"Oh, sure, like they can do that!" he bellowed. "We haven't seen any solid evidence that this mythical lost city you talk of actually exists. I fear that you may have had a wee *dram* too many before beddy-byes, then had a wee *dream* about the whole thing." As he mimicked Parry's Scottish accent, the Prime Minister was obviously delighted with the pun he'd just made; like a braying donkey he put his head back and unleashed a torrent of laughter, the whole table joining in with him.

All of a sudden, the picture of the Prime Minister and his War Cabinet stuttered, then froze.

What Chester and Parry were left looking at on the screen didn't seem quite right — as if everyone, the Prime Minister included, were suddenly much closer to the camera, as if they'd all been thrown across the table.

And, in that captured instant, none of them appeared to be laughing any longer; however, the delay between picture and sound meant that their raucous laughter still resonated in the cabin for a moment longer.

Then there was nothing but an eerie silence.

The President of the United States swallowed and then cleared his throat as the frozen picture was lost in a snowstorm of static. "Bob, can we find out what happened to the feed?"

Parry was back in his chair, his hands tightly clasped together. "Oh, no," he whispered.

Chester had never seen him look so pale. "You don't think . . . ?" the boy asked him.

"I truly, truly hope not," Parry replied.

"No signal? None at all?" the President was saying to Bob,

who had two phones on the go at the same time. "Well, can we get some eyes on the Houses of Parliament? Have we got any drones over the area?"

"A drone? There?" Parry asked, but his question was ignored as Bob conferred with the President, who was rapidly running out of patience. "Well, if we *have* got satellite coverage, get it on-screen right now," he said, thumping the table.

The left-hand display came back to life with an aerial view of London, the Thames in the center of the picture glinting with the first light of dawn.

"Yes, magnify to a quarter quadrant, and amp up the definition with some digital enhancement, will you," Bob said, now only using a single phone as he issued instructions.

Chester couldn't believe what the spy satellite was capable of, the picture enlarging in successive jumps until the roofs of individual buildings along the banks were visible. And as the enhancement for low light was applied as Bob had requested, the clarity also shot up, the Thames appearing like a silvered snake.

"Tower Bridge," Parry said, as he recognized it from the aerial view.

"Bear with us — we're going to track along the course of the river," Bob informed them, and the view sped along the Thames, past the different bridges.

Then the view steadied as the camera on the satellite reached its destination.

"Oh, God, no," the President said.

"What is that?" Chester mumbled, confused by the image.

Parry put a hand to his temple. He was trembling. "It's one almighty hole in the ground."

Chester saw what he meant. Even as he watched, buildings were crumbling and falling in at the edges of the ever-widening fissure, as if in slow motion. There were no Houses of Parliament anymore, no Big Ben, and no Westminster Bridge — and as the Thames swirled down into the coal-black opening, stretches of the riverbed were exposed.

"They actually did it," Chester said breathlessly. "They blew the roof of the Eternal City. Just like Drake guessed they might."

There was silence as everyone tried to deal with what they were seeing. The President's head was in his hands, his face hidden. "How am I going to tell your Prime Minister's wife and kids about this? They're staying at Camp David. What the hell am I going to tell them?" he said to no one in particular. Then he looked sharply up at Parry. "What about your asset, Commander . . . your mole in the Stikes's ranks? Why did you have no forewarning of this?"

"Sir," Bob cut in. "That information's not for dissemination."

Chester shot a glance at Parry, who was grimacing. He appeared extremely uncomfortable.

"We're way beyond any such niceties now," the President snapped at Bob. Then he shook his head. "We'll get back to you, gentlemen," he said.

Chester was left with the image of the President making a rapid cutting motion across his throat as he turned toward Bob, then the screens simply shut down.

■ ■ ■

"You poor old thing, you look done in. They are a handful, aren't they?" Mrs. Burrows said, stroking Colly's head. Stretched out on her side as the kittens suckled hungrily, the cat was exhausted, but she still made the effort to purr loudly.

As someone entered the room, Colly looked up, and her purring became more subdued. "It's all right, girl," Mrs. Burrows said, trying to reassure her. Like all Hunters she was extremely protective of her young, hissing and growling at anyone who came near, although Mrs. Burrows had proved to be the exception to this.

"I'll be glad when I've got my kitchen back," the First Officer grumbled, stepping over the toys the kittens had left scattered across the floor. It was an age-old tradition for Colonists to help out when a Hunter had a new litter, as it was quite an undertaking to care for and clean up after the lively offspring. Numerous gifts of food and old blankets had been left by the front door, but another favorite gift was the cloth toys people made for the kittens to play with. With their cotton-thread whiskers and shiny bead eyes, these generally resembled the different varieties of rats the cats would be expected to hunt in adult life.

The First Officer sat down, then groaned with the effort as he leaned forward to scoop up a toy that had caught his eye. This was no rat, but a little man dressed in black with a white face, and in its hand it had a tiny cloth book with the letter C embroidered on it. "Ha, a Styx, and he's even holding the *Book of Catastrophes*! Someone's got a sense of humor," the First Officer said with a chuckle. "If they'd caught anyone doing this, it would have merited Banishment or even death by hanging."

Mrs. Burrows turned toward the First Officer. "Oh, it's a Styx, is it? I thought that was meant to be you, love," she said, raising an eyebrow.

The First Officer chuckled, then stopped himself as he wondered if she had been joking or not. Although Mrs. Burrows's sight was heavily impaired, most of the time her incredibly developed olfactory sense more than compensated as she went about the Colony, helping the First Officer to run things. But every so often he was reminded that she could hardly see at all.

"No, I'm pretty sure it's meant to be a White Neck," he said. He jiggled it around by one of its chewed legs. All of a sudden one of the kittens, who'd noticed what he was doing, made a lunge for it. "Whoops!" the First Officer exclaimed as it was snatched from his hand and the kitten shot under the table with its trophy. "Nearly lost a couple of fingers there!"

Colly wasn't purring any longer, but was making a low growling sound as she stared gimlet-eyed at the First Officer.

"And tell that bloody Hunter I'm no threat to her babies, will you?" the First Officer said. "After all, she was *my* Hunter, once upon a time."

Mrs. Burrows laughed. "She doesn't mean it. And she'll be your Hunter again the moment her hormone levels are back to normal."

The kitten emerged from under the table and jumped up so that both of its forepaws rested on the First Officer's thigh. It may have been less than two months old, but it was already larger than any Topsoil domestic cat.

With a shake of its head, the Hunter kitten dropped the Styx rag doll in the First Officer's lap. "Well, will you look at this? I think I've made a friend here. He wants to play."

"Oh, that one." Mrs. Burrows exhaled. "He's the biggest and greediest of them all. Just like Bartleby."

"He's the spitting image of his old man, too. So maybe that's what we should call him — Bartleby, in memory of his pa," the First Officer suggested, as he sent the rag doll flying to the other end of the kitchen for the kitten to fetch. Colly growled again, even louder this time. "But I don't think his mother wants to let him go, though."

There was a heavy silence in the room until Mrs. Burrows spoke. "Talking about letting go, the more I think about it . . . I should never have let Will go off on that mission. What sort of mother am I?" She didn't give the First Officer time to answer as she added, "He's been gone for such a long time now, and I have a terrible feeling something must have happened to him."

The First Officer gave a nod, but then gestured toward the ceiling. "But everything's falling apart up there. He might have got back and be lying low somewhere . . . somewhere safe. After all, Drake and the others were with him. They would have looked out for him, and maybe none of them can get messages through to us because of the lockdown."

Under Mrs. Burrows's and the First Officer's direction, the Colony had shut itself off from the surface because the scale of the problems Topsoil was so great, and there was the constant nagging fear that the Styx might eventually focus their attention on the Colony again and re-establish their rule. There had been lockdowns in the past, but these had been imposed by the Styx, the most recent when Will had escaped with Cal after failing to spring Chester from the Hold. But this new lockdown wasn't to punish the people of the Colony but to protect them. And the good news was that other than going without their consignments of fresh fruit, they were almost self-sufficient again when it came to feeding themselves. The replanted penny bun fields were beginning to produce harvests, and the livestock breeding program was also well underway.

"You'll see — he'll turn up here one day soon. Everything will be just fine," the First Officer tried to reassure Mrs. Burrows. As the kitten reappeared with the toy and jumped up again with its paws on his leg, the First Officer rubbed the skin on its broad head. The kitten let out an appreciative mew. In an instant, Colly was up, her back arched.

"I think you'd better leave Bartleby kitten alone before she goes for you," Mrs. Burrows advised.

"Righty-ho," the First Officer said with a sigh, getting up slowly from his chair with both palms in the air as if he was surrendering. "Far be it from me to rock the boat. It's only my house and my kitch —"

"Something's very wrong," Mrs. Burrows burst out, snapping her head around to look at the bare wall. "Something just happened!"

"What — with the wall?" the First Officer asked.

Mrs. Burrows's eyes had rotated upward so that only the whites were showing. "Water — so much you wouldn't believe . . . and it's heading our way."

"Where . . . how far away?" the First Officer asked urgently.

Mrs. Burrows shuddered, her eyes righting themselves. "Far side of the Colony . . . that direction." She pointed at the wall.

The First Officer was already rushing toward the door. "It must be coming through the Labyrinth!" he shouted. "There must be a cave-in somewhere." He paused in the doorway, Bartleby kitten watching him curiously. "My God — if it's the Labyrinth, maybe the breach is in the Eternal City! Remember what Eddie told Drake about a fracture in the roof? Maybe it's that."

Once in the street outside, Mrs. Burrows and the First Officer collared the first person they came across to raise the alarm. Well into her seventies and showing no sign that she was going to stop doing the job she'd held for half a century, Ruby Withers was carrying her stepladder as she went about dusting the glowing orbs at the very top of the streetlamps. The First Officer quickly told her to go to the nearest temple and raise the alarm by ringing the bell.

Ruby caught on quickly. Every Colonist lived with three principal fears: the Discovery (when Topsoilers would learn of the city and invade it), a major fire, and lastly being caught in floodwaters.

Within minutes, the single bell ringing in the nearest temple led to a second sounding in a neighboring area, and then another, until there was ringing and shouting coming from all over the Colony.

At first there was confusion among the people because there was no apparent danger, and even the First Officer allowed himself the hope that Mrs. Burrows had been mistaken and that it was a false alarm. But as they came to the edge of the South Cavern, water was already gushing down the track in the middle of the steep tunnel leading up to the Quarter.

"It's started," Mrs. Burrows said.

The First Officer lumbered quickly up the sharply inclined tunnel and into the first passage that branched off from it. Right at the end of this was a heavy iron door, one of the many that led into the Labyrinth from the Colony. It had been welded shut, and although there was a small trickle of water at its base, there was no sign that anything was amiss.

Not until the First Officer cleaned the glass inspection port in the door and tried to shine his lantern through.

"Oh, no," he said.

Mrs. Burrows didn't need to be told that he'd seen the water level rising rapidly on the other side. Her supersense was warning her that all the portals to the Labyrinth were increasingly coming under pressure as thousands of gallons of water poured through its tunnels.

More Colonists were turning up every second. Even the new Governors were mucking in; the First Officer saw Cleaver using his not inconsiderable bulk to haul a cart laden with stone blocks as Squeaky and Gappy Mulligan pushed from behind.

Although many of the skilled artisans — the stonemasons, engineers, and other specialists that maintained the Colony's caverns and utilities — had been whisked away by the Styx for their breeding program, those who were left quickly mobilized. And the carts of stone and equipment drawn from the Colony's building yards kept coming.

With the knowledge that a full-scale breach would lead to their underground city being swamped by thousands of gallons of water, and very likely make it uninhabitable, the Colonists labored tirelessly to reinforce and shore up the portals into the Labyrinth by constructing reinforcing walls across them. And where the portals were judged to be strong enough to withstand the weight of water, the Colonists hammered caulking into the joints around the edges of the metal doors in an attempt to stem any seepage.

Mrs. Burrows was on hand to give as much information as she was able, although it was becoming more difficult for her as the huge volume of water completely filled the Labyrinth network, stopping her olfactory probes from penetrating into it.

And it was the best part of twenty-four hours before the Colonists took a break from their efforts. Tired, soaked, and covered in dirt, they all gathered on the main track, where the flow of water continued but didn't seem to be getting any worse.

"That much water can't come from anywhere else but the Thames, can it?" Mrs. Burrows asked the First Officer.

"I'm afraid that's right," he answered. "They blew the canopy over the Eternal City. Exactly as Drake said they might, one day."

Mrs. Burrows shook her head. "But if they've gone that far, what else are the Styx doing? We have to find out what's happening Topsoil," she said. "They might need our help."

"I don't know . . . ," the First Officer said, placing his hefty boot on one of the small streams of water, and watching it find a new course in the damp dirt. "We've got troubles enough of our own here. Last thing we want is to open up a portal and have the White Necks swoop in on us again."

They walked in silence, Will occasionally throwing glances at Elliott as he wondered what was wrong, because she didn't seem to be herself at all. While he was used to her being candid with him, Elliott's behavior toward Jürgen had been out of character, and Will didn't know the reason for it.

Only when they came nearer to the tower could they appreciate its sheer scale as it spiked into the bright sky. The exterior was completely smooth and gray, with only the odd patch where soil marked it. The overhanging disk-type structure at the top was difficult to look at because of the intensity of the sun, but once they were close enough at least it provided them with some shade.

And there was Woody, standing like a sentinel by the base of the tower where the ground was littered with piles of shattered rock and large boulders. Will put this down to the fact that the tower had burst up through the ground, bringing up strata from deep in the crust.

Woody was watching Elliott attentively as they headed toward him. He didn't seem to have any qualms about meeting her eyes now. In fact, since the inexplicable event at the pyramid, the diminutive man in his sunglasses and silly hat had gone through a transformation from an eccentric-looking but harmless member of the party to a rather ominous one, to the extent that both Will and Jürgen were actually rather wary of him.

But Elliott evidently didn't have any such reservations as she went right up to the bushman. He stepped aside to reveal that behind him was another of the symbols with the three diverging rays.

There was no other feature that Will could see on the curved exterior of the tower — just the three rays indented into the perfectly smooth and unmarked wall. "That looks like the panel you touched back at the pyramid," he noted.

And, as if there was some kind of tacit understanding between Woody and Elliott, the bushman's eyes were glued to the three indentures as she stretched a hand toward them.

"No you don't! No way!" Will shouted immediately, lunging at Elliott to seize hold of her and pull her away from the symbol. "I'm not going to let you do that!"

Elliott reacted calmly. "It's okay, Will. There's no danger to any of us. Really."

He released her, letting his arms hang limply by his sides. "Just think about the last time you did this."

She shook her head. "That's not going to happen again."

Will's voice lifted a tone as his frustration grew. "Oh, sure, and you really *know*, don't you? Based on what? We're right in the middle of something we don't understand, and who knows how it's going to turn out if you go sticking your hand into that? You might really be hurt this time." He glared at Woody. "Ask him what this tower is, and what it's here for, will you?"

Elliott spoke to the bushman in Styx, and he replied, his expression inscrutable. She asked another question and again he answered in the rasping Styx language. "He doesn't know any more than we do," Elliott told Will.

"He doesn't give that impression," Will countered.

Elliott sighed in exasperation. "Look, I've tried to ask him. All he says is that this was meant to be. He's using a word I don't recognize, but I think it must mean destiny or fate, or something like that. Maybe it's old Styx." She stooped to put her rifle on the ground by her feet, then straightened up again. "Can't you feel it, Will?" she said. "It's all around us."

Will shook his head. "You keep saying that. Feel what, exactly?"

"There's something here, and it's, like, so much bigger than us," Elliott replied.

Will and Jürgen exchanged glances. A raggedy flock of vultures was picking over the churned-up soil, and a trio of the largest and most unpleasant-looking ones, which resembled burst cushions, was fighting over a tasty morsel. They were making harsh, grating calls as they squabbled, but somehow it suited the moment.

"No, I don't feel anything different." Will peered up at the top of the tower with evident misgiving. "Look, I want to find out what all this is about as much as anyone, but we have to be careful. We haven't the faintest idea what this tower is here for, so we have to take this one step at a time."

"I'm sorry, Will. Nobody tells me what to do," Elliott stated flatly. "This is my choice."

Will sighed, not knowing what else he could say to persuade her. He'd made his reservations clear and, short of physically restraining her, there wasn't anything more he could do. So he kept his mouth shut as Elliott took one last look at him and moved toward the symbol. But in case she was thrown backward again, he made sure he was in a position to catch her.

Elliott slowly reached out and placed her fingers in the three indentures.

She stepped back as a circular opening with a diameter of around ten feet suddenly appeared in the tower to the left of the symbol. There was no sound, except some loose stones scattering across the floor inside the new opening.

Will remained where he was, but Jürgen immediately slipped past Elliott and began to examine the entrance. "The outside skin is a couple inches thick. I can't see where the door or panel has gone. How . . . where has it retracted?"

"It was the same with that trapdoor in the pyramid," Will said. His tone was such that Elliott gave him a quick glance. Despite all that was going on, he felt thoroughly let down by his friend. She hadn't listened to him.

Jürgen was unaware of this as he continued his investigation, tapping various spots around the opening, his knuckles making barely any sound. "I can't tell you what this material is — seems to be neither stone nor metal."

"See — there wasn't any danger to us, was there? What did I tell you?" Elliott said to Will, trying a smile on him as she went to collect her rifle from the ground.

Will didn't reciprocate, instead pretending to stare inside the opening. Then he waved a hand toward it. "So what now? We go inside? What if it closes again, and we're stuck in there?"

Elliott looked at him blankly. "Wow, you're one big scaredy-cat these days! What happened to the great explorer? Maybe you *are* just getting old!"

"I am *not* getting old," Will replied. He immediately stormed straight past Jürgen, who watched him with some surprise as he entered the tower without a second thought.

7

CHESTER AND PARRY had been deposited back on the shore by the marines in one of their high-speed inflatables. After all that had happened and the excitement of being on a submarine, it felt strange to be on the wind-lashed beach again.

"So do you reckon we can count them out? The Americans?" Chester asked, as they began to walk toward the cliff.

"Looks like it," Parry replied, his expression grim. "I'm not surprised that the President dropped us like a hot potato — even if he were to commit his forces, there's no one left to govern this country now."

For what seemed like hours they had both hung on in the cabin of the submarine, waiting to find out if the conference would resume. But despite many attempts to speak to the White House, the blue-suited man accompanying them couldn't get confirmation that they would be granted another audience with the President. Finally the captain of the submarine had entered the cabin, saying that he had orders to get under way, so Chester and Parry would be escorted back to shore.

"All the trouble — all the killing — seems so far away," Chester reflected as the sun crept up over the far horizon of the sea, and the cliffs began to glow dimly with the rose-hued light of the new day. Although his mind kept returning to what he'd witnessed in London, something from the final moments of the conference was nagging at Chester. "Parry, the President mentioned something about a mole in the Styx ranks — is that right? Have you managed to get someone in there?" he finally ventured, as they came to the coastal path at the top of the cliff.

Parry muttered, "No, it was nothing," but Chester noticed that the old man averted his eyes and also increased his pace as they turned inland toward the cottage, making their way through the clumps of gorse.

Parry didn't speak again until they were on the last stretch. "Thank you for coming with me, Chester," he said. "It was a lot to ask after the tragedy with your parents. I'm sorry to get you involved all over again."

"That's OK," the boy said. "I think it was good for me to get out. I'd sort of got myself stuck down in the dumps." He smiled affectionately at Parry, pleased that his presence was appreciated. "Not sure I really helped you much, though."

"You did, immeasurably," Parry replied. "The President must have read a thousand reports on what's been happening in our country, until he was overwhelmed by it. But you gave our plight a human side, and I could see that it was getting through to him and beginning to tip the balance in our favor. Maybe that was why the Styx took action when they did."

"Yes, how did they know to blow the cavern roof at that very moment?" Chester asked, as it occurred to him.

"The Styx had someone on the inside — must have been easy enough, because my recommendation to carry out regular

Purger checks had been ignored," Parry said. "So someone in the Prime Minister's team tipped them off."

Chester nodded.

"Here we are," Parry said as they emerged from the gorse and the cottage came into view. Chester couldn't see any lights on inside, but that was par for the course — Old Wilkie was a stickler when it came to blacking out the windows at nighttime.

And as Parry pushed open the front door, Old Wilkie was in his usual position in his chair in the hallway, his shotgun in his lap, and very much awake. They went into the main room where the embers were still glowing in the hearth. Stephanie had also stayed up, wrapped in a blanket to keep warm.

"You're back! You were gone for ages!" she said brightly, then frowned. "But where did you go, anyway?"

"You won't believe what we . . . ," Chester began, then caught himself. "Is it all right if I tell her?" he asked Parry.

Parry nodded. "Go ahead — she should know. And I'll brief Old Wilkie in the kitchen." He glanced at his watch. "I hope everyone's packed because we haven't got long before extraction." He and Old Wilkie crossed to the doorway on the other side of the hearth and went into the kitchen.

When they were alone, Stephanie said, "Come on, I want to hear all about it." She touched Chester's arm, then drew her hand back. "You're soaked! Is it raining that hard outside?"·

"Oh, that was the trip back from the submarine," Chester replied. "Where we were talking to the US President and the Prime Minister . . . well, the Prime Minister for a short time until something terrible hap —"

"Are you pulling my leg?" Stephanie was looking at him, a smile hovering on her lips. He noticed then that she'd made an effort with her hair and also put on some makeup, and how very pretty she was. "D'you know — I don't mind if you *are* teasing me," she said. "You're acting like your old self again. I've missed that. I've missed you."

Before Chester had time to answer, she had taken him by the arm and was leading him over to the sofa. She'd managed to tune in to an overseas radio station, and they sat there with the music in the background as she listened to him talk about the outing with Parry. She couldn't believe it when he told her what had happened in Westminster with the huge opening in the ground that swallowed up the buildings.

As the radio lost the signal and the music stopped, Chester realized how croaky his voice sounded. "What with giving the President my life story, I don't think I've ever talked for so long before!" He laughed. "I could really do with a drink."

He began toward the kitchen door, which was open a crack. Although Parry was speaking softly, the cottage was so quiet that Chester didn't have much difficulty hearing what he was saying. As Parry sounded so serious, Chester held back from going straight in, thinking that he should announce himself first.

There was the low rumble of Old Wilkie's voice, to which Parry immediately retorted, "No, how can he be told? Not after the calamitous way it played out in the Complex."

"What's the matter, Chester? Why've you stopped there?" Stephanie whispered from the sofa.

But Chester didn't answer, because something was troubling him.

He edged a little closer to the door so that he could hear Old Wilkie's side of the conversation, too. "I'm glad you didn't tell me before — it would have put me in a very awkward position with the lad." There was a pause before Old Wilkie continued. "I realize the infiltration play has been crucial, but Danforth's too much of a loose cannon for his own good, and ours," he was saying.

"Danforth?" Chester mouthed, shaking his head, as the President's words came back to him: *Your mole in the Styx ranks.*

The realization hit Chester with all the force of a bullet. He would never in a million years have guessed what Danforth had been up to. For the briefest moment, Chester didn't know whether to break down and cry, or to scream with all the anger welling up inside him.

The anger won out. Blinded by a red mist he threw the door open with such force that it almost came off its hinges. Behind him, Stephanie let out a yelp.

Mouths agape at Chester's abrupt entrance, Parry and Old Wilkie were at the table, glasses in their hands and a bottle of whisky on the table between them.

"So my parents died because of Danforth's stupid plan!" Chester said, his voice shaking with fury. "Is that right, Parry?"

For once, Parry was at a total loss. He was stuttering something as he rose to his feet. "Chester," he began. "I know it sounds th —"

"No! No more lies!" Chester shouted at him. "You knew what Danforth was up to — you knew exactly what he was doing," he ranted. "But you didn't bother to tell me, did you? They were only my parents!"

Parry took a step toward Chester, but the boy grabbed Old Wilkie's shotgun from the table. Snapping the breech shut, he slipped off the safety. Chester didn't go as far as to point it at Parry or Old Wilkie, but he was holding it as if he meant business.

Parry's tone was conciliatory. "I know how this appears, but you have to calm down, lad, so you can listen to wh —"

"What? Listen to more lies about that traitor?" Chester interrupted. "If Danforth's on our side, why did he knacker the systems in the Complex so we almost ran out of air? We couldn't even call for help because he'd messed with the equipment."

Parry shook his head. "He's nothing if not thorough — he wanted it to be convincing, and he also didn't want us hanging around in the Complex in case the Styx discovered its location." Parry shook his head. "Look, Chester, he really didn't think that Jeff would try anyth —"

"Don't you dare even *say* my father's name! You're not worthy of it!" Chester yelled. "And you didn't come here because you were worried about us, did you, Parry?" he was ranting. "Oh, no, you came because it was convenient for your rendezvous with the Americans. You don't give a flying fig about me, or any of us."

"Chester?" Stephanie said, as Chester reversed back into the main room. He felt vulnerable that the girl was behind him, aware that she was quite capable of disarming him if she wanted to.

"No, you keep away from me, too," he told Stephanie, stepping sideways with his back to the fireplace as he made toward the other door.

Parry and Old Wilkie were following as Chester entered the hallway, where he paused for a moment. "I can't stay in this place," he said. "I'm leaving."

"Please don't be so hasty, Chester," Parry implored him.

"But where will you go?" Stephanie asked in a small, frightened voice.

Chester was still beside himself with fury as he yanked open the front door and stormed through it.

"You can't leave like this. Let's talk, then you can decide what you want to do," Parry said, the steeliness returning to his voice as he and the others joined the boy outside.

"Why won't you wait a moment . . . and hear what Parry wants to say?" Stephanie begged. She was standing there with tears in her eyes, the blanket still around her shoulders.

Chester had been striding away, but came to an abrupt halt and wheeled around. "No! I'm warning you — don't any of you try to stop me!"

"You don't know what you're doing, Chester. You're not yourself," Parry said, taking several steps toward the boy and reaching out his hand.

"Stay back!" Chester said, bringing up the shotgun.

Old Wilkie was slowly edging around to the side.

Parry took another step. "I knew nothing of it in advance, but let me explain what Danforth was trying to achieve, and in the scheme of things how important it is to us."

At the mention of Danforth, Chester screamed, "I don't give a stuff about any of that! And I don't even want to ever *hear* that stinking traitor's name again!"

"Danforth's done the impossible and successfully infiltrated the Styx. He's put his neck on the block — he's been risking his *own* life, because he's been working for us. What he's doing is vital for our intel," Parry argued.

"Yeah, well, he's not much good at it, is he? He didn't warn you that our Prime Minster was about to be sucked down a hole, did he?" Chester countered.

"He isn't always able to get messages thr —" Parry began, but was interrupted as Chester began to shout, because he'd suddenly noticed how far Old Wilkie had moved around to his side.

"No, you don't! Trying to come at me from different directions, are you?" he accused Old Wilkie and Parry. Chester hiked the shotgun toward the sky and fired one barrel over Old Wilkie's head. The report of the shot echoed all around.

Old Wilkie was holding up his hands to show he was unarmed. "I wasn't trying anything," he said.

"Like I believe you. Don't move another inch! Any of you!" Chester threatened.

"I wish you hadn't done that," Parry said under his breath.

"Why — because your soldier boys will come running?" Chester said.

"No, because it will carry for miles. The Armagi might pick up on it," Parry replied.

"Oh, yeah, sure. There's nothing around here. You're just trying to put the frighteners on me," Chester sneered. "Well, I couldn't care less anymore. The Armagi can h —"

One moment Old Wilkie was there, hands still raised, the next he was hurtling through the air. He came to rest halfway between Chester and Parry, facedown and unmoving.

"Gramps!" Stephanie shrieked.

Old Wilkie moaned. His clothes were ripped up his back, revealing that the flesh had been lacerated.

"Criminy!" Chester muttered.

Where Old Wilkie had been standing was something almost transparent as the winter sun refracted through it. The height of a man, when it had touched down on the frost-covered grass it had barely made a sound.

The Armagi had slashed at Old Wilkie with the edges of its batlike wings and now tucked them away behind its back. They could have been made from glass, the way they caught the light.

One of Parry's satphones began to vibrate. Chester guessed that it was the nearby SAS team waiting with the helicopter, and that they had heard the shot. But Parry certainly wasn't going to answer it. Instead, barely moving his lips, he murmured to Chester, "You've got the only weapon here, laddie."

But Chester didn't react, paralyzed with shock.

Except for its black compound eyes, it was difficult to make out the Armagi's features on its beaked head because internal organs of varying translucency were visible inside its skull. Fluid seemed to be coursing around veins or arteries, and something with a dirty green hue throbbed at the top of its cranium. But it had turned its head to Parry as he spoke, then began toward him.

"Chester . . . CHESTER!" Stephanie screamed.

Chester finally reacted. Bringing the shotgun to bear on the Armagi, he squeezed the trigger. But as he'd swung the weapon around, Chester had fired prematurely, letting off the second barrel before it was lined up on its target.

The shot didn't hit the Armagi in the thorax as Chester had intended, but clipped what approximated its shoulder. Myriad glittering pieces of it scattered into the air, like windborne ice.

Despite the force of the blast, it remained upright, one clawed foot gripping the ground, the other poised in the air. Then the Armagi swiveled toward Chester.

"Ohmigod," he said. "I'm toast." He threw a glance over at Stephanie. "Bloody run!" he yelled. "I'll keep it busy."

There was no question that this time the Armagi was coming for him.

He chucked the shotgun at it, but it fended the weapon away with a deft flick of its undamaged limb. It may have been injured, but the creature was still just as much of a threat.

Chester didn't bother to run.

He closed his eyes, sinking to his knees, waiting.

In that brief moment he thought of his parents. "I'll be with you soon, Mum and Dad," he whispered, trying to control his fear. But he couldn't, and, at the top of his lungs, he screamed, "Help me!"

There was a swishing sound.

He opened his eyes.

Parry was still there, his arm around Stephanie.

The Armagi had folded to the ground, something protruding from the nape of its neck.

Chester turned to look behind him.

"Martha! I don't bloody believe it!"

She'd stepped out from the gorse bushes and was standing there, her red hair as bedraggled as it always had been, her voluminous clothes just as filthy.

"Hello, dearie," she said, walking over to him and stroking his cheek.

Chester couldn't get his words out. "Where . . . How the . . . How . . . ?"

"My wonderful boy, you only had to ask for help," she said, looking at him adoringly, as she brushed his hair from his forehead. "You knew I'd always come, didn't you?"

Chester looked from the crossbow in her hand to the motionless Armagi. "Did you kill it?"

He did a double take as he saw what was there now.

Instead of the creature, stretched out and facedown, was a naked Styx.

"No, it's not dead . . . it's only stunned," Martha replied. "There's one place behind the head where, if you can get a bolt into its spine, a single shot will do the job. Skill and luck," she added, obviously very pleased with herself.

Still not believing his eyes, Chester ventured a step closer and peered down at the Styx. "But . . . but . . . it's changed . . . ," he stuttered.. "How did it do that?"

Martha also moved over to the prostrate Styx and cast her eyes over him. "It's the only way I'll ever get a naked man to throw himself at my feet," she said wistfully. Then she took Chester's arm and began to pull him away. "Careful — not too close."

"But he has to be dead," Chester insisted. "He certainly looks it."

Martha shook her head. "Not dead, not with these things. Only way to be sure is to burn every last bit of them, toe clippings 'n' all."

"Yes, they regenerate," Parry said, taking a step forward.

As if Chester had completely forgotten where he was, he now looked up at Parry, taking a moment to focus on him. "No you don't! You just stay away from me!" Chester growled.

"Lad, you have to underst —" Parry started saying, but never finished as Stephanie shrieked again, pointing over at the trees of a nearby copse.

A second Armagi alighted on the ground some twenty feet away. It appeared to be looking for the other creature.

"Your crossbow?" Chester said to Martha, remembering she'd just fired it.

"Nothing doing," Martha replied. "Can't reload in a hurry. Only got one good hand after the Bright caught me."

The Armagi was moving toward her and Chester, but she seemed perfectly calm.

"Martha . . . what do we do?" Chester asked frantically. He'd believed they were out of danger, but he couldn't have been more wrong.

"I might have lost a hand to the Bright, but —" Martha interrupted herself to whistle.

Chester thought something was wrong with his vision. From all sides, white objects converged on the Armagi. As they swooped in, they were every bit as fast as the creature. They may have been slightly smaller than the Armagi, but it didn't stand a chance. As if caught in the middle of a tornado, the Armagi was torn to pieces, body parts flopping on the ground all around where it had been standing.

"— that doesn't mean that I didn't catch it, *and* tame it," Martha finished.

"Tame it?" Chester asked, not really taking in what she was saying.

"Yes, I tamed the Bright," Martha said proudly.

As the tornado stopped, Chester was left looking at not just a single Bright but a whole host of them. They were hovering in the air above the remains of the Armagi, their brilliant white scales reflecting the light.

"Angels." Chester laughed, remembering what Dr. Burrows had said about them. "But there are so many — not just one!"

"Yes, seven." Martha whistled and waved with her good hand. In less than the blink of an eye, the Brights had swooped through the air to surround her and Chester, their wings making a gentle thrumming as they hovered in a circle, their halos shining gently. There was something so repellent about them, and yet they had a certain beauty, too.

"They're amazing!" Chester laughed again.

"They're my protectors. And now they're your protectors, too." Martha stroked Chester's head lovingly. "With them we'll be safe wherever we go."

"But I don't understand. How did you know where I was?" the boy asked.

Martha indicated the Brights with her hand. "Once you give them a scent, they can track it like hounds — even across hundreds of miles. That's how I could always find you, wherever you went."

"Er, Chester," Parry said. He was still protecting Stephanie with an arm around her as both of them gawped at the spectacle of Martha and her Brights. "You're not *seriously* thinking of leaving with that woman, are you? Not after what she put you through?" he asked.

Chester retrieved the shotgun, then went back to Martha and very pointedly slipped his arm through hers. "Yes, I am. When we were in Norfolk, she was just watching out for me — I understand that now. She really cares about me, which is more than you've ever done. Look what you did to my mum and dad."

Martha's grime-covered face with all its broken veins was a picture of happiness as she listened to Chester. "Yes, I was only watching out for you. I knew you'd been under the Dark Light and were trying to signal to the Styx. I knew that."

"So this is good-bye," Chester said to Parry.

"You might want to see to your friend," Martha suggested, as Old Wilkie groaned and began to stir. Stephanie immediately went to him, but Parry remained where he was, shaking his head in disbelief. "Chester, at least take this with you, in case you need to get in contact." He tugged a satphone from his pocket and held it out.

Chester didn't say a word, but Parry lobbed it over to him, and he caught it.

"It's fully charged," Parry said. "Turn it on and listen to the messages every so often, will you? Promise me you'll do that?"

Tucking the phone in his pocket, Chester still didn't respond as, their arms linked, he and Martha turned in the direction of the sea and began to walk away, the seven Brights rotating around them like a carousel.

AS THE SMALL LAUNCH careered up the subterranean channel, scudding over the surface of the river,
Jiggs's main concern was that the hull would last the journey.
It had taken some major repairs to patch up the damage the
Limiters had inflicted on it and anything else that still floated
before dumping the wrecked vessels in the bottom of the harbor. And Jiggs hardly had the ideal materials at his disposal
to repair the launch — some time-expired resin and old
fiberglass matting — but he'd gotten there in the end.

And he was also very concerned for Drake, who was hud-
dled in the bottom of the boat. Although, with much grumbling,
Drake had eventually consented to wrapping himself in a poncho from the quartermaster's stores, the spray was bitterly
cold, and Jiggs himself had lost much of the sensation in his
hands and face.

Jiggs was still worrying about his friend and wishing that
there were some way to stop and check on him when he felt the
launch slow. It was decelerating as though it had met with
resistance in the river.

It had. Through his Russian monoscope, Jiggs caught a
glimpse of a steel cable strung right across the width of the river

channel. It was cleverly positioned, just high enough to avoid any flotsam, but at the perfect height to snag a passing craft.

As the cable reached breaking point and snapped, the loud twang could have been a sound effect from a cartoon. It might have been funny if the consequences weren't so dire.

Jiggs yelled, "INCOMING!" at the very top of his voice as the loose ends of the cable whipped away on either side of the channel. Drake didn't seem to hear the warning under his poncho.

With instincts honed through countless deployments in areas where antipersonnel devices were an everyday hazard, Jiggs reacted in a fraction of a second. Ramming the throttle on full, he yanked the outboard over, steering the launch into the middle of the channel, as far away from the sides as he could get.

He was praying that the Styx sappers had been intending to catch anyone traveling in the opposite direction — *down* to the deep-level shelter — and not *up* from it. It made a world of difference to where the explosives would be planted. It made all the difference as to whether he and Drake were going to escape with their lives.

As the explosives detonated, Jiggs was crouching and trying to protect his head. The surge of water threw the launch up the river, and the tunnel behind was thick with smoke and a cascade of flying stone.

Jiggs knew at that moment the trip wire had been set for boats going in the opposite direction. "Thank you, God!" he shouted. He was still offering up his gratitude as reports of the blast echoed back and forth in the tunnel. Then, as he followed a bend in the channel, there was just the sound of the outboard and the gushing river again.

Drake stirred, his head peering tortoiselike from under the poncho. "You want something?" he asked. "You nudged me."

"No, not me, and everything's fine. Just get some rest," Jiggs replied, trying not to laugh.

After another ten hours, they broke the journey to stop at one of the way stations along the route. Here Jiggs stocked up with fuel from the rusty storage tanks on the quay, while Drake took respite from the constant freezing spray of the speeding river.

They resumed the journey and, many hours later, finally pulled into the long harbor that lay below the disused airfield. Jiggs tied up the launch and helped Drake onto the quayside. After a change of clothes and a hot drink he went off to investigate.

"I've cleared the booby traps," Jiggs told Drake when he eventually returned. "There were three trips on the way to the exit."

Drake nodded. "I'm amazed they left the river unprotected. If it had been me, I would have planted one there for sure."

Jiggs just nodded, a small smile playing on his lips. "Yes, me, too," he agreed. "Odd, that." Then he helped Drake to his feet, and they set off.

The interior of the tower reminded Will of a modern cathedral he'd once visited with his father. It might have been the way that their footfalls were reverberating through the large space, or perhaps because the interior with its plain walls and ceiling, all of the same gray material as the exposed pyramid, gave the impression of both solemnity and majesty.

Of power.

Will was beginning to think that there was something in what Elliott had been saying. Maybe he was sensing it, too, now.

And adding to this impression were the two large columns directly opposite the entrance. As he moved toward them across the dusty floor, it felt to Will as if he was approaching an altar. His eyes swept over the peculiar spiky letters that were inscribed across both of them over twenty feet up.

"Does that writing make sense to anyone?" he inquired.

"No, I don't recognize it," Jürgen replied. "Those letters don't share any characteristics with the scripts or the glyphs I've been studying."

"And you?" Will asked Elliott coldly. He still hadn't quite forgiven her for the way she'd ignored his advice before they entered the tower.

As she shook her head, Will indicated the twin cylinders. "There's no sign of any doors, but you don't suppose those things are elevators, do you?" He chuckled because this building, which had just been thrust out of the ground, had to be many millennia old, and it felt like such an odd question to ask.

"That would make sense, given the height of the structure," Jürgen suggested, but he was already making his way over to the bushman, who was standing by what appeared to be a circular flight of stairs that began to the far left of the columns and continued up behind them.

"Why don't you ask Woody what this place is? . . . Ask him what we're getting ourselves into here," Will prompted Elliott.

Elliott immediately began to speak to the bushman in Styx. After a couple of exchanges, she turned to Will. "He says he doesn't know, and I believe him. He keeps using that same word — *destiny*," she said.

"Well, there's one way to find out," Will said. "Let's go!"

With Woody leading, they all began to race up the circular stairs.

"These are exactly like the ones inside the pyramid," Elliott noted.

"Yes, the dimensions are quite odd. Almost as if they weren't meant for people," Jürgen pointed out; they were all finding the steps very awkward to climb. In order to negotiate them at any speed, the trick was to attempt two at a time, although that meant taking inordinately long strides. After a while the action became automatic, and they would only stumble when they lost the rhythm.

As Woody continued to lead everyone upward, the steps seemed to go on forever around the central columns. Finally, they came to a landing with another circular opening. They were all out of breath but bursting with curiosity as they entered it.

"I assume we're in the wider structure at the top now," Jürgen panted.

"Yeah, but there's nothing in here. So what's all this for?" Will asked.

Nobody could give him an answer. They completed a full circuit of the space, ending up where they'd begun. It was completely empty — just the curved external wall with four console-type blocks of the gray material rising out of the floor at regular intervals around the central well.

Jürgen knocked exploratively against the outer wall. "Feels cold," he said.

Elliott had moved toward one of the blocks on the floor and seemed to be about to touch it, but then stopped herself. She looked rather flushed, although Will wasn't sure if this was simply because she was recovering from the rapid climb up the stairs, or if something else was bothering her.

"Everything OK?" he asked.

"Sure. Yes," she mumbled, already moving toward Woody at the entrance.

With a shrug, Will began to do the same when he stopped abruptly. "Hold on," he said.

"What is it?" Jürgen asked.

Will had been examining his hands, then began to peer at the ceiling above them. "There aren't any windows or lights in here," he said. "So how come we're not in complete darkness?"

Jürgen also held up a hand and was moving it around to examine it from different angles. "You're absolutely right," he said. He seemed to be even more flummoxed as he lowered his hand toward the floor. He suddenly got down on his knees to rub the dust from an area of the floor.

"What are you doing?" Will asked him.

Jürgen stood up again. "The light seems to be omnidirectional — there are no discernible shadows." He raised his outstretched hand with the palm parallel to the floor. "Notice that the underside of my hand is illuminated even though the floor is coated with dust, and there are no obvious sources of illumination down there anyway. Or anywhere, for that matter. You're right, Will, this is extraordinary."

Jürgen wasn't finished. "And unless this is some kind of

engineering feat and light from outside is being channeled in, there must be an energy source to do this."

"Yeah, I think we know that. It also opened the door for us downstairs, and blew the old pyramid apart, and raised this whole tower from the ground," Will reeled off.

Jürgen nodded a little sheepishly as Will noticed how impatient Woody was. "Let's try the next floor and see what we find there," he suggested, still watching the bushman carefully. Will really didn't trust him anymore.

"Well, there's nowhere else to go now. We must be at the very top of the tower," Jürgen observed as they came to the last of the stairs and emerged into one large circular area, this time without any obstruction in the middle from the twin columns.

Instead, right in the center there was a circular podium some twenty feet across, on which stood a tall, central, block-like console surrounded by smaller blocks.

Again, the walls, floor, and ceiling were of the same material as the rest of the tower, and the same uniform light lit the whole space.

"Whoever built all this, they liked to keep things simple," Will commented.

Jürgen was walking around the wall as Will stepped onto the central podium to inspect the different blocks, running his hands over them. "And all this feels like stone, same as on the floor below, same as everywhere."

Elliott and Woody had gone straight to the tallest console in the center of the podium. They were both staring at it, at the very top. They both looked troubled.

Will exhaled sharply. "I know something's wrong. If you don't tell me what it is, I swear I'll never talk to you again," he threatened Elliott.

"Something's missing from here," she said.

"What do you mean?" Will asked, becoming even more disconcerted by the way his friend was acting. "What's missing? And how could you know that?"

"I don't know how I know," Elliott gasped. "It's like in a dream when something terrible happens — the worst thing you can possibly think of — and you wake up with that awful feeling of dread, but you can't remember why exactly." As her gaze met Will's, he noticed that a tear was tracing its way down the dirty skin of her face. "I wish I could tell you exactly, but something doesn't feel right. Something that should be here isn't."

"What else can you feel then?" he challenged her, trying to keep his voice calm.

She moved to one of the smaller consoles. "Well, I also know that if I do this . . ." She splayed out her fingers and pressed her palm onto the top of the console.

The circular wall around the space suddenly came alive with bright pictures. Jürgen was so startled that he took a rapid step backward and lost his balance, ending up on one knee.

Different images of the Earth's surface — apparently from a viewpoint out in space — covered every inch of the external wall.

"How . . . ?" Will gasped. Through wispy patches of cloud cover, he was looking at multiple images of continents and oceans. The different views were moving, passing around the walls, overlapping as they went.

"And I know if I do this," Elliott said, swiping a single finger across the console, the surface of which was now glowing with blue lines and strange symbols, "then I can get closer."

Jürgen was muttering something as he remained on the floor, his mouth agape as he watched the different scenes.

"And I also know if I do this . . . ," Elliott continued; she slid a finger over the panel and one image spun around the walls and stopped where they could all see it just in front of Jürgen, ". . . then this is where I'm meant to be."

Will's eyes darted from the image to Elliott and back. "Me, too," he said very quietly. "Because that's England."

Elliott took her hand from the console and the images were suddenly gone, and everything was as it had been before.

Except Woody was on his knees and gabbling away to himself, his hands pressed together as if he was praying.

Elliott turned toward Will as her shoulders shook and she began to sob. "Will, I'm frightened," she managed to say. She held her arms toward him and tried to take a step in his direction, but almost fell. "What's happening? Please, can you just hold me?" she begged him. "Please."

9

AS HE WALKED ALONG the cliff path with Martha, Chester thought he caught the sound of a helicopter's rotors over the wind. "Good bloody riddance," he said under his breath, because it was likely to be Parry leaving.

Now that she had Chester back, there was a very big grin permanently stretched across Martha's grubby face. "I've got us a nice place to go, dearie," she said. "We'll be all nice and warm there."

"Great," Chester replied with forced cheerfulness. He was still so angry that he could barely think about anything else.

"And I bet you could do with something to eat, too," Martha added.

"Um," Chester began uncertainly. "Just one thing on that front."

Martha looked at him. "Yes, my love?"

"About my food — from now on I want to know *exactly* what's in it. Would that be OK?"

"Of course, my sweet boy," Martha said, "and about that time. I h —"

"No, please don't tell me. Don't want to hear. Don't want to hear," Chester was repeating, holding his hands over his ears.

"Ha, all right," Martha cackled. "All I'll say is *needs must*," she added as they continued on their way. "Needs must, dearie."

Glad that he'd gotten that off his chest, Chester was wondering if they were a little exposed, on a track that was obviously well used, and particularly as it was broad daylight.

Martha divined what he was thinking, and rubbed his shoulder affectionately with what was left of her damaged hand. "We're safe wherever we go, love — don't you worry." She took the stubs of her fingers from him, then swept her hand toward the sky. "My little fairy protectors are up there, always watching out for me. They never sleep — not for long, anyway. They'll let me know if anyone's close."

"So you caught that first Bright in Norfolk," Chester asked, curious to know what had happened.

"Yes — after we fought long and hard, I tricked her into the water," Martha replied. "I trapped her there, but I didn't kill her."

"Her?" Chester echoed.

"Yes, I fed her and kept her captive, and to my surprise, she had her bairns."

Chester's brow furrowed. "Bairns? What's that?"

"You know — babies," Martha replied. "That was why I'd been able to overpower her. She was with young, and it made her slow. The bairns were born in little bags, and from them came tiny Brights, like little fairies. Smaller even than the miner birds you get in the Colony."

"And they didn't go for you or attack you or anything?" Chester asked.

"No, because of their mother. I'd kept her tied up, and I kept the bairns all well fed with rodent catches while my hand

and ribs healed." Martha rubbed her rather rotund chest to emphasize how painful it had been for her. "And when it was time to move on I didn't have the heart to kill them. So I cut her free, but she stayed with me, and as you can see she's still with me, and looking out for me."

"Truly a guardian angel," Chester said, laughing.

Martha nodded. "I reckon at one time they lived up here on the surface, because in a matter of weeks they grew used to the gravity. You can see how fast they are now."

"So maybe Dr. Burrows was right," Chester said. "They *were* up here once, and maybe they're why we have those stories about mythical creatures. The idea for angels, even."

At the mention of Dr. Burrows, Martha stopped grinning. "But, my sweet, you've had a rough old time of it, haven't you? I told you not to trust Topsoilers. They'll never be your friends. That man back there did for your family, didn't he? What made him do that?"

Chester didn't feel prepared to go into it right there and then. "Parry? It wasn't him exactly, but he was in on it. Look, Martha, I'll tell you all about it later, but my mum and dad got caught up in someth —"

He ducked as two Brights crossed right in front of them, in opposite directions. "My God, they're quick," he said. He'd only had the briefest flash of white intersecting with white before they were both gone.

"Shhh!" Martha said. "And load this for me, will you?" she asked, keeping her voice low as she passed her crossbow over.

Chester took it from her. She'd been parted from her ancient-looking crossbow back in Norfolk, and this replacement was definitely Topsoil-manufactured, the lighter materials making it more suitable for single-handed use. And Martha had made a few modifications to it, which included a few strips of muddy sacking wound around it and a few clumsy dabs of paint to camouflage it.

"Sure," Chester confirmed. He cocked the weapon, then from the quiver over her shoulder selected a bolt. As he seated this in the crossbow, he noticed the shaft was stained with blood, and that tiny pieces of meat were stuck to the point.

Martha was scanning behind them.

"What is it?" he whispered.

"See how they're flying low and to the sides," she said. Chester could just about make out the blurry streaks as the Brights zipped above the trees to the left of the path and in the lee of the cliff on the other side. It was as if they were stalking prey. "You see, my fairies warn me if anyone comes close," Martha continued. "Let's get in here and wait for them."

They moved into the trees, and Martha raised her crossbow. After a short while, Chester spotted a head bobbing along as someone climbed the path up a slight incline. He turned to Martha. "Looks like just one person. Will the Brights attack them?"

"They won't do a thing without my say-so," Martha whispered. "You know that person, don't you? Wasn't she with you?" she asked, pointing with her chin.

As Chester looked back, his heart skipped a beat.

Where the path rose from a slight depression, a single figure was in full view and striding purposefully along.

"It's Steph!" he exclaimed. "But what the blazes is she doing all the way out here?"

Martha was immediately suspicious. "Could be some kind of trap they're setting for you. But if it is, then she's alone. I can tell from the way my fairies are shadowing her."

Stephanie was completely unaware of the lethal animals circling not far above her and under the lip of the cliff only feet away.

She had almost reached where Martha and Chester were hiding when Martha stepped out, her crossbow leveled at the girl. "What do you want?" Martha shouted, her voice cold and threatening.

Stephanie nearly jumped out of her skin. "Oh, hi, is Chester with you?" she asked, her voice quavering. "Oh, you are," she said, as Chester emerged from the trees. In her warm coat and woolly hat, and with the rucksack on her back, she looked like she could be on a school outing.

"What are you doing here?" Chester demanded. "Why didn't you fly off with that lying bastard and your grandfather?"

Stephanie bit her lip nervously.

"They have gone, haven't they? I thought I heard a helicopter," Chester said.

Stephanie nodded.

"So what are you still doing here?" he repeated.

"Um . . . ," she replied. "I couldn't let you go off thinking that I'd known about Danforth and what happened to your mum and dad, because I didn't. I swear I didn't know anything at all about it. Nobody told me."

"Fine, but you're not answering my question," Chester said urgently. "What are you doing here?"

Stephanie's voice was very small under the sound of the wind and the waves crashing at the bottom of the cliff. "Um, I came because I was really worried about you . . . and you left before I could speak to you. So while Parry was helping Gramps — he wasn't hurt that badly — I sneaked away. I grabbed as much of your stuff as I could because I thought you'd want it." She swung around slightly so he could see the Bergen filled to bursting on her back, then looked awkwardly down at the ground. "I . . . er . . . I wondered if maybe I could come with you, Chester. If we could be together."

It was clear to Chester that she was embarrassed and would have said more if Martha hadn't been there. And he had no idea what to say in response. He'd been so consumed with anger that he'd been numb to everything else. The truth was that at the moment the first Armagi had made its entrance, part of him hadn't actually cared whether he lived or died.

But this wasn't about him now. During the weeks in the cottage Stephanie had shown him nothing but kindness and affection, and he'd rebuffed her. He liked her very much, and at this moment he was very frightened for her; Martha was incredibly possessive, and that made her unpredictable. And, Chester didn't doubt, murderous.

By following him, the girl had well and truly put her head into the lion's mouth.

"You have no place here," Martha growled. Chester saw her tense her arm as she steadied her aim, lining the weapon up for a shot at Stephanie's chest. "We don't need no one along to slow us down," Martha added, glancing up and obviously considering whether she should instruct her Brights to tear Stephanie apart as an alternative to using a bolt on her.

"Wait a moment," Chester said quickly, and stepped closer to Martha. It was no accident that he laid a hand on the woman's rounded shoulder and kneaded it while he whispered into her ear.

As she listened, Martha scratched her chin with the stumps of her fingers. "Is that right?" she said eventually, turning to him.

"Absolutely," he replied.

Martha was looking penetratingly into his eyes. "And that's all?" she asked.

"Definitely," Chester confirmed, putting on his sweetest, most endearing smile. Martha lowered her crossbow and let out a whistle to her Brights. "Come over here, girlie, and join us," she said to Stephanie, grinning with all her black teeth on display.

Chester quietly sighed a huge sigh of relief.

"I expect a slug of this wouldn't go amiss," Jürgen said, offering Will the hip flask that he'd taken from his rucksack.

Taking it from the New Germanian, Will sniffed at the neck of the flask, then wrinkled his nose in distaste. "Oh, no, I don't think so," he said, quickly handing it back. "What is it, anyway?"

"Schnapps," Jürgen replied, about to offer it to Elliott but then thinking better of it.

They had decided to return back to the base of the tower,

not least because Elliott was in such a state. Will had never seen her this distraught before, and had been forced to help her all the way down the circular flight of stairs. As the two of them sat together on one of the fractured boulders, her head was buried in Will's shoulder. She'd stopped crying, although he could still hear her take the odd involuntary breath as if the tears weren't far away.

Jürgen glanced at the bushman, who was hunched over on the ground ten or so feet away from everyone else, then leaned back against the tower and took another, even bigger mouthful from his flask. He swallowed noisily and then exhaled just as noisily. "This stuff is jolly wizard for steadying one's nerves," Jürgen remarked after a moment.

"Jolly wizard?" Will repeated, wondering why all of a sudden the New Germanian's language had become so odd.

Jürgen grinned. "Sorry, that's probably something I picked up from the English books we had in the city library. The Jeeves and Wooster stories somehow found their way onto a helicopter when the first settlers flew in."

Jürgen's radio suddenly crackled, and he pushed himself upright to fumble in a pocket and retrieve it. As he spoke to his brother in German he was waving his flask demonstratively in the air.

Although Will didn't understand what was being discussed, Jürgen's side of the conversation grew rather terse after only a short time.

Will used the opportunity to speak to Elliott. "Are you feeling better now?" he asked her softly.

She nodded but still didn't show her face.

"It's all been too much for you — for all of us. You've had a bad shock — that's all," he tried to rationalize to her.

She nodded again, simultaneously shivering despite the heat.

"You don't ever have to go back inside again," Will said. "No, maybe that would be for the best. We can leave this place — you and I — and never come back here again."

Jürgen finished his conversation on the radio. He looked angry.

"What's the matter? Are Werner and Karl going to join us?" Will asked him.

"They are, but my brother says I must be mistaken about what we've found. He even went as far as to accuse me of drinking too much when I described what we all saw. My own brother doesn't believe me." Jürgen had been about to take another swig from his flask, but instead he suddenly jerked his head as if something had stung him. "What *are* we talking about here, Will?" He was silent for several seconds before he continued. "If we accept that the new, exposed pyramid and the tower are connected, and all indications point to that . . ."

"And Woody's ancestors built on top of the pyramids many thousands of years ago . . . ," Will put in.

". . . then we've just seen a display of technology that could *predate* us — *Homo sapiens* — as a species by . . . well, who knows how long? And the big question is how it came to be here. And maybe the right answer is that it's nonterrestrial."

"Nonterrestrial?" Will repeated with a frown. "But my dad's Ancients must have been around at the time, because they saw those views of the planet."

"How do you figure that?" Jürgen immediately challenged.

"Because they were able to draw their maps inside the pyramid from them. That's why they were so accurate," Will replied. "So it follows that the technology was in use then."

"Maybe," Jürgen said, holding up his flask as something occurred to him. "But talking about those views . . . they're from outer space . . . but from what exactly?" he asked, his voice oddly flat. "And from when? I mean, from what time?"

Will hadn't had the opportunity to examine the scenes in any detail as they'd circulated around the walls, but because of the size and appearance of London in the images it hadn't occurred to him that they were anything but current. He was about to comment on this when Elliott stirred.

"From now," she said, her voice barely audible because her face was still pressed against Will.

"So they are from now? You mean they're live images? How do you know that?" Will asked her gently.

"I just do," she answered.

Jürgen had been staring out over the fields of soil that were gradually turning gray under the fierce heat of the sun, but now he swung his head toward Will. "It's evident that the technology . . . all the technology we've seen so far . . . appears to have some form of empathy with your friend. Except for her, none of us has any degree of control over it. And the reason for that has to be because she has the blood of the invaders in her."

"You mean the Styx," Will said, tightening his arm around Elliott to comfort her. He'd have preferred that she wasn't hearing any of this. But he also felt that it would be unreasonable to ask the now slightly inebriated New Germanian to put a sock in it, as he might take it badly.

And, besides, Will's mind was buzzing with all the possibilities, too.

"Yes, the Styx." Jürgen took a single step forward as if bracing himself. "So, Will, does that mean that the Styx — or their predecessors — were . . ." His voice seemed to give out. He cleared his throat. "Are we talking about . . . ?"

Will met the man's eyes, waiting for the next word.

"Talking about . . . ?" Jürgen half whispered.

There in the shadowed lee of the tower, with just the calls of the birds and the odd snatch of Woody's muttered prayers reaching them, neither Will nor Jürgen felt prepared to say the word.

It was just too outlandish, too bizarre, and how did it tie in with the evolution of humans?

And with the history of the world?

The implications were too great to contemplate.

Will tightened his arm around Elliott again.

"Aliens?" he said.

10

WITH STEPHANIE TAGGING along at a distance behind them, Chester and Martha had been walking briskly down a fenced-off track between two fields.

"Nearly home, my sweet," Martha cooed, as Chester spotted the small farmhouse up ahead.

Then, as he happened to glance over the fence to one side, he stopped dead as something caught his attention. "My God! What on earth did that?" he gasped, recoiling at the sight of carcasses of the dead sheep strewn around the place. They had been eviscerated, their bodies brutally ripped apart and all their organs strewn over the ground. "Armagi?"

"No, that was my Brights," Martha answered proudly. She hadn't slowed as she headed toward the farmhouse. "They have to eat — just the same as us."

"Not quite the same as us," Chester whispered. Remaining where he was, he continued to watch as, farther along the track, Martha gave a couple of low whistles and waved her hand. She could have been directing sheepdogs, not the weird and strangely wonderful creatures from the depths of the Earth.

The Brights zipped over Chester's head, so fast that it was impossible to see them clearly, like smoke or mist caught in a high wind. Martha whistled once again, then flicked her fingers in the direction of the field.

"Oh, there they are," Chester said to himself, as several of the Brights appeared over the field, as if they'd just materialized out of thin air. They were hovering some hundred feet up or so, and for once remaining in one place long enough for him to make out their insectoid bodies and their white wings as they beat the air.

"What are they doing?" Chester muttered, then noticed a small herd of sheep grazing directly beneath the Brights. The sheep stared vacantly in Martha's direction, probably wondering what the crazy woman was doing, making silly noises and waving her arms around.

They had no idea what was about to hit them. With another whistle from Martha, the Brights simply plummeted toward the ground as if in a deadfall. Chester had a glimpse of the nearest of Martha's *fairies*, its mouth wide open and displaying vicious rows of jagged spikes. With their ivory-white wings outstretched, each Bright landed on the animal it had selected and pinned it flat to the ground so that it was nearly impossible to make out any of them against the rime-covered grass. And it was also impossible to see what they were doing to the poor sheep under them, something for which Chester was very grateful.

"That's sick," he mumbled, looking at the mutilated sheep closer in the field once again as Stephanie stopped alongside him.

"Yeah, gross," she agreed, as she leaned against a fence post. "But I'm just so very glad I managed to catch up with you, Chester," she said, smiling. "I really didn't think I was ever going to see you again."

From where the nearest Bright was feeding on a sheep, there was that sucking sound that flesh makes when it's torn. As the Bright beat its wings once, then settled again as it continued to gorge itself, something glistening with blood was cast aside and came to rest in the frosty grass. Chester grimaced as he saw it was the sheep's heart. It was still beating.

From her lack of reaction, Stephanie obviously hadn't noticed. "And thank you for dealing with Martha back there. I didn't know she was like that," she said.

Chester had been completely preoccupied by the grisly spectacle in the field, but now shot a glance at Martha to see if she was watching him and Stephanie, at the same time taking a hasty sidestep away from the girl.

"But what did you, like, say to her?" Stephanie asked.

"Not now!" Chester replied in a whispered growl, intentionally not looking at her. "Keep right away from me while she's around. She's jealous, and she'll bloody well kill you."

"Oh," Stephanie said, and Chester immediately set off toward Martha in the direction of the farmhouse. Stephanie remained where she was for a moment or two, looking a little taken aback, then she, too, continued down the track.

It was a basic farm building of red brick, but after the night he'd had on the submarine and the revelation about Danforth, Chester was grateful just to be out of the cold and somewhere he could sit in quiet for a while. Without taking off his coat, he flopped onto the sofa in the main room, still holding the empty shotgun as he watched Martha light the fire. She fussed over it until there was a hearty roar warming the room. Stephanie, heeding Chester's warning, carefully chose herself somewhere to sit on the opposite side of the room where she was browsing through an old magazine she'd found.

"So there was nobody in this place when you got here?" Chester asked.

"It was all locked up," Martha replied, moving toward the doorway. "Are you hungry?"

"You bet. What's on the menu?" Chester said.

"Sheep," Martha answered. "That's the one thing there's plenty of around here."

"And you really mean *just* sheep?" Chester said, pulling himself upright on the sofa.

"Yes, just sheep. Nothing else. I promise," Martha said, giving him a crooked smile.

"O . . . K," Chester said through a yawn, as Martha scurried off to the kitchen.

As soon as she'd gone, Stephanie cleared her throat to get Chester's attention. As he turned toward her, she shot him a *what-was-that-all-about?* frown, but he merely shook his head.

They could hear Martha crashing around in the kitchen at the end of the corridor.

"She's busy in there — she can't hear us," Stephanie whispered.

"Don't count on it," Chester whispered back. "It's not worth the risk."

With a shrug Stephanie went back to her magazine and Chester dozed on the sofa until Martha finally reappeared with some bowls of steaming food, which they ate at the table in complete silence.

Well, almost complete silence. Chester was struck by the stark contrast between his two dining companions as they ate: Martha, with table manners typical of most Colonists, occasionally mumbled to herself as she slurped the juices from her spoon and chewed with her mouth wide open. The noise was frightful, as if she was trying to make herself as repugnant as she possibly could.

And then there was Stephanie at the other end of the table, strikingly attractive, her manners impeccable as she daintily used her fork.

The only thing that the two of them had in common was their ginger hair — other than that they could have been from different species.

God, I'm beginning to sound like Will, Chester thought to himself. And with that he began to think about his friend, hoping that both he and Elliott had survived their mission and were safe somewhere. Chester remembered the times they'd had together — although they'd by no means been easy, at least they'd shared the burden and endured them together. An aching hollowness inside reminded him how much he missed their companionship.

"All right there, my dearie?" Martha inquired, as she noticed he'd stopped eating. Chester could see pieces of lamb stuck in the gaps between her dirty teeth.

Nodding, he resumed on his bowl, swapping a secret smile with Stephanie while Martha's head was down and she was shoveling the stew into her mouth.

But despite Stephanie's presence there, Chester felt so alone.

He sighed as he finished his bowl of stew, which had actually been quite appetizing. As Martha, too, finished, Stephanie offered to clear the table. Martha wouldn't have it; she carefully stacked the bowls one on top of the other, then went to the front door and simply slung them outside, where they landed on the paved yard with a crash.

"There — that's all done," she said, rubbing her hands together.

"That was great, Martha. Thank you," Chester said, slightly surprised at what she'd just done, but not about to comment on her very weird form of domestication.

"Yes, thank you," Stephanie said.

Martha, who hadn't once looked in the girl's direction, during or after the meal, was gawping at Chester with her usual wide grin on her face.

"I'd better fetch some more wood so we can keep the fire stoked up," Martha said. "Want to keep it nice and snug for you in here."

Chester gave her a grateful nod, and as Martha went outside, he moved to the window where he could see her, and leaned on the windowsill. Although she was around thirty feet away, she was aware that he was there and kept glancing at him and giving him that odd little wave.

Chester pretended to scratch his nose to hide the fact that he was talking. "Stay on the other side of the room," he told Stephanie. "You don't know how close Martha came to killing you. What on earth were you thinking when you followed me? Anything can set Martha off. She can turn into a right nutjob."

"I don't understand — why did you go off with her, then?" Stephanie asked.

"Because I didn't care. I *don't* care and, anyway, it's better than hanging around Parry with his stinking lies."

"He didn't know what Danforth was planning at the time," Stephanie countered.

"But he did afterward, and he was too much of a coward to tell me. That's what hurts," Chester said. Although he was full of anger, he managed to grin at Martha as she gave him another wave. "Better if we stop talking now. She might get suspicious."

"First tell me what you said to her," Stephanie demanded.

Chester sighed. "I had to come up with something quick. It wasn't easy for me to say it, but I told her that she was my mother now that my real mother was dead. And I also told her the only reason you and I were friends was because you reminded me so much of my sister." He took a breath. "You know that she was knocked down and killed by some idiot in a stolen car when I was young?"

"I didn't know that," Stephanie said quietly. "Is that true? Do I remind you of your sister?"

"Nah," Chester replied. "You're nothing like her. She was shy and sort of dumpy and short. But I had to give Martha a good reason or she would have assumed you were my girl-friend, and it would have been *lights out* for you."

"So am I your girlfriend?" Stephanie asked after a moment, searching out Chester's eyes with her own.

Chester tried to suppress a small smile, not least because Martha was heading back to the farmhouse with an armful of firewood. "I suppose you are. If both of us live long enough for that to mean anything."

Werner was far enough away from the *Kübelwagen* that Karl couldn't hear him muttering and cursing after he'd finished the conversation with his brother over the radio.

If it wasn't enough that they'd endured a hailstorm of rock and half the jungle seemed to have been dropped around them, Werner was finding what his brother had to say very difficult to believe. Something about a new tower in which Jürgen had seen views of the Earth from outer space. Had his brother completely lost it, or had he been drinking? *"Gott im Himmel,"* Werner spat, kicking a chunk of stone lying on the track, then wishing he hadn't as he discovered it was heavier than he'd anticipated.

Hobbling the remaining distance to the vehicle, he got Karl ready, and they set off on foot. The trail, now littered with debris, was impassable in the small-wheeled *Kübelwagen*. So their options were either to fetch the half-track from where Jürgen had left it and try to bulldoze their way back down the trail and return to the city, or to walk all the way to where Jürgen was.

And Werner was in turns concerned for his brother and curious about what the usually level-headed anthropological scientist had been babbling about over the radio. But the evidence was all around him that something significant had taken place, and Werner wanted to get to the bottom of it for himself.

However, the journey turned out to be far more of a challenge than he'd anticipated; once he and Karl had left the main track and entered the jungle, it wasn't the occasional large chunk of masonry that hampered their progress, but the substantial amount of mashed-up foliage that was strewn everywhere.

All this uprooted and shredded vegetation was still settling, and every so often whole branches or tangles of roots that had been suspended up in the giant trees fell to the ground. So not only were he and Karl clambering over the debris between the unaffected trees of the jungle, they were also forced to keep an eye out for anything that might drop on them from above.

As they trekked through the jungle the amount of displaced greenery increased, until they were trying to circumnavigate small hillocks of it. Then, finally, the trees thinned, and they stepped out onto the huge area of bare earth.

Karl glanced inquiringly at Werner.

"I know — it's incredible," his uncle said. "Just look at it."

And they did for a moment, at the new form of the pyramid and then the incredible sight of the tower in the distance.

"Maybe my brother's not losing his mind after all," Werner said under his breath, and they began across the fields of sun-dried dirt in this new landscape.

By the base of the tower, Jürgen had been looking out for them and, as he spied them in the distance, rushed off to meet them.

Elliott, still slightly shaken, had moved into the entrance chamber of the tower accompanied by her new shadow, Woody. The moment she was back inside the tower, a marked change came over her and she seemed far more at ease. She also took up Will's suggestion that she lie down with her head propped on her rolled-up jacket, and soon drifted off to sleep.

Jürgen finally arrived back with his brother and son. Seeing Elliott was soundly asleep, he gestured to Will that he was intending to take the other two upstairs, and they tiptoed off.

Will found himself at a loose end. Not wanting to go too far from Elliott in case she woke up, he passed the time by making an exhaustive examination of the walls of the entrance chamber, knocking against them to see if he could find anything. Then he turned his attention to the two large columns, trying to work out what they were, and also seeing if he could produce any sort of change by touching their surfaces just as Elliott seemed to be able to do. He'd nearly finished exploring every inch of the columns he could reach when a voice from behind made him jump.

"Here, let me," Elliott said. Rubbing her eyes, she didn't seem to be fully awake as she took a step forward and brushed the column in front of him with her hand.

There had been nothing to show that the particular area she'd selected was any different from the rest of the matte gray surface, but under her fingertips a three-pronged motif glowed blue. To the right of the symbol a door in the cylinder slipped silently open to reveal a chamber filled with creamy light.

Will was speechless. He could have been performing a strange new dance as, moving from foot to foot, he tensed his arms in frustration and tried to shrug at the same time. "I don't understand," he finally burst out, wheeling around to Elliott. "Why is it that only *you* can make this stuff work?"

"I don't know," she said, massaging a shoulder to ease her muscles after her nap on the hard floor. She appeared far more relaxed now — the rest seemed to have helped her to get over the shock of what had happened at the top of the tower. But now Will was the one who was becoming increasingly unnerved.

"But what makes you different from the rest of us? Is it because you're half Styx?" he suggested, then narrowed his eyes with suspicion. "Or is there something you're not telling me? Because why didn't Woody and his mates have a love-in with the Rebecca twin . . . or Vane . . . or any of the other Styx, for that matter, when they showed up in this world?"

"Maybe my blood changed him," Elliott said with a frown. "Or maybe because Woody and all the other bushmen kept their distance. He told me they thought the Styx were like the New Germanians — just another load of people muscling in on their land." She was silent for a moment, her frown deepening as she touched the column twice, closing and then opening the door in it again. "And how I know these things — well, I told you, it's the same as something you remember from a dream. It feels so real, but at the same time you know it can't be real because it didn't actually happen."

"Thanks — that's made it all clear . . . ," Will said, cocking an eyebrow and grinning, ". . . as mud."

"I know it sounds crazy." Elliott looked at her feet as she rubbed her forehead. "And I feel as though there's more in here, although I can't tell you exactly what right now."

"There is? But you must have some idea what it is," Will shot back at her.

She laughed with the strangeness of it all. "I won't know what I know until I need to know it."

"Can you run that by me again?" Will chuckled, but he was shaking his head in confusion at the same time. He turned to the column where the door had remained open. "But maybe we ought to find out what Jürgen and his brother are doing upstairs. That's if I'm allowed in the elevator, and don't have to take the long way up like the rest of us lowly humans."

Elliott punched him gently in the chest, laughing. "Come on, lowly human," she said.

Predictably, Woody wasn't going to be left out of the running, and slipped inside the elevator, too.

Elliott touched a plain panel, sliding her hand up it, and the door immediately closed.

Will was peering around him as he muttered, "Safe as houses."

"What?" Elliott said.

"No, nothing — I just remembered how much Chester hated elevators," Will explained. "After that dodgy one in the Colony."

"I hope he's OK, wherever he is," Elliott said.

"So do I, but come on — Woody and I are here and waiting — why haven't you hit the *up* button?" Will asked.

"I already have," she said.

The door slid back to reveal Jürgen and Werner having what appeared to be a heated exchange while Karl listened in, his eyes wide with alarm. The two New Germanian brothers instantly fell silent, their expressions quite comical as they watched Elliott step from the elevator with Will and the bushman on either side of her.

"Oh, hi," Werner said.

"Elliott," Jürgen cut in before his brother could say more. "I suppose it's asking a lot, but would you mind proving to these two," he said, indicating Werner and Karl, "that I wasn't hallucinating up here? Could you give them a demonstration of what you can do on the next floor up?"

Will was outraged on Elliott's behalf. "She's not a performing monkey, you know!" he exploded, repeating a phrase he'd heard Dr. Burrows use once. "I don't think it's fair for you t —"

"No problem," Elliott interrupted him, moving toward the flight of stairs that led to the uppermost level of the tower. As soon as she was at the top, she went straight to the small console and laid a hand on its surface.

They all watched in stunned silence as the circular wall was again filled with multiple images of Earth, of the ink-blue oceans and the wispy clouds up in the atmosphere and the brown-greens of the land masses.

Will was again mesmerized. "I don't understand. These views have to be from something floating around the Earth, like a satellite, or satellites . . . but why wouldn't they have been discovered by now? Especially because they must have been there for donkey's years," he reasoned out loud, turning to the New Germanians. However, they seemed to be too stunned to say anything at all.

Karl had taken his father's hand as the two watched in wonder, and Werner was laughing and shaking his head and saying "How is this possible?" over and over as they watched the images of the outside world that none of them had ever actually been to.

Then Werner stopped. "But is this really from *now*?"

Will was standing beside Elliott as she touched different areas of the console, the blue lines and symbols glowing as her fingertips danced over them. "Sure it is," she answered.

"Then can you show me Germany, please?" Werner requested.

Elliott had been moving her fingers over the console, but now she leaned toward Will. "You'll have to help me find it."

Will realized then that of course she wouldn't be familiar with the world's topography — why would she, when she'd spent virtually her whole life in the Colony and the Deeps?

"There," Will said, pointing. "Close in on that area where the sun's setting."

The whole of central Europe now filled the walls, although to the west a dark shadow was advancing across it as evening set in.

"And now zoom in on that area . . . ," he directed her, pointing at part of the wall, ". . . but more over to the left."

"Look, Jürgen, there's the Ruhr!" Werner said in an excited voice. "And there's Cologne . . . and Essen, where our parents grew up. Isn't that incredible!"

It wasn't that easy to see the river and the surrounding valley itself because dusk was settling over the area, although the various towns and cities along it were sparkling with all the many lights in them.

"OK, now can we go west toward England? I'd like to have

another look at it," Will said, again pointing so Elliott knew where he wanted her to move the focus. The wall flickered, then settled down as France appeared, its cities iridescent against the evening sky.

"Now go up," Will directed, as Elliott moved the view across the English Channel, and then stopped. "There it is again!" he exclaimed excitedly, then was silent for a moment. "But why's it so dark?"

Although nothing had appeared amiss the last time they'd seen England, it had been in daylight. The picture that greeted them now was alarmingly different. There was none of the wash of illumination you'd expect to find in London, or indeed any of the major cities in the South East.

"That can't be right," Will said, trying to find an explanation for the darkness. "Zoom in a bit closer, will you?"

Elliott did, so they could see that there were a small number of areas in the capital that were lit up, although these were few and far between. And several areas radiated a different type of light, with a red hue.

"No. Are those fires?" Will asked, his voice thin. "What's going on down there?" He looked at Elliott. "Unless there's some sort of major power cut right across the UK, it's all gone horribly wrong."

"So maybe my father and Parry didn't stop the Phase and —" Elliott began.

"And the Styx have already done *that* to England," Will finished for her, unable to tear his eyes from the ominous darkness across London.

Elliott took her hand from the console and the image was

immediately extinguished. "Not just them," she said. "Maybe it's the Armagi."

Grinding his fist against his palm, Will was filled with foreboding. "I have to find a way to get back," he said. "If it's not already too late."

In broad daylight, Drake and Jiggs stole through the disused airfield until they found the Portakabin where the security men were usually based. The door was unlocked and nobody was inside, nor was there any sign of a vehicle.

Jiggs tried the light switch, clicking it on and off. "No power. Somebody forgot to pay the bill," he commented.

Drake had gone straight to the telephone on one of the desks. "This is dead, too," he said. As he replaced the receiver, he noticed some unfinished tea in a polystyrene cup. "There used to be an around-the-clock guard on this place, but there's mold growing on that drink. Appears that nobody's been here . . ." He made a face as he peered at the mold in the cup. ". . . in weeks. Wonder why that is." For a moment Drake considered the bars of light coming through the strip blinds, where motes of dust danced slowly. "Anyway, the priority is to get in touch with my father or Eddie. Let's figure out the fastest way to do that without compromising ourselves."

There in the cabin they carried out an equipment check, laying each item of kit out on the floor. The problem was many of the items that Drake had had on him or been carrying in his Bergen had been badly burned in the nuclear blast.

"This is totally kaput. The circuits are fried," Drake said, lobbing his satphone over to Jiggs, who also tried to make it work.

"So we've got some weapons and ammo, a couple of empty booster rockets, my lens, a tracker, and a couple of beacons."

"And my knackered shortwave radio, which won't get us anywhere," Jiggs added, putting it on top of the pile. As he began to pack the equipment away again, Drake slumped into a chair at one of the desks.

"We have to get to the nearest house with a phone and leave a message on the remote server," Drake said. "As we have no idea where Parry's got to, it's the only way I can think of to contact him, and find out how the operation's gone up here on the surface."

"I agree, but unless we're lucky and find a vehicle, we're going the slow way — on foot," Jiggs replied, swinging the Bergen onto his shoulders.

"So be it," Drake said, hauling himself up wearily.

Although it was still winter, the sun was shining brightly in the clear sky as they ducked through an opening in the airfield's perimeter fence and headed across a field of wild grasses toward the nearest road.

"Warm for the time of year," Jiggs commented, undoing another button on his shirt.

Drake tried to catch the rays on his face. "This is glorious. Funny how much you take for granted," he said poignantly, allowing his eyes to shut for a moment. "I've probably been out in the morning sun on a thousand days precisely like this one, but this is the first time I've really *felt* it."

They pushed through a hedge and scrambled down a grass verge, finding themselves on a minor road. Their boots thudded on the tarmac as they walked as fast as Drake could manage, neither of them remarking on the branches and debris scattered everywhere. The road shouldn't have been in such bad condition, unless there'd been recent storm winds, and neither of them could see any other evidence of this.

Drake pointed at a small wooded area. "That's where I hid the Range Rover when I dropped Will and the poor old Doc off." He laughed to himself. "It wasn't that long ago, but it feels like a lifetime now."

"Hold up," Jiggs cut in, bringing them both to a halt. "See the vehicle up ahead?" He unclipped the top of his holster but didn't take his handgun out.

"Got it," Drake said.

They advanced slowly toward the car, taking their time because it had been left at an angle right across the road, making it impossible for anything to get past.

"Someone stopped in a hurry," Drake noted, directing Jiggs toward the skid marks. "What happened here?"

But Jiggs was already by the driver's door, staring intently at it. "This is odd." The door panel itself was pushed in as if it had been hit with some force from the side, and the window had been broken — pieces of it were scattered over the road. "The key's still in the ignition, and there's dried blood on the seat," Jiggs said as he ducked his head inside the car.

"Here, too, where someone's been dragged," Drake said, as he stepped slowly away from the car, following the dark smears of blood. "But no sign of a body, just some personal belongings." He picked up a wallet and cell phone from a drainage ditch at the side of the road.

"I don't understand," Jiggs said, as he tried to piece together what had happened. "Something impacts the car — hard — then the driver is yanked out through the window?" he asked, as he squatted to examine the pieces of torn-off cloth that had snagged on the broken edges of window, and all the blood on the exterior of the door itself.

Drake was trying the cell to see if it was working. "Typical! No signal," he said, "although it could be because the battery's low." Then he flipped through the wallet he'd found. "The driver was local," he began saying, but then abruptly dropped the wallet and began to sway on his feet.

Noticing something was wrong, Jiggs helped him over to the car.

"Sorry," Drake said. "Legs went on me all of a sudden."

Jiggs was looking at him with concern, at the sheen of fresh sweat on his face and the way he was shaking as he leaned against the car. "You'd better get in, and we'll make tracks for the nearest village," he suggested. "I need to get you to a hospital."

The car started without any problem, and they set off along the road. They hadn't been driving for more than five minutes when they went over a small humpback bridge, only to squeal to a halt because the road was blocked by a group of around twenty men. Some were wielding shotguns and small-caliber rifles, while others had pickax handles and even pitchforks.

"Good grief — are we about to be butchered by a lynch mob?" Jiggs said.

"I suppose we are in Norfolk," Drake replied.

A portly man in a tweed jacket stepped forward from the group. "Would you two gentlemen please step out of the car?" he asked. "And for all our sakes, kill that engine!"

Drake began to cough — it sounded so raw that it was painful to listen to him. Jiggs leaned out of the broken window, but left the engine running. "Why?" he asked. "And what's the story here?"

"Turn off the engine and step outside the car, then we'll tell you," the portly man said impatiently. As Drake continued to cough, the man glimpsed his head and all the bandages covering his burns. "Your friend . . . he doesn't look in great shape."

"He's not," Jiggs said, studying the portly leader. He guessed the man must be in his sixties, while a number of others appeared even older. Then there were some young bucks in the mob who clearly liked being armed. Jiggs could tell that from how they were holding their weapons, and he immediately began to worry about twitchy trigger fingers.

"OK, I'm coming out," Jiggs agreed, switching off the ignition and opening his door slowly. Then, with his assault rifle held high in one hand, he stepped out onto the road. He turned to Drake, who seemed to have recovered from his coughing fit. But as Drake emerged from behind the car door and finally raised his head, in each hand he had a Beretta pistol. Trying to ignore the pain from his wounded shoulder, Drake was aiming one pistol at the portly leader, while moving the other over the rest of the group.

"Who are you lot?" Drake demanded. "Because I feel as though I've just wandered onto the set of The Wicker Man. And I never liked the way that film ended."

"Very droll," the portly man replied. "We're just people from this area, trying our best to stay alive. And every second we dillydally here makes that less likely. So I suggest we all put our weapons away," he ordered, casting an eye over the other men around him, who immediately complied. "And you should do the same," he said to Drake. "Then come with me to somewhere a little less exposed than this."

Catching Drake's eye, Jiggs gave him a nod. Drake lowered his handguns, and then, with the portly leader walking between them, they left the road, following up a slightly inclined field.

"You two soldiers? We've had quite a few boots through here," the man asked, his eyes flicking from Drake to Jiggs. The man was wheezing from the exertion by the time they reached the top, and turned toward Drake. "And what's the matter with you? Your breathing sounds as rough as mine. Asthma?"

"No, radiation sickness," Drake gasped, his chest heaving as he broke into another coughing fit. It took him a moment to recover, then he said, "You have to tell us what's been happening recently." He frowned. "I mean, what's with all the weapons? And why aren't the mobile networks working?"

"You really have no idea?" the man asked with astonishment.

"Assume we know nothing," Drake replied.

The man drew in a wheezy breath before he began to speak. "The TV and newspapers reported that there were terrorist attacks when it first kicked off, and then it turned into something far worse." The man gave Drake a curious look, as if suddenly suspicious of him. "So you don't know how it's brought about the collapse of . . . of everything?" he answered, groping for the right words. "You two been hiding in a hole or something?" he asked.

"You're not far wrong," Drake told him as the portly man waved them over to a copse of trees.

"If you've missed out on all the fun and games while the country's gone to rack and ruin, you might want to watch this," he said, pointing down the slope to where several of the younger men had remained with the car. They had the hood up, while another was playing out a cable from a drum. "We reckon they're highly sensitive to the vibrations engines give off. It draws them in from miles away."

"Draws who?" Jiggs quickly asked.

"The glass beasts — you'll most likely see one for yourself in a jiffy."

"Glass beasts?" Drake repeated in a croak.

"We honestly don't know what they are. There's a group of them by the old airfield in West Raynham — if you drove close to it, you were damned lucky to get this far. But because you brought that car into our area, they'll not be long in turning up, and we can't have them nearby or we'll be overrun like the other villages."

"But you said *glass beasts* — what exactly do you mean?" Jiggs pressed him.

"It's hard to describe them," the man replied. "They drop out of the sky, and they sometimes come by water, but those ones look different," he replied. "However they arrive, it doesn't matter; they're all equally savage, and more of our people than I care to remember have been taken by them."

Drake and Jiggs met each other's gaze. "Armagi?" Drake said.

"You know something about these beasts, then?" the portly man put in.

Drake was shaking his head. "Not much, but we had an inkling this might happen."

"Better get out of sight now," the portly man said, and Drake and Jiggs followed his example as, with much grunting, he lowered himself down onto the ground. Once there, he clicked his fingers, and another man in the group immediately came over with a holdall containing some quite sophisticated telescopes on small tripods and handed them out. As Drake raised his eyebrows at his scope, the portly man explained, "Got some die-hard twitchers in our village — you know, bird-watchers — so we're always spoiled for scopes."

As the car could be heard starting up, the portly leader explained, "We leave the engine running by weighing down the accelerator — nothing too loud, but if they're on the trail, it'll bring them in quickly, like mice to cheese. You see, the glass beasts always seem to travel in pairs, and if we don't stop them here, they just keep looking till they find someone."

The men on the road were quickly moving away from it now. "Focus your scope on the car, then keep an eye out around it. You don't want to miss the grand entrance," the portly leader said, chuckling. "Bit different from watching sandpipers over at Blakeney Point."

Then, as they waited, in a muted and grim voice he began to recount to Drake and Jiggs what had been happening on the surface; about how the police and army seemed to have disbanded, and how all the utilities — electricity, gas, telecommunications — all of it had simply stopped. "You know, you two remind me of some curious people we had through the village a while back," the man said suddenly. "They didn't seem to know where they were, either. And why they just came to mind is because they were both plastered with mud and appeared as though they'd just been pulled out of the River Wensum, same as you."

Drake raised an eyebrow. "What did these people look like?"

"They strolled into my village shop early one morning before opening. I said to my wife at the time that I had a feeling something was in the offing — and it wasn't long before all these funny goings-on started, and the country went to pot."

"Can you describe them?" Drake asked.

The portly leader thought for a second. "There was a lad, wild-looking, with long hair as white as snow, and an older man, also with very long hair, who appeared to be his fath —"

"The older one wore glasses?" Drake interjected, a big smile spreading across his face. "What sort of shop did you say you have?"

The portly man pulled an unhappy face. "*Had*. Afraid I was forced to close it after I couldn't get any deliveries through, but it was the village shop — you know, a convenience store with food and newspapers and . . ."

Drake had begun to chuckle. "So you sold chocolate. Did, by any chance, the older of the two stuff himself silly on it that morning? Did he? Because the Doc always loved chocolate."

"He did!" the portly man burst out. "He bought several bars, and I saw him scoffing them outside on the pavement."

"Will and Dr. Burrows," Drake told Jiggs, who was looking confused, "when they first traveled up from the fallout shelter."

The portly man was also looking rather confused. "But how did y —"

"Shhh," someone behind them hissed. "The first beast has landed."

Jiggs had been concentrating on the car as the other two spoke, and had spotted the Armagi swooping down from over the trees and alighting close to it.

And Drake caught sight of the second one as it sprang from the river flowing under the bridge. "My God – there! That's an Armagi!" Drake whispered in horror. "Adapted to live in water."

"And the other is obviously capable of flight," Jiggs added.

"They can alter themselves," the portly man said. "But watch this."

The two Armagi approached the car, one with its wings folded behind its back, the other looking like liquid crystal as the water on it reflected the bright sunlight. There was a moment when they turned to face each other over the roof of the vehicle, as if they were communicating.

"And zambo!" the portly man murmured.

The member of the group hidden in the field applied a current to the wires running to the car's full tank of gas. The explosion lifted the vehicle clean off the ground, the two Armagi blasted into pieces by the huge fireball.

The oddest thing was that for the briefest instant both Drake and Jiggs caught a glimpse not of the transparent beasts against the flames, but of the distinct outlines of two men in silhouette.

The portly leader was already on his feet, and telling them to get up. "We'll come along later to check that nothing escaped the fire. You see, we incinerate every last chunk of those foul beasts we can find."

"Why do that?" Jiggs asked. "That looked pretty conclusive to me. They must be dead."

"You might think so," the portly man said. "But they can come back to life. We've seen it happen."

Drake was frowning as he thought of something. "If we can't use a vehicle with a combustion engine, how are we ever going to reach Parry? I can't really walk it, not the way I am."

The same thought had occurred to Jiggs. "What if we keep the revs low? Or if maybe we can somehow insulate the engine — soundproof it, that might —?"

The portly man smiled broadly as he cut in on their conversation. "If you can convince me that it's important enough, I have a better idea for you. It's not the latest word in travel, but it'll get you where you want to go."

11

IN THE TWO DAYS they'd been at the farmhouse, Chester, Martha, and Stephanie had already settled into a routine, albeit a rather strange one. Martha and Stephanie rarely had anything to do with each other, while Chester was incredibly restless and ill at ease, throwing himself around the place like a bear with a bad hangover. When he wasn't in his room — the master bedroom, which Martha had insisted he have, while Stephanie was relegated to what must have been one of the children's cramped rooms — he would take himself off for long walks.

Stephanie would watch as he left the farmhouse without a word to anyone, then stomp off across the fields. Martha would often rush out after the boy in an effort to accompany him wherever he was going. But she was never gone long as she found it difficult to keep up with her short legs.

And at all times Chester and Stephanie maintained their distance whenever they were in the same room. Even when Martha was far enough away not to hear, Chester didn't seem to be in any mood to talk.

But Stephanie couldn't put up with the silence any longer.

It was the start of the third day and they'd just had their break-fast, which hadn't been a very appealing meal because they'd been forced yet again to eat their cereal with water because there was no way of getting hold of any milk. Martha had just gone outside into the yard to throw the dirty bowls away when Stephanie decided to speak to Chester. "You're still terribly upset, aren't you?" she said softly.

"Oh, just a bit," Chester answered. With a sour expression, he carefully picked off a soggy cornflake from where it had fallen on his shirt and flicked it away.

"I'm sorry you are. I can't pretend to know how you feel." Stephanie said this genuinely because the last news Old Wilkie had received was that her parents and brothers had managed to escape abroad and were safe. Chester had lost everything. "I just wish I could do something to help you."

"There's nothing you can do, but thank you, anyway," he said, his head jerking as they heard the crash of the crockery shattering on the cobblestones out in the yard. "You know, if Parry had opened up to me about it as soon as he'd found out, I might feel differently. But no way can I forgive him now."

"Maybe he was going to tell you after that meeting you went to," Stephanie suggested.

"Well, he didn't, did he?" Chester snapped. "And if he had, then it would have only been because the US President put his foot in it." Chester snorted angrily. "No, I can't get over the fact that my mum and dad died because that creep Danforth had cooked up a stupid, screw-brained scheme all by himself. If that's actually the case."

"But Parry said he didn't know Danforth was going to do it. You don't believe him, then?" Stephanie asked.

"Who knows with these people? These army types are in such a mad rush to save lives that they end up killing everyone in the process," Chester said. "Collateral damage and practical military necessity, laddie," he added, moving his head haughtily and doing a passable impersonation of Parry, complete with Scottish accent. "Drake could be a bit like that, too, sometimes, but with Will and Elliott it was different — we always played it straight with each other. We would never have let each other down like that. *Never.*"

"I'd never let you down, either, Chester," Stephanie said, but Chester didn't seem to register this as he began to work himself up into a lather.

"I mean, why couldn't bloody Danforth have just *pretended* to the Styx that he'd done the dirty on us? He didn't have to go all the way." Chester had jumped to his feet and was pacing furiously around the room. "I wonder if he really enjoyed killing my parents! The sick bastard!" he spat.

Chester was as big as a fully grown man, and his aggression made him very intimidating. Stephanie began to think that it hadn't been such a good idea to try to talk to him.

He abruptly stopped his pacing and said, "The murdering bloody bastard." With a curse, he aimed a kick at one of the chairs around the table. An alarming smile spread across his face as a leg broke off and clattered onto the tiled floor. Then he really went for the chair, kicking and punching it again and again, until there was nothing more than splintered wood where it had been standing. Panting from the exertion, he shouted, "And what the hell am I still doing here? In this bloody armpit of a place?"

Martha had walked in and was looking at the wrecked chair. Chester didn't acknowledge her as he pushed by and went into the hallway. There he snatched up a pair of gloves and a hat from beside the front door and stormed outside.

"What was that about?" Martha demanded, narrowing her eyes at Stephanie. "I hope you haven't been botherin' him."

"I really don't know what set him off. I didn't say a word. All of a sudden he started to go on about his parents and Danforth, and . . ." Stephanie didn't finish as Martha moved quickly over to the window.

"But why doesn't he talk to *me* about it?" she complained.

He came back later that evening after many hours' absence, arriving just in time for supper. His face was blank and nobody dared to speak to him as he took his place at the table. It was easy to tell what they were eating from the smell — it was what they always had — lamb stew. Martha elbowed open the door as she brought it in, plunking it clumsily down on the table in front of them.

As she took her usual seat, Chester was simply staring down at his food. "Um, Martha," he said.

"Yes, my sweet?" she replied.

Using both hands he held up his plastic bowl, as if inviting comment from her. Along the side of the bowl was DOG in large, unmistakable letters, and while it must have once been a rather striking red color, it was so worn and the plastic so abraded by years of cleaning that its color had dulled and the edges begun to flake off. In comparison, Stephanie hadn't come off too badly with the chipped melamine bowl she'd been given.

"Running low on plates. Nothing much left in the cupboards," Martha said by way of explanation, dipping her spoon into her bowl, which was a battered enamel dish probably also used by the owners' pets.

Chester had put his dog bowl carefully back on the table. "I can't take any more," he said hoarsely.

"What — of my stew?" Martha asked.

"No, no, of feeling like this," he mumbled. His head was bowed, and Stephanie couldn't be certain if he was crying or not, but she thought that she spotted a tear dropping into his bowl.

"Oh, my poor sweet boy!" Martha rushed over to him, and hugged him tight. "What is it? What can I do to make things better for you?"

Of course Stephanie knew how severe his depression had been during the weeks in the cottage, but this display of vulnerability shocked her. He was more fragile and more disturbed than she'd ever imagined.

"Tell me what to do," Martha told him, almost pleading. Her eyes, too, were brimming over.

Chester sniffed. "You said that your Brights can find anyone for you?"

"Yes, that's right," Martha replied. "They can. Just as they could always lead me to you, wherever you went. If you have something with a trace of scent on it, my fairies will keep on looking, even over hundreds of miles, and they won't stop until they're successful."

"Purger," Chester mumbled. It was barely audible.

"What did you say, my sweet?" Martha asked.

Chester's shoulders heaved with a sob. "I've got one of his Purgers in my Bergen. It will smell of him."

"Whatever that is, I'm sure my fairies can use it," Martha said. "I'll send them out."

It was obvious to Stephanie that Martha didn't really understand what he was asking for, but right then she was prepared to agree to anything to ease his pain.

"Thank you," Chester croaked. Martha was still hugging him, and he put his hand on her forearm and squeezed it back. As he raised his head, Stephanie could see how his eyes shone with his tears. But she could also see how firmly he'd set his jaw. He stared into Martha's eyes. "I want him so badly. Can you really find him for me . . . find Danforth? Will you do that for me?"

"You know I will," Martha replied, the tears streaming down her face. "You only have to ask," she said, repeating the words over and over.

For the next twenty-four hours the New Germanian contingent hovered around Elliott, as if they were hoping that she'd perform one of her miracles for them again.

She didn't, and they had obviously grown tired of waiting when, out of the blue, Werner announced that they should all return to the city to stock up on supplies and gather some equipment that they needed. It was true that food was running low, but Jürgen's priority was clearly the research; he was firing on all cylinders as he planned a full scientific evaluation of the tower and the pyramid, and also an expedition to the other two pyramids to assess the changes there.

Will didn't take any part in the discussions but listened with interest as Werner and Jürgen kicked around ideas about how they might use seismic equipment in the tower to detect even the smallest vibrations if anything mechanical was operating. They also debated about using a portable X-ray machine on its walls, and how they might measure the level of any electrical activity in the tower.

The final topic on their agenda was to film a record of the *space views*, as they referred to them, of the Earth the next time Elliott operated the console. It was then that Will really picked up on the sense of disappointment emanating from the two New Germanians because Elliott wasn't revealing more of the tower's secrets, if indeed there were any. She'd become very moody and uncommunicative again, spending much of the time asleep, although the two brothers weren't so bold as to try to force her to do anything that she didn't want to.

But when Werner made the suggestion that they all prepare to head back to the city, Elliott reacted strongly to it. At first she was shaking her head and saying she wouldn't go, and when Werner talked to her and tried to convince her, she began to shout, declaring there was absolutely no way she was leaving the tower. The bushman was standing beside her, his body language increasingly belligerent, as if he was prepared to take on anyone who tried to strong-arm Elliott.

Werner remained calm, but refused to take no for an answer, saying that he wasn't even prepared to leave Woody behind, either. "What if we have discovered a weapon here?" he posed. "We have a responsibility — all of us — to ensure that it isn't misused, particularly by the tribesman, who may know more than he's telling us."

Elliott wasn't having any of this, and simply went over to her sleeping bag and slid down inside it, pulling it over her head. Werner then asked Will to try to reason with her, but she wouldn't speak to him, either. And when Will raised his voice in frustration because she was continuing to hide herself, the bushman stepped close, standing over Elliott's cocooned form in the sleeping bag.

"Woody, what do you think you're doing? Keep your bloody nose out of this!" Will barked at him.

When the bushman steadfastly refused to move, Will's temper snapped. "This is nothing to do with you!" he shouted at the bushman. "Go on — make yourself scarce, twig brain."

The bushman jabbered something back at him, his expression unpleasant.

"You shouldn't insult Woody. He understands more than you know," Elliott said, her voice muffled in the sleeping bag.

"Oh," Will said, feeling rather small. As Elliott clammed up again, and Will knew he wasn't going to get anywhere with her, he made a counterproposal to Werner. He suggested that he remain behind to look after her, and also keep an eye on

Woody. There was sufficient food to tide over three people for several days, and Will promised that he would update them regularly over the radio, calling them the moment anything unusual happened.

Short of kidnapping Elliott and forcing her to go with them, Werner didn't have much choice but to accept this suggestion. So, within an hour, he, Jürgen, and Karl had gotten themselves ready and trooped off across the bare plains toward the half-track.

It was a lonely time for Will after they'd gone, because if Elliott wasn't asleep, she shunned any contact with him, roaming aimlessly around the tower. But she never once put a foot outside, as if she couldn't bear to leave the tower, although Will sometimes caught her by the entrance. At these moments, she seemed to be staring out across the fields of dried-out earth, as if waiting for someone to appear on the horizon.

Elliott's continued reluctance to have anything much to do with Will made him question what had changed so radically in their friendship. He didn't delude himself that the carefree way of life that had meant so much to him in the weeks after the nuclear explosion had gone for good. When the traction beam, as Jürgen had called it, had stripped away the old pyramid, it had also obliterated any trace of the base in the nearby tree that had been their home. It was emblematic to Will because he knew that they could never go back to those halcyon days again, particularly not with the New Germanians and the ever-watchful bushman in attendance.

Will let out a long sigh. There was an inescapable inevitability to his life, as if some higher power was intent on disrupting it as soon as he found anything approaching happiness and contentment. *But why did it have to be that way? Why didn't anything good ever last for long?*

And now, as he lay in his sleeping bag in the entrance chamber of the tower, he was staring despondently up at the walls, and at the twin columns housing the elevators. Part of him wished they'd never come back to the pyramid and found the tower, while another part was burning with curiosity about who had built it and what its true purpose was. There was something so contemporary, so incredibly modern about the interior, although it was nothing of the sort because it had remained hidden in this world probably since time immemorial.

As if to emphasize this, the bushman's hushed, repetitive mumbling, like some sort of religious incantation passed down through the centuries, drifted over to Will. Woody had lit a fire just outside the entrance, where he was cooking some grubs he'd foraged from the new fields, and every now and then the wind fanned smoke into the tower.

"This is hopeless. I can't sleep," Will announced, throwing a look across at where Elliott was curled up. The bushman was occupied with his food, so Will quietly pulled himself from his sleeping bag and went to sit near Elliott.

"I don't know what's the matter . . . but I wish you'd at least talk to me and let me in on it." Will's voice turned to a croak with all his emotion, and he swallowed several times before he was able to continue. "You know, I've never felt so alone. I don't have anyone anymore. Mum's a thousand miles away, and Dad's gone, and all the others like Chester and . . ." Will couldn't think who else to add to the list, so quickly moved on. "Well, there's no one. No one except you. So please tell me what's wrong, because —"

A distant shout echoed through the tower.

"Huh?" Will said, suddenly very concerned, because it had sounded like Elliott. He leaned over and pushed the sleeping bag. Something rattled inside. Whatever Elliott had stuffed into it was hard and nothing like a human body.

The bushman had heard the shout, too. He abandoned his food and came inside, going straight to the flight of stairs.

"Bloody hell!" Will exclaimed, as he grabbed his jacket and Sten gun. He was angry with himself because he must have dozed off long enough for Elliott to trick both him and the bushman. Although he was just as much to blame, he took his annoyance out on the bushman. "Woody, you idiot! Why'd you let her pull that stunt on us?" he demanded.

Knowing that the elevator wouldn't work for him, he tore up the stairs with Woody close behind.

"Elliott!" Will shouted as he came to the first landing. She didn't answer him, but through the archway he saw her standing very still. She was staring fixedly at a particular spot on the outside wall, her eyes unblinking.

"Why were you shouting? And why are you up here by yourself?" he asked as he came alongside her. As soon as he could see her face, he was alarmed by the change in her: Her expression was haunted and anxious, and there were shadows as dark as bruises under her eyes. He lowered his voice as he spoke to her again. "Elliott, I need to know what's going on with you. And we'd agreed that you and I were going to stick together because we don't know wh—"

"Something's not right," she interrupted him.

"What — over here?" He went over to the wall she was still facing, and had a cursory look at it for himself. Nothing seemed to be any different there, so he returned to her. "And what do you mean? What's not right? And why did you sneak up here?" he asked gently, trying to take her hand.

She pulled away from him, then moved to the nearest of the four consoles around the central well. "A long time ago," she began, "something was taken from here."

"You mean from the next level?" Will asked, pointing at the floor above as he recalled what she'd said up there.

She nodded slowly. "It was never meant to be away for long, but something happened, and it was lost. I have to get it back. It's in the wrong place. We're all in the wrong place."

Will rubbed his chin, wondering how much he dared ask her in her present state. She didn't look like herself at all, as if she'd been in the grip of a terrible nightmare and wasn't fully awake yet. But he had to find out what she was talking about, what was troubling her so much. "Right . . . so if this *something's* not in the right place, how do we go about fixing that?"

Elliott laid a hand on the edge of the console, continuing to speak as if she hadn't heard his question. "I have to find it." She switched her gaze to Will. "And I have to bring it back."

Will shrugged. "Fine. We'll do it together. Where is it? Somewhere close?"

Without even looking at what she was doing, she stretched out and touched the top of the console. There was a burst of light from the wall behind Will, which settled down in a shimmering square of silver.

He needed a couple of seconds to collect himself after the surprise. "What's that? That's not another aerial view. What have you done?"

"It'll take me close to where the object is." Although she'd removed her hand from the console, the large silver square remained. "I'm going Topsoil to find it."

As he absorbed what she'd just said, Will was shaking his head. "You mean that's a way to get to the surface? But how, precisely?"

Elliott just looked at him blankly, so he began to move toward the flickering square. It was about seven feet square, and while the surface appeared to be in constant flux, the edges didn't vary at all.

"Don't get too close," Elliott warned.

It seemed vaguely reflective — he could just about see himself and Elliott in it. "Mirror, mirror," Will mumbled, transfixed by the square. He made himself focus on what he should be doing. "So, what, does this magically transport us somewhere?"

"Yes," Elliott answered.

Will thought for a moment. "OK, let's put that to the test, shall we?" he suggested dubiously. He hunted around in his jacket until he found something with suitable mass. "He'd never forgive me for this," he said, as he held up Dr. Burrows's old brass compass.

Will got himself ready, then gently lobbed the compass at the silver square. When it was approximately a foot from the surface of the square, its trajectory was completely altered, as if something had hit it. The compass was pulled at such speed into the square that in the time it took Will to blink, it had simply vanished. And there was no sound to suggest that it had struck any kind of surface such as the wall behind, or dropped on the floor below. "Wow!" he whispered. "Now you see it, now you don't!"

He turned to Elliott. Her eyes were gleaming — the haunted look almost gone. "Does that mean you'll come with me? Please, will you?" she begged.

He took a breath. "You're really telling me that if we walk into that square, we'll instantly be in London?" Will said. "Where Dad's compass has just gone? Just like magic?"

"That's right," she confirmed. "And it's not magic."

"And you're absolutely sure it'll be London? Not outer space or somewhere else?"

"London . . . absolutely. That's where I have to go."

Will took in a breath as his mind raced with the possibilities. "So if you're correct, and we don't just get vaporized or something, I can come along and help you, and I'll also be able to find out what's happening back out there on the surface?" He laughed with the improbability of it all. "We'll both get out of this world?"

She nodded.

But Will had thought of something. "We can't go. And no

way can you go, either — because of the virus. We'd take it straight through with us. We'd kill everybody!"

"I have to . . . ," Elliott began.

Will was adamant. "No, you can't. Remember what Werner said — the virus is everywhere down here because the birds are spreading it." At this point his eyes fell on the bushman. Will stuck his finger in the air, much like his father had been apt to do when he'd had a brain wave. "Wait a moment — I've got an idea."

"You have?" Elliott said.

"Yeah, I'm the man!" Will proclaimed, puffing out his chest and strutting around in a kind of victory dance because he was so pleased with himself.

This expression was completely lost on Elliott. "You're the man? What man?"

"Yes, I *am*. I am the man!" Will said, a big grin on his face. "What we do is send Woody over to the pyramid to get us all the decontamination gear we took there — you know, when Jürgen was worried that we'd crash in on a load of Woody's mates and give them the virus."

"And we set it up in front of that," Elliott said, indicating the silver square as she caught on.

"Yep, and we make sure we take every precaution under the sun before we step into your mirror. And you make Woody understand that he's to stay put and not to try to follow us through." Will was still finding this all a little difficult to believe. "And if this square is really what you think it is, I can be home in, like, the click of my fingers. And I can be there to help Chester and Parry and . . ."

"I believe that we can *really* help them, if it's not too late," Elliott said. "Because what I have to do is connected to this blood in me, to my father's blood. I know that somehow it's connected to the Styx." She paused before she added, "And the Phase."

Will just nodded.

12

"**THIS ONE?**" Mrs. Burrows asked, as she came to a door on the worn stone staircase.

The First Officer frowned as he stopped beside her and considered it. "I seem to remember it was blocked up. Let's try farther up," he suggested.

After another short flight on the claustrophobic stairwell, there was another landing with an identical iron-framed door of old worm-eaten wood. But when the First Officer turned the handle and attempted to open it, nothing happened. "Stand aside, please," he said self-importantly to Mrs. Burrows, limbering up his arms and taking a moment to prepare himself. Then he stepped back and, like a charging rhino, threw himself at it with all his might.

There was a splintering sound and the door did open, but only to butt up against a solid brick wall. The sloppily applied mortar between the joints of the bricks had the appearance of toothpaste, suggesting that the wall had been built from the other side.

"Humphhh," the First Officer said in disappointment. "Please stand farther back," he told Mrs. Burrows.

"Stop coming over all *policeman* with me, will you," she muttered a little crossly.

He took no notice of this, again stepping back as far as he could on the tiny landing, and then launching his not inconsiderable bulk at the wall. He did this for a second time. And a third.

"Losing your touch, dear?" Mrs. Burrows asked him with a smile on her face.

But then, on the fourth attempt, the wall suddenly gave way. After the First Officer had clawed the bricks out to enlarge the opening, he discovered a layer of new plasterboard, which he broke through as if it were a sheet of paper.

"Modern bloody building materials," he muttered, as he and Mrs. Burrows finally stepped out into a room.

"Where are we? What can you see?" Mrs. Burrows asked.

The First Officer described what was there — how it was obviously in the middle of an extensive refurbishment. All the surfaces had fresh plasterboard on them, and from the cables everywhere on the walls and dangling from the ceiling it was evidently being rewired.

"So someone's doing some improvements," Mrs. Burrows said, as she went straight to the window. It was still light outside, although it was raining so heavily and the sky was so overcast that everything appeared dull and gray. She sniffed. "This place is familiar," she said.

"Gladstone Street," the First Officer helped her.

Mrs. Burrows nodded and sniffed again. "Just another rainy day in Highfield." As she stood at the window, her hand touched something pinned to the new window frame. "What's this?" she asked.

The First Officer pulled off the old dog-eared photograph that one of the builders must have come across and pinned there. "It's a daguerreotype of a very old lady wearing thick glasses, with some cats."

"They call them photographs in this century," Mrs. Burrows said, adding quickly, "This old lady . . . does she have white hair . . . with wiry, odd-looking curls?"

The First Officer brought the photograph closer to see. "She does," he confirmed.

Mrs. Burrows nodded. "Ah, I know why this place is so familiar. I bet you that's Mrs. Tantrumi. She lived in one of the almshouses around here, and chances are it was this one, because the Styx obviously had a quick way to reach her if they wanted her."

"Mrs. Tantrumi?" the First Officer asked.

"Yes, she was a Styx agent. And the old witch is the reason I was caught on Highfield Common and put through all that Darklighting," Mrs. Burrows replied, her voice bitter. Then something dawned on her. "And, do you know, the luminescent orb that led my husband, Roger, to discover the Colony was found under this house. This is where it all started!" She looked fondly at the First Officer. "You and I would never have met if it hadn't been for that."

The First Officer nodded, keen to focus on the job at hand. "So what now? Do we go outside and investigate wh —"

"No," Mrs. Burrows said abruptly, her head snapping

back toward the window. "God, no! Quickly, get back through that door!"

"Why, what is it?" the First Officer asked, more than a little confused at what she'd evidently picked up with her supersense.

"There's nobody left alive in Highfield . . . but there are things out there that I've never smelled before." Mrs. Burrows was pushing the First Officer back toward the door. "And if just one of those things gets into the Colony, we're all done for."

"Do you think we've done this right?" Elliott shouted from inside the decontamination tunnel. She and Will had spent hours at the top of the tower slotting the aluminum sections together in different configurations until finally the double skin of dark green outer rubber could slide into place over it.

"I don't know . . . I think so — it looks as though it's more or less there now. It would have been so much easier if it had come with instructions," Will said, as she joined him and they stood back to take in the long, tentlike structure. "OK," he said, going to the crates. "Now we fit it out with this stuff."

They began to install the shower and bank of ultraviolet lights. They had a general idea of how to do this because they'd seen what the decontamination chamber had been like in the New Germanian hospital, so all they could do was to try to reproduce it in this portable version.

"I rigged up something just like this in a tunnel years ago," Will said, as he connected a lead acid battery similar to that from a car so it would power the small bank of ultraviolet lights.

Elliott's task was equally involved because she was trying to work out how to install the shower using the many feet of tubing and a hand pump.

Finally, they thought they were ready for a trial run.

"Hit the switch," Will shouted from inside the tent, and was bathed in the light from the ultraviolet panel as Elliott did as he'd asked. "That's fine — turn it off!" He moved down inside the tent until he was in the first compartment. "OK, now try the pump."

She began to work the hand-operated pump, giving it her all. She was watching the blue germicidal fluid pulse hypnotically through the tube system when she became aware of Will's shouts.

"Stop! Stop! That's enough!" Will's face appeared at the mouth of the tent, his face and white hair dripping with the blue fluid. "I just knew that was going to happen," he spluttered, but nevertheless he looked very pleased. "Well, it all seems to work." He looked at Elliott. "So, are we going through with this?"

She nodded vigorously.

From the very start he'd known there was no way she was about to chicken out and, despite his reservations, there was nothing on — or *in* — Earth that was going to stop him, either. He couldn't wait to find out if the silver square did what she claimed it would. "OK, if you help yourself to one of those germ suits, you might as well get started on the decontamination." He swung toward the bushman, still speaking to Elliott. "And do you think you can get Woody to help? If not, there'll be no one outside the tent to process me when I go through."

"Don't worry about him — just sort out what kit we're taking with us," she answered, already heading to where they'd laid out two of the white plastic suits identical to those that Jürgen and Karl had been wearing the first time they'd bumped into them in the city.

While Will checked through all the equipment in their Bergens, Elliott issued instructions in the Styx language to Woody, who was outside the tent. She was in the shower section of the tunnel being completely drenched by the germicide, which was sprinkling down from the overhead syphon. Some of the fluid trickled into her eye, stinging it so badly that she had to step from under the shower and wash it with water from a canteen before she could go on. "I hope we're doing this properly!" she shouted grimly to Will.

"Oh, I truly hope so, too!" Will shouted back. Shaking his head, he let out a humorless laugh. "Or we'll be responsible for killing all several billion people up on the surface." His head reeled at the thought. Just saying those words brought home the implications — even the smallest of mistakes that allowed one single, tiny virus to be carried to the outer world would be more disastrous than words could express.

Elliott was similarly affected. Still blinking her eye, she didn't move for a moment. "Then . . . do you think I should go through the shower again?"

Will glanced at the plastic tanks beside Woody. "Might be a very good idea. We've got buckets of the blue gunk."

Once Elliott had showered for a second time, Will slid their Bergens and their equipment into the entrance, and Elliott soaked it all in the germicide.

Dragging all the kit with her, Elliott then moved farther down the tent where she stood under the bank of ultraviolet light that Woody had turned on. Having donned her plastic suit — which was a task in itself because the germicide covering it made it slippery — she finally put on the cylindrical helmet. Making sure it was seated properly in the seal around her neck, she clicked the two catches shut, and then turned on the valve to the small canister of air. She slung this over her back where it hung from a strap. Then she called out to Will that she was ready.

"My turn," he said to Woody, uncomfortable because the bushman made no effort to avert his eyes as Will stripped off all his clothes. "Elliott, I'm coming in. No peeking!" he shouted, and entered with his germ suit under his arm. He, too, went through the shower twice and finally stood under the lights while Elliott faced in the opposite direction, arms crossed and humming impatiently.

When he was dressed, he joined her at the far end of the tunnel, and they stood side by side, ready to step into the shimmering mirror that lay directly outside the tent.

"It's still there?" Will asked nervously.

Elliott unzipped a few inches of the door flaps to check. "Yes," she replied.

"And you're sure about this?" He picked up his Bergen and hooked his Sten over his shoulder, then looked rather undecided. "Tell me one last time — this is really going to zap us through to the surface? Like something out of *Star Trek*? How do you know we won't just burn up or something?"

She frowned at the mention of *Star Trek*, but answered simply, "It's going to work."

"Yeah, yeah, you can't tell me how, you just *know* it," Will grumbled.

Without a further word, Elliott unzipped the door flaps, and they faced the glimmering portal together, their equipment and suits dripping with germicide.

"Let's do it," Will said quietly. He took her hand and squeezed it as they both left the tunnel, walking toward the portal. "Feels cold," he said.

They hadn't even entered the square when a force took hold of them, wrenching them with such power they couldn't have resisted even if they'd wanted to.

For less than a beat, all they heard was the rush of air. Despite the suits, they felt it on their skin like a sudden blast of wind.

And they knew they were no longer in the inner world.

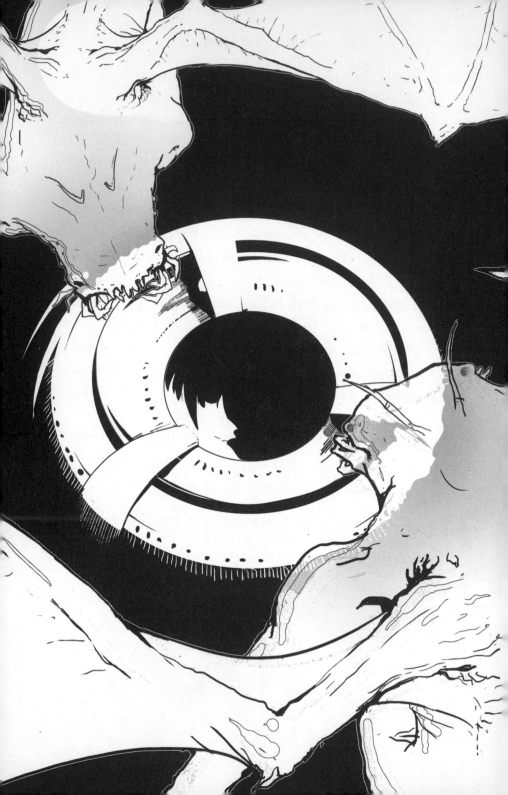

PART 3

```
      B
      I
      S
      H
W O O D
      P
      S
```

13

THEY FELL SEVERAL FEET onto something hard. The jolt made them drop their Bergens and their weapons.

It was pitch-black and bitterly cold.

Will immediately reached out for Elliott and found her on the ground beside him.

"You OK?" he asked.

"Yes," Elliott replied, then pointed to her helmet. "Is it safe to take this off now?"

"S'pose so. We're going to have to, sooner or later, because the air will run out. And if we've got the decontamination wrong, then . . ." He trailed off. He released the seal around his neck and removed the plastic helmet from his head. Elliott followed his example, and they both took their first breaths, drawing the freezing night air down into their lungs.

"Brrrr," Elliott exhaled, her teeth already beginning to chatter.

It hit them both right then just how unprepared they were for conditions like this after the tropical climate of the inner world. And it was exacerbated because not only were their thin plastic suits little protection against the cold, but they were both still damp from the decontamination process.

"We didn't bring any proper clothes with us," Elliott realized.

"We didn't think this through," Will agreed.

Their voices sounded small and there was no echo. Wherever they'd arrived, they were definitely out in the open.

"At least we're still alive! We made it!" Will declared, as it sank in that they had survived the journey through the shimmering portal.

Elliott was more subdued, as if she'd expected nothing less. "Yes, great, but where exactly are we?" Rising to her feet, she used her rifle scope to look around. "Trees? All I can see are trees," she said. "And I feel really sick," she added with a moan, sitting back down on the ground again as she clutched her stomach.

Will had opened up his Bergen and was rummaging through it, but stopped what he was doing as the nausea also gripped him. "Me, too. I suddenly feel really awful," he said. He lowered his head, then brought it up again quickly, at the same time burping at great volume. "Ah, that did the trick." He turned to Elliott in the darkness. "You try it."

"What? Burp?"

"Yes, go on. Must be a buildup of air, because of the change in pressure or something."

"Well . . . OK." There was a pause as she inhaled and held her breath, then she let it out in the most almighty belch — far louder than Will's — which reverberated around the trees. "That *is* better," she said.

"Very ladylike," Will chuckled, diving back into his Bergen to look for Drake's light-intensifying lens. It had been redundant in the inner world with its constant daylight, but he'd still carried it with him everywhere he went through force of habit.

"Haven't used this for a while. Hope it still works," he said, fitting the strap around his head and then hinging the lens down over his eye. As he flicked the switch on the small box that dangled by a cord from the unit, all he could see was the usual orange snowstorm before the view settled down. "Yes, trees — I've got them," he said, as he glanced around. "And is that a stream over there?" he asked, indicating where the nettles and undergrowth parted and something glistened in the small amount of moonlight penetrating the thick cloud cover.

But Elliott was busy peering through her scope in the opposite direction, surveying the short slope beside them as she tried to make out what lay at the top. "I wonder where we are," she said.

"It certainly doesn't look like London. We must be in the country somewhere," Will said. "And before we freeze to death, we need to get out of this," he added, stamping his feet on the ground in an effort to keep himself warm.

It was then that Elliott spotted the frosted tarmac of a path running up the incline. "What about up there?" she suggested to Will.

Gathering their equipment together, they began up the path, but Will suddenly stopped. "Just a moment." He returned to where they'd been, and had only been peering around the ground for a second or two before he stooped to pick something up. "I really hoped this would be here," he said, holding up his father's compass.

But then he also noticed something else about the spot they'd come through. "Hey, will you look at that! We made a fairy ring," he said with a laugh. Around him was a perfect circle, nearly six feet in diameter. Not only had the long grass been cut through by whatever force had transported him and Elliott there — the area right in the center of the circle had also been scooped out to such an extent that the frozen soil was visible. "Do you think that's how all fairy rings are made?" he suggested less than seriously.

But Elliott was already at the top of the incline where she was crouching behind a low metal railing. She touched the top of her head in an *on me* hand signal, which immediately warned him to be on his guard. She'd found something. And as Will scrambled up the slope toward her, his Sten gun at the ready, she patted the air in another signal, indicating he should keep down.

They were by the side of a wide road that swept around a corner to their right. It followed a slight gradient down to their left, and on the other side of this section of road there were buildings.

"So we're not in the countryside," Will whispered, as they both took in what lay before them. "We *have* been brought to London after all," he added.

"Yes, I'd worked that out for myself," she whispered back.

"But those are *some* houses," Will said. He knew from their size that he and Elliott had to be in one of the wealthier areas of the city.

Elliott craned her neck to the left to see what was farther down the road. "No lights anywhere," she whispered. She hadn't much experience of Topsoil cities, and added, "That's not usual, is it?"

Will didn't respond immediately, listening to the distant barking of a fox. "No, something's definitely wrong." Almost directly across from them was a side road lined with more large houses. "Let's take a look over there," he suggested, then peered up at the sky. "I've no idea how late or early it is, but we don't want to be stuck out in the open when it gets light."

"Yep," Elliott said. "So cover me." She ran in a half crouch across to the corner of the road opposite, then kept watch as Will did the same. They tucked themselves in against a wall, glancing at the vehicles abandoned along the road, around which rubbish and even some articles of clothing were strewn.

Will's gaze fell on a sign. *"Bishopswood Road?"* he whispered, trying to think if he'd heard of it before.

"Mean anything to you?" Elliott asked.

Will shook his head. "No, but from the postal code, this is North London, but not as far north as Highfield."

"Been a fire in that one," Elliott said, pointing to the house opposite where heavy smoke shadows stained the white Georgian frontage.

"What about the next house along — spot anything there?" Will asked, squinting as he tried to see it through his lens.

"If we want somewhere safe to stay, how about the place right behind us?" Elliott suggested. "Nice high wall around it."

Will took a moment to consider the house, noting the gates that seemed to be firmly shut. "Sure. Let's give it a closer look."

Once over the wall they crossed the paved drive, checking each window for signs of life. Will tried the front door, but it was locked, so they crept around to the back, on the way passing a large conservatory.

They came to a back door with glass panels in the upper half, and positioned themselves flat against the wall on either side. Will tried the handle, but again it was firmly locked.

"So . . . do we break the glass to get in?" he posed. "What about the noise?"

Elliott didn't answer right away, and they both listened to the fox continuing to bark in the distance, and the bitterly cold wind as it raked the bare branches of the trees in the garden.

"I'm bloody freezing," Will grumbled. "Typical, isn't it? I've been moaning about the sun and the heat for weeks, and now I get this." He glanced up at the sky. "Complete darkness and brass-monkey weather."

"Come on — smash it," urged Elliott, making up her mind. "We can't stay out here."

"Breaking and entering — here I go again," Will muttered. He swung the metal stock of his Sten at one of the panes of glass, grimacing as the pieces landed on the floor inside with a clatter. Reaching through the hole he released the catch on the interior of the door. "That's it. We're in."

The hallway was paneled with dark wood, and hung with several chandeliers. Will and Elliott split up and worked their way methodically through the ground floor, then met up at the bottom of the stairs before doing the same with the bedrooms on the next floor. Will shook his head. "Talk about homes of the rich and famous. I've only seen places like this before on Mum's TV programs," he remarked.

They chose the largest of the bedrooms and began to search it for warm clothes. Will opened a door in the corner, only to find that there was a walk-in closet with beautifully made cedar-wood shelves stacked high with men's clothes. He called Elliott over and they helped themselves to whatever came to hand, donning sweaters and then another layer on top in an effort to keep warm.

For the remainder of the night they took turns keeping guard at the doorway, while the other slept.

Will had been right to get them under cover, as it wasn't long before dawn broke. Turning his lens off, he gently shook Elliott awake. She had sunk into the sumptuous king-sized bed, pulling the duvet right over her head. They both tiptoed downstairs, the light from outside allowing them to take in how extravagant the interior was.

"This is nothing like your house," Elliott observed, standing on the polished marble tiles in the hallway as Will went into the large conservatory, which had a grand piano in it, surrounded by some rather thirsty-looking palm trees in large earthenware pots.

"You don't say." He laughed. "Which way's the kitchen?"

They found it — an incredibly expensive-looking room with white tiles everywhere and similarly white fittings. And in the first cupboard they checked they came across packets of chocolate digestive biscuits.

Will wasted no time in tearing open one of these, passing Elliott a handful of biscuits. "A little soggy, but wow, taste that chocolate!" Will mumbled through a mouthful. He stood in front of the twin sinks beneath the window, staring out at the garden, and continued to munch his way through the whole packet. He didn't take much notice as Elliott went off to explore the house.

Hearing a sound behind him, he spun around.

A man, in his fifties with a gray beard and untidy hair, stood there with a handgun aimed straight at Will's head. "What are you doing in my house?" he demanded in a growl.

With crumbs dropping from his mouth, Will tried to answer.

"I see you've broken one of my windows. What are you? A bloody looter?" the man said, his voice low with anger. "Some lowlife up from the Archway come here to clear me out?"

Will managed to swallow his mouthful. "No, not a looter," he replied.

"If you don't get off my property, so help me . . . I'll put a bullet in you," the man threatened, taking a step back from Will as if giving him the option to leave without a fuss.

Will sighed. "Why am I always the one who gets the gun pointed at him?" he asked wearily.

"What?" the man asked in a rush of breath, amazed that Will was taking the situation so coolly.

And Will *was* taking it coolly. After what he'd been through over the past couple of years, it took more than this to rattle him. Particularly because he'd noticed something. "So you're going to shoot me with that poxy air pistol, are you? Then what?" Will asked. "Because it's not going to do much damage to me, and by the time you've cocked it and put a new pellet in, I'll have cut you in half with my Sten." He turned slightly to allow the man a glimpse of the submachine gun slung over his shoulder.

"That's a Sten?" the man said, looking markedly less confident.

There was a click as Elliott did her party trick, slipping off the safety on her rifle with the barrel prodding the man in the nape of the neck. "Need any help there, Will?" she asked.

"No, we're fine," Will said. "Me and beardy man are just talking, aren't we?"

The man slowly lowered his air pistol, but regarded Will and then Elliott with some indignation. "If you're going to nick my clothes, do you think you could take something other than my best suits? Those are both bespoke Savile Row, and bloody expensive."

Will hadn't paid much attention to what they'd found in the wardrobe, but now examined the gray suit jacket he was wearing, and the double-breasted blue suit that Elliott had picked out, with the sleeves and trouser legs rolled up so that it was a better fit. They were both very fine suits.

"Sorry," Will said. "We didn't come here to steal from you, but we were just both bloody freezing. It was early in the morning when we arrived, and we needed clothes and somewhere warm."

"Why? Where did you *arrive* from?" the man inquired. "Because I haven't heard a single vehicle come this way for weeks now."

Will nodded. "It's a long story."

The man glanced past Will to look out through the windows into the garden. "Well, if you're not intending to go back out there while it's light — which would be a very fast way to get yourselves killed — I suggest you both follow me."

The man didn't wait for a response as he walked straight past Elliott and left the kitchen, heading for a room toward the front of the house. Here he went over to a heavy tapestry on the wall behind a large dining table and lifted one corner to reveal the door hidden there. "Welcome to my lair," he said.

Once Will and Elliott were down the steps, the man swung the thick metal door shut behind them, bolting it at the top and bottom. Switching on his flashlight, he then escorted them along a corridor, pointing at the various doors that led from it. "Cinema, wine cellar, and this is the bathroom. There's been no electricity or gas for a month now, but the water seems to still be on."

He stopped beside a substantial door and slapped it with the palm of his hand. "And this is the panic room."

"What's that?" Elliott asked quickly.

"It's an armored safe room where you can lock yourself away in an emergency. I had it installed for my family after there was an armed robbery at a neighbor's." The man was silent for a moment, as a shadow passed over his face. "I'm telling you about it because along with a telephone line direct to the police station, it had full access to the house CCTV system. And before the power went off for the last time, I was able to watch what was happening in the street. . . ."

"So what did you see?" Will asked.

The man shook his head. "There were things — I can't really describe them — moving in the road, but it wasn't so much what I saw, but what I *heard* that night. The screaming and the cries for help." He looked down at his feet. "It was terrible."

Then the man seemed to pull himself together as he continued along the corridor. "Anyway, these are a couple of storage rooms where I've stashed all the food, and this is where I've been living," he said, playing his flashlight beam on the double doors before swinging them open. "The games room."

"Cool," Will whispered as they entered. Lit by a kerosene lamp hissing away on a table in the center, the room was almost the size of a basketball court.

"This was an indulgence for my kids," the man said.

At one end of the room stood a Ping-Pong table and a large television with some video consoles. The other half of the room was less cluttered, with a bed pushed into the corner and several crates of clothes and books. "Amazing. So has this always been here?" Will asked.

The man shook his head. "I had the basement dug out when my family was still living here." He indicated the vents above their heads. "Although there's been no electricity for the fans, fresh air still comes in through those." He indicated the ceiling with both hands. "You see, where we're standing right now, we're directly beneath the garden." Then he looked around the room. "When I heard all the screaming in the road, I'm ashamed to admit I ran straight down here. And I've been hiding here ever since."

"I don't blame you," Will said.

The man glanced in the direction of a radio beside the unmade bed. "I thought I'd wait for some news before I ventured outside, but all I can get are European stations, and they don't seem to have any idea about what's going on here in the UK." He removed the clothes from a couple of chairs for Will and Elliott, then perched on the edge of the bed as he continued to talk.

The man's name was David, and it was obvious that he was grateful for some company. He said he lived alone at the house because his wife had left him, taking the children with her. "They went six months ago, and I suppose I haven't been out of the house much since. But when I —"

"What's this?" Will interrupted him. He'd begun to wander around the room and had spotted an ancient-looking map in a frame on the wall. *"Bishops Wood,"* he said, squinting at the name written across an area of woodland. Because the legend was *Biſhops* with an *f* instead of the first *s*, Will knew from what Dr. Burrows had told him that it had to be several centuries old. "That's interesting. We're on Bishopswood Road, aren't we?"

"Yes, the name originated from an ancient wood. When the builders were using their backhoe to dig out this basement, they uncovered some very old and very rotten pieces of timber, and the planners had to check that we weren't destroying anything of archaeological importance." David turned to point at the wall directly behind him. "You see, in that direction, just across the main road, is the park where they believe the original Bishops Wood was situated."

"That's where we were last night," Will said to Elliott. "So there was an ancient wood there?" Will asked David.

He nodded. "The person from National Heritage said it was some sort of Druidic site dating way back." David made a face. "And an intersection between two ley lines to boot, if you believe in all that."

"I think maybe I'm beginning to," Will said, eliciting a look from Elliott.

David rubbed his hands together. "Well, I don't know about you but I'm starting to seize up from the cold. I usually wrap myself in a couple of duvets at night to keep warm, but frequent cups of something hot also take the edge off. Can I interest anyone?"

When David went off to make them both tea in one of the other rooms, Elliott turned to Will. "What's all that about *ley lines*? What are they?"

"My dad thought the theories about them were a load of codswallop. They're supposed to be where the Earth's energy is channeled or something," Will replied. "He had this book that said rituals often took place on them, and also some old monuments like Stonehenge had been built where they ran."

Elliott shook her head. "I don't understand. So what are they exactly?"

Will took a breath. "It all sounds pretty flaky, but the book said they marked where Neolithic people thought natural energy flows through the Earth. *Magical* energy, if you want to call it that." He smiled. "If we came through on the intersection that David mentioned, maybe they were right. Maybe these ley lines *are* a source of power, from your tower in the center of the world."

David returned balancing three mugs of steaming tea on a tray, and they began to drink them appreciatively. "So tell me — I'm dying to know how you came to be here," he said.

Will quickly told him about the Styx, and the Colony, leaving out anything about the inner world and New Germania because it would have been too much for the man to take on board.

"So you climbed out on the surface a stone's throw away," David said. "Given what's been happening around here, I suppose I'm prepared to believe anything. But where are you heading for next?"

Will deferred to Elliott with a wave of his hand. "Ask her — she's the one with the plan," he said.

14

THE LIGHT WAS FADING rapidly as they
stepped out into the garden. Will and Elliott were
wearing more of David's clothes — corduroy trousers and
thick trench coats over sweaters — this time taken with his
blessing.

They had waited for nightfall, then said good-bye to him,
and left the basement through the door in the dining room.
The smell of burning laced the crisp air as they stole across the
back of the house. Will peered at the lawn underfoot as they
went, thinking how strange it was that David was just
below, hiding away in his modern-day version of a cave in the
hope that everything would somehow return to normal again.
Will wondered how many others were doing the same all over
the country.

"Just a second," Will said, rummaging right down into the
bottom of one of the side pockets in his Bergen. He smiled as
he found what he'd been looking for and, as though he was
about to perform a magic trick, produced a small black box
with great flourish.

"Is that what I th —?" Elliott asked, peering at the box,

which was the size of a pack of cards with a wire antenna trailing from it.

"Sure is," he interrupted her. "I completely forgot I still had any beacons left until I was getting Drake's lens out." Will held up the electronic device. "This was a spare in case we needed more of them to mark the route to the inner world." He found the tiny micro switch next to the antenna and moved it over. "There," he said. "I've activated it."

Elliott frowned at the beacon. "Is that such a good idea?"

Will shrugged. "Short of slogging all the way up to Parry's estate in Scotland — which might be a total waste of time because he's probably never gone back there — we've got no means of letting him or Eddie know we're Topsoil again, have we?" Will lobbed the transmitter a short distance up in the air and caught it again. "But you never know — they might pick up the signal put out by this. And if they do, it'll lead them straight to us."

Elliott was nodding. "I suppose there's nothing to lose — unless the Styx are able to trace the signal, too."

"I think we should take that risk," Will said, not believing for a moment that there was one.

An insistent pinging alarm had sounded across the floor. Like a shot Danforth was over at the screen where the indicator was flashing. Silencing the alarm, he'd just pushed the person manning the station to the side so he could see the screen properly when the old Styx came striding into the room.

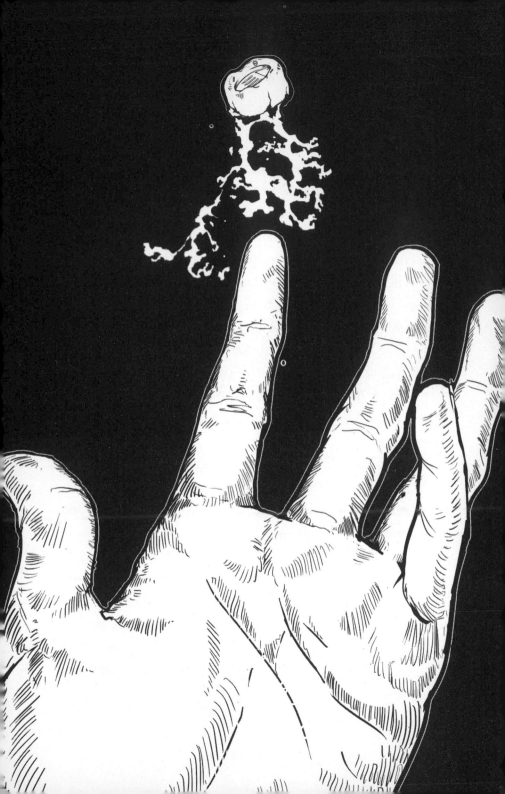

"What was that?" he demanded.

"A VLF . . . a very low-frequency signal," Danforth replied with a degree of surprise, as he watched the long waveform meander across the bottom of the grid on the display. "But according to the sensors it doesn't have any sub-coding."

"Meaning?" the old Styx said.

"It doesn't carry any information. It's merely a marker of some kind." He indicated the next screen along on the desk. "And it's just come on in London."

"Any guesses who it might be?" the old Styx said. "Is it military in origin?"

"I wouldn't necessarily jump to that conclusion. It's not a frequency they use — it's so low it's scraping along at the very bottom of the spectrum."

The truth was that Danforth knew full well what it was likely to be, because he'd developed the VLF technology that had been used on the various missions to the inner world, particularly the last one to seal it off. And Danforth couldn't reveal to the old Styx why he was so interested by this new development; it meant that someone had made it back from this last mission. It was the very first indication that there were any survivors.

If Danforth had anticipated one of the beacons popping up on the surface like that, he would have limited the range of the detectors, or programmed in a black spot to hide it. He just wished that he hadn't been so thorough when he'd supercharged the detection system for the Styx at this installation, but he'd wanted to prove his worth to them. "Are we going to do anything about it?" he asked the old Styx.

"We know where it is — we can dispatch some Armagi to the location to have a look, but it's not a priority right now," the old Styx said, clasping his long pale fingers together in front of his chest. "Because I have some pleasing news for you."

Danforth waited for him to continue.

"We've decided to proceed with the offensive on GCHQ. We're going in later today. And I know you would like to come along, too."

"That's wonderful. Thank you." Danforth nodded, although it was one of the last places on Earth he wanted to be.

Drake was leaning over the fence at the side of the field, propping himself up with his good arm as he was violently sick.

Jiggs regarded him with concern; the nausea was clearly intensifying, just as he'd expected it to.

"Our heavy friend back in the Norfolk village was right about providing us with old-fashioned transportation," Drake croaked without looking up. "Talk about being thrown back into the Middle Ages."

"They do the job," Jiggs replied.

Drake groaned. "Sure, but being jogged up and down on that bloody animal isn't helping me one little bit."

"Don't you listen. He doesn't mean it, old chap," Jiggs whispered to Drake's horse as he stroked its neck. Jiggs was holding its reins and those of his own mount as he waited for Drake to recover. "He thinks you're really a wonderful horse. He's just not himself at the moment," he added conspiratorially to the horse.

"If you're talking about me behind my back to that refugee from a glue factory, I'll n —" Drake said, but stopped as the cramp in his stomach made him want to double up.

Jiggs shook his head sadly, wishing that he was able to do more for his friend. They'd been giving main roads and any built-up areas a wide berth, which wasn't ideal, because a hefty dose of antiemetics from a pharmacy or a hospital would have improved Drake's condition.

Although Jiggs didn't really need to consult it because of his exceptional sense of direction, he slid the map from his pocket and re-checked the cross-country route they were intending to take to Parry's estate in Scotland. In normal circumstances they would have naturally gravitated toward London, as it would have been a good place to try to pick up on Parry's whereabouts. But if things were as bad down south as the portly man and the villagers had made out, it wasn't somewhere that Jiggs wanted to tangle with, not with Drake in his condition. So they'd decided that Parry's estate was the next best place to head for; even if Parry wasn't there, there was likely to be a satphone or two hidden away in the house.

Jiggs was just putting the map away when he heard a faint clicking from close by. "Hello, what's that?" he asked, frowning. He listened intently, and when it came again a few seconds later he realized that it must be coming from the Bergen roped to the back of his horse.

As Drake shuffled back he found Jiggs between the horses, his Bergen at his feet, staring at a tracker.

"This just woke up," Jiggs said, holding it up so Drake could see the needle, which was showing tiny fluctuations at the lower end of the scale and giving off the occasional rash of clicks, like a drowsy cricket.

"What's the direction of the signal?" Drake asked weakly. "It's probably an echo from one of the subterranean beacons."

"That's the surprising thing. I don't think it is," Jiggs replied as, holding the tracker in front of him, he turned ninety degrees to the direction they'd just come. "In fact, it's originating from the south."

"The south?" Drake repeated.

Jiggs moved the tracker in small increments until the signal was at its strongest and making a regular ticking sound, with the needle holding remarkably steady. "No question about the direction. And from the bearing, I'd put my money on London as the source."

"Well, what do you know?" Drake said, visibly perking up. "But the only reason anyone would activate a beacon here on the surface is if they wanted to attract attention . . . ours, because who else is likely to have the technology to spot a VLF signal, or even be on the lookout for transmissions at that end of the scale?"

"And none of the beacons were left on the surface, were they? They were all taken down to the inner world. So how did this one find its way back?" Jiggs said, anticipating the second point Drake was about to make.

"Eddie and I were able to locate and rescue Chester from Martha because of his beacon, but it's not him this time. So it has to be someone from our team," Drake concluded. "Someone's made it home again, even after the nukes went off."

"Will?" Jiggs suggested.

Drake shrugged. "Or Elliott or Sweeney — or, if our mission went completely pear-shaped, it could even be the Styx," he said, heaving himself up onto his horse. "There's only one way to find out. We're going to London."

"Do you really feel up to it?" Jiggs asked. "It would be wiser to stick to the original plan and head for your father's house."

"Not on your nelly," Drake replied. He reached forward to stroke the mane of his horse. "I just wish this thing came with better suspension."

"So tell me," Will whispered, "we've now jumped a total of four fences and gone through three back gardens, but where are we heading? Do you actually know?"

Since they'd left David's house, Elliott had been leading them uphill through his neighbors' gardens to avoid using the road. Without any hesitation, she now raised her arm and pointed. "Yes, that way."

"Any particular reason you want to go that way? Because we're not too safe out here, you know."

Elliott began to answer, but he gently placed a finger on her lips. "Don't worry — you don't need to answer me. Remember I'm only a lowly human, here to do your bidding."

"Oh, do shut up, Will," she said, as she ducked away from his hand, but she was smiling.

She led the way, and he followed without question as they clambered over the next fence, landing silently on the other side.

This house was massive, even compared to David's, but Will noticed something as he studied it through his lens. "Old people's home," he remarked, as he saw a single walker on the terrace. It was in front of the conservatory that ran across the rear of the property, and in which many armchairs were facing the garden.

"We had quite a few of these in Highfield for the oldies, but why's that walker been left out there?" Will wondered. As he examined the back of the building in more detail, he could see that there were several more walkers on the terrace and the lawn, but they had been knocked over. And some of the large panes of glass in the conservatory had been shattered.

"I wonder where they went, the old people," he muttered to himself, because Elliott was up ahead and out of earshot as they kept moving, repeating the process of climbing over the fences and crossing through garden after garden.

They'd just landed in yet another when Will stopped all of a sudden. "Wow!" he exhaled, adjusting the lens over his eye as the moon broke through the clouds to wash the scene with an ethereal light. "Wow," he said again, at the topiary animals dotted around the garden; a cockerel and an eagle faced each other, but it was impossible to see what the other creatures were supposed to be because the bushes hadn't been trimmed for a while. As Will and Elliott walked between them, they were conscious of the dark windows of the house; it felt like they were being watched.

Will began to take an interest in the house. "The garden's

pretty cool, but get a load of that," he exhaled. The roof rose to an acute point, with ornate eaves carved in a dark wood. And the windows were all very narrow and stylized.

"It's just a house," Elliott replied.

"Yeah, but it's like something from a story. Dad would have given anything to live somewhere like this," Will said. "A fine example of Gothic architecture," he added, sounding a lot like Dr. Burrows.

As with all the other houses, it appeared to be unoccupied, but it was impossible to tell for certain. Elliott turned toward the building and looked at it carefully before striding toward it. Will hurried to catch up, taking hold of her arm.

"Um, I don't mean that we should go inside," he said, "if that's what you're thinking."

Elliott indicated the house with a sweep of her hand. "Why not? We heard what David said, but don't you think we should find out what's been happening for ourselves? After all, we've got a long way to go yet, and we need to know what we're likely to come up against."

"Have we? Do we?" Will tried to say as Elliott suddenly put on a burst of speed toward the house. With a grunt of exasperation, he sprinted after her.

They found the front door wide open. For a moment Elliott seemed to hesitate as she stared up at the first floor, and Will thought she'd had a change of heart. But then she clicked the safety off her rifle and made her way inside.

They entered together, their weapons at the ready. There was no entrance hall as such, but a large room that seemed to extend across most of the ground floor. Will saw a magnificent grand piano with many shelves of books behind it, then his gaze came to rest on the far wall.

"Looky here," he said. Glass-fronted cabinets stretched the length of the wall. For the moment, Will forgot where he was, unable to resist a closer examination of the archaeological artifacts they housed. Fragments of glazed pots, tools, and jewelry were all on display. "Roman," he said, peering at the first cabinet, before heading to the second. "Greek, I think . . . yeah . . . and these vases might be Etruscan. Amazing," he muttered over and over.

"Yes, amazing," Elliott said, although with little enthusiasm. It was clear that someone passionate about history had lived here, but this was hardly the time to dwell on it.

Particularly so because while Will walked from cabinet to cabinet, eagerly taking in the different items, Elliott had found something disquieting. She hadn't noticed before but several articles of furniture had been knocked over farther inside the room, and her finely honed sense of danger went into overdrive when she spotted a dark trail on the polished wooden flooring. Examining it more closely she found that the trail was streaks of dirt and possibly blood, which traced a route from the front door to the staircase.

"I'm going up to check upstairs," she informed Will, pointing to the floor above.

"Be with you in a minute," he said.

She climbed the stairs, on the way up finding a discarded shoe and a set of false teeth. At the top of the stairs there was a wide landing that led to an equally wide corridor. Moonlight flooded in through large picture windows at each end, allowing her to see where the dark trail went.

She stuck her head into each room as she moved down the corridor, finding they were empty and the beds all made. But then, halfway along the corridor, the dark trail continued up a small flight of carved wooden stairs to the next floor, which she assumed to be the attic. Pointing her rifle ahead of her, she began up the stairs.

However, as she reached the top, her foot caught against something and she toppled forward. As she tried to stop herself from falling, her finger twitched against the trigger, and her rifle fired.

The shot resounded deafeningly around the large room.

"Oh!" she exclaimed, quickly picking herself up.

It was cold. The skylights in the steeply slanted roof on either side of her were mainly broken, so the attic was exposed to the elements.

Which explained why she hadn't smelled the many dead bodies in various states of mutilation.

She'd been brought down by one of the cadavers stretched out at the top of the stairs, but they were everywhere.

Some were half eaten, and some very much full of life as Styx grubs burrowed away inside them.

"Oh —" she breathed again, swallowing hard as she realized what she'd blundered into.

This was obviously where the Armagi had brought the occupants of the houses for breeding. Some of these poor unfortunates had been impregnated, while others were there for food. And many of the victims had been elderly — she could see that from the wispy gray hair and aged features. That explained why the old people's home had been empty.

A terrible wailing sound came from just feet away. She wheeled toward the area of roof closest to her.

One of the younger Armagi — a lizard-type creature some four feet from nose to tail — was clinging to it. Its head swiveled toward her.

The head of a human child.

Its nostrils flared as its forked tongue flicked toward her.

It wailed again, then another lizard took up the cry, then another. The sound of her rifle had frightened them. She could see it in their shining eyes.

They were everywhere, probably as many as twenty of them, but there was no way she was about to stop and count. And they were all clinging to the roof timbers, watching her through their slit pupils, their mouths wet with blood.

In addition to the lizards, she glimpsed large objects tucked into the corners of the roof space. They resembled the cocoons of moths or butterflies, but on a giant scale.

She heard Will calling her name, but she held absolutely still.

The lizard nearest to her was sniffing her, but it had stopped wailing. However, some of the others continued in a random pattern, much like chickens when they've been disturbed. And these young Armagi were still very clearly alarmed by her appearance.

The closest lizard sniffed her once more. Elliott braced herself, wondering if it was about to use its rows of needle teeth on her.

Then the most remarkable thing happened. It appeared to simply lose interest, scurrying up to the apex of the roof with a *tac-tac* noise as its clawed feet dug into the surface.

Elliott remained stock still, not even allowing herself to breathe.

Will's panicked voice came again from the floor below. Elliott heard a door slam — this seemed to agitate the lizards all over again, making them scuttle in every direction. Then another door slammed on the floor below. Will was looking for her. Of course he was — he'd heard the rifle shot.

And at any moment he'd come up the stairs and into the attic.

Elliott had to do something.

She took a step backward, then another, lifting her foot over the gored cadaver. Then she was on the wooden staircase. She spun around and threw herself down it, only to cannon straight into Will at the bottom.

"For God's sake!" he cried. "Where have you . . . what happened?"

"Just shut up," she said, pushing him backward. She kept going until he was up against the corridor wall, where his shoulder knocked a painting to the ground.

As it hit the wooden floor with a crash, Elliott pressed herself hard up against him, so that he was sandwiched between her body and the wall.

"This isn't really the time or the pl —" he said, with a nervous chuckle.

"Idiot," she snapped, hearing the commotion from the floor above. She was petrified that they might swarm down the wooden stairs. But more than this, she knew — with almost complete certainty — that the calls of the frightened lizards were summoning the adult Armagi. She knew this because the wails of the lizards had been piercing to her, something she found impossible to ignore, as if those young creatures had been her own children, her own babies, crying out for help.

"I think I can save you," she said to Will. She was crying now, her breaths short.

"You can *what?*" he demanded.

"The Armagi are coming. They'll get you," she shot back.

"Me? Well, let's get out of here," he shouted.

"*You* won't be able to run from them," she gasped.

"What about you? Why not you, too?" he asked.

"I don't know. I'll be OK." She felt around Will's waist. "Where's your knife? Give it to me! Quick!"

Will reached to the scabbard on his belt and pulled it out.

Elliott snatched it from him, then whipped off her mitten. She held the knife over her palm, then pushed it down hard, cutting her hand open.

"What — why?" Will gasped, seeing how deep the incision was. She reached for his face, wiping her blood over him, smearing it down his cheeks.

"What the . . . ?" he shouted.

"Keep quiet," she whispered urgently. "I can hear them."

And he could, too. Unless it was the wind, he was sure that there was a humming sound. Something *was* coming.

She continued to pump her hand to produce more blood, spreading it all over him, over his arms and down his thighs.

"If I can just fool them into thinking . . . ," she was saying as they heard a loud thump from above. Something had landed on the roof.

"Is that one?" he asked. Without knowing what he was doing, he began to pull away from Elliott, trying to extricate himself from between her and the wall.

"No, for God's sake, just keep still," she said, gritting her teeth as she raked the tip of the knife across her palm again. Even more blood was flowing from it as she ran her hand all around his head, streaking his white hair with it.

"Keep absolutely still," she hissed at him again.

There were two crashes, the floor under their feet vibrating with each impact.

A pair of Armagi had flown in through the windows at either end of the corridor.

Will and Elliott hardly dared draw breath, let alone move.

They could hear and feel each impact of the Armagi's clawed, griffinlike feet as the fearsome creatures advanced down the corridor from both directions. And through his lens Will was able to make out more of their appearances as they came closer, their transparent feathers gleaming in the moonlight, the muscles in their limbs slipping over each other like slabs of polished ice.

One headed straight for the wooden staircase, the other

closing in on Will and Elliott. She had her back to what was going on in the corridor and couldn't see.

But Will could.

The floorboards creaked under the Armagi's weight as it came toward them, and stopped right behind Elliott. The height of a tall man, it had compound eyes like an insect, and they now rested on Will and Elliott.

Its head was translucent, the wall of the corridor visible through it, but fluids pumped around inside its cranium, and something pulsed like a tiny black heart at the very top of its exoskeleton.

Will could see the Armagi so clearly through his lens. It had a beak like a bird's. But as it took another step closer to Elliott, Will could see that it wasn't a solid beak because it had opened up into four insectlike mandibles.

Elliott's body stiffened against Will's as the Armagi inclined its head and scraped the upper pair of mandibles along the top of her shoulder. All the time, it was drawing in air, sniffing.

Then it was still for a moment, as if it had picked up a scent.

Will couldn't breathe — he didn't dare.

The Armagi swiveled away from him and Elliott, making a quarter turn. It had a small pair of transparent sticks at the nape of its neck — they were the diameter of knitting needles. Will watched as they began to beat together, faster and faster until they were moving so quickly they became a blur. They were vibrating together, but he couldn't hear anything. He wondered if Elliott could. Then he realized that they weren't that dissimilar from the insect legs that sprouted from the same spot on the Styx women's spines.

But Will couldn't think about that now. For a moment he dared to let himself believe that he and Elliott were going to escape with their lives. Or, if Elliott thought that there was no danger to her, then *he* might be about to escape.

But then the Armagi swiveled back around toward them, its head jerking in the twitchy movement reminiscent of reptiles.

It sniffed at Elliott again. Then, for the longest time, it seemed to be just poised there, observing her and Will.

Will couldn't tell if Elliott's plan was working and the creature was confused, or if it was about to lurch at them and claw them both apart. It was rather like trying to divine the emotions of a heavy statue that was about to tip over and crush you.

Will could feel Elliott's heart pounding against his, and her blood dripping down his face. His eye with the lens was protected, but the other one wasn't, and some of her blood had run straight into it. It made him desperate to blink, but he couldn't.

Then, with another loud creak, the Armagi shot over to the wooden stairs, and disappeared up them.

Only now did Will dare to release his breath. "They've gone," he whispered barely audibly, blinking his eye a few times.

Elliott didn't respond for a moment, then she replied equally as quietly, "We have to get out. Now."

She moved back from him, and together they tiptoed along the corridor, then down the stairs and out through the front door. Once in the open, they clambered over the low wall at the front of the house, and kept going through several more drives until they'd reached one with thick undergrowth, where they could hide and catch their breath.

Will saw Elliott trying to move her hand and wincing at the pain. From a pocket of his coat he took out one of David's handkerchiefs that he'd helped himself to, and gently bound her palm. Then he just held her in his arms.

Eventually, as he began to relax, Will said, "Well, that was quite something." He blew out through his lips at the sheer understatement, his relief so great that he wanted to laugh. But he didn't. "At least now we know what an Armagi looks like."

Elliott mumbled something, but Will didn't catch it. "And I don't know quite *how* you knew to do that back there — that trick with your blood," he added.

She remained silent.

"But thank you," he said.

As Drake lay on the ground, with his eyes closed, Jiggs was scanning the distant motorway through his binoculars. "There are a couple of trucks on the hard shoulder . . . then we've got an army transporter, and some cars in a small pile-up . . . but sod all is moving."

As the horses grazed, one of them snorted loudly. Drake copied it, then said, "So if we swapped the horses for a car, we could be there in under an hour. If only those pesky Armagi didn't have a thing for engines."

The horse snorted again.

"That's about it," Jiggs agreed. "If you're finding this too much, we can drop the idea of going to London. What we're going to run into when we reach the outskirts is anyone's guess. Wall-to-wall Armagi? Are we really going to fight our way into the center? And for what?"

"To find someone with a satphone, or where some military is holed up?"

"If anyone's actually left," Jiggs countered.

"Someone has to be. . . ." Drake groaned as he sat up. One of the dressings on his head had come loose and was flapping in the breeze. He tugged it off, examining the stains on it with distaste. "This isn't getting any better."

"It's a radiation burn. It takes time to heal," Jiggs said.

"Tell it that if it doesn't get a move on, there won't be any point," Drake said, then turned to Jiggs as something occurred to him. "We've just left Cambridgeshire and we're in Essex now — is that right?"

Jiggs nodded.

"I've got a suggestion. Remember that hush-hush underground train my father took us on, that got us all the way into London? The one that the government built during the Cold War, so they could save their hides if Russia attacked?"

"Yes, of course I do. It went as far as the BT Tower. I was on that train with you," Jiggs said with a wry smile.

"Oh, yes, I forgot. The invisible man," Drake replied. "So, tell me, approximately how far is the station from here?"

"Fifteen miles," Jiggs said. "But there's no electricity so the train won't be able to run."

"Of course not, but how about if we ride the gee-gees like the clappers over there, then use the tunnel? We can take it all the way in, on foot," Drake proposed. "Sure beats being strafed by Armagi when we hit the 'burbs."

Without a further word, they got back on their horses and began to ride toward the secret station under the reservoir.

"It's so quiet," Will said, as they remained hidden in the overgrown border at the front of the house. "This is London. Normally there'd be cars, voices . . ."

More from shock than anything else, he'd been talking in an attempt to fill the silence, but trailed off as he realized he didn't have anything to add. He began to rub Elliott's blood from his face with his sleeve.

It had been a while since she'd spoken, but now Elliott cleared her throat. "Don't do that," she said.

He looked at her through his lens, but didn't ask her why.

"You wouldn't have believed what was in that room," she said tonelessly. "Styx lizards like the one in the warehouse that bit Chester's father. Grubs . . . in bodies, and the bodies were mostly the old people from down the road. That's where they'd been taken. And these large pod things. There were Armagi in them, waiting to hatch." She shuddered. "But the bodies were just terrible . . . so many and half eaten . . . just terrible."

Will nodded.

She adjusted the handkerchief dressing he'd put on her injured palm. "And the weird thing is that I sort of knew what I was walking into. I had a feeling what I'd find in that house . . . up in that room. . . ."

"You did?" Will said. "But I don't understand. Why did we go anywhere near it, then?"

"I had to. It was as if they were calling out to me," she tried to explain, barely finishing the sentence before she gushed, "Oh, Will, you should be with Stephanie, not me. I'm not like you. I'm something else. I'm this monster, and it's not good that you're with me. . . . I'm dangerous."

Will swallowed uncomfortably. "Stephanie . . . *what?*" he managed to get out.

Elliott was shaking her head slowly. "I could tell you liked her," she said, then lowered her voice. "And I know that you two spent time together when we were trapped in the Complex."

Hit by this bombshell, Will was speechless for a moment, then gabbled, "No, I didn't . . . I think she wanted . . . but nothing . . ."

Elliott leaned against him, her shoulder touching his arm. "It's OK."

"No, it's not OK," Will said.

"It is. Really it's OK. Because I can't tell you how long we've got together. And you shouldn't be alone," Elliott said, her voice barely audible.

"I don't believe this!" Will objected, becoming very upset.

"Not so loud," she warned him. She looked up at the roof-top of the Gothic house, which was just visible down the road. "The Armagi are still there, and we don't want them to come looking." She rose to her feet. "I should never have brought you with me," she declared. "If I could take you back, I would."

Will spluttered with indignation. "Wh . . . what do you mean — you're talking like you're in charge of me or something!"

Putting her head back, Elliott looked at the night sky. "I am," she said simply. "All of you. Because I can put an end to all this." She lowered her gaze to Will. "And I know now that I can protect you from the Armagi. I can do that." She held out her injured hand as if considering it. "But I can't do anything about Limiters, not for either of us. So we have to take it slowly and be very bloody careful as we go, and only move at night. And we need somewhere safe before dawn's here."

There was a muffled *phut* sound as the lock blew on the iron door. In fact, the sound of the door swinging open on its hinges and hitting the wall beside it was louder and more noticeable.

"Nicely done," Jiggs said, then he and Drake quickly made their way back to where the small plastic explosive charge had gone off. They both stopped to peer down the crumbling concrete steps in the gap in the embankment around the reservoir, where the now open door was waiting for them.

"We're in," Drake said, and they descended the damp steps. After several flights they walked out into the train station. As they shone their lights along the platform, on which large drums of cable, rotting sandbags, and rusted metal parts had been left, there was the train they'd ridden for their previous journey to BT Tower.

"Feels odd being here again without Elliott and Will and the rest of the team," Drake said. "And no sign of that guy from the Old Guard who looks after the place. Parry said he effectively lives down here."

"Maybe we caught him on his tea break," Jiggs joked. "We go that way," he added, and they moved to the far end of the platform.

"Into the guts of hell," Drake whispered and, for a moment, they both held still, staring into the dismal darkness in front of the locomotive. The brickwork around the tunnel opening was stained with lime and efflorescence, and the air reeked of stagnant water.

"I seem to have spent my whole life going into dark places I didn't want to," Drake said wearily. "I suppose there's no reason why that should change now."

Jiggs stamped his feet as if he had enough energy for the two of them. "Come on, Drake, chin up, old man. What do they say about there being light at the end of the tunnel?"

"Don't believe them," Drake said. "They have no idea what they're talking about."

15

MARTHA WAS BURSTING with excitement when she returned to the farmhouse.

"Come to me, my dearest boy, come to me," she bellowed, beckoning Chester over. Stephanie noticed her hands were spotted with blood and grime; no doubt that meant another sheep had met its end and was heading for her cooking pot. "Have I got some news for you!"

She threw her arms around Chester and squeezed him while he just regarded her impassively.

"Well, have you?" he asked.

"Yes, I have!" she cried. "One of my fairies seems to have picked up the scent trail of your nasty man."

"Danforth? You're sure?" Chester said, his whole manner transforming. "You've really got him for me?"

"Yes, my fairy can take us to him," she replied.

"Oh, you wonderful woman," Chester shouted, only now responding to Martha's embrace. He pressed his cheek against hers. "I could eat you!" he said.

Be careful what you're saying, Stephanie thought wryly to herself. *She could eat you, too!* Stephanie had been told about Martha's penchant for human flesh, but hadn't thought too much about it until she'd actually met the woman. She could quite see Martha was capable of it.

"Where is he, then? Where's Danforth?" Chester asked.

"I can't tell how far away he is, but my fairy can show us," Martha replied.

"How does that actually work?" Chester said rather sharply, as if he had suddenly begun to doubt what she was telling him. "Do your fairies speak to you or something?"

Martha nodded. "In a way, yes, they do. You see, I've learned to understand the signs they give each other — they give them to me, too. And one fairy has just flown back to me, while the other is keeping a watch on Nasty Man for us."

Chester seemed satisfied with this answer, and Stephanie shook her head as the two of them continued to hug each other tight, making *mmmm*ing noises. Both of them were unhinged in their own ways: Martha because she'd lost her son and then been subjected to years of isolation, and Chester because of what he'd been through at the hands of the Styx, culminating in his parents' untimely death. Two people, both deeply injured, and united by their losses. But Stephanie didn't kid herself that their relationship was anything other than delicate, like two plates spinning on poles beside each other. At any moment, either one — or even both — of those plates could come crashing down.

Finally relaxing his grip on the rotund woman, Chester held her at arm's length. "We should get going, then."

Martha hesitated. "Why don't I ask my fairies to do the job for us, and kill Nasty Man? Then we don't need to go anywhere."

No, no, no. Stephanie was willing Chester not to agree. She had seriously considered running away to extricate herself from this incredibly bizarre situation, but Chester had told her to forget that as an option. Not just because of the risk from the Armagi — he'd said that he wouldn't be able to stop Martha from setting the Brights on Stephanie the moment she walked out.

Chester hadn't replied to Martha's suggestion. In fact, he looked thunderous.

"Why don't I just tell them to finish him off, my dearie?" Martha asked him again. "Then there'd be no need to move from here, where we're happy and safe."

"No way! That creep is mine. And you bloody tell your Brights not to touch a bloody hair on his foul head. In fact, I want them to protect him . . . and keep him safe for me," Chester growled, his eyes flashing. "He's mine!"

"Of course, dearie, it's all right, it's all right," Martha cooed, stroking his hair at the temple. "Of course, I'll do that for you. Anything."

Chester suddenly let go of Martha, and pulled away from her. He stood still for a moment, pressing his lips together as if in deep thought. "If we don't know how far away Danforth is, then we need transportation . . . something with some oomph. Wait here," he said, going into the hallway and grabbing his jacket from the hook. Then he threw open the front door and stormed out from the house.

There was no way that Stephanie could follow him, so she settled back in her usual armchair, clutching the old goose-down comforter around her that she'd taken from a bedroom, and simply stared out of the window. It wasn't as if there was anything else for her to do in the place — no new magazines, and on most days not even a radio station to listen to. Several hours passed, and she had slipped into her usual stupor — the only way she could get through the day — when an engine roared outside.

Stephanie and Martha, armed with her crossbow, were immediately at the window, peering out to see who it was. Chester stepped from the vehicle, a four-wheel drive that was caked in mud. He gestured for them to come outside.

"Found this four-by-four on a nearby farm the other day when I was having a look around, and thought it might come in useful. There were some spare cans of diesel around the farm, too, so I've put them in the back, and some canned food so we don't have to eat sheep glop any longer," he said, glancing into the rear of the vehicle. Then, as he walked around the front, he slapped the hood decisively. "Come along, you two! Get your acts together. We're hitting the road!"

"I don't fancy it. I'm not riding in one of them contraptions," Martha said. She had a deep-seated mistrust of anything more complicated than her crossbow. "Anyway, who's going to steer?"

"Steer? You mean *drive*? I'm going to, because that piece of scum Parry taught me." Chester went right up to Martha. "Come along — you said you'd do anything for me. Well, I'm asking now." She looked undecided, but Chester was determined to have his way. "You know you want to help me — you know you do, Mum." He planted a big, noisy kiss on her peeling lips.

"Oh! Oh! Oh!" Martha fluttered breathlessly. She immediately colored up, swinging her shoulders like a little girl. "Oh, all right, my darling boy," she said.

"Unless it's stray animals giving us false positives, looks like the party's heating up," Parry announced.

Two of his men had simultaneously raised their hands as the thermal sensors they'd been monitoring on their laptops registered signals. On the top floor of the block of flats there were a dozen such men in total, some drawn from the SAS and others from Parry's Old Guard, all staring at their computers on various pieces of furniture they'd scavenged from the deserted floors below. Surrounding the men were the building's air-conditioning plant and the motors for the elevators, which of course hadn't been in operation for several months because of the lack of power.

Another of the men at the laptops stuck up his hand at that moment. "Over to the northwest, too, boss. Strong signal," he reported.

"Yes, it would appear that we're in play," Eddie agreed, meeting Parry's eyes. "And it's what we expected: The sensors are picking up Limiters as they move into position around the installation to catch anyone who tries to make a run for it." He switched his attention to a nearby screen, which showed a live view of GCHQ, the government's communications and signals agency. It was some five hundred yards away from where they were now, the image being piped in from one of the cameras positioned on top of the apartment building. "So the frontline troops, the Armagi, will lead the attack, with my former comrades, the Limiters, acting as the mop-up squad," he added.

"*Mop-up squad?* I never thought I'd ever hear the Styx elite being described quite like that." Parry smiled, but his eyes told a different story. Stepping closer to Eddie, he lowered his voice. "We've both sacrificed far too many men in recent weeks so Danforth's cover with the Styx could be preserved. I want you to know that the selfless behavior of your former Limiters will not be overlooked."

True to form, Eddie's response was devoid of any emotion. "Thank you, but they knew what the stakes were when they joined me," he said. "As for what's about to happen, more Limiters may die, and even though they are still blindly obeying the Styx hierarchy, I'd like to think that we can save as many lives as we can. They're only following the diktat laid down by the ruling class."

"And the Armagi?" Parry asked.

"They're a different matter entirely," Eddie replied. "I have no qualms about their destruction because I don't regard them as *people*. They're purely biological hardware, machines for killing, produced as a result of the Phase, and they have no useful place on this Earth."

Parry nodded, turning to the men in the room to address them. "Listen up. All of you switch over to the cameras now. I want you to watch the approaches. Danforth is likely to be showing up with some high-value Styx targets. Keep your eyes peeled for him, because the old Styx, and even Alex and the Rebecca twin, might not be far away. And it's also a priority for Danforth to be extracted alive. He's already taken enough risks to get us this far, and I want him out of there in one piece."

The Limiter drove into the underground parking garage and began to slow. The vehicle had barely stopped when the old Styx leaped from it, followed by Danforth.

"What kept you?" Alex snapped at them, as she slid from the backseat of the jet-black Bentley already waiting there. Striding across to a doorway, she shouted, "Come along, Rebecca, get a move on! And for God's sake, just *you* come with us. Don't bring your performing monkey with you."

As Rebecca Two emerged from the front seat, Danforth noticed that the old Styx gave her a sharp look. Or, to be more precise, he gave the young blond New Germanian officer behind the steering wheel of the Bentley a sharp look.

"Still it persists, that unholy coupling?" the old Styx said to Alex, as he caught up with her.

"Time for us to bring it to a close," Alex replied, her voice low and cold. She strode through the doorway of the parking garage and into a dark corridor with a concrete floor littered with puddles of water. "It doesn't do to have passengers," she added, shaking her head, her insect legs clicking together where they poked from behind the collar of her thick fur coat.

Danforth couldn't be sure because, in deference to their authority, he walked several paces behind Alex and the old Styx, but he was pretty certain that the Styx woman's head had turned ever so slightly in his direction as she'd uttered these words. He knew from the old Styx that the Rebecca twin's human companion was frowned upon, but he had the strongest feeling that Alex had also been talking about him. It didn't bode well. The Styx woman was unpredictable, and he felt incredibly insecure. He instinctively ran his tongue over the false tooth containing the miniaturized radio, wishing he had an opportunity to send a transmission.

They went through several more of the unlit corridors

before climbing a short flight of steps to a door. As they emerged into the daylight, stepping out onto the pavement, Danforth saw precisely where they were.

"There it is," Alex whispered. "One of the last bastions of this country's pathetic defense system, about to drop into our laps like a ripe plum."

"GCHQ," Danforth said through his gritted teeth. They all kept well in to the side of the street, which passed through several junctions as it ran all the way down to the doughnut-shaped building that he had been so instrumental in helping establish and equip.

He pointed at the high fence just visible in the distance. "You are aware that the outer boundary will be heavily monitored?" He cast his eyes around the street. "Although there's unlikely to be electricity in the rest of the town, GCHQ has its own geothermal supply, so its systems will all still be up and running."

Danforth quickly took in how many Limiters he could see along the street — three or four at the most, all tucked into doorways. "And you didn't consult me about any planned assault, so how much do you know about GCHQ's defense capability? There will be numerous — and I mean numerous — highly trained armed response units ready to counter any breaches. That capability will have been bolstered due to th —"

Alex put her head back and laughed harshly. "You funny little human!" she sneered. "Do you think that we care one iota about any of that?" She turned her attention to the installation up ahead. "And who said we'd go in through the perimeter? Watch this."

The old Styx and Rebecca Two stepped away from her as she lowered her coat from her shoulders. Her insect limbs extended to their full length and came together, beginning to vibrate.

When Danforth caught his first glimpse, he assumed that the wind had whipped up the passage of the clouds in the sky. It quickly became evident that what he was seeing was nothing to do with the weather conditions, and something very sinister.

In a vortex Armagi were swarming up high, their forms refracting the gray-blue of the sky. They began to converge together and then to descend, a solid gyre of them, like an upside-down waterspout, straight into the opening of the middle of GCHQ.

"I wonder what your fellow flesh bags will make of that," Alex said with a smirk, "for the remaining minutes they have left to live." She suddenly swung to the old Styx. "We can jettison this fool now. We have no need for him, and I find his presence tedious."

The old Styx raised his hand and a pair of Limiters appeared from nowhere, one on either side of Danforth. Then the old Styx turned his dead eyes on Danforth. "It's true. We never needed you, and we can't allow you to stay with us. There isn't any room for humans."

"We had a deal," Danforth replied, keeping his voice even. "You're going to renege on it?"

"If you'd handed us Drake's, Elliott's, and the Burrows child's heads on a platter, we'd have been more convinced of your commitment. But you didn't."

"Nevertheless, they're all dead," Danforth insisted.

The old Styx gave him a skeptical look.

"You haven't seen hide nor hair of them since I came over to you, though, have you?" Danforth pointed out.

"That may be correct, although we still have had no word from our party sent into the inner world, which is surprising. And our subsequent teams dispatched to find them have not reported back, either," the old Styx said. "That makes us suspicious that all is not as it seems."

"If something's happened to them, it's nothing to do with me," Danforth argued. "You're making a big mistake." Although he remained outwardly calm, his mind was racing. Top of his list was how he could remove his tooth and make an SOS transmission with the Limiters watching his every move.

"Take him away and finish him," the old Styx ordered, then lowered his voice. "And while you're at it, get rid of that New Germanian at the same time. Make sure the bodies are hidden out of sight." He'd lowered his voice to ensure that Rebecca Two hadn't overheard his order, but in any case she was too intent on the deluge of Armagi.

As one of the Limiters began to push Danforth down the street, in the opposite direction from GCHQ, he managed to grab another glimpse of the continued cascade of Armagi from the sky.

"Move it," the Limiter growled, striking him in the kidneys with the stock of his rifle.

Despite the pain, Danforth allowed himself a small smile. At that very moment, the Styx woman was under the impression that she was going to achieve a significant victory. But she was about to get a rude awakening. If everything went according to plan, at least he'd have helped to deal a major blow against the Styx before he lost his life. And he still hadn't given up all hope; if the timing fell to his advantage and the strike took place before he'd been killed, it might create enough of a diversion for him to escape.

No. He sighed. That was hoping for too much, with this pair of deadly soldiers on the case. They were too well trained for that. Nothing, short of an armed intervention, would put them off their mission. He was dead. He accepted that.

He pretended to stumble.

"Faster," one of the Limiters scowled. "Stop sandbagging."

The soldier was right. Danforth was trying to buy time. He peered up at the rooftops of the buildings around him, wondering if Parry had a camera on him. He thought it unlikely — he was too far from the Doughnut.

As they went past the entrance to the underground parking garage, one of the Limiters peeled off. The other soldier continued to shove Danforth along the main street, then took him around a corner and into a side road.

There the Limiter slammed him against the wall of the building, with such force that he fell to the pavement.

"Stay down," the Limiter growled, slipping a scythe from the scabbard on his belt.

Danforth looked from the dull steel of the blade to the leafless branches of the trees dotted along the road, then to the sky.

So was this where it would end for him? In a rather ordinary road, in an ordinary town in England. It was ironic considering the places he'd been in his life.

Both Danforth and the Limiter turned to the end of the road as the other Limiter finally appeared, pushing Captain Franz before him.

"On your feet," the Limiter with the scythe growled at Danforth.

Danforth knew that when the young New Germanian arrived, they'd both be executed just as the old Styx had instructed.

"What is going on?" Captain Franz demanded, trying to straighten his chauffeur's hat as the Limiter prodded him in the back again. "Where is my Rebecca?"

Captain Franz stopped in front of Danforth.

"She's not going to be able to help you now," Danforth told him.

The New Germanian had that slightly befuddled expression that came of too many Darklighting sessions.

"Fetch Rebecca! Right now!" Captain Franz ordered the Limiters. "This is all a mistake."

Danforth took a deep breath before he spoke. "Save it. You won't get anywhere," he said to the New Germanian. "These two pathetic excuses for troops can't think for themselves." He smiled sourly at the Limiter nearest him, who had the scythe ready at his side. "You're nothing more than robots. I've known many professional soldiers in my time, and you don't come close."

Danforth was silent for a beat, trying to gauge what effect his jibes were having, but the Limiter was impossible to read. The sunken eyes in the scarred face were simply watching him. "What's the matter? Need your bug lady to tell you what to do next?"

The Limiter with the scythe struck him across the face. Danforth dropped to the pavement, and although his glasses had been broken and there were flashes of light in his eyes, he couldn't believe his luck. The Limiter hadn't used his scythe.

Not yet, anyway.

"You broke my tooth," Danforth said, adopting a whining voice but cheering inside. He reached into his mouth and detached the false molar, palming it.

"On your feet," the Limiter with the scythe rumbled.

Although it was slippery with his blood and saliva, Danforth had just managed to press his thumbnail into the radio to activate it when the Limiter lashed out at him again.

The radio went flying.

Blast it! Danforth thought.

The Limiter pointed at him with the blade. "Little man, you've earned the right to die first."

The Styx soldier took hold of Danforth's lapels and hoisted him to his feet with the one hand, the scythe poised in the other.

Captain Franz was mumbling something incomprehensible in German. It may have been a prayer.

The Limiter plunged his knife hand toward Danforth.

It happened so fast it was as though the Limiter had simply disappeared.

Danforth tottered on his feet and, squinting through his bloodied eyes, met Captain Franz's even more befuddled gaze. "Where'd he go?" he mumbled.

Then they both saw the Limiter.

He was stretched out on the far side of the road, without his head, his body mangled.

Despite Danforth's taunts to the contrary, Limiters were consummate professionals, and the other soldier wasn't fazed by the death of his comrade. He wasn't going to wait around for any explanations before he reacted. Moving on pure instinct, he swooped at Danforth and seized hold of him.

He may have been thinking of using Danforth as a shield instead of killing him right away, but the Bright still struck, biting off a good part of the Limiter's face and neck. His head lolled to one side, a fountain of red spurting from his severed jugular. Then he simply folded to the ground at Danforth's feet.

"Was war das?" Captain Franz cried, gaping up at the sky, although the Bright was now nowhere to be seen.

"I have absolutely no idea," Danforth said, retrieving his glasses. One lens was missing, but the other was still held in the frame, despite it being cracked. "And I'm not about to stick around to find out."

There was a yelp from the corner. "Johan! What are you doing here?" Rebecca Two had come sprinting down the main road, but now slid to a halt as she spotted her beloved New Germanian.

"Oh, Rebecca," the New Germanian replied, looking shellshocked as he held out a limp hand to her.

"I thought something was wrong. . . . I sensed it," she said.

Danforth wasn't in the mood for any sentimentality.

For a small man, he still knew how to handle himself. Throwing his arm around Captain Franz's neck so he had him in a half nelson, Danforth pressed the Limiter scythe to the man's throat. Thinking it might come in useful, he'd retrieved the weapon at the same time as his spectacles. "Hold it!" he ordered Rebecca Two.

"OK — just please don't hurt him," she implored Danforth, then spotted the Limiter's blood on Captain Franz's face. She went to take a step. "But what happened to you, Johan? You're bleeding."

"I'm warning you! Stay put!" Danforth said.

"What did this man do to you?" she asked, throwing a furious glance at Danforth.

"It's not my blood," Captain Franz replied, before Danforth increased the stranglehold to stop the New Germanian from saying more.

"You killed these Limiters," Rebecca Two accused Danforth, but she didn't sound very sure of herself as she made out the headless body of the soldier across the road, and the other's lethal wounds.

"Your men had orders to execute both of us," Danforth told her.

"Why?" she cried.

"Isn't that a bit obvious? We're both superfluous humans," Danforth replied. "Now I want you to keep your voice down, because you're coming with me."

"I am not," Rebecca Two retorted.

"You are if you want your boyfriend to live," Danforth threatened. He dug the tip of the scythe into Captain Franz's throat.

"No, don't! Please don't hurt him," Rebecca Two implored Danforth. "I'll do what you say."

"And before we go, I need you to find something for me," Danforth said. He peered at the middle of the road. "It looks like a tooth."

"A tooth?" Rebecca Two had just asked, when the ground under their feet shook and there was a cranium-rattling bang. The Rebecca twin was knocked from her feet by the blast, a huge cloud of dust billowing down the street toward her.

Danforth swore, glancing at Rebecca Two where she had fallen. "Looks like it's just you and me, then, blondie," he whispered into Captain Franz's ear.

"Nein, Rebecca, *nein, nein,"* the New Germanian was mumbling.

"Don't get your knickers in a twist; I doubt that she's dead," Danforth said as he pushed Captain Franz into the road where he'd spotted his miniature radio. Once he'd retrieved it, Danforth gave Rebecca Two another glance. "Shame I can't take her with me. She'd have been an interesting subject for interrogation," he said with regret.

Captain Franz was also looking at her with regret. *"Nein, nein, nein,"* he was still mumbling, as Danforth frog-marched him quickly away.

"There she blows," Parry said, as the pictures from the cameras flickered from the explosion. As they settled down, the views of what was left of GCHQ were obscured by palls of dust and smoke. The detonation had been timed for the moment the stream of Armagi finished their aerial entry and were inside the installation, and searching in vain for anyone to kill.

"So zero fatalities on our side?" Eddie asked.

"I sincerely hope so. It was evacuated some weeks ago, except of course for the skeleton staff needed to keep up the appearance that it was business as usual," Parry replied. "And they should have escaped through the underground evacuation tunnels — there are several of th —"

"Sir," one of the soldiers manning a laptop cut in. "We've just received a burp from Danforth. He's asking to be extracted. And he says he's got a hostage with him."

"The rest of you pack up your kit! We're moving out now!" Parry ordered, as he went over to the soldier. "OK, where did Danforth say he was?" he asked.

Alex and the old Styx had been fortunate. They'd been tucked well into the side of the street when the blast hit, but it had still thrown both of them to the ground.

Alex was laughing as the air began to clear and she saw what little remained of GCHQ. The Doughnut had been reduced to a pile of rubble, the few parts of it still standing enveloped in flames. "So they planted charges and waited for us to turn up, then blew the whole place. . . . Is that the best that the poor little flesh bags can come up with?" she said.

"They saved us the effort of demolishing it," the old Styx said, gazing at what was left.

Alex had stopped laughing and was instead making a clucking sound as she noticed how much dust had settled on her coat. "Although it pains me to lose some of my children, they're Armagi, and there are just so very many of them now," she said, as she began to pat her coat down, using her human limbs for the front and her insect ones for the back. "It's not the same as when they took my Warriors from me. The humans only made things worse for themselves when they changed the game."

"Yes, and they haven't quite realized that anything they attempt now is futile," the old Styx agreed, nodding. "It's too late for them."

But Alex wasn't listening. She'd stopped brushing her coat, and there was a sadness in her eyes. "But I will never, *ever* forgive Will Burrows and the rest of them for slaughtering my Warrior Class — my true children — in that warehouse," she said in a low, smoldering voice.

The old Styx had his mind on more pressing matters. Now that the smoke and dust were clearing, he'd been glancing at the street around them, and a frown had appeared on his normally expressionless face. "But where did Rebecca go?" he asked.

16

"**WHOOP! — THERE WE** go again," Chester said, switching on the window wipers as pieces of Armagi and the liquid that coursed through their veins splattered the windshield for the umpteenth time.

He'd been driving like a lunatic, not easing off on the speed even when the motorway was full of obstacles. On several occasions he'd clipped discarded vehicles in the way, almost losing control of the four-by-four and weaving all over the road because he'd been going so fast. And each time there had been a collision, he'd laughed it off, although Martha looked petrified as, sitting beside him, she hung on to her seat belt for dear life. And Stephanie didn't allow herself a moment's rest, because if they were about to crash, she wanted to be ready for it.

They'd had a welcome respite from the journey when they'd stopped to heat up some cans of food. But before they'd eaten, Martha had wandered off. Stephanie spotted her at the top of a small hill, where she seemed to be simply staring at the sky. When Martha finally returned, she told Chester that she'd learned from the Brights that "Nasty Man" was on the move, but they were still going in the right direction to reach him. And she said that a Bright would be remaining with him at all times, to continue to track his movements.

Despite what she'd told Chester, Stephanie had no idea how Martha could learn this from these large mothlike creatures that rarely seemed to stop zipping around the place. Chester didn't seem to be very interested in this piece of news, instead keeping a whole can of baked beans with cocktail sausages to himself, while Stephanie had to share the second can with Martha.

And then, after Chester had topped up the tank with diesel, they were off again. For once the stretch of motorway ahead was relatively clear, so it didn't matter that Chester had his foot down.

But after more pieces of Armagi had showered down over them, Martha kept craning her neck to peer up at the sky through the front windshield. "They're getting tired," she said eventually.

Chester didn't reply, instead rocking his head from side to side as if he was listening to a piece of music that only he could hear. And he made no effort to slow the car. "You know, dearie, they can't keep this up all day," Martha tried again. "They need to rest just like us."

Chester began to fiddle with the controls of the air-conditioning, turning it up and angling the vent so that the breeze was blowing full in his face and ruffling his air. "Getting a bit hot in here," he said.

What he didn't say was that the combination of the warm

fug in the vehicle and Martha's lack of hygiene was particularly unpleasant. Stephanie had been shouted at by Chester and Martha when she'd opened her window in the back because they said it was too dangerous. And any benefit from the air-conditioning was minimal where she was sitting. So instead, she'd fished out her bottle of perfume from the wash bag in her Bergen and had been taking the top off to sniff it from time to time, to give herself a momentary relief from the smell. She'd gone so far as to pour a drop or two on her scarf, but this elicited such scathing looks from Martha that she didn't dare do it again.

"If we don't slow down and take it more gently, one of my fairies will be killed by those Armagi," Martha said. There was no answer from Chester, who wobbled his head again, his mouth puckered as if in a silent whistle.

"We really do have to slow down, dearie," Martha murmured, sounding quite desperate now.

Stephanie had just slipped the stopper from her perfume again and was taking a sniff when Chester yelled at Martha, "Shut up, will you?"

Stephanie was so shocked by his reaction that she almost dropped her perfume. She found she was seized by the almost irrepressible urge to punch Chester in the back of the head. He was being so selfish, dragging them all on his insane quest for revenge without the slightest consideration for anyone else. *Not even for me,* Stephanie told herself.

Suddenly she had had all she was prepared to take. Maybe it was the stifling and rather unpleasant atmosphere in the car, or possibly her fatigue, but she didn't care anymore.

"Stop the car. I want to get out!" she shouted right in Chester's ear. As she'd barely uttered a word for the whole journey, her outburst came as even more of a surprise.

"What?" Chester gasped, the four-by-four swerving wildly on the road.

"I saw a sign for motorway services up ahead," Stephanie replied. "Drop me off there."

Chester didn't wait that long, pulling over onto the hard shoulder. As both he and Martha turned to Stephanie in the backseat, she said nothing, simply grabbing her wash bag and getting out. As she began to walk away from the car, Chester hurried after her.

"What the hell is wrong with you?" he asked.

Stephanie came to an immediate halt. "What is wrong with *me*?! What about *you*?" She shook her head. "OK, let me spell it out. You are being a colossal jerk and I've had enough."

He swept a hand at the open fields on either side of the motorway. "But we're in the middle of nowhere. You'll die."

"Like you care," she snapped back at him. "Anyway, I'd rather take my chances out here than with you in that stinking car."

"Whatever," he spat, turning on his heels and stomping back toward the car. "Do whatever you want."

"You'll kill us all anyway if you keep driving like that!" Stephanie shouted after him. She snorted to show her disdain. "You're such a hypocrite! I bet your sister was run over by an idiot like you driving too fast."

Chester froze on the spot, but remained facing away

from her. He didn't know how to respond. Stephanie's remark had struck him to the very core; at that moment, something penetrated his anger and the all-consuming desire for revenge.

Stephanie wasn't finished. "And what's so stupid is, haven't you noticed there are only Armagi when we're near towns? So if we lose some Brights now, like, how will we manage when we get to London, which seems to be where we're heading?" She shrugged. "It's probably full of Armagi. So without Martha's *fairies*, we're as good as dead."

"I have to say she's right, dearie," a voice suddenly declared. Martha had come over to listen. "We need to let my fairies have a breather and some food. And you do need to steer a little slower."

"It's *drive*, Martha. You *drive* a car." Chester turned to Stephanie and cleared his throat. "Yes, maybe I've been pushing it, and I reckon we could all do with a proper break. How many miles to these services you saw?" he asked.

Stephanie didn't reply.

"Come on. Put your stuff back in the car. London isn't that far, and you love London," he argued, trying to be consolatory as he gave her a sheepish smile.

Stephanie humphed. "Yeah, so what'll we do when we get there? I just know it's going to be, like, the most terrible place on earth," she said. "I just know it."

"But it's still London, with all the shops you love. And there's bound to be something open," Chester said, maintaining his smile. He was obviously making a huge effort to be pleasant to her, but Stephanie could see the deranged light hadn't left his eyes. "Come back to the car, will you, Stepho?"

"Stepho? Nobody calls me Stepho," Stephanie said under her breath. But against her better judgment, she began walking toward the vehicle, dragging her feet and asking herself what on earth she was doing.

"And we thought it looked bad the last time we were here," Drake whispered. He and Jiggs had crawled over to the windows and were poking their heads up just high enough to gaze out over London.

With numerous stops along the way to allow Drake to recuperate, they had walked the length of the train tunnel, all the way from Essex to Central London. When they finally arrived at the platform below the BT Tower, they had immediately taken the stairs up to the same floor in the tower from which they had observed the results of the Styx's first efforts to stir things up in the capital. But that had been several months ago, and it was immeasurably worse now.

"No power anywhere. So the whole grid must be down," Drake said. "I was hoping we might be able to fire up one of the tower's dishes and get a signal through to Parry."

"See, over there on that office block," Jiggs suddenly said, squinting through the darkness as night began to set in. "It's easy to miss them in this light, but can you make out what's on the roof?"

"Crikey!" Drake replied, as he saw the many crystalline forms of the Armagi teeming on the rooftop. "How many are there?"

"Actually, the whole place is crawling with them. They're everywhere," Jiggs added, as he spotted more on other roofs.

"It's gone too far," Drake said, as he slumped down on the floor. "How do we ever pull ourselves out of this?"

Jiggs checked the tracker before answering. "The beacon has definitely shifted since we went underground." When Drake simply lay there, Jiggs was concerned. "I know that hike through the tunnel must have felt like several marathons to you. How are you holding up, old man?"

"Cream crackered, sick as a dog, everything hurts . . . shall I go on?" Drake mumbled. "And, worst of all, this leg feels like it's on bloody fire," he added, touching it just above his knee and grimacing.

"Let me take a look," Jiggs said, crawling over to him. Starting by his ankle, he rolled up Drake's combat trousers until he could see the dressing on his lower thigh, which he then peeled slowly back. He recoiled slightly. "I'm afraid the burn here is badly infected."

Drake nodded stoically. "I wondered what the smell was."

Jiggs patted his Bergen where he kept his medical kit. "Let's get away from the windows and I'll change all your dressings."

"OK, but I want to check something first," Drake said, pulling his trouser leg down, then hauling himself along on his belly across the old carpet tiles until he'd reached a section of window farther around on the tower. "Remember that army checkpoint in Charlotte Street?" he said to Jiggs. Then, grunting with the effort, he raised himself up so he could see the view below.

"You're hoping that they left a radio," Jiggs guessed. "You know that it was more than just a checkpoint there. I had a mosey 'round last time, and didn't notice any comms equipment, but there were some heavy-duty munitions in that resupply truck," he said, indicating the solid-looking truck beside the khaki awning.

Despite his discomfort, Drake was grinning. "You managed to snoop around in there, right under their noses?"

Jiggs nodded. "Piece of cake. We could really do with an ammo restock if they left anything behind when they ran for the hills."

Drake was frowning as he continued to study the scene below. "Um . . . yes, that would be great . . . but . . . shouldn't we be setting our sights a little higher?"

Jiggs was intrigued. "Why, what have you got in mind?" he asked.

Drake pointed beside the truck that Jiggs had been referring to. "If I'm not mistaken, that's a brand-spanking-new Challenger Two parked down there, ripe for the picking."

Jiggs nodded as he contemplated the latest model British Army tank. "Now that would be a stylish way to get around town," he said with a chuckle.

"Wouldn't it just?" Drake said.

Some of the buildings were shops, so badly damaged by fire that it was impossible to tell what they'd been selling.

And in other buildings, curtains flapped in the upper windows as the wind sucked down the street, and when it blew at its hardest the paper and rubbish strewn across the pavements and road began to dance and swirl.

"This place hasn't changed much," Will said as they crept along, Elliott protecting him every inch of the way.

"Careful!" she suddenly whispered, and froze.

From the door of a pub one of the young Styx lizards scuttled out. It looked at them.

There was the sound of slithering and the clicks of opening and closing jaws.

Before they knew it, other lizards were out in the open, from windows all over the same corner building, darting across its stucco facade.

The blood Elliott had spread on Will seemed to still be doing the trick because after their initial interest none of the lizards paid them much attention. As all the lizards returned inside the building again, there was the crash of a glass breaking. For the briefest moment Will could imagine that it was business as usual in the pub, and one of the punters had missed the bar with his pint.

But then Elliott nudged him on again, and he had a glimpse of the cocoons hanging from the faux-rustic beams across the ceiling of the pub — fibrous-looking pods in which Armagi would be growing.

Farther on, as they edged along the wide road filled with shops, the sky began to show the first cold gray signs of dawn. From somewhere in the distance, there was terrible screaming.

"Brrr. That's awful," Will said, also speaking for Elliott. The dark and the cold and the sheer desolation were getting to both of them.

Elliott was staring at a cinema across the street. "We should find a place to hole up. How about there?" she said.

"Sure," Will said, immediately moving with her toward it. At the entrance of the multiplex cinema, Will caught sight of the poster for a film that must have just been released when the Armagi had begun to spread. It depicted an advancing mob of zombies with leached green faces and mouths smeared crimson.

"Not so clever now, is it?" he said, indicating the poster. "People wanted gore, and they've got it big time."

Elliott didn't reply as they climbed a stationary escalator to the foyer with counters for popcorn and ice cream; then she led them into one of the smaller auditoria, with its rows of seats and blank screen.

"This'll do until it's dark again," she said, dropping heavily into one of the seats.

"You OK?" he asked, worried because she seemed so drained of energy. Will knew he was making life harder for her and slowing her up when she was in such a desperate hurry to get wherever she needed to be. And her hand was a terrible mess because she'd repeatedly sliced it open to squeeze more blood from the wound for his benefit. He wondered if this was making her feel faint.

"What's that noise?" he asked suddenly, as he heard noises above them.

"We're under a nest," she answered. "Like in that house we went into." Without lifting or moving her head, which rested against the back of the seat, her eyes slid upward to the ceiling. "The Armagi are breeding up there."

"Oh, great. So why on earth did you pick this place to stop, then?" he demanded.

Elliott yawned cavernously. "Better to be right under their noses — it's safer."

Will remembered what she'd said about being drawn to the nest she'd blundered into in the attic. "Yeah, but for who — you or me?" he asked.

He never received an answer because Elliott had fallen asleep in her chair.

"You don't know her. She's not a bad person." Captain Franz dragged appreciatively on the cigarette he was holding in his free hand, while the other was handcuffed to the end of the table.

Parry and Danforth were both scrutinizing him, and Parry's expression was unsympathetic. "Are you having a laugh, laddie? The Rebecca twin isn't *bad*, after everything she and her sister have done? After all the lives that have been ruined by the Styx, the death and destruction spread by the Armagi as they gut our country? Not a bad person? You can't be serious. Because if you are, you're more stupid than you look," Parry barked at the New Germanian officer.

"She's nothing like the others," Captain Franz insisted.

Danforth had picked up one of his Purgers from where he'd left it on the table and was repeatedly flicking the purple light on and off. "Maybe this one is a dud, which is why I've failed to deprogram our friend here?" he suggested sarcastically.

Captain Franz was indignant. "I know what I'm saying. And I've told you as much as I can remember and, yes, I witnessed some terrible things. Maybe I was walking around in a cloud because of the Darklighting, but I saw her good side, too. She has to go along with what's expected of her. She's only following orders."

"Pah!" Parry exploded. "That old chestnut. *I was only following orders.* No, your little Styx girl is as evil and driven as any of them."

"You've got my Rebecca all wrong," Captain Franz said indignantly. "And anyway, she's more than a girl. The Styx grow up faster th —"

Parry held up a hand. "For God's sake, man, I've heard enough." He noticed that Eddie and one of his men were waiting in the entrance of the tent.

"Stay there," Parry said unnecessarily to Captain Franz, then rose from his chair, putting more weight than usual on his walking stick due to his fatigue. Danforth followed him to where the two men were waiting.

"Pretty boy's all yours. See if you can get anything useful out of him," Parry said in a low voice to Eddie, glancing over his shoulder at the blond New Germanian, who was contemplating the burning tip of his cigarette.

"So he hasn't said anything useful?" Eddie asked.

"No, unless you're interested in ladies' fashion or the Styx's predilection for luxury cars," Danforth chimed in.

Parry shook his head. "He's not at all clear about where he's been, and all the places he has pointed us to are historic. The Styx have long since vacated them. He's also completely deluded about that Rebecca twin. I don't know how much of it's because of the neural damage from being over-Darklit, or from his infatuation for her."

"The infatuation is genuine?" Eddie asked.

"Seems to be," Parry replied, his gray brows hiking with incredulity.

"So you want me to use more extreme methods on him," Eddie offered.

Parry nodded. "But don't rough him up too much, because he might come in handy if we need some leverage on the Rebecca twin," Parry replied, and he and Danforth left the tent.

Danforth stopped with surprise as he noticed the row of black helicopters in the field beside their temporary camp. "When did they show up?" he asked.

"While we were in with Captain Franz," Parry replied. "Five of the very latest US Sikorsky UH-60 Blackhawks — a generous peace offering from my friend Bob. The Americans have been moving more of their fleet over to our side of the Atlantic, and these have just been delivered to us straight from one of their carriers."

"I didn't hear them arrive," Danforth said.

Parry rubbed his hands together in anticipation. "That's rather the point. They're the latest word in stealth, with highly damped engines and filtered exhaust manifolds, so the heat trace is minimal. I reckon Bob has only been so generous because he wants to see if the Armagi can hear them."

Danforth's eyes flashed with interest. "Maybe I can suggest a use for them right away." They saw a soldier emerging from one of the many tents with a small device in his hands. "If my apprentice over there has built me the scanner I asked for to track the signal from that VLF beacon I picked up before, maybe we should find out who's at the end of it."

Parry was thoughtful for a moment. "Yes, if it's one of our team back from the inner world, then maybe — just maybe — they'll have something that can help us." He looked up at the ominous clouds collecting in the sky. "Right now, I'd settle for even a minor miracle."

17

ELLIOTT SEEMED TO HAVE no hesitation when it came to choosing which way they needed to go, although there was the odd occasion when she simply stood there, as if listening to a voice that Will couldn't hear. Then she was off again, always keeping him right at her side, as they both ducked from doorway to doorway along the street, scouring the darkness ahead for Limiters or Armagi.

"I recognize this," Will told her as they came to Euston Road, and began across it using the vehicles as cover. And then later, as they continued in their painstakingly slow stop-start way, they came to a place that triggered a flood of memories for him.

"Russell Square," he told Elliott, as they turned into it. Then they saw something that halted them in their tracks. Right in front of them, in the middle of the road, was the tail section of a passenger aircraft. From the way the piece of fuselage had crashed down on top of the traffic, with many twisted and scorched cars underneath, it had happened when the troubles had only just started and people were trying to leave London as quickly as they could. And leave the country itself, if they could find a seat on an airplane.

Will gazed at the burned and peeling paint on the blue-and-white tail fins, and was only stirred into action when Elliott nudged him on. They went diagonally across the square, moving through what had been an area of grass where people once ate their sandwiches on the benches at lunchtime. It was very different now; the burning aviation fuel had scorched every inch of the ground, and the trees were reduced to severe black spikes of charcoal.

There were more sections of the aircraft to negotiate at the far corner of the square, then, as they entered the road that led from it, a change came over Elliott. She seemed to throw caution to the wind, pulling ahead of Will without taking the usual care to shield him. He didn't complain but went with it, quite relieved that they were no longer moving at a snail's pace.

As they advanced farther down the road, it struck Will why the area was so familiar — he'd walked this very same route on many occasions with Dr. Burrows, and the large building Will could see was where his father had often taken him on weekends. Sure enough, on the railings were several posters advertising the latest exhibitions, and confirming that Will was right.

He tapped Elliott on the shoulder. "So this is where we've been heading all the time?" he asked her, to which she nodded. "You do realize it's the British Museum," he told her excitedly, pointing at the three-story wing set back about twenty feet behind the railings.

She'd been staring fixedly at the building, but now turned her attention to the railings, taking hold of them as if she was considering scaling them. "How do we get in?" she asked.

"Let's go around to the front," he replied.

Elliott began to run, and Will had a job to keep up with her.

"Wait a moment," he said to her as they reached the corner. "What's the big hurry? And are you really sure this is where you need to be?"

"It is," she replied immediately.

Will took her to the main gates. Although they were closed, there was a smaller pedestrian entrance to the side, which allowed them to enter the museum grounds. Despite the fact that everything was in pitch darkness, Will had Drake's lens over his eye, which rendered the scene as clearly as if it were daylight.

As Will followed Elliott onto the forecourt, the strong connection with his past buoyed him up. This museum, with its impressive Greek-temple facade, was something he knew so well, and was so dear to him.

For a moment Will was transported back to happier and more certain times. Many of his earliest memories were from excursions to museums, particularly this one, although Dr. Burrows had had his own agenda for each visit and made little or no provision for his son, rarely stopping to explain any of the exhibits to him. But as Will had grown older and more independent, he'd left his father to go off and do his own thing, only meeting up with Dr. Burrows again by the entrance when it was time for them to return to Highfield.

But as the wind blew and all the rubbish on the museum forecourt was whipped into chaotic animation, it looked so desolate. No more was the place bustling with tourists as he remembered it from sunny Sunday mornings, with the constant squeal of London cabs pulling up to drop off or pick up people.

"They're like the lights in the Colony," Elliott said abruptly, pointing at the lampposts dotted around the grounds. Other than the fact that they didn't have the glowing luminescent orbs atop their iron posts, she was right; Will could see the similarity. He was about to agree with her when Elliott came to a stop, holding her head as if she was listening to her inaudible voice again.

She began to run toward the middle of the three doors at the main entrance. As she reached it, she was pulling on it and rattling it with such force that the sound was reverberating all around the forecourt. She was wasting her time because it was firmly locked. Then she tried the other glass doors, making just as much noise.

"Hey!" Will hissed. "Are you *trying* to draw attention to us or something?"

He could see that she was frantic to get inside, her eyes darting back and forth over the entrance as if she couldn't believe that one of the doors wasn't open.

"Are you sure this is where you want to go?" he asked.

"We've got to break in," she babbled, kicking the glass panel at the bottom of the door. "Or blow our way in."

"Stop it. For God's sake, calm down, Elliott," he urged her, shaking her by the arm. "We can't do that. Let's try over there." He pointed to the side wing of the museum at the far end of the forecourt.

She began to race where he'd indicated, to a building that was set back from the front of the museum but constructed of the same pale Portland stone.

Someone had used a car to ram the doors open, abandoning it on the steps once they were in. Will and Elliott climbed over it to reach the black-painted door, which creaked open on a single hinge.

A little way inside sheets of grimy-looking cardboard had been laid on the marble floor, with some old blankets left in a heap. Judging by the empty candy wrappers and food packets, someone had been living there, although there was no sign that they were still around.

Will made sure the door was shut behind them. He'd never been in this part of the museum before, and he quickly deduced from the signs on the doors that they were administrative offices. Then he caught up with Elliott, who was already heading in the direction of the public galleries. Whether or not she was following whatever was driving her on, they didn't need to employ any detective work to find the way through because of the scuff marks on the floor and the trail of items left there, including more candy wrappers and empty drink cans.

They went through some doors, which, from the splintered wood around the locks, Will could see had been forced, and then into the ancient Greek and Roman galleries. Will was taking in the Minoan and Mycenae items in the display cases, many of them old friends, on the way.

And then they found themselves in the museum quadrangle, a large space that had formerly been open to the elements but which was now enclosed by a modern tessellated glass roof. In the middle of the quadrangle sat the circular building called the Reading Room. Their boots echoed through the massive space as they headed toward it.

Will noticed that Elliott wasn't making the slightest effort to check around them. "S'pose we're pretty safe in here," Will said, more to assure himself than trying to make a point to her. "And whoever was here seems to have gone now. I guess a museum isn't the first place you'd think of for food," he said. His stomach had other ideas, rumbling loudly as he wondered if all the supplies of candy and Coke had been plundered by the ram-raiders in the car.

Elliott came to an abrupt halt, her head cocked to one side, as if she was listening again.

"Where to now?" Will whispered.

Holding up her hand, she shushed him, then closed her eyes.

"Well, you have the choice of African, Middle Eastern, or Eur —" he began, trying to impress her with his knowledge of the various departments, when she began to talk over him.

"No . . . up there," she said slowly, blinking her eyes open and edging farther around until the walkway extending between the Reading Room and the back wall of the quadrangle came into sight.

"Great choice," Will said. "That's the way to the Mesopotamian and ancient Egyptian gallery."

"Just tell me how to get up there," Elliott snapped.

Will held up his fingers and moved them in a walking motion. "Stairs. Other side of this. You walk up them — around and around," he replied in a sarcastic, clipped way, taking a few angry steps forward so that he could point out where the circular flight of stairs started at the side of the Reading Room. But the fact that he was irritated with Elliott was totally lost on her as she dashed toward the stairs and then sped up them without saying a word.

With a groan Will followed, and when he finally reached the

walkway at the top, he went across it and into the first room of exhibits. She wasn't there, so he moved into the adjoining room. Puffing from climbing so many stairs, he called out to her, his voice sounding very small in the network of interconnecting rooms.

"I'm here," she mumbled.

He scanned around until he located her in the dead center of the room he'd been in, standing so still he'd completely missed her. Her eyes were closed.

"Oh, there you are!" Will laughed. "This room really is a great choice. Ever since I was young I used to come here to see the mummies because . . ." He trailed off, stepping over to a rectangular display case. In it was an open-topped casket of roughly hewn wood. Will pressed his head against the glass case to peer at the mummy so familiar to him from all his visits through the years. The small body was curled up in a fetal position on a bed of sand in the bottom of the casket. "Because they're so cool," he finished saying, gazing down at the dried skin and cracked flesh of the mummy's face, its brown teeth showing through its ruptured cheek.

"It's in here," Elliott said quietly.

"What?" Will replied, hurrying over toward the corner. She was by a huge stone sarcophagus, its surface covered in glyphs.

"What do you mean, it's in there?" Will asked. "It can't be. That won't have anything left in it."

Having removed her Bergen and put it together with her rifle on the floor, Elliott was running her hands over the lid of the sarcophagus. "No, it's right here," she repeated. "I can feel it."

"Oh, brilliant," Will exhaled wearily. "Trust you to choose the most humongous sarcophagus in the whole place."

Elliott's hands had come to a stop on a panel showing two entwined snakes along the middle of the chunky lid. "Right here," she whispered, moving her fingers over the snakes. She seemed to be in a desperate panic as she began to try to hook her fingers under the lid and lift it. It was futile; Will knew that she didn't have a chance because of the sheer weight.

"OK, just hold on," he said, dumping his Bergen and Sten on the floor beside Elliot's kit. "We need to find a lever of some kind. A piece of metal will do."

Elliott refused to budge from beside the sarcophagus, so Will began to search around. He eventually discovered a fire point out in the corridor where there were some buckets and a hose coiled on a roll. Next to this was an ax in a Perspex-fronted case, which he broke open with a kick. He came back with the ax, and even though he could just get the tip underneath the eroded stone of the lid, it was going to be of no use in lifting it.

"This is hopeless," he muttered, as his eyes fell on the large stone idol — a massive pharaoh's head carved in stone and some ten feet in height — beside the sarcophagus. He walked around the head to examine it from different angles, then checked very carefully how far it was from the sarcophagus. Last of all, he went behind the head to find out how much clearance there was between it and the wall.

"I wonder . . . ," he said under his breath, as he flicked the lens up from his eye to look at the head in the moonlight that poured in through a window higher up on the wall.

Then he nodded to himself. "Elliott, I need you over here. If we can tip this over, I reckon it should fall on your sarcophagus and maybe break it open."

It took him a while to persuade her to leave the sarcophagus and come with him to the rear of the pharaoh's head. Then she seemed to understand what he was proposing. As he tried to tell Elliott where he wanted her to be, she suddenly clutched her hand to the nape of her neck.

"What's wrong?" Will asked.

"I don't know — just had a really bad pain here," she answered. "It's gone now."

As she seemed to be all right, Will explained his idea again, and then, with their backs to the wall and their feet braced against the pharaoh, they both eased themselves up until they were five or six feet above the floor.

"Three . . . two . . . one," he counted down, and they pushed with all their might. The pharaoh's head rocked slightly. "There! We moved it!" Will exclaimed enthusiastically. "Elliott, this could really work!"

For a moment he turned his head to glance through the window, his eyes lingering on the moon. "Howard Carter, if you're up there and watching this, I just want you to know I'm sorry," he muttered. "Right," he said, addressing Elliott. "We get into a rhythm until this bust goes over. And I just hope it goes the right way, or we'll be squashed like . . . very squashed things."

Will repeated, "Push . . . push . . . push . . . ," again and again as the pharaoh rocked backward and forward, and then with a last "PUSH!" it overbalanced and was tipping forward. Will and Elliott jumped to the side as it toppled straight on top of the sarcophagus with a floor-shaking thud.

They had both skipped around to the front to watch as the sarcophagus, in what felt like slow motion, also went over. Its huge lid slid onto the ground, smashing the glass display case before it finally came to rest.

"What have I done?" Will said, as he saw the damage to the pharaoh's head, the sarcophagus lid, which was broken in half, and to the mummy in the glass case.

But Elliott wasn't the least bit concerned about any of these. She squatted down by the broken lid to pick something up from among the pieces. The lid hadn't been completely solid — inside it there had been an object.

She stood up with it. It was some sort of baton, almost two feet in length.

"My God!" Will exclaimed. "It looks exactly like the tower!"

And it did; with the same section at the tip, it could have been a model of the tower from the inner world. It also seemed to be made from the same material as the tower, its surface smooth and gray.

And when the bare skin of Elliott's hand had come into contact with it, a band around the shaft glowed with an intense blue light. It was identical to the light that they had witnessed before in both the tower and the pyramid.

"Ah, so the batteries are still good," Will whispered, trying not to laugh with the strangeness of it all.

"This is what I came for," she murmured, as she got to her feet and held the object reverentially up before her.

"But what is it? A weapon of some kind — a mace?" Will asked, then something occurred to him. "I hope it won't suddenly change into another tower, will it?"

"It's a scepter, and I have to take it back," Elliott said, her eyes locked on it.

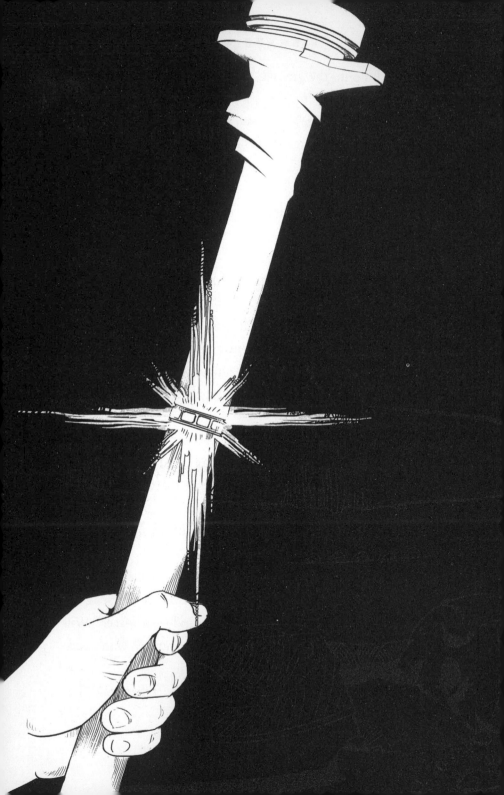

At the mention of the word, Will gave a small shrug. "OK, it's a scepter, then. Can I see it?" He stepped forward with his hand out, but Elliott snatched the object away.

"No, don't," she said sharply. "You shouldn't touch it."

"Fine, be like that." He shrugged again, instead going to examine the broken parts of the lid from the sarcophagus where the scepter had been concealed. There was a circular channel bored right into the middle of the thick stone of the lid, which of course was now empty. "So this scepter thing of yours could have been hidden in there for centuries, and nobody had the faintest idea," he thought out loud. "And, of course, all these relics were brought back to England by Victorian collectors, like, a century or two ago, so this sarcophagus would have been in Egypt for all the centuries before that. Is that where your scepter was lost?"

But Elliott had already gathered up her rifle and Bergen and was heading out of the room.

"Hey, you with the magic stick! Where are you off to now?" Will shouted as he heard the door slam shut behind her.

Grabbing his Bergen and Sten, he rushed across the walkway and had just caught up with her several flights down when there was the sound of gunfire hammering away so loudly windows were rattling. Both of them froze on the spot.

"That's close!" Elliott shouted. "And it's an automatic weapon."

"Could be the army?" Will suggested.

It was coming from outside the museum, and Elliott was right — it was very close. They raced farther down the circular staircase until they could see through the main entrance.

There was another burst of gunfire and a huge crash.

"A tank!" Will shouted. "Bloody hell!"

It had shot up the front steps and rammed straight into the doors, crashing through them and mangling the metal and glass.

It stopped there, half of it in the building and half outside. The automatic fire came again — the volume earsplitting in the confines of the museum, as the forecourt beyond the tank was sprayed with rounds.

The hatch opened and someone climbed from it.

Elliott was the first to recognize who it was through her rifle scope.

"Drake!" she cried.

"Elliott?" he yelled back.

Will and Elliott flew down the stairs. Drake had climbed down from the tank. "We picked up the signal from your beacon," he said, as Elliott threw her arms around him and held him tight. "But I didn't believe it could really be you two!" he added. Shaking his head, Drake smiled at Will. "But how did you get back here?"

"That'll take a bit of explaining," Will said, then interrupted himself as his friend's appearance registered with him. "Drake, what happened to you?"

Elliott had also taken a step back so she could see his deathly pallor and not only that his arm was strapped up, but that this head and hands were covered in bandages.

"It was the explosion in the Pore," Drake replied. "The radiation caught me."

"Oh, no," Elliott said, barely audibly.

Just then the machine gun began to hammer away again. As it stopped, there was urgent yelling from inside the tank.

"Who's that?" Elliott asked.

"Jiggs," Drake said. "The Armagi are building up outside, so we have to make tracks."

Jiggs was shouting so much his voice sounded hoarse. "Bloody hurry it up out there!"

"We've got to go!" Drake said urgently, already climbing back onto the tank.

The machine gun opened up again, drowning out Elliott as she said, "I've got to protect this." Simply throwing her rifle aside, she tucked the scepter inside her jacket and clamped her arm over it. Drake had seen what she'd just done and was finding it difficult to believe that she would discard her weapon like that. But now wasn't the time for explanations.

"They're wall-to-wall! I can't keep them off!" Jiggs shouted, opening up at the Armagi again.

"Get a move on, you two!" Drake shouted, beckoning frantically at them from the turret.

Elliott reached him and Drake grabbed her by the hand. "No! No room! Ditch the Bergen!" he shouted. She threw it aside, and he pulled her into the hatch.

Already up on the tank, Will had shrugged off his Bergen to pass it to Drake. "Bloody leave that, too!" Drake shouted.

The gun was firing continuously now.

"No way!" Will insisted. "Got all my stuff in there!"

Drake looked furious but snatched the Bergen from the boy's grip and was thrusting it down inside the tank when Jiggs cried, "Breach! They're through!"

There was a crash as the glass panels directly above the tank and above the two doors on either side burst inward.

Even though he lost a second or two as he shielded himself from the shower of glass, Will might still have made it if the turret hadn't swiveled around at that point. Taking a step back in surprise, he slipped and fell on his knees.

"Drake!" Will shouted, reaching out in desperation toward his friend, who was doing the same from the hatch.

Not just glass was falling around Will, but heavier objects. Armagi.

Something nearly tore off Will's arm as it gripped it with its claws and yanked.

The last thing Drake saw before he slammed down the hatch was the boy being heaved from the rear of the tank by two Armagi as others landed inside the museum.

"No, no, no, no," Elliott was wailing as she struggled with Drake inside the tank. "We can't leave him! We have to go back!"

"I'm sorry. He's gone," Drake told her, trying to shake some sense into her. "There are too many of them."

"Drake, I need you on the L94," Jiggs said, now he was driving instead of operating the tank's chain gun. As he steered through the gates and along the road at the front of the museum, there were dull thuds as Armagi slammed against the hull.

Jiggs was swearing under his breath. It wasn't because there was any remote possibility that the Armagi could penetrate the Chobham armor of the tank, which was twice as strong as steel, but because he was having immense difficulty seeing where he was going. The sheer number of Armagi in the way was making it impossible. And as he drove on, guessing where the road was, the Challenger was colliding with abandoned vehicles in the road. "If I can bloody see anything at all, I'm going to take a left into Southampton Row," he announced breathlessly. "Then head north. We'll have to figure out how to l —"

Elliott suddenly stopped crying. "No! Go right!" she ordered.

"Go right? But you don't know . . . ," Drake had begun as she pulled the scepter from her jacket. For a moment both Drake and Jiggs were silent, amazed by the blue light that filled the tank.

"I think we need to shake these blessed Armagi off our tail," Drake said, "then find somewhere quiet where we can catch up."

"How about the tea rooms at Fortnum's?" Jiggs quipped grimly.

As he was yanked from the tank, Will landed flat on his back. He hit the ground hard and was completely winded. All he could do was lie there, trying to get his lungs working again.

And when he did finally get his breath back and sucked down some air, the tank's powerful diesel revved and a cloud of hot exhaust fumes swirled all around him.

It was the worst sound in the world because he knew full well what it meant. Drake and Elliott couldn't do anything for him now.

They were leaving.

Without him.

As the tank trundled off, he was trying his best to focus on his immediate surroundings. He hadn't been wearing Drake's lens, so it wasn't a matter of his eyes adjusting to the moonlight, but his senses were still badly scrambled. Shapes shifted around him, many shapes.

And in the relative calm after the sound of the tank's engine retreated into the distance, he could hear the Armagi moving close to him, their feet grinding the broken glass.

For a second or two as he remained on his back, nothing happened. But as soon as he tried to lift his head, something struck him in the mouth. The blow was so powerful that he heard the crack as one of his teeth snapped off.

Will didn't delude himself that the situation wasn't desperate. For an instant he wished that the tank had reversed over him and killed him, because help wouldn't be coming. Not now that he was in the midst of all these beasts, which would stop at nothing — he couldn't plead with them for his life as he might with a human being.

He stole a look at them. He saw the dark inhuman eyes against the translucent planes of their bodies. He saw the serrated edges of their wings like so many glass daggers.

He was going to die.

And Will knew it was probably the last thing he should do, but he tried to sit up.

One of them suddenly lashed out at his chest, so hard that he was flung back against the marble floor again.

Then another blow. A kick to the head from something spiky. This time he had a glimpse of it coming toward him — it resembled the hind leg of a huge bird.

There was blood in his eyes. All he could hear was the kettledrum *thump-thump* of his own pulse.

I'm going to pass out, he thought. *But that's OK.*

Then there was something else. Another sound.

He only just caught it as the black blanket of unconsciousness began to fall over him.

It was a car horn.

Then he did pass out.

"They're sticking with us," Jiggs said. Kingsway was reasonably clear of vehicles, so he didn't hold back, pushing the tank almost to its top speed of thirty-five miles per hour. Even so, the Armagi kept doggedly following, flying around it like a swarm of angry wasps.

In the commander's station Drake seemed exhausted as he watched the creatures pursuing them on the rear periscope. "We've got to find a way to shake them off," he mumbled.

"Remember the Ghost Crab Maneuver?" Jiggs asked.

"Sort of . . . but was that what it was called?" Drake replied.

Jiggs turned the tank into the Aldwych. "I'm not sure, but you know what I mean. There's got to be a suitable building around here."

"Why don't you keep going around this block until we spot something?" Drake said.

Jiggs followed his suggestion, and looped around Bush House and the other buildings in the middle of the Strand, so that within minutes they'd returned back onto the Aldwych from the east side. "And, Elliott, we're going to need to blow some smoke, as they say. Have a look and see if you can find controls for —"

"L8 smoke grenades. Should be by the elevation control,"

Jiggs cut in. "If not, there's another way to do it, by cooking off the diesel in the exhaust manifolds."

"How do you know that?" Drake asked.

"Went for a joyride in one of these once," Jiggs replied.

"OK, I think I've found it," Elliott said, pointing to a series of numbered switches.

"Arm them," Jiggs told her. She clicked a master switch on the panel and waited.

"Jiggs, I've got us a likely candidate," Drake suddenly announced. "See that restaurant right on the corner of Kingsway? If you can miss the trees and hit it right, maybe we can flatten the main columns."

"Looks promising," Jiggs replied.

"What are you trying to do?" Elliott asked Drake with concern.

"He's trying to bury us," Jiggs said.

"It's an old trick. Create some confusion with smoke, then if we motor into the right building and it works out how we want it, we lie low under the debris," Drake explained, then turned to Jiggs. "Let's give it a shot next time around," he said.

As they looped once more around the buildings on the island in the middle of the Aldwych, and the restaurant came into view again, Drake gave the order for Elliott to fire the grenades. They rebounded off the buildings on either side, exploding and spreading a thick gray cloud across the road.

"Now, brace yourselves," Jiggs warned as he powered the Challenger straight toward the corner building. "And wish me luck, because I've got zero visibility."

Seconds later there was a huge crash, and the tank slowed to a sudden halt, throwing them all forward. But Jiggs rammed down on the throttle again, and the tank eased forward a little, before he killed the engine.

Then there was just a grinding sound, and the noise of debris hitting the hull outside.

Jiggs looked over his shoulder from the driver's seat, giving the thumbs-up.

"Keep absolutely quiet now," Drake told Elliott.

The maneuver had been a success. The tank had penetrated the front of the restaurant and, as it knocked several supporting columns away, a section of the floor above had collapsed on top of it, completely covering it. As the wind began to sweep the smoke away, the tank was almost totally hidden, and the Armagi had nothing on which to direct their attention.

"What do you think?" Jiggs whispered after a while.

"Did it work?" Elliott asked.

"Can't see anything through the periscopes, but I think it has. I suppose we'll only know it hasn't if the Armagi call in the Limiters to use high explosives on us," Drake replied. "I just hope there's enough air for all of us in this sardine can." He shook his head as he looked around the cabin. "I could never have been a tankie . . . I hate small spaces." He turned to Elliott. "OK, so what's the story with that oversized glow stick in your jacket?"

PART 4

MAYHEM

18

WITH THE DIESEL engine roaring, the tank thundered down Fleet Street, either barging cars out of the way or simply riding straight over them. As soon as Jiggs had backed it out from beneath the rubble, Drake had vacated the commander's position for Elliott. She knew precisely where she wanted them to go, and was now monitoring the way ahead using the periscopes.

Drake was suffering badly from the radiation sickness and welcomed the chance to rest, although he was doing his best to keep up with what was happening. "You calling the shots again, just like old times," he chuckled, as the girl issued directions to Jiggs in the driver's compartment at the front of the tank.

Elliott shot him a smile, then shouted to Jiggs as they came to an intersection. "Straight across. Keep going."

"Ludgate Hill," Jiggs announced, the engine note changing as they began to climb the slight gradient.

"There! Up there!" Elliott shouted, pointing.

Peering through his periscope, Jiggs took a moment to respond. "St. Paul's Cathedral?" he asked. "You're kidding."

"No, I mean it! Just keep going!" she called back. "I need to get inside — can you get us through the doors?"

"Inside? Whatever you say," Jiggs laughed. "We've already walloped one British institution today, so why not another?"

"Once we're in, I want you to stop," Elliott added.

Drake shook his head. "If we do, the Armagi will be all over us again before we know it. So use the same MO — go in about-face and keep them at bay with the L94," he said.

"Gotcha," Jiggs acknowledged. "Hold on tight!" he yelled, as they struck a couple of the stone bollards at the edge of the pedestrian area in front of the cathedral, snapping them off like rotten tree stumps. Then he swung the tank into a sharp turn, in the process managing to clip the statue in front of St. Paul's. "Whoopsy! I think I just clouted Queen Vic!" he said, as he put the tank into reverse and stood full on the throttle.

Drake and Elliott hung on as, gauging where he was going through the reverse periscope, Jiggs aimed straight for the pair of wooden doors at the top of the steps. Unfortunately there were a couple of massive stone columns with not quite sufficient clearance between them. With a low, resounding clang, the tank became stuck between them and came to a sudden halt.

"Hey, are you steering this thing or what?" Drake said, looking rather shaken from being jostled around so much.

"I'm doing my best," Jiggs retorted. "Considering there *are* a couple of bloody big columns in the way," he added under his breath, as he backed the tank off to take another run up the steps.

This time he was more successful. With an almighty crash, one of the columns toppled over, and although the tank was lifted up on one side by what was left of the shattered column, it was still heading for the tall oak doors with some momentum. There was a loud crunch and both doors were knocked clean off their hinges. "We're home, James," Jiggs said, standing on the brakes.

"Remind me not to let you drive again," Drake said to him, before turning to Elliott. "OK, we're really exposed here in the daylight. Let's do whatever you've got to do, then head out as quickly as possible. And I hope this isn't just some wild frolic."

Drake followed Elliott as she climbed through the hatch in the turret, then leaped down from the tank. After checking that the interior of the cathedral was clear of any Styx, they sprinted down the nave. On reaching the area under the huge dome of St. Paul's and the Whispering Gallery, Drake continued on for some way in the direction of the altar before realizing he was by himself. He turned to find Elliott had stopped directly under the dome.

"This is it," she said, closing her eyes.

Drake frowned. "What is? I don't get it. What could be here that's going to be of any help to us at all?" he demanded, the desperation evident in his voice.

"I honestly don't know," Elliott replied, opening her eyes and holding the scepter before her.

Drake came back toward her. "But this is a cathedral — what are you looking for here? And why here, in particular? What's so special about this place?"

"I really don't know yet," Elliott admitted. "Will thought it was to do with ley lines — which might be why this has always been a holy place."

Drake lost it at this point. "*Ley lines? A holy place!* What sort of New Age claptrap is that? I know we need a bloody miracle, Elliott, but that's so f —"

He never finished the sentence because Elliott, with both hands gripping the scepter, twisted the shaft halfway along.

"What's this?" Drake breathed, as he and Elliott noticed the most bizarre phenomenon. It was as if the light on them and the ground around them had gone through some sort of spectrum shift.

This effect was becoming more pronounced by the second, until they found they were in the dead center of a hemisphere of shimmering azure light, some forty feet across. The edge of the hemisphere was fluxing and shifting in the same way that an oil film does on water.

With no warning, a strong wind swept through the interior of the cathedral, strong enough to send pews scraping across the floor and hymn books flapping into the air like untidy birds taking to the wing.

It was followed immediately by an immensely loud creaking and cracking sound, as if the whole fabric of the building was coming under strain.

"Get down!" Drake shouted, peering above them.

In less than the blink of an eye, the dome of St. Paul's lifted off.

And, just as quickly, it had completely vanished from sight.

"What did you just do?" Drake demanded, as he had his first glimpse of blue sky above. He moved toward Elliott, ready to protect her from the pieces of masonry and timber that were dropping to the ground around them, but it proved unnecessary. None of it had actually fallen within the blue circle where they were.

Drake continued to peer above him, completely bemused.

"Where did it go?" he mumbled, shaking his head in sheer disbelief. It was as if some giant being had simply lopped off the top of a boiled egg with a spoon.

Elliott merely shrugged. "We saw something like this before, at the pyramid."

As he continued to shake his head, Drake was still trying to take it in. "Well, you got me." Then he laughed. "Against all the odds this building survived the Blitz, and we've just trashed it!" He turned his attention to the shimmering blue bubble surrounding them. "And what's with the light show?"

Elliott shrugged again, not offering any explanation. Instead she was peering around as if she was disappointed, as if she'd expected more.

As the L94 in the tank began to hammer away from the front steps, Drake was brought back to the seriousness of their situation. "OK, that's it," he decided. "We're sitting ducks in here. Time to get going."

As if to prove his point, something swooped in through the open roof. The first Armagi touched down, and fortunately didn't attack immediately, giving Drake the time to empty a magazine from his assault rifle into it. Pieces spun off the creature like chunks of flying ice before it dropped to the ground.

Several more Armagi landed on the cathedral floor, but as Drake changed magazines, they didn't seem to be attacking.

He cocked his rifle, watching them as they remained stock-still. "What's wrong with them? Why aren't they coming for me?" he asked. Still not one of the Armagi made a move, as if they didn't want to step into the circle of blue light.

Drake and Elliott exchanged glances, neither speaking for the moment.

More and more Armagi were landing inside the cathedral, but still they didn't advance. "I know you're safe from them, but I'm not. What's going on?" Drake asked.

"Maybe it's because of this light," Elliott suggested.

Drake shrugged, glancing across to the entrance of the cathedral. "I bet it won't keep us safe from Limiters. That tank is our only way out of here, but how can I possibly reach it now? I can't shoot our way through all those," Drake said, scanning the motionless Armagi. All of a sudden, he sat down, as if all his energy had deserted him.

Elliott realized what an effort it had been for him, and that he was in real trouble from the radiation sickness. She immediately went over to him.

"Save yourself if you can," Drake pleaded with her. "Look at me. I'm done for anyway."

"What in God's name is that?" Parry shouted into the headset as his helicopter led the formation over London.

He and everyone on board were mesmerized by what appeared to be a tornado against the morning sky. It seemed to begin as a dark spout just above the level of the rooftops before broadening out into a spinning dark cyclone reaching up toward the clouds.

"Some sort of explosion?" the pilot suggested.

"That's not any blast pattern I've seen before," Parry replied, as pieces of debris began to drop all around them. "Anyone got any bright ideas what's going on?"

"I can't help you with that, but there was the mother of all energy spikes just then," Danforth reported, as he watched the LED display on the device he'd been using to locate the beacon signal.

The pilot cried out as a large section of lead roof plummeted uncomfortably close, and he swerved the helicopter a little after the fact. The falling debris wasn't very dense, but a direct hit from some of the more substantial pieces of stone or timber would have been enough to bring down a helicopter.

"Everyone still with us?" Parry asked, as he turned to check that the other helicopters hadn't been damaged.

Eddie was watching the fallout scattering the streets below, some of it striking the buildings. "But what could have caused this?" he wondered out loud.

"I think we're about to find out," Parry replied, pointing at what still remained of the strange phenomenon ahead. "Isn't it directly on our bearing, Danforth?"

"You could be right," he replied. "The beacon's been stationary for a while now, and it appears to be at the epicenter of whatever that is." He checked the LED display again. "And we're almost over it . . . in a thousand yards . . . five hundred . . . and X marks the spot!"

"Good Lord!" Parry burst out, as their helicopter skimmed straight over St. Paul's Cathedral and they saw the gaping hole where the dome should have been.

"That's one of our tanks on the steps," the pilot observed.

"I saw it. And someone's picking off Armagi using the tank's chain gun," Parry said. "All right — whoever it is down there, they're on our side, and I'm sure they'd be grateful for some help." He spoke over the radio to the other helicopters. "I want two-man sniper teams put down on top of the buildings around here, and make it snappy."

"No! What are you doing?" Drake cried weakly, as Elliott began to cut into her forearm.

"Close your eyes and keep still," she said, bringing her arm up to his face. "I'm going to cover you in my blood. It worked for Will, so I don't see why it won't work for you."

Drake did as she'd told him, and she began to smear her blood all over him. "This situation is a bit different, you know — we're going to be knee-deep in those overgrown prawns once we step outside this light ring. It's not like we're just avoiding a couple of them along a street," he said.

"I know that," she replied.

Drake was silent for a moment before he spoke again. "You've been a good friend. You were always there for me in the Deeps when I needed you."

"Don't get all over-the-top with me, and let me finish wiping my blood on you," she chided him, laughing.

They moved to the edge of the blue bubble, and had just gotten themselves ready to go when the tank engine fired up. It began to reverse toward them, smashing pews under its tracks as it came. The engine stopped again, and Jiggs opened the hatch a few inches, peering out.

"Thought you could do with a lift," he said, looking around.

The Armagi in the cathedral were almost all completely still, although every now and then one of them would open and close its wings like a resting bird.

"Good timing," Drake said, and with Elliott supporting him they edged through the shimmering border of blue light.

"Hey, that's trippy," Drake muttered.

Elliott was quiet, keeping watch on the Armagi, who were following their every movement.

As they reached the tank, both Elliott and Drake stopped for a moment. One of the Armagi hadn't managed to get out of the way in time and had been pinned under the tank, its head crushed by the track. It was the strangest thing to watch because the Armagi was continually transforming into the long, thin body of a Styx and then back into an Armagi, over and over again. It was trying to regenerate, but the point at the back of its head that Martha had identified was under pressure from the tank track, and it was stranded somewhere between its two forms.

"Nice," Drake muttered sarcastically. "Now you see one monster, now you see another."

"Come on," Elliott urged him, supporting him as they skirted around the shape-shifting creature and then clambered up onto the tank.

Once the two of them were safely inside and the hatch had been secured, Jiggs looked at Elliott and then at the blood smeared all over Drake. "So the masking trick really works. Your blood fools them."

Without waiting for either of them to speak, he inclined his head toward the controls for the chain gun. "I don't want to worry either of you unnecessarily, but you should know that we're almost out of rounds. And we've been making a hell of a racket here, so we need to make ourselves scarce before any Limiters decide to join the party."

Parry and his men were on top of an office block overlooking St. Paul's. From behind the parapet at the very edge of the roof, they'd seen the Challenger reverse into the cathedral and out of sight. And now huge numbers of Armagi were arriving, but stopping on the cathedral forecourt as if waiting for something, waiting for a command.

Parry was just about to consult with Eddie about the situation, and particularly the way the Armagi were behaving, when his satphone went off.

"Hi, Parry, it's me, Bob," the caller said.

"Bob, can this wait?" Parry told him. "I'm a bit tied up at the moment."

"It can't," Bob replied.

Parry frowned. "OK — go ahead."

There was a slight delay before Bob spoke again. "Just a courtesy call. I thought you should know we're about to send a nuclear missile your way."

"What! Here?" Parry gripped the satphone so tightly the plastic casing creaked. He waved frantically at Danforth and Eddie to switch their headsets over so they could listen in.

"Yessir. One of our subs in the Atlantic has been given the firing sequence and is waiting for the final order from the President. That means you've got about fifteen minutes to get the hell out of Dodge."

"Can I ask why you're doing this?"

"Sure, although rather than have me try to explain the situation, I want you to see something. I'm breaking every darned rule in the book, but I'm going to give you a secure link to look at. Are you near a screen there?"

Danforth moved to the nearest laptop, where one of Parry's men was working, and typed in the link address as Bob reeled it off. An aerial image came on screen. It was clearly from a drone flying at some altitude. "Right, it's up," Parry confirmed. "What do you want to show me?"

"Hold on," Bob said.

The drone changed course and then Parry saw the need for urgency. Along a stretch of the Thames around Canary Wharf, huge numbers of Armagi had come together and were moving in dense columns across the ground. As Parry watched the video feed, the light reflecting from these columns of creatures made them look like runnels of molten silver as they reached the riverbank and slipped straight into the Thames.

"That's the story all the way along the river from Canvey Island to the estuary. A mass transit's currently in progress," Bob said. "And we've been tracking their movements once they're in the water, and they're migrating out to sea. Our best guess is that this is an invasion force on its way to the rest of the world."

"The cell breaks open, and all the new viruses spill out," Parry recalled.

"What was that?" Bob asked, not understanding.

"Something my son used to say about the Styx," Parry replied. "So, Bob, I agree there's no question that the Armagi are on the move, but is the threat that great?" Parry asked, trying to see if there was any reason he could find to divert the missile attack. "I mean, why aren't the Armagi airborne? That way they could spread more quickly."

"For reasons of stealth, I guess. They're harder to detect in the water," Bob answered. "Or, maybe, by swimming they're conserving energy, so they can cover greater distances. Say to the US, for example? That's what one of our scientific advisers is suggesting, anyway. But your guess is as good as mine."

"And precisely who's approved this strike?" Parry said, his voice uncompromising. "By what authority is this being done, because I hope it's not the good ol' US playing world policeman again all on its tod?"

"Er, Parry, I have no idea what most of that meant, but it's actually strikes, plural — there's a series of nuclear strikes scheduled. And, basically, every nation in the world has endorsed the action," Bob answered. "The US Senate and the Pentagon . . . Russia, all the Arab states . . . and there's unanimous consensus from the European Military Council, and throughout the whole of Eastern and Central Asia except for . . . er . . . Kazakhstan, who don't seem to be able to make up their minds. So we've effectively got full and unconditional global consent for a preliminary hit in London, followed by a join-the-dots sequence along the Thames, your southern coastline, and your international waters."

"You make it sound so clinical," Parry said. "This is my country you're talking about."

"Sorry, but like us, the rest of the world doesn't want the contamination to spread any further than Engl —" Bob started to reply.

"You've got to buy me some time," Parry interrupted him sharply. "Can you delay the strike?"

"And why should I do that?" Bob challenged.

"I'll give you the address for another satellite link, and we'll get a camera on the situation where I am. We believe some of our people made it back from the inner world, and something very strange is taking place. We may be close to getting some new information that can help us," Parry said.

Bob wasn't convinced. "You're not giving me anything I can use at this end."

"I haven't got anything yet," Parry admitted. "But you'll see from the video feed that the Armagi are congregating here in huge numbers, but then they're not moving. Seems that something's drawing them here, and — who knows — this latest development could be a game changer."

"Look, I'll see what I can do," Bob said hesitantly. "But I need something concrete from you, and yesterday."

"Understood. Bob, I'm going to hand you over to one of my men for a moment, but stay on the line," Parry said, passing the satphone to the soldier at the laptop. Then he immediately went back to join Eddie and Danforth at the parapet. "As if we don't have enough on our plate already."

Drake had stretched out on the cabin floor with a rolled-up tarpaulin for a pillow. His eyes were closed and his face was so drained and pallid he appeared more dead than alive.

"I wish there was more I could do for him," Jiggs whispered to Elliott as they looked at Drake with concern.

"Please don't talk about me as if I'm not here," Drake said, keeping his eyes shut, but managing a grin.

"Didn't think you were still with us, old man," Jiggs laughed.

"Two fish in a tank," Drake mumbled. "One says to the other, 'How do you drive this bloody thing?'"

"That bad?" Jiggs groaned, exchanging glances with Elliott. They both knew Drake only too well — the worse the situation, the worse the joke.

"'Fraid so," Drake mumbled. "Now, can we just fire up this bloody thing and ride it out of here?" he begged. "Maybe making ourselves a new door at the other end of the building in the process, as no doubt there'll be more prawns out front by now."

"No!" Elliott burst out, with such vehemence Drake opened his eyes. "I can't go. Not yet."

Tucked down against the parapet by the edge of the roof, Parry was using his binoculars to try to see inside the cathedral where the tank had reversed. "We need to know who's in that Challenger, and what they're doing here. Because whatever they're up to, it's acting like a magnet to the Armagi."

Eddie nodded in agreement. "No question that they seem to have diverted from their original route to the Thames, and instead they're beating a path here."

Danforth had been running another check on the signal from the beacon and its direction. "Maybe it's an obvious thing to say, but my money's on the tank for the VLF signal — it has to be where it's originating," he said.

Parry had switched his attention to what was left of the cathedral's domed roof as he thought out loud. "That wasn't a conventional explosion. Something very strange happened here, and I just pray that we're on to something we can use to get ourselves out of this corner, or at least buy a little breathing space." He was silent for a beat before he added, "But we're running out of time. We need to get someone inside the building for a recce."

Danforth cleared his throat. "I'll go. I can get some comms up and running with whoever's in the Challenger. I'm the obvious choice to do it."

"It's unlikely you'll make it through with that lot to contend with," Parry said, peering down at the ever-increasing hordes of Armagi.

"In the scheme of things, I don't think it makes a whole lot of difference if I stay up here or try my luck down there. As it stands, the chances of us coming through this aren't very promising," Danforth said.

Parry grimaced as he shot a glance over the London skyline. "I'm afraid you're right — the choppers are too far out. Even if I ordered them back right now, it's doubtful that any of us could get clear of the blast radius."

"So why not let me go down there and have a recce around the place?" Danforth asked.

"I'm not going to try to argue you out of it," Parry replied, glancing at his watch. "Take a couple of my best men — travel light, so you don't attract too much attention. You can use the pedestrian subway to get as close as you can to the cathedral, then you're going to have to play it by ear." For a moment they all focused on a point twenty feet or so from the entrance to the cathedral where a London Transport sign marked a flight of steps leading down under the pavement.

Danforth rushed off to put some equipment together in a shoulder bag and, minutes later, he and a pair of SAS soldiers emerged onto the street at the rear of the office block. All three of them checked the immediate area for Armagi, but there were none in sight. The creatures seemed to be concentrating themselves directly around the cathedral, which made life easier for the moment, but would cause Danforth problems as he got nearer.

With one soldier positioned behind him and one in front, Danforth began to edge along the wall of the building, all three of them hugging it and moving as quietly as they could.

Once they'd reached the corner, the entrance to the pedestrian subway was in spitting distance and, on the assumption that no Armagi had wandered down there, it would bring them up at the cathedral forecourt in no time at all. Danforth was trying not to think about the last twenty feet he'd need to cover, through the throng of creatures. He didn't delude himself that this whole exercise had the smell of a desperate suicide mission.

He was almost at the corner when a shout rang out from behind.

"Danforth!"

Danforth and the two soldiers spun around.

Chester was standing there, his shotgun pointing straight at Danforth. Martha was beside the boy, her crossbow also leveled at Danforth, while Stephanie was standing several paces behind, looking very frightened.

"Chester, this isn't a great time," Danforth replied, keeping his voice low.

"I've been wanting to talk to you," the boy growled, "about what you did to my parents." He advanced toward Danforth, showing no fear despite the fact that the two soldiers had their assault rifles trained on him.

"Do you want us to remove them?" one of the soldiers asked Danforth.

"Remove *us*?" Chester said, his lip curling viciously.

"Hold on," Danforth said, shaking his head. "Chester, we seriously don't have time for this. The US is lining up a nuclear strike on us here in London. We need to g —"

"Remove us?" Chester repeated. He turned his head toward Martha and gave her a small nod.

Like a streak of white lightning, the Brights struck the two soldiers hard, lifting them in the air and hurling them both against the wall. As they slipped down to the pavement, their bodies were twisted and broken.

Danforth had his hands up around his head. "That was unnecessary," he said, his voice even despite what had just happened. "And I see you *are* using Brights. I was wondering what saved me from those Limiters when GCHQ was hit."

"You're next, Danforth!" Chester said. His eyes were crazed, his face contorted with his hunger for revenge.

"No!" Stephanie cried, not able to take her eyes from the two dead men. "What are you doing? You didn't need to . . ." She didn't know what to think about Chester's crusade against Danforth, but to kill two men who had happened to get in the way was more than she could live with. Stephanie's eldest brother had joined the army in the months before all the troubles started, and she couldn't help but picture *him* slumped there, his blood smeared down the wall. She took a shallow breath as waves of nausea hit her. "This has to stop," she said.

Martha simply ignored her, her crossbow still raised.

Chester moved closer to Danforth, jabbing the barrel of the shotgun at him. "You were saying something about removing us, you creep? Like you removed my mum and dad?"

Danforth still had his hands up, but never once flinched as Chester brandished the weapon at him. "Chester, whether I was wrong or right to do what I did . . . in a few minutes it's all going to be immaterial," Danforth said. "Why don't you listen to what I'm telling you? We've been targeted for a missile strike!"

"I couldn't care less," Chester said, his voice a low rumble.

But Stephanie did care. She had no reason to disbelieve Danforth — the urgency in his voice sounded genuine enough, and it certainly didn't appear that he was still in cahoots with the Styx or he wouldn't be skulking around and hiding from the Armagi. And, besides all this, she did care very much about the two dead soldiers.

She did the only thing she could think of.

She slipped the huge hunting knife from Martha's belt and, grabbing hold of the woman's filthy hair, yanked her head back with the blade at her throat.

As Martha swore, Stephanie tried to get the boy's attention.

"Chester," she called out. "You've gone too far. You're not going to hurt anyone else."

"Keep out of it!" he barked, not even turning to look at her. "Let me enjoy this moment. The moment I kill this stinking traitor."

"No, Chester, you're not going to do that," Stephanie said, trying to keep her voice calm, despite the thumping of her heart. "Let him go, or I'll stick this knife into Martha."

Only now did Chester tear his eyes from Danforth for a quick glance behind him. But his insane, unblinking gaze was back on Danforth almost immediately, and he began to guffaw. It was loud and disturbing and made his whole body shake. "Go ahead, Stepho," he said. "Kill her, then. Do your worst."

"Chester?" Martha asked quietly. "You don't mean th —"

"Oh, shut up, you smelly old bag," Chester interrupted her.

"Chester." Martha gulped. "It's me — it's your ma speaking."

Chester's bloodlust was up. He wasn't thinking when he spoke. "You're bloody joking! My mum? You're about as much like her as a bucket of dead slugs."

Chester began to speak to Danforth in a furious whisper, the barrel of the shotgun rammed against the man's temple.

Stephanie felt Martha's body tense.

"I'm sorry you feel like that, dearie."

Martha pulled the trigger.

The bolt from the crossbow struck Chester in the back. He didn't cry out in pain or surprise, but an involuntary spasm made him fling his arms out to each side.

Danforth seized hold of the shotgun, pulling it from the boy's grip as he folded to the ground. "Phew. Thank God," Danforth whispered, not because he was safe from Chester now, but because if the weapon had discharged, the Armagi would have come flocking. "I have to go. You've got things under control here?" he said to Stephanie, speaking so rapidly the words were barely comprehensible. He didn't wait for an answer as he rushed to the corner and slipped out of sight.

Stephanie swallowed hard.

She remained in the same position, with the knife pressed to Martha's throat. "Chester," she whispered, trying to deal with what had just happened as she stared at the motionless boy. The blood drained from her head and her vision swam as she thought that she might pass out.

Then Stephanie felt the disturbed air and caught glimpses of the Brights sweeping close overhead. Martha had dropped her crossbow after taking the shot, but she still had the deadliest weapons at her disposal; her "fairies" would do anything to protect her.

It immediately brought Stephanie to her senses. She realized the precarious situation she was in. *I am not going to die here,* she told herself.

"Move!" Stephanie snapped at Martha, quickly heaving the woman across the pavement with her. And when Stephanie felt her back was against the wall, she pulled Martha in as close to her as she could, making sure she was tucked well behind the portly woman and her tentlike clothes.

Stephanie knew she might be safe from the Brights for the time being, but she had no idea where she was going to go from there. She wondered about the door Danforth and the soldiers had emerged from, but she couldn't see it from where she was.

Martha was sobbing silently. Stephanie could feel her body shaking against hers.

"It's all right, girlie," Martha said after a moment, in a rather pathetic voice. "I don't blame you. He wasn't a nice boy. Nothing like my sweet Nathaniel. Nothing."

Stephanie and Martha regarded Chester where he lay, face-down, the bolt protruding from his back.

"He's really dead, isn't he?" Stephanie asked.

Martha shrugged, then replied, "You have nothing to fear from me. I don't blame you for anything. You and I were both taken in by him."

Stephanie considered this. If what Danforth had said was true — and this was a gamble, given his past form — it didn't matter much if the Brights killed her, because they were all going to be dead soon from the American missiles, anyway.

"OK," Stephanie said eventually, removing the knife from Martha's throat and letting go of her. "I'm sorry I did that to you, but . . ."

Martha took several steps to the edge of the pavement.

She didn't turn, but slowly stretched her hand with the mangled fingers up into the air, and gave a sad, dejected little whistle.

Here it comes, Stephanie thought, bracing herself. *I'm going to end up like those dead soldiers.*

And the Brights did come, but instead of attacking Stephanie, they collected around Martha, enclosing her as their wings thrummed the air.

It was hard to count how many were there, but Stephanie thought it might be all of them, all seven.

Then, before she knew what was happening, Martha's feet had lifted from the pavement.

She rose into the air, borne aloft by her fairies.

And she rose farther and farther up into the sky, her head sagging forward onto her chest. Then the Brights whisked her away over the buildings, like some Gothic, nightmarish version of Mary Poppins.

Stephanie almost smiled at the thought.

Martha Poppins.

Let's Go Fly a Bright.

She knew Chester would have found that amusing. Poor, twisted Chester, who had been put through so much and lost so much, and been broken by it.

She found she was staring at his lifeless body, but couldn't go near it. She had been attracted to him, to his recklessness, and maybe deep down she'd believed that she could help him. Save him from himself. But now she felt nothing for him.

And she was hit by the realization that maybe she was like him.

Broken.

19

ARMAGI OCCUPIED the entire square in front of the cathedral — there were so many it was standing room only. They waited silently, their compound eyes turned toward the splintered doors at the entrance. As a jet-black Bentley slipped smoothly up the hill from Ludgate Circus, they moved aside to let it through. The car horn was sounding insistently as it drew to a halt.

"Something happening out front," Jiggs reported. He was using his periscope to try to see through the cathedral doorway, but the massed Armagi made it difficult. "I think a limo has just pulled up," he said incredulously.

"Give you one guess who that is," Drake said, as Elliott peered through her periscope, but couldn't see very much, either.

"Want me to blat them with the big peashooter?" Jiggs offered, pointing at the aiming controls for the tank's 120-millimeter cannon. "Can't promise I'll get anywhere close, but it's worth a try."

They heard the car horn again.

"Don't bother. They're not that careless," Drake said. "They wouldn't show themselves unless there was something they wanted."

"Careless . . . very careless," Parry said as he watched the doors of the Bentley being flung open. "Look at them — they can't have any idea we're up here. They've grown overconfident," he whispered. He was itching to give the command to his men to open fire, but instead he continued to assess the situation. "We've got ourselves a full house — the old Styx, the Rebecca twin, the Styx woman, and . . ."

Alex dragged someone from the back of the car. His face was puffy and bruised, and his eyes barely open. "Make an effort, will you?" Alex mocked him as she propped him up against the car, his head lolling drunkenly.

"My God! It's Will!" Parry whispered. "So at least some of them made it back. But he's been badly roughed up. Just hope he didn't bring any of that supervirus back with him from the inner world if it was released. That would really put the cat among the pigeons with the Yanks."

"I heard that," Bob said indignantly over Parry's headset. "What supervirus?"

"If you're going to listen in, keep it zipped," Parry told him. "Now I want all stations to report to me."

Parry's earpiece crackled. "Confirmed head shot on Styx woman," the first of the soldiers said. Then, one by one the other snipers on the rooftops all around the cathedral began to update Parry.

"OK, but fingers off triggers," he said when they had finished. "No action to be taken yet — I repeat — no action," he told them over the radio. "Just make sure you stay zeroed in on those targets, and await my word."

"Parry," Eddie prompted him. Two Limiters had appeared from nowhere. They caught Will as Alex pushed him away, then began to drag him in the direction of the cathedral.

"They're going to parade Will. That means that there must be others from the team in the tank. They're going to use the boy to bargain with, aren't they?" Parry asked, lowering his binoculars to look across at Eddie.

The former Limiter nodded. "That's what I would do."

Strutting around by the car, Alex began to shout at the cathedral. "Hello, hello! Come out to play!"

Inside the tank, they all heard her voice, and were looking at each other.

"Listen to that. It's Big Bug, isn't it?" Jiggs said. "They want a parley. You were right on the money, Drake."

"I know you're there," Alex called. "We've been tracking that radio signal you've very helpfully been putting out."

Elliott's eyes flicked around the floor of the tank until they fell on Will's Bergen. "I'm such an idiot! That's how they found us so quickly. I forgot the beacon was still switched on."

As he continued to peer through the tank's periscope, Jiggs suddenly gave a small whoop. "Yes! I've got eyeballs on that Styx woman — the one who escaped before we hit the warehouse. Come on, Drake — if I roll this heap forward a bit, we can do what we failed to do last time, and blow her into next week."

Drake had managed to get to his feet so he could take

Elliott's place in the commander's seat. Before he could say anything, Jiggs swore. "Nope, I've lost her. That was a golden opportunity," he said. He was still peering through his periscope as he breathed in sharply.

"Oh, no," Drake mumbled.

"What is it?" Elliott asked. There was an ominous silence as she waited for one of them to answer.

"Tell me what it is!" Elliott burst out, not able to stand the suspense any longer.

Drake took his face away from the periscope and simply looked at her. "Bad news, I'm afraid," he said.

Elliott pushed Drake aside to see. Will was being supported by one of the Limiters, while the other was staring at the tank over the heads of the Armagi. "What have they done to him?" she said.

"Don't be bashful. Join me out here, won't you?" Alex shouted. "Will is *dying* to see you."

Elliott lost sight of Will as the Limiters took him away.

"They've moved him," she said to Drake. "We have to find out what the Styx woman wants."

"Don't be daft," Drake said. "There's no way I'm letting you put a foot outside this tank, let alone outside the cathedral."

"They've got Will out there!" Elliott yelled at him. She couldn't stop herself from crying, but then took a breath as she tried to gain control of herself again. "She might be prepared to do a deal. They always want to do deals."

"Sure, and they always renege on them. No, if anyone's

going outside, it should be me," Drake argued. "I don't have that long. If they waste me, it's purely a timing difference."

"No, you don't understand," Elliott said, examining the glowing scepter, then locking eyes with Drake. She was only beginning to understand it herself. "I *need* to go out there. It's the only way to stop this madness. I really think I can stop it."

Jiggs suddenly sat bolt upright. "Listen to this," he said, indicating a speaker by his head and then leaning over to turn up the volume. "It's being sent over to the tank's shortwave radio."

The radio signal wasn't that strong and there were occasional dropouts, but the message was clear enough: "*. . . speaking to the occupants of the Challenger inside St. Paul's. I don't know who you are, but you've got one of my VLF beacons with you. Be aware that the commander has received confirmation that the US military are intending to hit London and the South East with nuclear warheads in a matter of minutes. If it's in your power to influence the situation, then you need to act, and act now.*"

"That's Danforth," Drake said, frowning at Jiggs.

"*You won't be able to respond to this. I'm transmit-only from a nearby location. I repeat, I am speaking to the occupants of the Challenger. . . .*"

"But whose side is he on now?" Drake posed. "Didn't he jump ship to the Styx?"

"In which case he's trying to trick us to go outside," Jiggs reasoned.

"But he isn't, is he?" Drake said. "He's not telling us to do anything other than help, if we can. He's not telling us to leave the tank so the Styx get us. He's telling us that there's a nuclear strike coming. Why would he do that?"

Drake's mind was working overtime. "And the reference to 'the commander' is in the message because he believes there's someone in this tank who knows Parry. It's meant for us."

"And Parry has connections at that level in the Pentagon," Jiggs put in.

Drake took a breath. "OK, sounds like the tock is clicking, and we haven't got anything to lose . . . any of us."

"You mean the clock is ticking," Jiggs corrected him.

"Whatever. And I'd really rather not ruin this wonderful suntan with more radiation. I've already had more than my fair share for this year," Drake muttered, placing his hand on the locking handle of the main hatch. He turned to Elliott, fixing her with a stare. "Do you mean what you say about going out there? You're prepared to meet them?"

She nodded grimly. "I have to go out — not just because of Will, but because I need to stop this."

"Right, let's you and me join the dance," he said to Elliott.

The Limiters had hauled Will back to the Bentley. They threw him on the hood, flipping him over onto his back. He was moving dazedly, and trying to speak but not making any sound.

"Leave him. I'll take it from here," Alex told the Limiters. She extended one of her insect limbs, pinning Will down on the hood with her pincers against his chest, although he was in no state to go anywhere.

As soon as Drake and Elliott had jumped from the tank, the Armagi stepped back so that there was a passage all the way down the nave to the main entrance. Keeping very close to each other, the two of them edged along it, the Armagi keeping their distance. It was more than just Elliott's blood protecting Drake this time.

And as the two of them emerged from the cathedral and out onto the top of the steps, the Armagi on the forecourt also parted so that there was a corridor all the way to the car. Drake and Elliott could see who was waiting for them at the Bentley . . . and see Will spread-eagled on its hood.

"My son," Parry said, as he watched Drake emerge from the cathedral and step into the daylight. "He's still alive!"

"And my daughter, too," Eddie said, as he spotted Elliott at his side.

"He doesn't look good," Parry observed as he increased the magnification on his binoculars to see his son more clearly.

"They must know Will's as good as dead. So why are they both putting themselves in the firing line like this?" Eddie said. "Unless they know the situation is desperate."

"Danforth must have done his stuff," Parry said. Changing to a separate frequency on his radio headset, he asked, "You managed it, then? Where are you?"

Danforth was halfway up the stairs to the entrance of the subway, pressed up against the wall, a radio transmitter still in his hands. All he could see out on the pavement were the lower limbs of the numerous Armagi assembled there. "I couldn't get all the way," he replied to Parry, "but I've done what I can. I tried to send a message to the tank's shortwave receiver, and I just pray they heard it."

"I think they did. My son and Elliott appeared outside the cathedral a few seconds ago," Parry said, and checked his watch. "Keep in touch. We haven't got long."

"Ah, my two jolly renegades," Alex said to Drake and Elliott. "I assumed it had to be you, going by the reports from the British Museum. My guys," she said, waving an arm at the sea of Armagi, "gave me a description of you."

Drake and Elliott slowly made their way down to the bottom of the steps at the front of the cathedral.

"You don't need that weapon," Alex told Drake. "Lose it now, or the boy gets his throat torn out." She pressed her claw down on Will's chest and he moaned loudly.

Drake shrugged, then threw down his Beretta. It rattled across the pavement, the only noise in the whole place.

"Good. Now don't be bashful. Come and join in with the fun," Alex ordered them.

With the two Limiters now on either side of them, the old Styx and Rebecca Two were standing together beside the Bentley. They said nothing — the Styx woman was clearly running the show.

"Right, that's far enough. Stop there," Alex ordered Drake and Elliott. "Was there anyone else in the tank with you?"

"What do you want to talk about?" Drake asked her.

"Answer me first," the Styx woman insisted, then almost immediately let the point go. "No, I see that it was just the two of you." Drake and Elliott wheeled around to see a Limiter at the entrance of the cathedral behind them. He'd obviously been inside to check the tank.

If either Elliott or Drake was in a less desperate predicament, they might have marveled at Jiggs's ability to completely blend into any situation he found himself in. As it was, there wasn't time to dwell on it.

"Tell us what you want," Drake repeated.

"I don't want anything, and you're in no position to ask for anything, are you?" Alex replied. "I just thought your half-breed would like a front-row seat as I consummate my union with her beau here."

"Let Will go," Drake said.

"Oh, I intend to," Alex said. "In two shakes of a puppy dog's tail." She was rather difficult to understand as the tip of the fleshy tube poked from her mouth and twirled energetically. As she threw herself on top of Will, the tube extended fully from between her lips and pushed its way deep into his mouth.

Drake and Elliott watched in horror as the muscles in the ovipositor contracted, and a large egg sac quickly squeezed down it. Will was coughing and choking and trying to resist, but then it was done.

The eggs had been deposited deep inside him.

"That's for slaughtering all my babies in the warehouse," Alex said, as she straightened up and with the back of her wrist wiped away the fluids that dangled in glutinous skeins from her black lips. "Oh, I've been saving that pod for a red-letter day like this. Only the very bestest and greediest Armagi will do for naughty Billy Burrows. The little darlings inside him are so ravenous, they'll be gobbling up his insides before you can say . . . *eat your heart out.*"

Elliott was white-faced with shock, but Drake was shaking with anger.

"We did what you asked. We left the tank and came out here," he growled, striding forward. "You could have spared Will that suffering. So help me, I'm going to take you apart with my bare hands, you abomination!"

Alex cackled unpleasantly. "God, you flesh bags are so petulant and so bloody t-e-d-i-o-u-s."

With a whiplash motion of her raised insect limb, she made a sound like someone snapping their fingers.

Two shots rang out almost simultaneously with each other, their reports echoing from the buildings.

As the bullets caught him in midstride, Drake dropped onto one knee. He clutched his hand to his chest, blood pouring from the twin wounds.

"Drake!" Elliott was beside him in an instant, helping him down to the pavement.

"He's hit," Parry said, hardly breathing as he spoke. "My son's down."

There was crackling over the radio but no one said a word, waiting for Parry's orders.

Eddie reached a hand out to him, taking hold of his arm for a moment. "I'm sorry, Parry, but . . . ," he whispered.

"Oh, yes," Parry said, struggling to make himself focus. "All positions . . . hold your fire." He was watching as Elliott knelt beside his mortally wounded son, a small figure among all the Armagi.

"That's why they're so relaxed," Eddie said. "They've got men in position in the buildings all around. Those shots weren't from any of the Limiters on the ground."

"You're right," Parry replied, and wasted no time in addressing his men again over the radio. "Did anyone get the location of those Styx sharpshooters? Check all the facing windows, and check them carefully — there are bound to be several teams around the place, maybe even on the floors below you. On my orders, I want them taken out. Got that — I want every single one of them slotted."

Eddie met eyes with Parry, who nodded once. One had lost his son; the other was likely to lose his daughter.

Then they again turned their attention to the cathedral square.

The situation was so tense that no one on the roof with Parry noticed as Captain Franz slipped away, then ran all the way downstairs to the street.

"You idiot," Elliott said tenderly as she cradled Drake's head in her lap. "You knew how it would turn out. So what did you do that for?" she asked, tears trickling down her face.

Drake grimaced as the pain gripped him. "To buy you some breathing space to . . . ," he whispered, ". . . to do whatever you're going to do. Do it now, girlfriend, and do it for me . . . for all of us."

"But I don't . . . ," she began, catching herself as she saw how close to death he was.

He started to choke.

"I can't think of a joke," he said.

He let out his last breath.

Elliott carefully lowered his head to the pavement and rose to her feet, a look of sheer determination on her face.

And no one noticed as she took advantage of the opportunity Drake had given her, sliding a hand beneath her coat to the small of her back. Neither Alex nor any of the other Styx had any idea what was tucked into her belt. But Elliott knew what she had there; she could feel it, feel the scepter, as if it was willing her to take it out, willing her to use it.

She began toward Alex.

Alex gave Elliott a sneering glance. "I just need to deal with this half-breed, then we're all done here. Nice to tie up some loose ends, and not before time." Alex turned to Rebecca Two and the old Styx. "Any reason you can think of why we need her alive?"

Neither Rebecca Two nor the old Styx said anything.

"Fine, then it's night-night and sweet dreams for the Drain Baby," Alex announced.

She raised her insect limb, ready to snap it again.

"Your sister died the worst death you can imagine," Elliott suddenly said to Alex, a cold smile on her face. "Vane would have been covered in buboes, all over her body. You can't imagine the pain when they burst from the pus and blood in them, but what got her in the end was the fluid in her lungs. From the lesions. She would have drowned in it."

Elliott threw a glance at the old Styx. "Every single one of your men in the inner world went that way. You see, there's a virus down there, and it's still there, spread by the birds."

"That's as may be," Alex said, her words clipped with her anger. "But who cares, because *this* world is almost back in our hands again."

Elliott ignored her, speaking instead to Rebecca Two. "And let me tell you about *your* sister," she said. "She was burned to a crisp by the nuclear explosion. Jiggs found her, but when he tried to examine her, one of her arms just broke off. She'd been turned to charcoal."

Rebecca Two said nothing, averting her eyes as Elliott took another step toward Alex.

"And you . . . what's so messed up is that this world has always been *in your hands*," Elliott said. "There's no need for any of this."

"What are you talking about?" Alex snarled.

"You won't remember — no Styx does — but many millions of years ago, our ancestors came to this solar system in a huge ship."

Alex gave a derisive snort. "Ship? What ship?"

"The ship that you're . . . we're . . . everyone's standing on right now."

"What — you mean the *Earth*?" Alex said, her voice rising with incredulity.

"That's right," Elliott confirmed. "You see, all that time ago, some of the atmosphere leaked out from the center, and we came Topsoil to put things right. But we never made it back, and with no one to helm the ship, it drifted into orbit around the sun. We were never meant to stay here."

"That's a very imaginative little tale — trying to buy yourself some time, are you?" It hadn't escaped Alex's notice that Elliott was including herself in references to the Styx. "And you evidently think you're one of us now? It's a little late in the game to switch teams."

Ignoring the remark, Elliott indicated the massed ranks of Armagi all around her. "In the beginning we looked more like that . . . and Styx and humans worked and lived together inside the ship, because we'd brought them on the journey with us."

"I really don't need to hear any more of this drivel," Alex said, snapping her insect limb as she'd done before.

The noise, like the single click of a castanet, reverberated around the place. But, to Alex's bewilderment, none of the Limiters had taken a shot. Elliott was still standing there.

The girl smiled at Alex's confusion. "We only began to resemble humans after our last Phase . . . to resemble the species that we'd bred and reared to serve us. Pretty ironic, isn't it?"

Alex snapped her limb again, and then again, growing more and more irate.

What she hadn't seen was the Limiter sharpshooters being sniped. Parry had given the order, and his men on the rooftops had successfully put the three Limiter teams out of action before they'd had a chance to fire even a single shot at Elliott.

Alex had stopped clicking her limb and was frowning.

"Anything wrong?" Elliott asked her.

"You! *You're* wrong!" Alex screeched, swinging to the old Styx and then the two Limiters on the cathedral steps. "And you," she shouted at them. "Do the honors, will you, and shut this tiresome brat up once and for all? She's boring me stiff."

The old Styx produced a handgun at the same time as the two Limiters brought up their long rifles.

There were sounds like distant whispers.

The old Styx was thrown forward onto the ground, a neat hole in the back of his head. Rebecca Two jumped back from beside him in surprise.

And the two Limiters on the cathedral steps were also knocked off their feet by powerful sniper rounds from Parry's men.

"Fiddlesticks," Alex muttered, as if their deaths were as bothersome as breaking a fingernail.

Elliott knew the sound of a silenced sniper rifle only too well. She realized then that she wasn't alone, that she had friends out there.

She raised her hand above her head, calling out, "Don't shoot her!" She pointed at Alex. "Leave her to me!"

"Get back in the car, you little fool! Don't just stand there!" Alex screamed at Rebecca Two, who showed no sign that she was going anywhere. Alex scowled at her, then turned on Elliott. "At least I can rely on the Armagi to do what I tell them."

She began to beat her insect limbs together, faster and faster.

Not a single Armagi moved a muscle. They were simply standing there in their droves, watching.

"What *is* wrong with them?" Alex complained.

"You just don't get it, do you?" Elliott said, "They won't attack me because I'm the same as you. I have your blood in my veins. I'm just as much Styx as you are."

"If you want anything done properly, you have to do it yourself," Alex grumbled.

The Styx woman launched at Elliott.

But the girl didn't just stay put.

She went to meet Alex.

As they came together, Alex lashed at Elliott's eyes with her insect limbs, but she got more than she'd bargained for.

Elliott cried out, the skin tearing apart between her shoulders.

And from the base of her neck, a pair of insect limbs snapped open to their full length. Like something newborn, they were speckled with blood. And they were also brown and far lighter in color than Alex's shiny black legs.

But they were every bit as strong.

Elliott's new pair of limbs caught Alex's in their pincers, stopping the Styx woman in her tracks and effortlessly holding her off.

Alex was speechless.

"Parry," Bob said over the headset. "Two minutes to impact."

"You've launched already? Aren't you watching the video feed?" Parry rumbled. "You have to abort."

"Sure, we're watching, and we're sharing it with the governments of all the other countries throughout the world," Bob replied. "But there's been no change to the status. Our drones are showing that the Armagi are still moving out to sea."

"I'll see what I can do," Parry said.

"What are you doing here?" Danforth asked Captain Franz suspiciously as the New Germanian appeared by his side, out of breath, and looking very nervous. Although he'd have rather been anywhere else but down in the pedestrian subway, Danforth had remained there in case there was anything more he could do to help. Although he couldn't actually see for himself how events were unfolding outside the cathedral, he was picking up most of what he needed to know on the main channel of the headset. But nobody had warned him that Captain Franz was joining him.

The New Germanian had caught his breath and was about to answer when Danforth was buzzed by Parry. He listened to what he was being told for a moment, then turned to the New Germanian.

"This is going to be fun," he whispered, his expression far from enthusiastic. "Because I'm going out there now." Danforth pointed at the throng of Armagi they could see at the top of the steps. "I'd be very grateful if you'd hang on to these for me, although I don't know if I'll be coming back." He handed the man his shortwave radio and another device he'd been using.

He readied himself, then climbed the steps, at the last moment putting on a burst of speed. As he emerged from the subway, he was shouting, "Excuse me! Excuse me!" as if he were trying to get through a crowd in Oxford Street rather than a scrum of fearsome creatures.

Elliott and Alex were still locked together, holding each other at bay with their insect limbs.

"Let him through," Elliott shouted, as soon as she heard Danforth.

But Danforth didn't want to come through and was looking around warily. One of the Armagi he'd barged out of the way opened its mouthparts and rattled them together, its inhuman eyes staring at him. "Oh, hello," Danforth said to it, taking a rapid step back. Then he quickly clambered on top of the railings by the entrance to the subway, so he could see over the heads of all the other Armagi.

"Um . . . sorry to butt in," he said apologetically to Elliott. "But Parry wants you to know we've only got a couple of minutes before the first missile hits us here."

As Danforth ducked from view, Will moaned loudly. He was still lying on the hood of the Bentley, but was obviously in the most terrible pain as he gripped his stomach and tried to roll over.

Alex laughed. "My little darlings are feeding, your boyfriend's dying, and even if you can do something about all that, there's no way you can stop us from spreading. I've sent the Armagi out, and it seems you're about to be vaporized by your American friends." She laughed again, high and clear. "There'll be no one left to recall the Armagi swarm. You're too late."

"You're wrong about that," Elliott said.

Still holding Alex off, Elliott slipped out the scepter from the small of her back that she'd been holding in readiness there.

"What are you doing?" Alex asked.

Gripping the scepter with both hands, Elliott didn't answer as, just as she'd done before, she twisted it halfway along the shaft.

The blue light flickered, then turned red. But that wasn't all. As Elliott held it out, the scepter began a transformation, rapidly increasing in length. And at one end, three prongs appeared, all in the same smooth gray material.

"What the hell *is* that?" Alex demanded.

"This," Elliott said, holding up the trident, "puts a stop to your madness."

"Elliott, if you're going to do something, you've got to do it now!" Parry's voice boomed from the rooftop through a bullhorn.

"Got you!" she shouted back.

With Alex still gripped firmly by her insect limbs, Elliott raised the trident.

"Time we all went home," she said.

She brought the trident down, striking the bottom of the shaft hard on the pavement.

Red light flooded her vision. It came from inside the cathedral, where the blue hemisphere had changed color, then burst out through the ruined roof, until the whole sky turned bloodred. For several seconds everything was suffused with a rosy glow, as if the sunset of all sunsets had come, but long before the end of day.

Then, as if an earthquake had struck, the ground began to shake. Whether they were on the rooftops or on the ground, everyone around the cathedral felt it.

The tremor subsided as quickly as it had begun.

There was a beat when everyone breathed a sigh of relief that it was over, and that they hadn't been hurt.

Then came a sound as if a million tons of fish had hit the ground, and the Armagi — every single one of them — disintegrated.

They didn't even have time to turn back into human form. The whole place was awash with oily pieces of their transparent bodies as they slopped across the road and the paved forecourt of the cathedral.

"Parry, what the bejesus was that?" Bob's anxious voice came over the radio. "We saw that red light all the way out here. And we also experienced some sort of seismic event. Tell me your people weren't responsible for that."

"Frankly, Bob, I haven't the faintest idea *what* just happened," Parry replied. "But look at the Armagi. I reckon it's time to call off that missile strike now."

Bob didn't answer.

Captain Franz poked his head out from the entrance of the subway.

Right away Rebecca Two spotted her New Germanian officer and called to him. He began to run frantically toward her, slipping and falling over several times in the sea of oily Armagi body parts.

"Oh, great, that's all I need," Alex muttered, but she was more intent on Elliott's trident.

Danforth suddenly appeared beside them, his pistol drawn. "I'll keep an eye on Big Bug for you," he offered to Elliott.

"Thanks," the girl said, releasing the Styx woman, then stretching her new insect limbs in the air. "I was beginning to get a cramp."

"What is that?" Alex asked Elliott, still staring at the trident. "Some kind of weapon?"

Elliott held it up. "Is it beginning to come back now? Are you beginning to remember? Because it all started . . . and ended with this." She held up the trident to consider it for a moment, then shook her head. "We were stranded up here on the surface when this was taken from us. Who knows how it happened — maybe the humans rebelled against us or something," she said with a shrug. "And without us there to control it, our ship never continued on its journey. Over the billions of years we . . . we Styx . . . simply forgot who we were."

"I don't feel . . . ," Alex said, staggering slightly, but Elliott had left her, rushing over to Will's side.

Jiggs had already crept out from where he'd been hiding and was tending to Will. He'd torn the boy's shirt open and was examining his abdomen and chest. Then, diving into his medic's bag, he quickly administered a phial of morphine to him. "That'll help with the pain," he said.

"How is he?" Elliott asked.

Jiggs shrugged. "We need to open him up and get the Styx larvae out." He looked around at what was left of the Armagi.

"We can't take the risk that they're not still alive, and even if they are dead we need to find out what damage they've already done."

"I need a moment with him," Elliott said.

"I . . . ," Jiggs began, unwilling to leave the boy.

"Just give me a moment," Elliott insisted.

There was something about her that made Jiggs obey without further question.

Elliott took hold of Will, shaking him by the shoulders. "Will, you have to wake up."

He coughed hard, blood and froth from his lungs speckling the sheer black of the Bentley's hood.

"Come on, Will, please. I haven't got long," she begged, shaking him again.

Then his eyes flicked open. "God, it hurts," he groaned, his face tensing with the pain.

"I know," she said.

"Elliott, it's you," he said, as he realized who had hold of him. "What happened?" As he managed to focus on her, he caught sight of one of her insect legs as it twitched over her shoulder. "That's new," he said, then laughed as the morphine began to take effect. "Hey, are you in a costume?"

And although Will's sight was rather blurred and he wasn't seeing clearly, his question wasn't that outlandish.

If Dr. Burrows had been there, he, too, would have had something to say about Elliott's appearance: the trident, the crimson glow it was emitting, and the insect limb poised behind her that Will had mistaken for a tail.

If all that hadn't been symbolic enough, there was also the fact that the Styx had their origins at the center of the Earth, where a small but fiery sun never stopped burning. Taken all together, it would more than likely have prompted Dr. Burrows to spout forth about the devil meme in the human subconscious.

But Dr. Burrows wasn't there.

And his son was hardly in a condition to think rationally.

"Is it Halloween?" Will asked, chuckling outrageously as the morphine did its stuff.

"No, it's not Halloween," Elliott answered patiently. "And you have to listen to me. I want you to remember what I'm about to tell you. Concentrate, Will, because I don't have much time."

Parry finished speaking to Bob, then turned to Eddie. "They've put a hold on the strike for the moment. All the images from the drones are indicating that the Armagi swarm is over." Parry briefed everyone over the radio, and there were cheers and shouts from the rooftops all around the place. But as Parry came off the radio, he was staring at Eddie. "What's wrong?"

"I don't know," Eddie replied. He had his hand raised in front of him, his fingers splayed.

As Parry watched, it was as if Eddie was blurred, vibrating, like a piece of film when it's out of the sprocket but still running through a projector. And on the roof around Parry the same thing was happening to Eddie's men.

And to Rebecca Two.

And to Alex.

And to Elliott.

But Elliott had been prepared for it.

Glancing up, she saw Stephanie approaching from the pedestrian subway, Martha's knife still in her hand.

"I think someone's coming to see you," she said to Will, but not vindictively.

"No, stay. Please," Will said weakly, trying to hold on to Elliott.

"I can't. Anyway, you wouldn't want me like this," Elliott said, her insect limbs twitching behind her.

"I don't care. I . . ." Will trailed off, barely conscious, as his hands slipped from Elliott.

"Good-bye, Will," she said softly to him, leaning over to kiss him on the forehead. Then she turned from the Bentley and took a few steps across the pavement. She was peering up at the top of the building where her father and Parry were.

"Dad!" she shouted at the top of her voice.

"Here," Danforth said, offering her his headset.

She took it from him and quickly put it on.

"Dad, can you hear me?" she asked.

"Elliott," he acknowledged, waving from the edge of the roof.

"I'm sorry," she said. "It was all or nothing," she said, staring up at him. "If I hadn't activated the recall, it would have all been over anyway, not just for us, but for the rest of the planet, too." She shook her head, her expression sad. "There wasn't anything else I could do."

"Well, you did it, Elliott. You stopped it," Eddie said, brimming with pride for his daughter. There was a pause before he asked, *"Recall?"*

Elliott never replied.

She, her father, and every Styx on the surface of the Earth began to blur out in a haze of red.

They were simply vanishing into thin air.

"Rebecca!" Captain Franz shouted desperately from the back of the Bentley. Sensing that something was happening to her, the Styx twin had stepped from the car, then promptly begun to disappear. The New Germanian threw himself at where Rebecca Two had been, trying to clutch at her as the red blur faded away. But for all the good it did him, he might as well have been trying to catch smoke. As there was nothing to stop him, he fell on his face, sliding in the oily mess left by the Armagi, and then he just lay there, sobbing uncontrollably.

And other than his sobs, there was nothing but a stunned silence all around the cathedral.

20

AS WILL CAME TO, he found he was lying in bed. A real bed, with a mattress and a pillow, and the feel of starched sheets against his skin. And there was pain, lots of it, mostly in his stomach and chest.

He let out a groan, not because of how he felt, but because he needed to know that he was really awake. Then he groaned again, louder this time, and managed to open his eyes. He had a glimpse of sunlight through a window, and at the same time became aware of someone sitting beside him in a chair. Whoever it was, they were holding his hand. They were speaking to him, but he couldn't hear what they were saying.

"Elliott?" he asked, trying to see.

And then he thought that he could make out the shadowy outline of a second person behind the first. "Chester . . . is that you, Chester?"

"It's just me, Steph," came the reply, and after a moment, "and . . . no, Chester isn't here."

It took Will a few seconds to process this. Then he managed to open his eyes again and focus on her. Her red hair was clean and perfect, and she was smiling. She radiated beauty, just like she had when he'd first met her on Parry's estate. It felt to Will as though he'd gone back in time.

"Oh, hi," he said, pretending to cough so he had an excuse to pull his hand away from her. "Where's Elliott?" he asked croakily. His mouth was chronically dry, so he began to reach toward the jug and plastic cup on the bedside cabinet.

"Water?" she anticipated. "Let me get you some. You must be, like, so thirsty."

He tried to sit up to take the glass from her, but the stabbing pain in his abdomen put a stop to that.

"No," she said, "you mustn't try to move."

With Stephanie's assistance, Will drank the water greedily. "Where am I?" he asked between mouthfuls.

"Hospital. They've got it working again. They've even got the electricity back on now, but they hadn't when they did your operation here."

"Operation?" he repeated, the water going down the wrong way and making him cough, for real this time. "Why, what did they do to me?"

Then it started to come back to him. He remembered the Armagi and Alex, and then — but only very vaguely — what happened on the hood of the black Bentley.

"Look, I should let Parry know you're awake. All right?" Stephanie said. She seemed in a hurry to leave the room.

It wasn't Parry who appeared a few moments later, but someone else. Will was rather startled as he hadn't heard anyone come in, and all of a sudden there was a man standing at the end of the bed.

"How are you doing, Will?" Jiggs asked.

"Who are you?" Will asked, narrowing his eyes at the unfamiliar figure, with his unkempt beard and grubby-looking fatigues. "You're not a doctor, are you? Where's Parry?"

"He'll be here soon. And no, I'm not a doctor." Jiggs laughed. "I forget that you and I haven't really met before, not formally. I'm Jiggs. You might have seen me before, but it would have been just for a moment . . . on the edge of the Pore in the inner world."

Will didn't answer.

"It's funny — I know you so well, but you don't know me. I came on that mission to seal off the inner world, with you and Drake and Sweeney and the rest of the team, and the time I'm talking about is when I ambushed a pair of Limiters," Jiggs said, trying to help Will out. "Don't you remember at all? I took out the first Limiter with a . . ." Jiggs made a slashing motion across his throat. ". . . and carried the second one over into the Pore with me."

Will was squinting at the rather nondescript man with his darting, alert eyes. "Oh, yes, *Jiggs*. Of course. You're the invisible man," he said. "Hello."

They shook hands, which was a little peculiar after all that they'd been through at the same time, but not quite together.

"I've spoken to Parry and he's on his way," Jiggs said. "He's got his work cut out for him right now. You know he's filling in as Prime Minister in the emergency government until they can get things back on track."

Will was staring through the window, feeling somewhat detached from everything. "More of it is coming back to me . . . more of what happened at the end," he said quietly. "She's gone, hasn't she?"

"Yes, Elliott, and all the Styx — they sort of disappeared," Jiggs confirmed.

"She told me she was going away. And, unless I've dreamed it, she had . . ." Will wasn't sure how to put it, so he tried to indicate a pair of insect legs by pointing behind his head.

"She did. When she was in the tank with Drake and me, she complained about pain in her neck. But it never occurred to me that . . ." Jiggs trailed off.

"And Drake?" Will asked all of a sudden. "I heard his voice after that Styx woman dragged me out of the car, and then . . . were there shots?"

Jiggs nodded. "That was it for Drakey, I'm sorry to say. But he'd been so badly irradiated when the bomb in the Pore went off, he didn't have much time left anyway."

Shaking his head slowly, Will didn't speak for a second. "And what about Chester?" he asked, very reluctantly, because he thought he already knew the answer. Otherwise his friend would have been there at his bedside, too.

Jiggs shifted uneasily as he answered. "No, he didn't make it, either. I'm afraid he was set on a collision course with Danforth. You see, the death of Chester's parents was never intended and very unfortunate. But Danforth was no traitor. Far from it. In his out-there, superclever-supercrazy mind, he'd figured we were on a hiding to nothing, and had cooked up a plan so he could infiltrate the Styx. And it worked, up to a point."

Will was silent for a moment. "So did Danforth kill him?"

"No, surprisingly enough, it was Martha."

"Martha!" Will said with surprise.

"Yes. She turned up with a bevy of Brights as her personal escort-cum-hit squad. Seems Chester and Martha went off together, but then had a falling-out. You should ask Danforth or Stephanie about it — they were both there when it happened."

"That's just terrible. Poor Chester," Will said. He could hardly bring himself to think about the loss of his friend. "It was because of me that he got into all this in the first place," Will added, almost in a whisper.

"Don't do that to yourself," Jiggs said firmly. "You can't beat yourself up over him. The way it played out with the Styx, not one of us was safe. Nobody knows yet precisely how many casualties this country has suffered, but it runs into the millions."

A twin-bladed helicopter thundered past the building, so close that the windows vibrated. Jiggs was grateful for the opportunity to change the subject as he turned to see the large pallet of crates strung below the aircraft on ropes. "Good — that looks like more medical supplies for us. The Americans are here in force now, and bending over backward to be helpful," he said. "Considering they were seconds away from blowing us all to kingdom come with a nuclear strike, I suppose it's the least they can do."

"Nuclear strike? Really?" Will echoed. "I missed so much," he said. "After the Armagi got me."

"Only to be expected," Jiggs said. "They wouldn't exactly have handled you with kid gloves. And, besides, Alex needed you out of it when she shoved those Armagi larvae down your gullet."

"So I really had those things in me?" Will said with a shiver, glancing down at his stomach.

"Yes, and I was first on the scene. I had no option but to . . ." Jiggs hesitated.

"Please. I want to know," Will urged him.

Jiggs was still hesitant. "Maybe it would be insensitive of me to tell you anything more. Are you really sure you want all the gory details?"

"Don't worry," Will said, trying to smile but achieving something more akin to a grimace. "After what I've been put through over the last couple of years, I'm not sure anything much can get to me now."

"Righty-ho," Jiggs said. "Well, I figured I had to take immediate action after Bug Lady impregnated you outside St. Paul's, and I was the nearest person with any sort of medical training."

"I was choking a lot, wasn't I?" Will whispered, putting a hand to his throat.

"You were," Jiggs confirmed. "And after the grubs were deposited inside you, your body quickly began to shut down, so I filled you up with morphine. The golden rule with any major trauma like that is to medicate immediately against the shock."

"I think I sort of remember . . . it was beginning to hurt like hell, and Elliott was with me, too, wasn't she?" Will said.

Jiggs nodded. "For a while. Anyway, we had to operate on you, there and then, in a tent on the forecourt of St. Paul's. We had no option but to act quickly because we had no way of knowing if the grubs had hatched out of the egg sac or not, or even if they were still in you."

Jiggs held his hand sideways to Will to emphasize the point he was about to make. "You see, there seems to have been a dividing line between the Styx, who magically did a disappearing act, and the Armagi, who degraded into a rather foul-smelling, fishy mass."

Will made a face.

"Anyway, I opened you up pretty sharpish, and found that the grubs had all died, but not before they'd begun to feed. So I located and removed each of them, stopped the bleeding, and patched you up the best I could. Then you were evac-ed here in a chopper, where a doctor opened you up again. You see, the dead grubs had degraded in you, leaving behind not just organic matter but other chemicals — enzymes, I suppose — which had to be painstakingly swabbed out, because we didn't know what effect they might have."

"So I'm OK now?" Will asked.

"The doctor believes so. Although you're not quite out of the woods yet. There's always a risk of infection, which is why you're dosed to the gills with antibiotics, and he's left some drains in place."

Jiggs pointed at the clear plastic tubes that hung over the side of Will's mattress.

"They come from me? Can I see?" the boy asked, peering down at his front.

Jiggs blew through his lips. "Are you sure you want to?"

Will nodded.

"OK," Jiggs said, lifting the sheet aside. He peeled back a large rectangle of bandagelike material that was across Will's body. There was a massive incision all the way from the boy's breastbone to his midriff, held together with monstrous black stitches that looked as though if you cut them he would simply burst open. And then there were the tubes running from inside the incision.

"Oh," Will said. He hadn't expected it to be so dramatic.

"Yes, and I apologize that the incision isn't neater, but I only had my old pocketknife on me at the time," Jiggs said.

Will looked up at him, but the man was smiling.

"Only kidding." Jiggs laughed. "You're going to have one blinder of a scar there to show the girls wh —" he added, catching himself as he realized how Will must be feeling about Elliott.

Jiggs put the bandage back in place, then laid the sheet over Will again. "Actually, old man, you're a bit of a rarity, because as far as we know, nobody else who's been impregnated by the Styx has ever survived."

"Why doesn't that make me feel any better?" Will said.

21

"**THERE SHE IS! KILL HER!**" Alex screeched, trying to get up at the same time as jabbing one of her pincers in Elliott's direction.

The combination of the ever-burning sun and the incredibly fertile soil at the center of the world meant that the bare earth in the fields around the tower hadn't remained bare for long. It was covered with a green baize of grass, new shoots, and tiny unfurling fronds. And dotted over this, like so many black skittles, the Styx had suddenly appeared when they'd been transported from the surface.

"Get her!" Alex yelled. Most of the Styx were completely disoriented and in the same state as she was, falling onto all fours as they'd materialized in a blur of crimson. But it didn't take the resilient and toughened Limiters more than a few seconds to pull themselves together. Many already had their rifles to their shoulders.

They opened fire, the rounds striking the tower around Elliott. She was only too aware that Eddie and his former Limiters would be out there somewhere in the field, too. They were hopelessly outnumbered by the other Styx, and obvious targets.

By bringing the trident down on the ground outside St. Paul's, not only had Elliott thwarted Alex's plan to send out the Armagi into the rest of the world, but she'd also passed an effective death sentence on her father. Elliott told herself that she'd had no alternative. And wherever he was in that plain of green, there was absolutely nothing she could do for him right now — she didn't even have her rifle with her.

But it wasn't the only death sentence that Elliott had dished out. Alex and Rebecca Two, along with every other member of the Styx race, were all going to be dead in a matter of days. None of them had been inoculated against the supervirus that was still present in the inner world.

Straining her eyes as she tried to find her father, Elliott remained in the entrance to the tower, standing there in a shepherdlike pose, the trident resting on the ground by her side.

Although she showed no fear as more rifle shots began to land around her, she wasn't going to push her luck, not while she still had a task she needed to complete.

"Kill that half-breed!" Alex wailed again, falling as she tried to run toward the girl.

Elliott merely gave the Styx woman a small bow of the head, then took a step back into the tower. As the door whisked shut, the pile of rocks that Will had thought were a safeguard against it doing precisely that were immediately pulverized.

As Elliott began toward the elevator, she took a moment to look around the entrance chamber. After she and Will had gone, the bushman had evidently lingered on in the tower for a while, from the remains of all the fires he'd lit inside it. There were small piles of burned roots beside which Elliott could see the husks of locusts and a couple of bird skulls. And some of the New Germanian brothers' equipment was still stacked against the walls, but there was nothing to show that they themselves had been there recently.

The elevator took her up the tower, but she had to climb the stairs to reach the very top level. She immediately went to the podium in the middle of the space and stepped up onto it, moving toward the largest plinth in the center. Taking a quick breath, she held the trident at arm's length, directly over it.

As she lowered the trident and the tip of the shaft made contact with the plinth, she saw concentric ripples spread out across its smooth and very solid surface. The effect was identical to what happens when a stone hits calm water. Elliott blinked, not believing her eyes, but in the next instant something even more outlandish happened. She was forced to let go of the trident altogether, because it was being pulled into the plinth and absorbed back into the fabric of the tower itself. A few moments later, only the prongs of the trident remained, then they too dipped below the surface of the plinth. Elliott touched the plinth, feeling where the trident had vanished, and how the surface was completely solid again.

For a while she stood looking at the plinth and the rest of the level around her, but nothing seemed to be different.

The very first time Elliott had been there, she'd told Will something was wrong, something was missing. Now that the scepter was finally back where it should be, all her pent-up fatigue hit her. She tried to take a step but her legs buckled and she sagged against the plinth, grabbing it for support.

Elliott had completed the quest that she hadn't understood in the beginning, and that she'd had no option but to complete. From the moment that she'd initiated the chain of events after touching the trident symbol in the pyramid, the blood she shared with the ancestors of the Styx had seen to that. She'd been under the spell of a genetic behavioral pattern that had removed her free will as surely as if she'd been a robot following its programming.

Programming to find and restore the trident to its rightful place.

Although nothing appeared to have changed inside the tower, there was a change outside it of which Elliott was only too aware. In the huge voids deep in the mantle of the planet — not just the zero-gravity belt that she and her friends had traveled across, but numerous others — the crystal belts had sprung into life. As the spheres in them rotated faster and faster, they gave off an intense light, far brighter than the triboluminescence Dr. Burrows had correctly identified.

And they also began to generate enormous amounts of energy.

For these spheres were the source of propulsion that had brought the Earth into orbit around the sun.

Finally, after so very long, they had been activated again.

The insides of the cavities around the spheres glowed with grids of blue light in patterns that only one person in the whole world — Jiggs — had noticed after the nuclear explosion in the Pore.

But as if sleeping giants had been roused from their deep slumbers, no human could do anything to stop the spheres' immense power.

And this power was being put to use.

22

THERE WERE PERIODS of intense activity at
the hospital as fleets of vehicles arrived with survivors,
most of whom — one of the nurses had told Will — were
being treated for malnutrition or exposure. He heard them
being wheeled along the corridor outside at all hours of the
day, and caught glimpses of the soldiers who seemed to be
running everything.

As he recovered from his operation, Will had been quite
happy to lie in bed and rest. But during one of the lulls in
which there was complete quiet in the place and he'd been
staring absently up at the ceiling, he was roused from his tor-
por. The door to his room nudged open a few inches as if a
breeze had swept down the corridor. He kept watching just in
case someone was about to come in to visit him. "Jiggs — is
that you?" he asked, wondering if it was the man with the ability to render himself almost invisible.

But there was no one there, and Will mumbled, "I'm going
doolally," feeling rather foolish.

Then the strangest thing happened.

With a scrabbling noise on the linoleum, a cat's head poked
up over Will's feet at the end of the bed.

"Bartleby!" Will exclaimed, truly believing he was seeing a ghost. The Hunter sniffed inquisitively at him, then put his snout down and began to scamper around the room. The animal was clearly detecting all sorts of new and interesting Topsoil smells that he hadn't encountered before.

"Not quite," Mrs. Burrows said, as she entered the room with the First Officer in tow. "But it is one of his kittens."

"Kitten? He's huge!" Will said, beaming at his mother. He was delighted to see her after what felt like so long.

"And how's my son doing?" Mrs. Burrows came over to Will and gave him a hug. "Jiggs said you're mending well after your op."

"Yes, we hear you've had the battle of your lives up here," the First Officer said, taking Will's hand in his huge ham of a fist and shaking it.

Bartleby Kitten, or just Bartleby, as the First Officer called him because it was easier, immediately took to Will and climbed up on his bed. The Hunter obviously wanted to play, as he rolled on his back and began to cuff Will with his over-sized paws.

"God, it really could be Bartleby," Will said. "He looks identical." The cat had noticed the translucent tubes poking out from under Will's blanket and was chewing on one of them. "No, not that!" Will told the cat quickly, trying to push him away.

Mrs. Burrows ushered the kitten off the bed, then began to chat with Will, telling him about how she and the First Officer were spending all their time up in Highfield, where many of the Colonists were helping with a clean-up operation, and where many of them had already chosen to relocate. "The ironic thing is that — in a roundabout way — the prophecies written in the *Book of Catastrophes* have come true," Mrs. Burrows told Will. "The Colonists *have* got the surface to themselves again. There's an empty town just waiting for those who want to go Topsoil. Because there's nobody left alive in Highfield."

"Nobody at all? They're *all* dead?" Will asked quietly.

There was a knock at the door and Parry entered.

"You're looking better, my lad," he said, before asking Mrs. Burrows and the First Officer if they would mind giving him some time to speak alone with Will.

"They've set up a makeshift canteen on the ground floor," Parry suggested. "If you ask at reception, they'll tell you where it is."

"Don't worry, I think I can find it," Mrs. Burrows replied, tapping her nose as she winked at Will. She and the First Officer shuffled out, leaving Bartleby asleep on Will's bed, his legs in the air.

"Jiggs told me that you're Prime Minister now," Will said, giving Parry a smile. "Does that mean I have to call you sir or something?"

Parry raised his eyebrows. "Hardly — and when did you ever show me any respect anyway?" He gave a shrug. "Besides, I'm only PM for just as long as it takes them to find someone from the old Cabinet to do the job."

Parry glanced through the window as another helicopter came in to land. "The emergency aid is starting to arrive from the international community now that the risk has been removed," he said.

"Has it, though?" Will asked. "Is it true that not a single Styx has been left Topsoil, or anyone who had any Styx blood in them, like Elliott?"

Parry's expression turned sad and for a second he looked away. "Yes, it's true. There's not one of them left, so I suppose we won in the end, but we lost some good people in the process," he said. "Elliott, of course, but also Eddie and his team." Parry sighed. "And then there's what happened to Chester. . . ."

"And Drake . . . I'm so sorry about Drake," Will said quietly, as he realized he needed to say something about Parry's son to him. And Will also didn't feel strong enough yet to think about the loss of his friend.

"Thank you." Parry nodded, then fixed him with a stare. "Will, unfortunately I'm not just here to see how you are. I also need to debrief you. There are still some gaps in what we know, and I need to hear your version of events."

"That does sound official," Will said.

"I'm afraid it is, and I'll need a full statement from you in due course. You see there's actually an international inquiry under way, not least because several of the world nations are accusing us of unauthorized subterranean atomic testing. They're suggesting that's why a tremor was felt around the world, and also where the Armagi, apparently a mutant species that was created due to the high radiation, originated. Well, that's what the French think, anyway." Parry chuckled, then raised an eyebrow quizzically. "And the Yanks don't know whether to give the lot of us Congressional Medals of Honor — or to convict us all of some international crime against humanity. You're on the list, too, Will, for both of them."

Will laughed uneasily.

Parry's expression became serious. "You spent more time with Elliott than anyone else," he said, his expression serious. "I need you to tell me everything you can remember about her, and what happened near the end."

"Sure, but my memory's a bit patchy after the Armagi nabbed me and I was brought to St. Paul's," Will replied. "And why is Elliott so important in all this anyway?"

"Because quite a few of us are terrified by the implications if some sort of alien force has taken control of all our destinies," Parry replied.

As Bartleby snored at his feet, Will recounted what had happened with Elliott during their time together in the center of the world, about the discovery in the pyramid, and then the appearance of the tower. Parry didn't interrupt once as Will talked about how he and Elliott had been transported back to the surface, and then had found the scepter in an Egyptian sarcophagus.

"So you can't shed any light on precisely what was guiding Elliott through all this?" Parry asked. "Because it seems that she knew exactly what to do at each step."

Will shook his head. "She didn't know herself. Perhaps my dad would have called it a race memory." Will touched his forehead. "Something deep in here because of her Styx blood — something that had been woken up by the tower or the pyramid, I suppose. I don't know how else to explain it."

Parry and Will chatted for a while longer until Mrs. Burrows and the First Officer returned to the room. Then, as Parry stood up to leave, Bartleby was roused from his sleep. He immediately scampered over to the window where, with his paws on the sill, he seemed to be staring out at the horizon.

"Silly kitten," Mrs. Burrows said affectionately. "What's got him so interested?"

Groaning with the discomfort, Will was trying to raise himself up so that he could say good-bye properly to Parry when something caught his eye through the window, too.

"What is it?" the First Officer asked.

"I don't know," Will mumbled, squinting. "But . . . but is it my imagination, or does the sun look smaller than usual?"

Chuckling as he heard Will's comment, Parry was about to leave, his hand on the door handle, when his satphone went off. He stopped to take it out and look at it. "America calling," he said.

"It does look smaller, you know," Will murmured, still transfixed by the pale circle in the sky. Bartleby hadn't shifted from the window, as if his animal intuition was telling him something, too.

"Yes, Bob, what can I do for you?" Parry asked.

"That's it!" Will burst out. "That's what she told me! The last thing Elliott said to me was that we were all going home . . . that she'd had to start some sort of *recall*."

"What do you mean, going home? Home where?" Mrs. Burrows asked.

"NASA is saying *what*?" Parry bellowed into his phone.

"Elliott said she had to start a recall in order to stop the Styx and the Armagi," Will said. "She didn't know where we were going, but she said this might happen. The whole planet, or spaceship, or whatever you want to call it, would begin to move."

"That all sounds a bit crazy, Will," Mrs. Burrows said. "How can you really believe in this whole planet-as-spaceship theory anyway?"

"You wouldn't dismiss it so quickly if you'd seen what I've seen in the center of the world. And no, it's not so crazy if you think about it," Will replied. "Why do you think humans have always gone underground at the first sign of any trouble? Because that's where we feel safe. Why do you think Sir Gabriel Martineau and all the Colonists built a city underground with the Styx?" Will posed to his mother and the First Officer. "Because that's our natural instinct. Because the center of the world is where we all came from, and maybe for all these thousands of years we've just been trying to get home again."

Parry hadn't finished his call with Bob, but had his hand over the microphone as he hurried to the window. Bartleby still had his paws up on the sill and regarded Parry with some curiosity.

After a moment, Parry turned to Will, his face ashen. "The latest positional information from NASA is that the Earth has begun to deviate from its orbit. NASA says it's unprecedented. They believe we've started to move away from the sun."

"Told you," Will said, as he struggled to sit up. "Mum, can you find out what they did with my clothes? And can you also find a doctor to do something about these tubes, because I can't get very far with them still inside me."

"Why? Where are you going?" Mrs. Burrows asked.

Will glanced at the view through the window again. "You need to get all those Colonists underground again, and I'm coming back there with you. Because I don't think any of us should stick around here on the surface any longer than we have to."

"Bob — sorry to keep you hanging on like that," Parry said. "Yes, you're right. Seems we've got ourselves another situation here. And it's dead serious."

23

ONE WEEK WENT BY, then a second, and the tower didn't allow Elliott to go outside. Although there was a risk that Limiters might still be alive and lying in wait for her, Elliott would try the door each day, but so far it had been to no avail.

And not much in the tower would allow her to operate it, with the exception of the elevator. Elliott had even tried the transporter on the penultimate floor, thinking that she might return Topsoil. She was incredibly concerned for Will, and had no way of finding out whether he'd survived the impregnation by Alex. But again, try as she might, the surfaces of the console had remained gray and lifeless, with not the smallest sign of the blue lights. And the remote viewing device was completely unresponsive to her.

Out of desperation, she also tried everything she could to extract the scepter again, but the plinth wasn't giving it up.

Elliott assumed that the tower, and whatever it was part of, was running some sort of program that restricted what could be done inside it, but for how long she had no way of knowing. It was as if the program, once activated, had to run its course.

And as she whiled away the hours in the tower, she wondered what had become of the New Germanians and the bushman. Perhaps, as the Styx had begun to materialize out of thin air, they had all fled. She couldn't imagine Woody going very far from the tower in her absence, so she assumed that the Limiters must have caught him early on.

And the three New Germanians might not even have been anywhere near the tower when the mass influx of Styx began. Perhaps they'd been safely out of the way in their city. However, it would have been the Limiters' first port of call, so she didn't give much for their chances unless they'd hopped on a boat and fled to one of the remote outposts she'd heard them talk about.

And she began to think of the tower as a living thing, some sixth sense telling her that processes were going on within it. But if it did possess some form of sentience, then she asked herself if it had any consideration for her, because she could quite easily have died of starvation or thirst if it hadn't been for the supplies left behind by the New Germanians in the entrance chamber. Elliott would make her way down there during the day, light a fire, and prepare herself meals, although it had to be said she never felt very hungry. Perhaps, she wondered, that was why the tower felt it could lock her in. Because perhaps she didn't actually need any sustenance while she was inside its walls.

And then one day when she pressed her hand to the wall by the doorway, the tower suddenly freed her.

The panel slipped open, and she stepped out into the now knee-high fields of green grass and saplings. She hadn't wandered very far when she came across a Limiter's body, almost stepping on it where it was stretched out in the new vegetation. Although the Limiter had already been ravaged by birds, he was lying with his rifle at his side, as if he had been waiting to ambush her.

Elliott kept walking through the fields, aware that she might stumble across her father's body.

And there, in all those lush fields, she felt so very much alone, imprisoned in the middle of the world, with just the flocks of birds to keep her company.

As her only traveling companions.

Because Elliott was only too aware that the planet was returning home. She had used the word *recall*, and that's what it was; having failed to reach its destination, the ship was being recalled to its rightful place. Back home again.

But where that home was, and what manner of beings would be there to greet her when they arrived, she couldn't even begin to guess.

But she had no option now.

She — and the world — were on their way.

EPILOGUE

"**COME ALONG. UP YOU GET,** Bart Kitten,"
Will said, patting the bed beside him. Apart from the occasional excursion outside to catch a rat or two, the young Hunter had been Will's almost constant companion since his mother had brought him down to the Colony with her to convalesce.

It was all rather fitting, because Will was being tended to in the very same room in which Mrs. Burrows had made her miraculous recovery after the Styx had left her for dead following her excessive Darklighting. The sitting room in the First Officer's house was precisely how it had been for her stay, the furniture moved aside to make space for a bed. And that was precisely where Will had spent the last couple of weeks, lolling around in bed and largely left to his own devices except for the odd house call from a doctor.

Truth be told, Will was having the time of his life.

Safe in the knowledge that the threat from the Styx had been removed once and for all, he was enjoying the opportunity to laze around all day long, sleeping as much as he felt like in his nice, warm bed.

And he certainly was being well and truly pampered — the First Officer's mother and his sister, Eliza, had been asked to do their bit and look after him in the daytime when the First Officer and Mrs. Burrows were busy with Colony matters.

The Colony had indeed become a very busy place again. Parry and his SAS unit had moved there, along with a contingent of Topsoil survivors from London and the South East. At least there'd been ample room for this influx of new residents because the Styx's merciless harvesting of the Colonists for the Phase had left whole streets empty.

Will found he didn't miss being Topsoil at all, although he knew there was much debate up there over how the atmosphere might be affected as the planet continued its inexorable drift away from the sun. Would the air be lost as the planet edged farther and farther from its orbit and, eventually, out of the solar system, or was there some form of field to keep it intact? And would surface temperatures plummet until they were only a few degrees above absolute zero, the temperature of deep space?

Human life, and *all* life, would become unfeasible in that situation.

But Will didn't linger on these fears for too long — he was more than happy to hide away in his darkened bedroom and wait for his next meal to be brought to him. He felt that he'd had more than his fair share of unpleasantness at the hands of the Styx, and it was someone else's turn now to solve the problems. So he was quite content to fill his days with trivial and insignificant things for a change, which included playing with the oversized kitten.

"Oh, do come on, Bart!" he said tetchily, patting the bed beside him even harder.

Much to his surprise, the cat narrowed his eyes and began to back out of the room, snarling at him. Then, with a last rumbling growl, Bartleby was off, haring down the corridor and into the kitchen.

"Stupid bloody moggy," Will muttered in a disappointed voice, folding his arms huffily across his chest.

Hearing the commotion, Mrs. Burrows came to investigate. "What's gotten into that cat?" she asked.

"I've absolutely no idea," Will replied. "Something must have rattled him. He's nothing like Bartleby — that's for sure."

For a moment Mrs. Burrows remained in the doorway, staring at her son with her sightless eyes. She sniffed, then said, "Supper's nearly ready. Hope you're hungry?"

"Certainly am, Mum," he replied.

At first it had felt a little peculiar to be part of his mother's new life in the Colony, her apparent domestic bliss with the First Officer. But in a way, Will believed that he had every right to be there; he was making up for lost time because he'd never known anything like it when they'd lived together in Highfield. All through those years, Mrs. Burrows had been far from a perfect mother as she occupied her days with her beloved television and not much else. Certainly not cooking meals for him!

"Can you guess what we're having?" she said, smiling as she and her son went through their little routine.

"Um . . . not penny-bun stew, by any chance?" Will replied, playing the game and acting as if this was some startling novelty when the large mushrooms were just about the only thing that Colonists ate, day in, day out.

Mrs. Burrows cleared her throat. "Eliza tells me that Stephanie came to see you yet again today," she said matter-of-factly because she knew Will was still missing Elliott terribly. "It wouldn't do you any harm to let the poor girl in and talk to her."

"Maybe . . . ," Will replied noncommittally. "When I feel better."

Mrs. Burrows wasn't going to push the point; she was just on the way out of the room when Will said, "If that cat isn't coming back, can you shut the door, please, Mum?"

"You really like the dark now, don't you?" she said.

He'd asked to have the luminescent orb removed from the fitting in the middle of the ceiling because, even shrouded, it had been keeping him awake. Of course it made no difference to Mrs. Burrows if there was light or not, and every Colonist had been raised to live with constant illumination, even during periods of sleep, because the orbs burned unceasingly.

"I do. Yes," he answered and, as she pulled the door shut, Will let out a long sigh, relishing the pitch-black in the room.

Ah, the wonderful, chocolatey darkness, he thought to himself, allowing it to lap over him now he was alone.

In the silence of the house, snatches of his mother's conversation with the First Officer carried down the corridor from the kitchen. She was talking about the Hunter's strange behavior, then there was a large crash as she dropped something and swore loudly. It sounded like a pan, so it was probably their supper hitting the deck. Mrs. Burrows evidently still had a lot of catching up to do when it came to domesticity.

There was the low rumble of the First Officer's voice — Will couldn't make out the words, but he sounded concerned. Then Will heard his mother announce, quite clearly because she was at the kitchen door and facing down the corridor, "I know you'll think me mad, but I tell you — I *can* smell Styx. It's faint, but it's in this house!"

The First Officer's booming laugh filled the building. "You *are* mad," he said with affection.

"Too right, mate. She *is* mad," Will echoed in a whisper, chuckling to himself.

He stopped chuckling as the realization struck home.

The way Bartleby was reacting to him.

His sudden yearning to be in the dark.

His mother's supersense, which was rarely wrong.

Will placed a hand on his stomach, gingerly feeling it. Jiggs had said that the Styx grubs might have left something behind: chemicals . . . enzymes . . .

Will sat up slowly.

Was he somehow changing?

Changing into something else?

Changing into a *Styx*?

He held quite still for a moment, then shook his head. "Does this never end?" he cried.

ACKNOWLEDGMENTS

I would like to thank:

Barry Cunningham, publisher and editor of the Tunnels series, without whom there would have been no beginning and no end. He has the patience of a saint (he's needed it when dealing with me), and the imagination, empathy, and the light touch that have helped and encouraged me through all these books. So, thank you for everything, Barry. We finally did it. We got there. Now where's that film you promised?

I would also like to thank . . .

. . . you. If it wasn't for all you readers out there, who have supported my series over the years, there's no way that I'd be writing these words at this very moment. So thank you. And, yes, I do care about what you think, and I do read your reviews!

The Chicken House: Rachel, Nicki, Steve, and Esther, and all the rest of the team who have made the books what they are.

Karen Everitt, who has been so instrumental in keeping me on the right track with each installment, and has spotted all the things I've missed. And there have been many!

And all those people throughout the world who have helped with the series and made such a difference. I know I'm going to put noses out of joint by not listing all your names, but I'd like to give the following a particular mention: Sirius Homes, Kirill Barybin, Mathew Horsman, Joel Guelzo, Simon Wilkie, Craig Turner, and Julian Power.

ACKNOWLEDGMENTS

And, of course, my hard-put-upon family, Sophie, George, and Frankie, who are now allowed back in my study again. I find I can only write books because I have an almost religious conviction that I'm doing the right thing, and I know that sometimes it isn't easy for those around me.

And lastly I want to say good-bye to my friend. Will, I'm really going to miss you.

Roderick Gordon

■ ■ ■

But if you leave me to love another
You'll regret it all some day;
You are my sunshine . . .
Please don't take my sunshine away.

■ ■ ■

WITHDRAWN